PENGUIN CLASSICS

SONGS OF A DEAD DREAMER
and GRIMSCRIBE

THOMAS LIGOTTI was born in Detroit in 1953. Considered one of the foremost authors of supernatural horror stories, he began publishing in the early 1980s. Following a tradition established by Edgar Allan Poe and perpetuated by H. P. Lovecraft, Ligotti is noted for his portrayals of characters who are outsiders to ordinary life, depictions of otherworldly dimensions, and uniquely dark vision of human life. His works are often praised by critics for their richly inventive imagination and evocative prose. Ligotti's first collection of tales, *Songs of a Dead Dreamer*, was published in 1985, and its follow-up, *Grimscribe*, in 1991. Among his other publications are the collections *Noctuary* and *Teatro Grottesco* as well as an influential philosophical work, *The Conspiracy Against the Human Race: A Contrivance of Horror*. Ligotti has received several awards, including the Horror Writers Association's Bram Stoker Award for his omnibus collection *The Nightmare Factory* and his short novel *My Work Is Not Yet Done*. He lives in Florida.

JEFF VANDERMEER's most recent fiction is the *New York Times*–bestselling Southern Reach trilogy (*Annihilation, Authority,* and *Acceptance*). His nonfiction has appeared in *The New York Times, The Guardian, The Washington Post,* TheAtlantic.com, and the *Los Angeles Times*. VanderMeer has edited or coedited many iconic fiction anthologies, taught at the Yale Writers' Conference and the Miami International Book Fair, lectured at MIT and the Library of Congress, and serves as the codirector of Shared Worlds, a unique teen writing camp located at Wofford College. He lives in Tallahassee, Florida, with his wife, the noted editor Ann VanderMeer.

THOMAS LIGOTTI

Songs of a Dead Dreamer
and
Grimscribe

Foreword by
JEFF VANDERMEER

PENGUIN BOOKS

PENGUIN BOOKS
An imprint of Penguin Random House LLC
375 Hudson Street
New York, New York 10014
penguin.com

Songs of a Dead Dreamer was first published in the United States of America by Silver Scarab Press in
1986. A revised edition with a different selection of stories was published in Great Britain by Robinson
Publishing in 1989 and in the United States by Carroll & Graf in 1990. A second revised version with
different content was published in Thomas Ligotti's *The Nightmare Factory* by Carroll & Graf in
1996. A third revised version was published in the United States by Subterranean Press in 2010.

Grimscribe was first published in Great Britain by Robinson Publishing in 1991 and in the United
States by Carroll & Graf in 1991. A revised version was published in *The Nightmare Factory* by
Carroll & Graf in 1996. A second revised version was published by Subterranean Press in 2011.

LIBRARY OF CONGRESS CATALOGING-IN-PUBLICATION DATA
Ligotti, Thomas.
[Short stories. Selections]
Songs of a dead dreamer: and, Grimscribe / Thomas Ligotti ; foreword by Jeff Vandermeer.
pages ; cm.—(Penguin classics)
ISBN 978-0-14-310776-7
I. Ligotti, Thomas. Grimscribe. II. Title. III. Title: Grimscribe.
PS3562.I4546A6 2015
813'.54—dc23
2015018805

Printed in the United States of America

27th Printing

Set in Sabon LT Std

Contents

The Voice of the Child

The Voice of Our Name

Foreword

Over the past thirty years, Thomas Ligotti has produced an extraordinary body of work in the short story form—evidenced herein by his first two collections, *Songs of a Dead Dreamer* (1985) and *Grimscribe: His Lives and Works* (1991). *Songs* was first published by Harry O. Morris's Silver Scarab Press in a three-hundred-copy edition with cover art and illustrations by Morris and an introduction by Ramsey Campbell. The book received its due acclaim after a wider release in 1989, but the first edition remains a jewel within our book collection. I remember leafing through it and feeling as if I were looking at an artifact that had slipped through from another universe. *Grimscribe* was, at the time of publication, seen by some as a typical second book, as if Ligotti had taken a step back in quality. Over time, however, readers and critics have recognized that the collection is, if anything, richer, more focused, and more mature than *Songs*.

Where within the fictional cosmos do Ligotti's stories exist? The same fixed, timeless position as those of Edgar Allan Poe and Franz Kafka.* Like that of Poe and Kafka, his fiction is transformative by virtue of the author's unique way of seeing the world and because it is innovative in ways both visible (formal experimentation) and invisible (stealth experiments that

---

*H. P. Lovecraft is a self-admitted early influence on Ligotti's work. However, in a kind of metaphysical horror story of its own, Ligotti early on subsumed Lovecraft and left his dry husk behind, having taken what sustenance he needed for his own devices. (Most other writers are, by contrast, consumed by Lovecraft when they attempt to devour him.)

reveal their presence only by how they affect the reader).
Unlike with Poe's fiction, this quality in Ligotti's work cannot
be emulated in any meaningful way and ferociously resists
commodification by the marketplace. Unlike in Kafka's stories, Ligotti's prose is too uncomfortably visceral and (although
deeply absurdist at times) too hostile to a certain kind of play-
fulness to enter into the traditional canon. But in all three
cases, a unique voice at the right distance from its subject matter prevents the work from becoming dated. A deliberate lack
of specificity follows from the author's natural preoccupations. Unnamed narrators and nameless towns, for example,
allow for a corresponding vagueness of either character or setting
that, perversely, creates the necessary anchor for even a reader
a century from now, traveling beneath strange stars, to be held
in thrall.

Perhaps these qualities also reflect that although Ligotti
came out of the weird and uncanny genres, he was always
passing through those regions. Recalling the horror scene in
the mid-1980s through the mid-1990s, I remember that it was
marked by a certain conservativism and a general devotion to
naturalism. In its most extreme manifestations, this worship
of pragmatic causality became the hyperrealism of subgenres
devoted to depicting explicit violence and sex. Set against such
trends were a handful of unique voices, including writers like
Kathe Koja, Caitlín R. Kiernan, Poppy Z. Brite, and Clive
Barker, who at times added elements of the surreal, Decadent,
New Gothic, or genuinely transgressive body horror.

Did Ligotti come out of this community? Not really. His
work, sui generis, just happened to be published in those envi-
rons during that time period. To suggest otherwise would be
like saying there is huge significance to the neighborhood in
which a physicist lives when he has a eureka moment due to
research at his laboratory. In this sense Ligotti is allied with
iconoclasts like Angela Carter, Haruki Murakami, the aforementioned Kafka, Alfred Kubin, and, to some extent, the great
Bruno Schulz. Indeed, brilliant one-off texts like Sakutarō
Hagiwara's dreamlike "The Town of Cats" (1935) and Eric
Basso's preternaturally Proustian "The Beak Doctor" (1977)

seem oddly Ligotti-esque even if they are not direct influences—precisely because, like Ligotti's work, they exist in a
unique space between horror and the surreal, between the visceral and the philosophical. It is a special place, found on no
map, where the supernatural resists being labeled and every
attempt at naming leaves the formal inquest flummoxed as to
whether a particular shadow or reflection was part of the natural or unnatural worlds.

In Ligotti's work, the supernatural exists in support of ideas
that serve as a sharp interrogation of the way we live, evoking
comparisons to literary realists as different as John Cheever
and Shirley Jackson. That may seem an audacious idea, but if
we pluck Ligotti from the clutches of weird fiction, we find
that his universality exists at an unexpected level—not because
weird fiction doesn't deal with complex issues and ideas, but
because the weird fiction context places the emphasis squarely
on the uncanny, obliterating our ability to see anything else.
Ligotti's fiction, temporarily unhooked from the weird, is best
understood as a continuing interrogation of the legitimacy of
our modern lives. He is exploring the underbelly of modernity—
personal and societal. His interest is in the blight beneath,
whether it occurs solely in the mind or is expressed through
actions. For this reason, the films of David Lynch and the fiction of Thomas Ligotti sometimes speak to each other in interesting ways.

Ligotti launches into this exploration, this kind of *Blue Velvet* approach, from the very first story collected in *Songs*, "The
Frolic." The banal start of this story set in the suburbs could
be the beginning of the average *New Yorker* tale—and if
Ligotti had wanted to he could have reinforced the truth of the
surface of modern life; he could have written a story of a husband and wife at odds, with the husband's work serving merely
to add fuel to their arguments. Instead, Ligotti serves notice
that he's interested in subversion: the window of the rational is
smashed to bits by the irrational. One might even make the
case that the window is smashed by the fears of the husband,
which in a strange way become a kind of perverted wish.

One of Ligotti's first forays into formal experimentation,

"Notes on the Writing of Horror: A Story," seems like the meta-fictional version of a smashed window at first, but accretes viscosity and layers of realism as the tale progresses. As in Vladimir Nabokov's "The Leonardo," Ligotti tells the reader that he is assembling certain fictional elements to convey his story . . . and then, like Nabokov, proceeds to make the reader forget a story is being read, the "fictive dream" closing around with a cocoon-like sense of claustrophobia. At the same time, "Notes on the Writing of Horror" mercilessly sends up certain approaches to supernatural fiction—it is caustically funny; funny with a sneer and a giggle. It gets under the skin in part because, miraculously, it earns the sneering. As a kind of veiled statement of intent from Ligotti, the story is a fierce, uncompromising work, and a proverbial high-wire act on the page. I can only imagine it as a cuckoo's egg laid in the nest of the horror field as it existed at the time.

These kinds of subversions continue in a more gentle fashion with stories like "Alice's Last Adventure," in which Ligotti uses a smidgeon of Lewis Carroll to send up the "twee fey" of both Edward Gorey and Gahan Wilson. The element of play is found not in the appropriation of childhood grotesqueries, but in the voice of the elderly author juxtaposed with a series of unnerving encounters. Once the window is broken, not only can things come through, but you can *get out*. Except, *what is there to get out to?* A plausible interpretation of the story could be that it is about the irrationality and contradictions of aging. A tweak here or there and this interpretation would be the surface of the story, not just part of the subtext.

In the same vein, *Grimscribe*'s major story "The Last Feast of Harlequin" creates its greatest effects as much through the mundane as through the uncanny. An anthropologist visits the town of Mirocaw out of curiosity about a pageantry festival that includes clowns. In a perfect deadpan tone that allows the author a tightrope walk between the absurd and the horrific, the metaphysical and the visceral, the anthropologist comes to realize he has made an irrevocable mistake. Much of the pleasure here comes from the narrator providing the reader with information previously left out and inquiries into clown activities that are often drily humorous. (Indeed, Ligotti has always been a very funny writer, a quality easier to enjoy once you become acclimated to his supernatural elements.)

But the story also expands on Ligotti's interest in a kind of middle-class experience, or ordinary life, that is disrupted by the extraordinary, which puts a lie not only to the narrators' view of their own selves but also to the idea that the ordinary is mundane, that the surface is also the subtext. In part, Ligotti here comments on modernity through the idea of ritual, and how ritual pervades our lives in both ordinary and outré circumstances. Ritual is a kind of mask that holds in check what happens in our most secret lives. Other stories in *Grimscribe* use objects as talismans to explore these same undercurrents, whether the eyeglasses of "The Spectacles in the Drawer," the "madness of things" in the house in "Flowers of the Abyss," or the idol/manuscript in "Nethescurial."

When we encounter ritual enacted in a grotesque fashion (that to some extent ridicules our own repetitions) we may at first try to reconcile it with our own preordained patterns; thus the absurd element of *politeness* or *reasonableness* sometimes expressed in true-life extreme situations. But if instead we recoil, run shrieking, might it be not only because what we see is macabre but because, for a moment, we recognize that this strangeness partakes of the same wellspring as our own regimented lives? That our (unthinking) rituals are only attempts not to succumb to what is going on beneath the surface, within our minds, with regard to the intolerability of life (i.e., eventual death)?

I must confess I am loath to discuss other favorites among these stories. Each has at some point appeared sharp and pale out of the murky darkness, had its moment, and then receded from my sight again, such is the impressionistic flavor of these particular stories. "Ethereal" is a terribly overused and imprecise word to describe weird fiction, but it's still the best description of how Ligotti's fiction exists in the moment of individual sentences on the page. Every time you read these stories, not only do you reimagine them, but they seem to change shape and substance through some power rising from behind the words. These are not uncanny effects—they're merely another manifestation of the universal in Ligotti's fiction.

With *Songs* and *Grimscribe*, Ligotti burst fully formed onto the literary scene. Had just these two collections been published, Ligotti would still be hailed as a writer of the first rank. What occurs later in his career is not so much a maturing and a leaving aside of earlier work as an interesting shift of attention: from the general preoccupations with what lies beneath modernity, often expressed through Everyman and Man of No Qualities characters, to a specific focus on the modern workplace in such long stories as *My Work Is Not Yet Done*. Turning the gaze of weird fiction toward the modern work environment—pushing past the blatant emptiness of the cubicle world to truths ever more horrific, subtle, and darkly hilarious—is just a natural extension of Ligotti's initial explorations in *Songs* and *Grimscribe*.

In writing about these more existential explorations, I don't mean to suggest that the supernatural in Ligotti's fiction is not convincing, terrifying, and cathartic in its own right. It is all of those things, and for another writer that might be the extent of our fascination, and quite enough for most readers. But the reason Ligotti lingers in our imaginations, why his work is so relevant to the twentieth and twenty-first centuries, is that so much else exists beneath the surface. Whether you are just now encountering Ligotti's fiction or rereading it, I envy you this chance to encounter the work of one of our greatest dark imaginations.

JEFF VANDERMEER

Songs of a Dead Dreamer

To my parents,
Gasper and Dolores Ligotti

DREAMS FOR SLEEPWALKERS

THE FROLIC

In a beautiful home in a beautiful part of town—the town of Nolgate, site of the state prison—Dr. Munck examined the evening newspaper while his young wife lounged on a sofa nearby, lazily flipping through the colorful parade of a fashion magazine. Their daughter Norleen was upstairs asleep, or perhaps she was illicitly enjoying an after-hours session with the new television she'd received on her birthday the week before. If so, her violation went undetected by her parents in the living room, where all was quiet. The neighborhood outside the house was quiet, too, as it was day and night. All of Nolgate was quiet, for it was not a place with much of a nightlife, save perhaps at the bar where the prison's correctional officers congregated. Such persistent quiet made the doctor's wife fidgety with her existence in a locale that seemed light-years from the nearest metropolis. But thus far Leslie did not complain of the lethargy of their lives. She knew her husband was quite dedicated to his new professional duties in this new place. Perhaps tonight, though, he would exhibit more of those symptoms of disenchantment with his work that she had been meticulously observing in him of late.

"How did it go today, David?" she asked, her radiant eyes peeking over the magazine cover, where another pair of eyes radiated a glossy gaze. "You were pretty quiet at dinner."

"It went about the same," said Dr. Munck without lowering the small-town newspaper to look at his wife.

"Does that mean you don't want to talk about it?"

He folded the newspaper backwards and his upper body appeared. "That's how it sounded, didn't it?"

"Yes, it certainly did. Are you okay?" Leslie asked, laying aside the magazine on the coffee table and offering her complete attention.

"Severely doubting, that's how I am." He said this with a kind of far-off reflectiveness. Leslie now saw a chance to delve a little deeper.

"Anything particularly doubtful?"

"Only everything," he answered.

"Shall I make us drinks?"

"That would be much appreciated."

Leslie walked to another part of the living room and from a large cabinet pulled out some bottles and some glasses. From the kitchen she brought out a supply of ice cubes in a brown plastic bucket. The sounds of drink-making were the only intrusion upon the living room's plush quiet. The drapes were drawn on all windows except the one in the corner where an Aphrodite sculpture posed. Beyond that window was a deserted street-lighted street and a piece of moon above the opulent leafage of spring trees.

"Here you go. A little drinky for my hard-working darling," she said, handing him a glass that was very thick at its base and tapered almost undetectably toward its rim.

"Thanks, I really needed one of these."

"Why? Problems at the hospital?"

"I wish you'd stop calling it a hospital. It's a prison, as you well know."

"Yes, of course."

"You could say the word *prison* once in a while."

"All right, then. How's things at the prison, dear? Boss on your case? Inmates acting up?" Leslie checked herself before things spiraled into an argument. She took a deep gulp from her drink and calmed herself. "I'm sorry about the snideness, David."

"No, I deserved it. I'm projecting my anger onto you. I think you've known for some time what I can't bring myself to admit."

"Which is?" Leslie prompted.

"Which is that maybe it was not the wisest decision to move here and take this saintly mission upon my psychologist's shoulders."

Her husband's remark indicated an even more acute mood of demoralization than Leslie had hoped for. But somehow his words did not cheer her the way she thought they would. She could distantly hear the moving van pulling up to the house, but the sound was no longer as pleasing as it once was.

"You said you wanted to do something more than treat urban neuroses. Something more meaningful, more challenging."

"What I wanted, masochistically, was a thankless job, an impossible one. And I got it."

"Is it really that bad?" Leslie inquired, not quite believing she asked the question with such encouraging skepticism about the actual severity of the situation. She congratulated herself for placing David's self-esteem above her own desire for a change of venue, important as she felt this was.

"I'm afraid it is that bad. When I first visited the prison's psychiatric unit and met the other doctors, I swore I wouldn't become as hopelessly cynical as they were. Things would be different with me. I overestimated myself by a wide margin, though. Today one of the orderlies was beaten up again by two of the prisoners, excuse me, 'patients.' Last week it was Dr. Valdman. That's why I was so edgy on Norleen's birthday. So far I've been lucky. All they do is spit at me. Well, they can all rot in that hellhole as far as I'm concerned."

David felt his own words lingering atmospherically in the room, tainting the serenity of the house. Until then their home had been an insular haven beyond the contamination of the prison, an imposing structure outside the town limits. Now its psychic imposition transcended the limits of physical distance. Inner distance constricted, and David sensed the massive prison walls shadowing the cozy neighborhood outside.

"Do you know why I was late tonight?" he asked his wife.

"No, why?"

"Because I had an overlong chat with a fellow who hasn't got a name yet."

"The one you told me about who won't tell anyone where he's from or what his real name is?"

"That's him. He's the standout example of the pernicious monstrosity of that place. A real beauty, that guy. One for the books. Absolute madness paired with a sharp cunning. Because of his cute little name game, he was classified as unsuitable for the general prison population and thus we in the psychiatric section ended up with him. According to him, though, he has plenty of names, no less than a thousand, none of which he's condescended to speak in anyone's presence. It's hard to imagine that he has a name like everyone else. And we're stuck with him, no name and all."

"Do you call him that, 'no name'?"

"Maybe we should, but no, we don't."

"So what do you call him, then?"

"Well, he was convicted as John Doe, and since then everyone refers to him as that. They've yet to uncover any official documentation on him. It's as if he just dropped out of nowhere. His fingerprints don't match any record of previous convictions. He was picked up in a stolen car parked in front of an elementary school. An observant neighbor reported him as a suspicious character frequently seen in the area. Everyone was on the alert, I guess, after the first few disappearances from the school, and the police were watching him just as he was walking a new victim to his car. That's when they made the arrest. But his version of the story is a little different. He says he was fully aware of his pursuers and expected, even wanted, to be caught, convicted, and put in a penitentiary."

"Why?"

"Why? Who knows? When you ask a psychopath to explain himself, it only becomes more confusing. And John Doe is chaos itself."

"What do you mean?" asked Leslie. Her husband emitted a short burst of laughter and then fell silent, as if scouring his mind for the right words.

"Okay, here's a little scene from an interview I had with him today. I asked him if he knew why he was in prison."

"'For frolicking,' he said.

"'What does that mean?' I asked.

"His reply was: 'Mean, mean, mean. You're a meany, that's what you are.'

"That childish ranting somehow sounded to me as if he were mimicking his victims. I'd really had enough right then but foolishly continued the interview.

"'Do you know why you can't leave here?' I calmly asked with a poor variant of my original inquiry.

"'Who says I can't? I'll just go when I want to. But I don't want to go yet.'

"'Why not?' I naturally questioned.

"'I just got here,' he said. 'Thought I'd take a holiday. Frolicking the way I do can be exhausting sometimes. I want to be in with all the others. Quite a rousing atmosphere, I expect. When can I go with them, when can I?'

"Can you believe that? It would be cruel, though, to put him in general population, not to say he doesn't deserve such cruelty. The average inmate doesn't look favorably on Doe's kind of crime. They see it as reflecting badly on them, being that they're just your garden variety armed robbers, murderers, and whatnot. Everyone needs to feel they're better than someone else. There's really no predicting what would happen if we put him in there and the others found out what he was convicted for."

"So he has to stay in the psychiatric unit for the rest of his term?" asked Leslie.

"He doesn't think so. Being interred in a maximum security correctional facility is his idea of a holiday, remember? He thinks he can leave whenever he wants."

"And can he?" asked Leslie with a firm absence of facetiousness in her voice. This had always been one of her weightiest fears about living in a prison town—that not far from their own backyard there was a horde of fiends plotting to escape through what she envisioned as rather papery walls. To raise a child in such surroundings was the prime objection she had to her husband's work.

"I told you before, Leslie, there have been very few successful escapes from that prison. If an inmate does get beyond the walls, his first impulse is always one of practical self-preservation. So he tries to get as far away as possible from this town, which is probably the safest place to be in the event of an escape. Anyway, most escapees are apprehended within hours after they've broken out."

"What about a prisoner like John Doe? Does he have a sense of 'practical self-preservation,' or would he rather just hang around and do what he does somewhere that's conveniently located?"

"Prisoners like that don't escape in the normal course of things. They just bounce off the walls but not over them. You know what I mean?"

Leslie said she understood, but this did not in the least lessen the potency of her fears, which found their source in an imaginary prison in an imaginary town, one where anything could happen as long as it approached the hideous. Morbidity had never been her strong suit, and she loathed its intrusion on her character. And for all his ready reassurance about the able security of the prison, David also seemed to be profoundly uneasy. He was sitting very still now, holding his drink between his knees and appearing to listen for something.

"What's wrong, David?" asked Leslie.

"I thought I heard . . . a sound."

"A sound like what?"

"Can't describe it exactly. A faraway noise."

He stood up and looked around, as if to see whether the sound had left some tell-tale clue in the surrounding stillness of the house, perhaps a smeary sonic print somewhere.

"I'm going to check on Norleen," he said, setting his glass down on the table beside his chair. He then walked across the living room, up the three segments of the stairway, and down the upstairs hall. Peeping into his daughter's room, he saw her tiny figure resting comfortably, a sleepy embrace wrapped about the form of a stuffed Bambi. She still occasionally slept with an inanimate companion, even though she was getting a little old for this. But her psychologist father was careful not to question her right to this childish comfort. Before leaving the room, Dr. Munck lowered the window which was partially open on that warm spring evening.

When he returned to the living room, he delivered the wonderfully routine message that Norleen was peacefully asleep. In a gesture containing faint overtones of celebratory relief, Leslie made them two fresh drinks, after which she said:

"David, you said you had an 'overlong chat' with that John Doe. Not that I'm morbidly curious or anything, but did you ever get him to reveal anything about himself? Anything at all?"

"Oh, sure," Dr. Munck replied, rolling an ice cube around in his mouth. His voice was now more relaxed.

"You could say he told me everything about himself, but all of it was nonsense—the blathering of a maniac. I asked him in a casually interested sort of way where he was from."

"'No place,' he replied like a psychotic simpleton.

"'No place?' I probed.

"'Yes, precisely, Herr Doktor. I'm not some snob who puts on airs and pretends to emanate from some high-flown patch of geography. Ge-og-ra-phy. That's a funny word. I like all the languages you have.'

"'Where were you born?' I asked in another brilliant alternate form of the question.

"'Which time do you mean, you meany?' he said back to me, and so forth. I could go on with this dialogue—"

"You do a pretty good John Doe imitation, I must say."

"Thank you, but I couldn't keep it up for very long. It wouldn't be easy to imitate all his different voices, accents, and degrees of articulacy. He may be something akin to a multiple personality, I'm not sure. I'd have to go over the tapes of my interviews with him to see if any patterns of coherency turn up, possibly something the detectives could use to establish who this guy really is. The tragic part is that knowing Doe's legal identity is a formality at this point, just tying up loose ends. His victims are dead, and they died horribly. That's all that counts now. Sure, he was somebody's baby boy at one time. But I can't pretend to care anymore about biographical details—the name on his birth certificate, where he grew up, what made him the way he is. I'm no aesthete

of pathology. It's never been my ambition to study mental disease without effecting some improvement. So why should I waste
my time trying to help someone like John Doe, who doesn't live
in the same world as we do, psychologically speaking. I used to
believe in rehabilitation, not a purely punitive approach to criminal behavior. But those people, those *things* at the prison are
only an ugly stain on our world. The hell with them. Just plow
them all under for fertilizer, I say." Dr. Munck then drained his
glass until the ice cubes rattled.

"Want another?" Leslie asked with a smooth therapeutic tone
to her voice.

David smiled now, his illiberal outburst having purged him
somewhat of his ire. "Let's get drunk and fool around, shall we?"

Leslie collected her husband's glass for a refill. Now there was
reason to celebrate, she thought. David was not giving up his
work from a sense of ineffectual failure but from anger, an anger
that was melting into indifference. Now everything would be as it
had been before; they could leave the prison town and move back
home. In fact, they could move anywhere they liked, maybe take
a long vacation first, treat Norleen to some sunny place. Leslie
thought of all these things as she made two more drinks in the
quiet of that beautiful room. This quiet was no longer an indication of soundless stagnancy but a delicious, lulling prelude to the
promising days to come. The indistinct happiness of the future
glowed inside her along with the alcohol; she was gravid with
pleasant prophecies. Perhaps the time was now right to have
another child, a little brother or sister for Norleen. But that could
wait just a while longer . . . a lifetime of possibilities lay ahead.
An amiable genie seemed to be on standby. They had only to
make their wishes, and their bidding would be done.

Before returning with the drinks, Leslie went in the kitchen.
She had something she wanted to give her husband, and this
seemed the perfect time to do it. A little token to show David
that though his job had proved a sad waste of his worthy effort,
she had supported his work in her own way. With a drink in
each hand, she held under her left elbow the small box she had
got from the kitchen.

"What's that?" asked David, taking his drink.

"Just a little something for the art lover in you. I bought it at that little shop where they sell things the inmates at the prison make. Some of it is quality merchandise—belts, jewelry, ashtrays, you know."

"I know," said David, his voice at a distance from Leslie's enthusiasm. "I didn't think anyone actually bought that stuff."

"Well, I did. I thought it would help to support those prisoners who are doing something *creative,* instead of . . . well, instead of destructive things."

"Creativity isn't always an index of niceness, Leslie," David warned his wife.

"Wait'll you see it before passing judgment," she said, opening the flap of the box. "There—isn't that nice work?" She set the piece on the coffee table.

Dr. Munck now plunged into that depth of sobriety which can only be reached by falling from a prior alcoholic height. He looked at the object. Of course he had seen it before, watched it being tenderly molded and caressed by creative hands, until he sickened and could watch no more. It was the head of a young boy, a lovely piece discovered in gray formless clay and glazed in blue. The work radiated an extraordinary and intense beauty, the subject's face expressing a kind of ecstatic serenity, the convoluted simplicity of a visionary's gaze.

"Well, what do you think of it?" asked Leslie.

David looked at his wife and said solemnly: "Please put it back in the box. And then get rid of it."

"Get rid of it? Why?"

"Why? Because I know which of the inmates did this work. He was very proud of it, and I even forced a grudging compliment for the craftsmanship of the thing. But then he told me the source of his model. That expression of sky-blue peacefulness wasn't on the boy's face when they found him lying in a field about six months ago."

"No, David," said Leslie as a premature denial of what she was expecting her husband to reveal.

"This was his most recent—and according to him most memorable—'frolic.'"

"Oh my God," Leslie murmured softly, placing her right

hand to her forehead. Then with both hands she gently placed the boy of blue back in his box. "I'll return it to the shop," she said quietly.

"Do it soon, Leslie. I don't know how much longer we'll be residing at this address."

In the moody silence that followed, Leslie briefly mused upon the now openly expressed departure from the town of Nolgate, their escape. Then she said: "David, did he actually talk about the things he did? I mean about—"

"I know what you mean. Yes, he did," answered Dr. Munck with a professional gravity.

"Poor David," Leslie said, lovingly sympathetic now that machinations were no longer required to achieve her ends.

"Actually, it wasn't that much of an ordeal, strange to say. The conversation we had could even be called stimulating in a clinical sense. He described his 'frolicking' in a highly imaginative manner that was rather engrossing. The strange beauty of this thing in the box here—disturbing as it is—somewhat parallels the language he used when talking about those poor kids. At times I couldn't help being fascinated, though maybe I was shielding my true feelings with a psychologist's detachment. Sometimes you just have to keep some distance between yourself and reality, even if it means becoming a little less human.

"Anyway, nothing he said was sickeningly graphic in the way you might imagine. When told me about his 'most memorable frolic,' it was with a powerful sense of wonder and nostalgia, shocking as that sounds to me now. He seemed to feel a kind of homesickness, though his 'home' is a ramshackle ruin of his decayed mind. His psychosis has evidently bred an atrocious fairyland which exists in a powerful way for him. And despite the demented grandeur of his thousand names, he actually sees himself as only a minor figure in this world—a mediocre courtier in a broken-down kingdom of miracles and horrors. This modesty is very interesting when you consider the egotistical magnificence that a lot of psychopaths would attribute to themselves given a limitless imaginary orbit where they could play any imaginary role. But not John Doe. He's a comparatively lazy demi-demon from a Neverland where dizzy chaos is the norm, a state of affairs on which he gluttonously thrives. Which is as good a description as any of the metaphysical economy of a psychotic's universe.

"There's actually quite a poetic geography to his interior dreamland as he describes it. He talked about a place that sounded like a cosmos of crooked houses and littered alleys, a slum among the stars. Which may be his distorted rendering of a life spent growing up in a shabby neighborhood—an attempt on his part to recast the traumatic memories of his childhood into a realm that cross-breeds a mean-street reality with a fantasy world of his imagination, a phantasmagoric mingling of heaven and hell. This is where he does his 'frolicking' with what he calls his 'awestruck company.' The place where he took his victims might possibly have been an abandoned building, or even an accommodating sewer. I say this based on his repeated mentioning of 'the jolly river of refuse' and 'the jagged heaps in shadows,' which could certainly be mad transmutations of a literal wasteland, some grubby and secluded environment that his mind turned into a funhouse of bizarre marvels. Less fathomable are his memories of a moonlit corridor where mirrors scream and laugh, dark peaks of some kind that won't remain still, a stairway that's 'broken' in a very strange way, though this last one fits in with the background of a dilapidated slum. There is always a paradoxical blend of forsaken topographies and shining sanctuaries in his mind, almost a self-hypnotic—" Dr. Munck caught himself before continuing in this vein of reluctant admiration.

"But despite all these dreamy back-drops in Doe's imagination, the mundane evidence of his frolics still points to crimes of a very familiar, down-to-earth type. Run-of-the-mill atrocities, if one can speak of the deeds he committed as such. Doe denies there was anything pedestrian about his mayhem. He says he just made the evidence look that way for the dull masses, that what he really means by 'frolicking' is a type of activity quite different from, even opposed to, the crimes for which he was convicted. This term probably has some private associations rooted in his past."

Dr. Munck paused and rattled around the ice cubes in his empty glass. Leslie seemed to have drifted into herself while he was speaking. She had lit a cigarette and was now leaning on the arm of the sofa with her legs up on its cushions, so that her knees pointed at her husband.

"You should really quit smoking someday," he said.

Leslie lowered her eyes like a child mildly chastised. "I promise that as soon as we move—I'll quit. Is that a deal?"

"Deal," said David. "And I have another proposal for you. First let me tell you that I've definitely decided to give notice of my resignation."

"Isn't that a little soon?" asked Leslie, hoping it wasn't.

"Believe me, no one will be surprised. I don't think anyone will even care. Anyway, my proposal is that tomorrow we take Norleen and rent a place up north for a few days or so. We could go horseback riding. Remember how she loved it last summer? What do you say?"

"That sounds nice," Leslie agreed with a ripple of enthusiasm. "Very nice, in fact."

"And on the way back we can drop off Norleen at your parents'. She can stay there while we take care of the business of moving out of this house, maybe find an apartment temporarily. I don't think they'll mind having her for a week or so, do you?"

"No, of course not, they'll love it. But what's the great rush? Norleen's still in school, you know. Maybe we should wait till she gets out. It's just a month away."

David sat in silence for a moment, apparently ordering his thoughts.

"What's wrong?" asked Leslie with just a slight quiver of anxiety in her voice.

"Nothing is actually wrong, nothing at all. But—"

"But what?"

"Well, it has to do with the prison. I know I sounded very smug in telling you how safe we are from that place, and I still maintain that we are. But this John Doe character I've told you about is very strange, as I'm sure you've gathered. He's positively a child-murdering psychopath . . . and then again. I really don't know what to say that would make any sense."

Leslie quizzed her husband with her eyes. "I thought you said that inmates like him just bounce off the walls, not—"

"Yes, much of the time he's like that. But sometimes . . ."

"What are you trying to say, David?" asked Leslie, who was becoming infected by the uneasiness her husband was trying to hide.

"It's something that Doe said when I was talking with him today. Nothing really definite. But I'd feel infinitely more comfortable about the whole thing if Norleen stayed with your parents until we can organize ourselves."

Leslie lit another cigarette. "Tell me what he said that bothers you so much," she said firmly. "I should know, too."

"When I tell you, you'll probably just think I'm a little crazy myself. You didn't talk to him, though, and I did. The mannerisms of his speech, or rather the many different mannerisms. The shifting expressions on that lean face. Much of the time I talked to him I had the feeling he was playing at some game that was beyond me, though I'm sure it just seemed that way. This is a common tactic of the psychopath—messing with the doctor. It gives them a sense of power."

"Tell me what he said," Leslie insisted.

"All right, I'll tell you. I think it would be a mistake, though, to read too much into it. But toward the end of the interview today, when we were talking about those kids, he said something I didn't like at all. He enunciated his words in one of his affected accents, Scottish this time with a little German flavor thrown in. What he said, and I'm reciting it verbatim, was this: 'You wouldn't be havin' a misbehavin' laddie nor a little colleen of your own, now would you, Professor von Munck?' Then he grinned at me silently.

"Now I'm sure he was deliberately trying to upset me. Nothing more than that."

"But what he said, David: 'nor a little colleen.'"

"Grammatically, of course, it should have been 'or' not 'nor,' but I'm sure it wasn't anything except a case of bad grammar."

"You didn't mention anything about Norleen, did you?"

"Of course I didn't. That's not exactly the kind of thing I would talk about with these people."

"Then why did he say it like that?"

"I have no idea. He possesses a very weird sort of cleverness, speaking much of the time with vague suggestions and subtle jokes. He could have heard things about me from someone on the staff, I suppose. Then again, it might be just an innocent coincidence." He looked to his wife for comment.

"You're probably right," Leslie agreed with an ambivalent eagerness to believe in this conclusion. "All the same, I think I understand why you want Norleen to stay with my parents. Not that anything might happen—"

"Not at all. There's no reason to think anything would happen. No doubt this is a case of the doctor being out-psyched by his patient, but I don't really care anymore. Any reasonable person would be a little spooked after spending day after day in the pandemonium and often physical danger of that place. The murderers, the rapists, the dregs of the dregs. It's impossible to lead a normal family life while working under those conditions. You saw how I was on Norleen's birthday."

"I know. Not the best neighborhood in which to bring up a child."

David nodded slowly. "When I went to check on her a little while ago, I felt, I don't know, vulnerable in some way. She was hugging one of those stuffed security blankets of hers." He took a sip of his drink. "It was a new one, I noticed. Did you buy it when you were out shopping today?"

Leslie gazed blankly. "The only thing I bought was that," she said, pointing at the box on the coffee table. "What 'new one' do you mean?"

"The stuffed Bambi. Maybe she had it before and I just never noticed it," he said, partially dismissing the issue.

"Well, if she had it before, it didn't come from me," Leslie said quite resolutely.

"Nor me."

"I don't remember her having it when I put her to bed," said Leslie.

"Well, she had it when I looked in on her after hearing . . ."

David paused. From the expression on his face, he seemed to be contemplating a thousand thoughts at once, as if he were engaged in some frantic, rummaging search within every cell of his brain.

"What's the matter, David?" Leslie asked, her voice weakening.

"I'm not sure exactly. It's as if I know something and don't know it at the same time."

But Dr. Munck was beginning to know. With his left hand he covered the back of his neck, warming it. Was there a draft coming from another part of the house? Theirs was not the kind of place to be drafty, not a broken-down, hole-in-the-wall hovel where the wind gets in through ancient attic boards and warped window-frames. There actually was quite a wind blowing now; he could hear it hunting around outside and could see the restless trees through the window behind the Aphrodite sculpture. The goddess posed languidly with her flawless head leaning back, her blind eyes contemplating the ceiling and beyond. But beyond the ceiling? Beyond the hollow snoozing of the wind, cold and dead? And the draft?

What?

"David, do you feel a draft?" asked his wife.

"Yes," he replied as if some sobering thought had just come to mind. "Yes," he repeated as he rose out of his chair and walked across the living room, ever hurrying as he approached the stairway, leaped up its three segments, and ran down the second-floor hall. "Norleen, Norleen," he chanted before reaching the half-closed door of her room. He could feel the breeze coming from there.

He knew and did not know.

He groped for the light switch. It was low, the height of a child. He turned on the light. The child was gone. Across the room the window was wide open, the white translucent curtains flapping upwards on the invading wind. Alone on the bed was the stuffed animal, torn, its soft entrails littering the mattress. Now stuffed inside, blooming out like a flower, was a crumpled piece of paper. And Dr. Munck could discern within the folds of that page a fragment of the prison's letterhead. But the note was not a typed message of official business: the handwriting varied from a neat italic script to a child's scrawl. He desperately stared at the words for what seemed a timeless interval without comprehending their message. Then, finally, the meaning of the note sank heavily in.

Dr. Monk, read the note from inside the animal, *We leave this behind in your capable hands, for in the black-foaming gutters and back alley of paradise, in the dank windowless gloom of some intergalactic cellar, in the hollow pearly whorls found in sewerlike seas, in starless cities of insanity, and in their slums . . . my awestruck little deer and I have gone frolicking. See you anon. Jonathan Doe.*

"David?" he heard his wife's voice inquire from the bottom of the stairs. "Is everything all right?"

Then the beautiful house was no longer quiet, for there rang a bright freezing scream of laughter, the perfect sound to accompany a passing anecdote of some obscure hell.

LES FLEURS

April 17th. Flowers sent out in the early a.m.

May 1st. Today—and I thought it would never happen again—I have met someone about whom, I think, I can be hopeful. Her name is Daisy. She works in a florist shop! *The* florist shop, I might add, where I paid a visit to gather some sorrowful flowers for Clare, who to the rest of the world is still a missing person. At first, of course, Daisy was politely reserved when I asked about some lilting blossoms for a loved one's memorial. I soon cured her, however, of this detached manner. In my deeply shy and friendly tone of voice I asked about some of the other flowers in the shop, ones having no overtones of loss. She was quite glad to take me on a tour of the shop's iridescent inventory. I confessed to knowing next to nothing about commercial plants and things, and remarked on her enthusiasm for her work, hoping all the while that at least part of her animation was inspired by me. "Oh, I love working with flowers," she said. "I think they're real interesting." Then she asked if I was aware that there were plants having flowers which opened only at night, and that certain types of violets bloomed only in darkness underground. My inner flow of thoughts and sensations suddenly quickened. Though I had already sensed she was a girl of special imagination, this was the first hint I received of just how special it was. I judged my efforts to know her better would not be wasted, as they have been with others. "That *is* real interesting about those flowers," I said, smiling a hothouse warm smile. There was a pause which I filled in with my name. She then told me hers. "Now what kind of flowers would you like?" she asked. I staidly requested an arrangement suitable for the grave of a departed grandmother. Before leaving the shop I told Daisy I might need to stop by again to satisfy some future floral needs. She seemed to have no objection to this. With the vegetation nestled in my arm I songfully walked out of the store. I then proceeded directly to Chapel Gardens cemetery. For a while I sincerely made an effort to find a headstone that might by coincidence display my lost one's name. And any dates would just have to do. I thought she deserved this much at least. As events transpired, however, the recipient of my commemorative bouquet had to be someone named Clarence.

May 16th. Day, as I now intimately called her, visited my apartment for the first time and fell in love with its quaint refurbishments. "I adore well-preserved old places," she said. It seemed to me she really did. I thought she would. She remarked what decorative wonders a few plants would do for my ancient rooms. She was obviously sensitive to the absence of natural adornments in my bachelor quarters. "Night-blooming cereuses?" I asked, trying not to mean too much by this and give myself away. A mild grin appeared on her face, but it was not an issue I thought I could press at the time. Even now I press it within these scrapbook pages with great delicacy.

Day wandered about the apartment for a while. I watched her as I would some exotic animal—a sleek ocelot perhaps. Then suddenly I realized I had regrettably overlooked something. She looked it over. The object was positioned on a low table before a high window and between its voluminous curtains. It seemed so vulgarly prominent to me then, especially since I hadn't intended to let her see anything of this sort so early in our relationship. "What is this?" she asked, her voice expressing a kind of outraged curiosity bordering on plain outrage. "It's just a sculpture. I told you I do things like that. It's not very good. Kind of dumb." She examined the piece more closely. "Watch that," I warned. She let out a little "Ow." "Is it supposed to be some type of cactus?" she inquired. For a moment she seemed to take a genuine interest in that obscure objet d'art. "It has tiny teeth," she observed, "on these big tongue things." They do look like tongues; I'd never thought of that. Rather ingenious comparison, considering. I hoped her imagination had found fertile ground in which to grow, but instead she revealed a moribund disgust. "You might have better luck passing it off as an animal than a plant, or a sculpture of a plant, or whatever. It's got a velvety kind of fur and looks like it might crawl away." I felt like crawling away myself at that point. I asked her, as a quasi-botanist, if there were not plants resembling birds and other animal life. This was my feeble attempt to exculpate my creation from any charges of unnaturalness. It's strange how you're sometimes forced to assume an unsympathetic view of yourself through borrowed eyes. Finally I mixed some drinks and we went on to other things. I put on some music.

Soon afterward, though, the bland harmony of the music was undermined by an unfortunate dissonance. That detective (Briceberg, I think) arrived for an encore of his interrogation re: The Clare Affair. Fortunately I was able to keep him and his questions out in the hallway the entire time. We reviewed the previous dialogue we'd had. I reiterated to him that Clare was just someone I worked with and with whom I was professionally friendly. It appears that some of my co-workers, unidentified, suspected that Clare and I were romantically involved. "Office gossip," I countered, knowing she was one girl who knew how to keep certain secrets, even if she could not be trusted with others. Sorry, I said, I had no idea where she could have disappeared to. I did manage to subversively hint, however, that I would not be surprised if in a sudden flight of neurotic despair she had impulsively relocated to some land of her heart's desire. I myself had despaired to find that within Clare's dark and promisingly moody borders lay a disappointing dreamland of white picket fences and flower-printed curtains. No, I didn't tell that to the detective. Besides, I further contended, it was well known in the office that Clare had begun dating someone approximately seven to ten days (my personal estimation of the term of her disloyalty) before her disappearance. So why bother me? This, I found out, was the reason: he had also been informed, he told me, of my belonging to a certain offbeat organization. I replied there was nothing offbeat in serious philosophical study.

Furthermore, I was an artist, as he well knew, and, as anybody knows, artistic personalities have a perfectly natural tendency toward such things. I thought he would understand if I put it that way. He did. The man appeared satisfied with my every statement. Indeed, he seemed overly eager to dismiss me as a person of interest in the case, no doubt trying to create a false sense of security on my part and lead me to make an unwitting admission to the foulest kind of play. "Was that about the girl where you work who disappeared?" Daisy asked me afterward. "Mm-hm," I noised. I was brooding and silent for a while, hoping she would attribute this to my inward lament for that strange girl at the office and not to the lamentably imperfect evening we'd had. "Maybe I'd better go," she said, and then did. There was not much of our date left to salvage anyway. After she abandoned me I got very drunk on a liqueur tasting of flowers from open fields, or so it seemed. I also took this opportunity to reread a story about some men who visit the white waste regions of a polar wonderland. I don't expect to dream tonight, having already sated myself with this arctic fantasy. Brotherhood of Paradise offbeat indeed!

September 21st. Day came up to the cool, clean offices of G. R. Glacy, the advertising firm for which I worked, to meet me for lunch. I showed her my cubicle of commercial artistry, and drew her attention to my latest project. "Oh, that's lovely," she said when I pointed out the drawing of a nymph with flowers in her freshly shampooed hair. "That's really nice." That "nice" remark almost spoiled my day. I asked her to look closely at the flowers mingling in the locks of the mythical being. It was barely noticeable that one of the flower stems was growing out of, or perhaps into, the creature's head. Day didn't seem to appreciate the craftiness of my craft very much. And I thought we were making such progress along "offbeat" paths. (Damn that Briceberg!) Perhaps I should wait until we return from our trip before showing her any of the paintings I have hidden at my home. I want her to be prepared. Everything is all prepared for our vacation at least. Day finally found someone to take care of her cat.

October 10th. Good-bye diary. See you when I get back.

November 1st. After a period of ruminative silence on the subject, I will now set down a brief chapter from Day's and my tropical sojourn. I'm not sure whether the events to be delineated represent an impasse or a turning point in the course of our relationship. Perhaps there is some point that I have completely failed to get. As yet, I am still in the dark. I've been here before with Clare and had hoped that my escapist interlude with Day would be definitive, or close to it, and not filled with dubiety. Nevertheless, I still feel that the episode to follow deserves documentation.

A Hawaiian paradise at midnight. Actually we were just gazing upon the beachside luxuriance from our hotel veranda. Day was tipsy from consuming several drinks that wore flowers on their foamy heads. I was in a condition similar to hers. A few moments of heady silence passed, punctuated by an occasional sigh from Day. We heard the flapping of invisible wings whipping the warm air in darkness. We listened closely to the sounds of black orchids growing, even if there were none. ("Mmmm," hummed Day.) We were ripe for a whim. I had one, not knowing yet if I could pull it off. "Can you smell the mysterious cereus?" I said, placing one hand on her far shoulder and dramatically passing the other in a horizontal arc before the jungle beyond. "Can you?" I hypnotically repeated. "I can," said a game Day. "But can we find them, Day, and watch them open in the moonlight?" "We can, we can," she chanted giddily. We could. Suddenly the smooth-skinned leaves of the night garden were brushing against our smooth-skinned selves. Day paused to touch a flower that was orange or red but smelled of a deep violet. I encouraged her to press on across the flower-bedded earth. We plunged deeper into the dream garden. Faster, faster, faster the sounds and smells rushed by us. It was easier than I thought. At some point, with almost no effort at all, I successfully managed our full departure from known geography. "Day, Day," I shouted. "We're here. I've never shown this to anyone, and what torture it's been keeping it from you. No, don't speak. Look,

look." Oh, the thrill of bringing a romantic companion to this dark paradise. How I yearned to show her this resplendent world in full bloom and have her behold it with ensorcelled delight. She was somewhere near me in the darkness. I waited, seeing her a thousand ways in my mind before actually gazing at the real Day. I looked. "What's wrong with the stars, the sky?" was all she said. She was trembling.

At breakfast the next morning I subtly probed her for impressions and judgments of the night before. But she was badly hung over and had only a chaotic recall of what she had experienced. Well, at least she didn't go into hysterics, as did my old flame Clare.

Since our return I have been working on a painting entitled "Sanctum Obscurum." Though I have done this kind of work many times before, I am including in this one elements that I hope will stir Day's memory and precipitate a conscious recollection of not only a certain night in the islands but of all the subtle and not so subtle messages I have tried to communicate to her. I only pray she will understand.

November 14th. Stars of disaster! Earthly, not unearthly, asters are what Day's heart craves. She is too much a lover of natural flora to be anything else. I know this now. I showed her the painting, and even imagined she was excited about seeing it. But I think she was just waiting to see what kind of fool I would make of myself. She sat on the sofa, scraping her lower lip with a nervous forefinger. Opposite her I let a velvet cloth drop. She looked up as if there had been a startling noise. I was not wholly satisfied with the painting myself, but this exhibition was designed to serve an extra-aesthetic purpose. I searched her eyes for a reflection of understanding, a ripple of empathetic insight. "Well?" I asked, the necessity of the word tolling doom. Her gaze told me all I needed to know, and the fatal clarity of the message was reminiscent of another girl I once knew. She gave me a second chance, looking at the picture with a theatrical scrutiny.

The picture itself? An interior done up very much like my own apartment—a refuge crowding about a window of a disproportionate breadth, so as to direct the viewer's sight telescopically outward. Beyond the window is a vista wholly alien to terrestrial nature and perhaps to all that we deem human. Outside is a gorgeous kingdom of glittering colors and velvety jungle-shapes, a realm of contorted rainbows and twisted auroras. Hyper-radiant hues are calmed by the glass, so that their strange intensity does not threaten the chromatic integrity of the world within. Some stars, colored from the most spectral part of the spectrum, blossom in the high darkness. The outer world glistens in stellar light and is mirrored by gleams from within each labyrinthine form. And upon the window's surface is the watery reflection of a lone figure gazing out at this otherworldly paradise.

"Of course, it's very good," she observed. "Very realistic."

Not at all, Daisy Day. Not realistic in either manner or matter.

Some uncomfortable moments later Day told me she had a prior engagement and was running late. It seemed she had made girl plans with a girlfriend of hers to do some girly things girls do when they get together with others of their kind. I said I understood, and I did. There is no doubt in my mind of the gender of Day's companion this night, and perhaps other nights I did not know about. But it was for a different reason that I was distressed to see her go. Something that I could read in her every move and expression, something I have seen before, gave away her suspicions about me and my private life. Of course, she already knew about the meetings I attend and all such things. I've even paraphrased and abridged for her the discussion which goes on at these gatherings, always obscuring their real meaning in progressively more transparent guises, hoping one day to show her the naked truth. Like Clare, however, Day has prematurely learned too much of the truth about me and the others. And I fear she may decide to relay her inside information to the wrong people. The dogged Detective Briceberg, for instance.

November 16th. Tonight we held an emergency meeting, our assembly in crisis. The others feel there's a problem, and of course I know they're right. Ever since I met my latest love I could sense their growing uneasiness, which was their prerogative. Now, however, all has changed; my romantic misjudgment has seen to that. They expressed absolute horror that an outsider should know so much. I feel it myself. Day is a stranger now, and I wonder what her loquacious self might disclose about her former friend, not to mention his present ones. A marvelous arcana is threatened with exposure. The inconspicuousness we need for our lives could be lost, and with it would go the keys to a strange kingdom.

We've confronted these situations before. I'm not the only one to have jeopardized our secrecy. We, of course, have no secrets from each other. They know everything about me, and I about them. They knew every step of the way the progress of my relationship with Daisy. Some of them even predicted the outcome. And though I thought I was right in taking the chance that they were wrong, I must now defer to their prophecy. Those lonely souls, *mes frères!* "Do you want us to see it through?" they asked in so many words. I consented, finally, in a score of ambiguous, half-hesitant ways. Then they sent me back to my unflowered sanctum.

I'll never again get involved in another situation of this kind, I promised myself, even though I've made this resolution before. I stared at the razory dentes of my furry sculpture for a perilously long while. What that poor girl saw as tongue-like floral appendages were silent: the preservation of such silence, of course, is their whole purpose. I remember that Daisy once jokingly asked me on what I modeled my art.

November 17th.

> To Eden with me you will not leave
> To live in a cottage of crazy, crooked eaves.
> In your own happy home you take care these nights;
> When you let your little cat in, please turn on the lights!
> Something scurries behind and finds a cozy place to stare,
> Something sent to you from paradise, with serpents to spare:
> Tongues flowering; they leap out laughing, lapping. Disappear!

I do this to pass the hours. Only to pass the hours.

November 17th. 12:00 a.m. Flowers.

ALICE'S LAST ADVENTURE

"Preston, stop laughing. They ate the whole backyard. They ate your mother's favorite flowers! It's not funny, Preston."

"Aaaaa heh-heh-heh-heh-heh. Aaaaa heh-heh-heh-heh-heh."
—PRESTON AND THE STARVING SHADOWS

A long time ago, Preston Penn made up his mind to ignore the passing years and join the ranks of those who remain forever in a kind of half-world between childhood and adolescence. He would not give up the bold satisfaction of eating insects (crispy flies are his favorite), nor that peculiar drunkenness of a child's brain, induplicable once grown-up sobriety has set in. The result was that Preston successfully negotiated quite a few decades without ever coming within hailing distance of puberty. In this state of arrested development, he defiantly lived through many a perverse adventure. And he still lives in the pages of those books I wrote about him, though I stopped writing them some years ago.

Did he have a prototype? I should say so. One doesn't just *invent* a character like Preston using only the pitiful powers of imagination. He was very much a concoction of reality, later adapted for my popular series of children's books. Preston's status in both reality and imagination has always held a great fascination for me. In the past year, however, this issue has especially demanded my attention, not without some personal annoyance and even anxiety. Then again, perhaps I'm getting senile.

My age is no secret, since it can be looked up in a number of literary reference sources. Over twenty years ago, when the last Preston book appeared (*Preston and the Upside-Down Face*), one reviewer rather snootily referred to me as the "'Grande Damned' of a particular sort of children's literature." What *sort* you can imagine if you don't otherwise know, if you didn't grow up—or not grow up, as it were—reading Preston's adventures with the Dead Mask, the Starving Shadows, or the Lonely Mirror.

Even as a little girl, I knew I wanted to be an author; and I also knew just the kind of tales I would tell. Let someone else give preadolescents their literary introductions to life and love, guiding them through those volatile years when *anything* might go wrong and landing them safely on the shores of incipient maturity. That was never my destiny. Instead, I would write about a puckish little character based on a real-life childhood playmate of mine whose deeds of mischief were legend throughout the small town where I was born and raised. As Preston Penn, my erstwhile chum could throw off the shackles of material existence and explore the mysteries of an upside-down, inside-out, faintly sinister, and always askew universe. The embodiment of topsy-turvydom, Preston gained a reputation as a champion of misbehavior and an adventurer who looked beneath the surface of everyday things—pools of rainwater, tarnished mirrors, moonlit windows—to discover a stunning sortilege, usually with the purpose of stunning in turn his perennial foe: the dictatorial world of adulthood. A conjurer of stylish nightmares, he gave his grown-up adversaries fits and sleepless nights. No dilettante of the extraordinary, but its personification. Such is the spiritual biography of Preston Penn.

But to give credit where credit is due, it was my father, just as much as Preston's original, who provided the spark for the stories I've written. To put it briefly, Father had the blood of a child coursing through his big adult body, flooding with fancy the overly sophisticated brain of Foxborough College's associate professor of philosophy. Typical of his character was a love for the books of Lewis Carroll, and thus the genesis of my name. When I was old enough to understand such things, my mother told me that while she was pregnant my father *willed* me into a little Alice. That sounded like something he would say.

I remember one occasion when Father was reading *Through the Looking-Glass* to me for the umpteenth time. Suddenly he stopped, closed the book, and said to me, as if in deep confidence, that there was more in the Alice books than anyone knew. But that *he* knew, and someday would tell me. To Father, the creator of Alice, as I later came to see it, was a symbol of psychic supremacy, the sterling ideal of an unstrictured mind manipulating reality to its whim and gaining a kind of objective force through the minds of others. And it was very important to Father that I share "The Master's" books in the same spirit.

"See, honey," he would say while rereading *Through the Looking-Glass* to me, "see how smart little Alice right away notices that the room on the other side of the mirror is not as 'tidy' as the one she just came from. Not as *tidy*," he repeated with professorial emphasis but chuckling like a child, a strange little laugh that I inherited from him. "Not tidy. We know what *that* means, don't we?" I would look up at him and nod with all the solemnity that my six, seven, eight years could muster.

And I did know what *that* meant. I felt intimations of a thousand misshapen marvels—of things going haywire in curious ways, of the edge of the world where an endless ribbon of road continued into space by itself, of a universe handed over to new gods.

Father's imagination seemed to work nonstop. Squinting at my roundish child's countenance—saying, "Ooooh, look how she shines so bright!"—he called me "Little Moon Face."

"*You're* a little moon face," I playfully talked back.

"No, *you* are," he would say.

"Am not."

"Are too."

We'd continued this back and forth until both of us burst out laughing. When I got older, my features became more angular, an involuntary betrayal of my father's conception of his little Alice. I suppose it was a blessing that he did not live to see me succumb to the despoilments of time, saved from this heartbreak by a sudden explosion in his brain while he was giving a lecture at the college. So Father never had the chance to tell me what it was that he knew about the Alice books that nobody else did.

But perhaps he would have perceived that my maturation was only skin deep, that I just superficially picked up the conventional behaviors of an aging soul (nervous breakdown, divorce, remarriage, alcoholism, widowhood, stoic tolerance of a second-rate reality) without destroying the Alice he loved. She *must* have been kept alive, or so I would like to think, because it was she who wrote all those books about her soulmate Preston, even if she has not written one for many years now. Oh, those years, those years.

So much for the past.

At present I would like to deal with just a single year, the one ending today—about an hour from now, judging by the clock that just chimed eleven p.m. from the shadows on the other side of this study. During the past three hundred and sixty-five days I have noticed, sometimes just barely, an accumulation of curiouser and curiouser episodes in my life. A lack of tidiness, one might say, which may be partly due to the fact that I've been drinking rather heavily again.

Some of the previously mentioned episodes are so elusive and insubstantial that it would be a real chore to talk about them, except perhaps in terms of the moods they leave behind like fingerprints, and which I've learned to read like divinatory signs. My task will be less taxing if I confine myself for the most part to the grosser incidents I have to recount, thereby making it easier to give them a modicum of the sense and structure I could use just now. A tidying up as it were—neat as a pin, straight and sure as the green lines on the yellow page before me.

I should start by identifying tonight as that immovable feast which Preston always devotedly observed, celebrating it most intensely in *Preston and the Ghost of the Gourd* (even if time has almost run out on this holiday, according to the clock ticking at my back; though from the look of things, the hands seem stuck on the hour I reported a couple of paragraphs ago. Perhaps I misjudged it before.). For some years I've made an appearance at the local suburban library on this night to give a reading from one of my books as the main event of an annual Hallowe'en fest. Tonight I managed to show up once again for the reading, even if I hesitate to say everything went *as usual*. Last year, however, I did not make it at all to the costume party. This brings me to what I *think* is the first in a year-long series of disruptions unknown to a biography previously marked by nothing more than episodes of conventional chaos. My apologies for taking two steps backward before one step forward. As an old hand at storytelling, I realize this is always a risky approach when bidding for a reader's attention. But here goes.

It was one year ago today that I cancelled my reading at the library to attend an out-of-town funeral of someone from my past. This was none other than that sprite of special genius whose exploits served as the *prima materia* for my Preston Penn books. The excursion was one of pure nostalgia, however, for I hadn't actually seen this person since my twelfth birthday party. It was soon afterward that my father died, and my mother and I moved out of our house in North Sable, Mass. (see *Childhood Homes of Children's Authors* for a photo of the old two-story frame job), heading for the big city and away from sad reminders. A local teacher who knew of my work, and its beginnings in North S, sent me a newspaper clipping from the *Sable Sentinel* which reported the demise of my former playmate and even adverted to his secondhand literary fame.

I arrived in town very quietly and was immediately overwhelmed by the lack of change in the place, as if it had existed all those years in a state of suspended animation and had been only recently reanimated for my benefit. It almost seemed that I might run into my old neighbors, schoolmates, and even Mr. So and So who ran the ice-cream shop, which I was amazed to see still in operation. On the other side of the window, a big man with a walrus mustache was digging ice cream from large cardboard cylinders, while two chubby kids pressed their bellies against the counter. The man hadn't changed the least bit over the years. He looked up and saw me staring into the shop, and there really seemed to be a twinkle of recognition in his puffy eyes. But that was impossible. He could have never perceived behind my ancient mask the child's face he once knew, even if he had been Mr. So and So and not his look-alike (son? grandson?). There we were: two complete strangers gawking at each other, both of us actors performing together on the same stage but playing out different dramas. It brought to mind one of my early books, *Preston and the Two-Faced Clock,* wherein time goes by so fast that it stands still.

I shook off the black comedy of errors at the ice-cream shop and proceeded to my destination, only to find that another farce of mistaken identity awaited me there. For a few moments I paused and looked up at the words on the lintel atop the double doors of that cold colonial building: G. V. Ness and Sons, Funeral Directors. Talk about time going by so fast that it stands still, or seems to. During the years I'd lived in North Sable, I had entered this establishment only once ("Good-bye, Daddy"). But such places always seem familiar, having that perfectly vacant, neutral atmosphere common to all funeral homes, the same in my hometown as in the suburb outside New York ("Good riddance, Hubby") where I'm now secluded.

I strolled into the proper room unnoticed, another anonymous mourner who was a bit shy about approaching the casket. Though I drew a couple of small-town stares, the elderly, elegant author from the big city did not stand out as much as she thought she would. But with or without distinction, it remained my intention to introduce myself to the widow as a childhood friend of her deceased husband. This intention, however, was shot all to hell by two ox-like men who rose from their seats on either side of the grieving lady and lumbered my way. For some reason I panicked.

"You must be Dad's Cousin Winnie from Boston. The family's heard so much about you over the years," they said.

I smiled widely and gulped deeply, which must have looked like a nod of affirmation to them. In any case, they led me over to "Mom" and introduced me under my inadvertent pseudonym to the red-eyed, half-delirious old woman. (Why, I wonder, did I allow this goof to go on?)

"Nice to finally meet you, and thank you for the lovely card you sent," she said, sniffing loudly and working on her eyes with a grotesquely soiled handkerchief. "I'm Elsie."

Elsie Chester, I thought immediately, though I wasn't entirely sure that this was the same person who was rumored to have sold kisses and other things to the boys at North Sable Elementary. So he had married *her,* whaddaya know? Possibly they *had* to get married, I speculated cattily. At least one of her sons looked of sufficient age to have been the consequence of teenage impatience. Oh, well. So much for Preston's vow to wed no one less than the Queen of Nightmares.

But even greater disappointments awaited my notice. After chatting emptily with the widow for a few more moments, I excused myself to pay my respects at the coffinside of the deceased. Until then I'd deliberately averted my gaze from that flower-crazed area at the front of the room, where a shiny, pearl-grey casket held its occupant in much the same position as the "Traveling Tomb" racer he'd once constructed. This part of the mortuary ritual never fails to make me think about those corpse-viewing sessions to which children in the nineteenth century were subjected in order to acquaint them with their own mortality. At my age this was unnecessary, so allow me to skip quickly over this scene with a few tragic and inevitable words . . .

Bald and blemished, that was rather expected. *Totally* unfamiliar, that wasn't. The mosquito-faced child I once knew was now repulsively bloated and saggy, swollen up and puffy-lipped like some unidentifiable corpse the cops might find in a river. Patently, he had overfed himself at the turgid banquet of life, lethargically pushing away from the table just prior to explosion. The thing before me was a portrait of all that was defunct, used up—the ultimate adult. (But perhaps in death, I consoled myself, his child self was even now ripping off the false face of the overgrown-up before me.)

After paying homage to the remains of a memory, I slipped out of the room with a stealth my Preston would have been proud of. I'd left behind an envelope with a modest contribution to the widow's fund. I had half a mind to send a batch of gaping black orchids to the funeral home with a note signed by Laetitia Simpson, Preston's dwarfish girlfriend. But this was something that the other Alice would have done—the one who wrote those creepy books.

As for me, I got into my car and drove out of town to the nearest fine hotel, where I found a nice suite—spoils of a successful literary career—and a bar. And as it turned out, this overnight layover must take us down another side road (or back road, if you like) of my narrative. Please stand by.

A late-afternoon crowd had settled into the hotel's cocktail lounge, relieving me of the necessity of drinking in solitude. After a couple of Scotches on the rocks, I noticed a young man looking my way from across the room. At least he appeared young from a distance. Emboldened by booze, I walked over to sit at his table. And with every step I took he seemed to gain a few years. He was now only relatively young—from an old dowager's point of view, that is. His name was Hank De Vere, and he worked for a distributor of gardening tools and other such products. But let's not pretend to care about the details. Later we had dinner together, after which I invited him to my suite.

It was the next morning, by the way, that inaugurated that year-long succession of experiences which I'm methodically trying to sort out with a few select examples. Half step forward coming up: pawn to king three.

I awoke in the darkness specific to hotel bedrooms, abnormally heavy curtains masking the morning light. Immediately it became apparent that I was alone. My new acquaintance seemed to have a more developed sense of tact and timing than I had given him credit for. At least I thought so at first. But then I looked through the open doorway into the other room, where I could see a convex mirror in a wood frame on the wall.

The bulging eye of the mirror surveyed the entirety of the next room, and I noticed that something was moving around in the reflecting glass. A tiny, misshapen figure seemed to be gyring about, leaping and twirling in a madcap way that should have been audible to me. But it wasn't.

I called out a name I barely remembered from the night before. There came no answer from the next room, but the movement in the mirror stopped, and the tiny figure (whatever it was) disappeared. Very cautiously I got up from the bed, robed myself, and peeked around the corner of the doorway like a curious child on Christmas morning. A strange combination of relief and confusion arose in me when I saw that there was no one else in the suite.

I approached the mirror, perhaps to search its surface for the little *something* that might have caused the illusion. My memory is vague on this point, since at the time I was a bit hung over. But I can recall with spectacular vividness what I finally saw after gazing into the mirror for a few moments. Suddenly the sphered glass before me became clouded with a mysterious fog, from the depths of which appeared the waxy face of a corpse. It was the visage of that old cadaver I'd seen at the funeral home, now with eyes wide open and staring into mine. Or so it seemed for a moment before I put on my glasses. And when I did all I saw was only my own face . . . a corpselike kisser if ever there was one. *Preston and the Looking-Glass Ghoul,* I thought, feeling almost inspired to take up my pen once more.

And this inspiration was again aroused a short while later when I was checking out at the front desk. As the clerk was fiddling with my bill, I happened to look out of a nearby window, beyond which two chubby children were romping on the hotel lawn. After a few seconds the kids caught me watching them. They stopped and stared back at their audience, standing perfectly still, side by side. Then they stuck out their tongues at me before running away. (And how much they looked like the odious Hatley twins featured in *Preston and the Talking Grave.*) The room took a little spin that only I seemed to notice, while others went calmly about their business. Possibly this experience can be ascribed to my failure to employ any post-debauch remedies that morning. The old nerves were somewhat shot, and my stomach was giving me no peace. Still, I've remained in pretty fair health over the years, and I drove back home without further incident.

That was a year ago. Now get ready for one giant step forward: the old queen is now in play.

In the succeeding twelve months I have noted a number of similar happenings, though they occurred with varying degrees of clarity. Most of them approached the fleeting nature of déjà-vu phenomena. A few could be pegged as self-manufactured, while others lacked a definite source. I might see a phrase or the fragment of an image that would make my heart flip over (not a healthy thing at my age), while my mind searched for some correspondence that triggered this powerful sense of familiarity: the sound of a delayed echo with oblique origins. I delved into dreams, half-conscious perceptions, and the distortions of memory, but all that remained was a chain of occurrences with links as weak as smoke rings.

But today, as pumpkins leer from porches and pillow-case ghosts swing on tree branches, this tenuous haunting has gained a more substantial consistency. It started this morning and continued throughout the day with increasingly more defined and evocative manifestations. Again, my hope is that I may tidy up my psyche by documenting these episodes, beginning with one that now seems a prefiguration of those to come. Lucid exposition is what's needed. Thus:

Place: the bathroom. Time: a little after eight a.m.

The water was running for my morning wash-up, cascading into the tub a bit noisily for my sensitive ears. The night before, I suffered from an advanced case of insomnia, which even extra doses of my beloved Guardsman's Reserve Stock did not help. I was very glad to see a sunny autumn morning come and rescue me. My bathroom mirror, however, would not let me forget the sleepless night I'd spent, and I combed and creamed myself without noticeable improvement. Chessie was with me, lying atop the toilet tank and scrutinizing the waters of the bowl below. She was actually staring very hard and deliberately at something.

"What is it, Chessie?" I asked with the patronizing voice of a pet owner. Her tail had a life of its own; she stood up and hissed, then yowled in that horribly demonic falsetto of threatened felines. Finally she dashed out of the bathroom, relinquishing her ground for the first time since she was a kitten.

I had been loitering at the other side of the room, a groggy bystander to an unexpected incident. With a large plastic hairbrush gripped in my left hand, I investigated. I gazed down into the same waters. And though at first they seemed clear enough, something soon appeared from within its porcelain burrow. However, it retreated too soon back into the plumbing for me to say what it was. All that remained was a squiggly imprint on my memory. But I could not bring it into mental focus. It was as if I saw the thing and did not see it at the same time. Even so, whatever it may have been engendered a flurry of impressions within me, as of a confused nightmare that leaves behind only a pang of horror upon its dreamer. I wouldn't even bring up this installment in my story if I didn't think it related to another that occurred later on.

This afternoon I began preparing myself for the reading I was to give at the library, the preparation being mostly alcoholic. I've never looked forward to this annual ordeal and only put up with it out of a sense of duty, vanity, and other less comprehensible motives. Maybe this is why I welcomed the excuse to skip it last year. And I wanted to skip it this year, too, if only I could have come up with a reason satisfactory to the others involved—and, more importantly, to myself. Wouldn't want to disappoint the children, would I? Of course not, though heaven only knows why. Children have made me nervous ever since I stopped being one of them. Perhaps this is why I never had any of my own—adopted any, that is—for the doctors told me long ago that I'm about as fertile as the seas of the moon.

The other Alice is the one who's really comfortable with kids and kiddish things. How else could she have written *Preston and the Laughing This* or *Preston and the Twitching That*? So when it comes time to do this reading every year, I try to put *her* onstage as much as possible, something that's becoming more difficult with the passing years. Oddly enough, it's my grown-up's weakness for spirits that allows me to do this most effectively. With each sip of Scotch that passed my lips today I felt more at ease.

The sun was going down in a pumpkin-colored blaze when I arrived at the little one-story library. Some costumed kids were hanging around outside: a werewolf, a black cat with a long curling tail, an extraterrestrial with fewer fingers than humans and more eyes. Coming up the walk was Tinkerbell escorted by a pirate. In spite of myself, I couldn't help smiling at the whole scene. For the first time in quite a while, this pageant of masqueraders brought back memories of my own childhood when my father took me trick-or-treating. (His love of this night was easily as avid as Preston's.) Having gotten into the spirit of this eve, I was feeling quite confident as I entered the library and confronted a flock of youngsters. But the spell was maliciously broken when some smart aleck called out from the crowd, shouting: "Hey, lookit the mask *she's* wearing." After that I propelled myself down several linoleum hallways in search of a friendly adult face.

Finally I passed the open door of a tidy little room where a group of ladies and the head librarian, Mr. Grosz, were sipping coffee. Mr. Grosz said how nice it was to see me again and introduced me to the moms who were helping out with the party.

"My William's read all your books," said a full-figured Mrs. Harley. "I just can't keep him away from them." Not for lack of trying, I thought, judging by the quietly infuriated tone of her voice. My only reply was a dignified smile.

Mr. Grosz offered me some coffee but I declined: bad for the stomach. Then he wickedly suggested that, as it was starting to get dark outside, the time seemed right for the festivities to begin. My reading was to inaugurate the evening's fun, a good spooky story "to get everyone in the mood." First, though, I needed to get myself in the mood, and pardoned myself to use the ladies' room, where I could refortify my fluttering nerves from a flask I had stowed away in my purse. As a strange and embarrassing social gesture, Mr. Grosz offered to wait right outside the lavatory until I finished.

"I'm quite ready now, Mr. Grosz," I said, glaring down at the little man from atop an unelderly pair of high heels. He cleared his throat, and I almost thought he was going to extend a crooked arm for me to take. But instead he merely stretched it out to indicate, in a stock gentlemanly manner, the way to go. I think he might even have bowed.

He led me back down the hallway toward the children's section of the library, where I assumed my reading would take place as it always had in the past. However, we walked right by this area, which was dark and empty, and proceeded down a flight of stairs leading to the library's basement. "Our new facility," bragged Mr. Grosz. "Converted one of the storage rooms into a small auditorium of sorts." We were now facing a large metal door painted an institutional shade of green. It looked for all the world as if it might lead into the back ward of a mad-house. I could hear screaming on the other side, which sounded to me like the cries of bedlamites rather than the clamor of rambunctious kids. "Which one will it be tonight?" asked Mr. Grosz while staring at my left hand. *"Preston and the Starving Shadows,"* I answered, showing him the book I was holding. He smiled and confided that it was one of his favorites. Then he opened the door for me, pushing its weight with both hands, and we entered what chamber of horrors I knew not.

Over fifty kids were sitting in or standing on or knocking over their seats. Shouting from the podium at the front of the long, narrow room, a pointy-hatted witch was outlining the party activities for the night; and when she saw Mr. Grosz and me arrive, she began telling the children about a "special treat for us all," meaning that the half-crocked lady author was about to deliver a half-cocked oration. "Let's give her a big hand," she said, clapping as I stepped onto the rickety-looking platform. I thanked everyone for inviting me to their party and fixed my book on a lamp-bearing lectern decorated with wizened cornstalks. Then I tried my best to warm up the crowd with a little patter about the story everyone was going to hear. When I invoked the name of Preston Penn, a few kids actually cheered, or at least one did at the rear of the room. I assumed it was William Harley.

Just as I was about to begin reading, something happened I had not been led to expect—the lights were switched off. ("It slipped my mind entirely," Mr. Grosz apologized afterward.) In the dark, I noticed that facing each other on opposite sides of the room were two rows of jack-o'-lanterns glowing orange and yellow from on high. They all had identical faces and looked like mirror reflections of one another, with triangular eyes and noses and wailing Os for mouths. (As a child, I was convinced that pumpkins naturally grew this way, complete with facial features and phosphorescent insides.) Furthermore, they seemed to be suspended in space, their means of support concealed by the darkness, which also hid within it the faces of the children. Thus, these jack-o'-lanterns became my audience.

But as I read, the real audience asserted itself with foot

shuffling, whispers, and some rather ingenious noises made with
the folding wooden chairs they were sitting in. I also heard a
"devilish giggling," in the words I employed to describe the
snickering laughter of the very imp whose story I was reciting.
Toward the end of the reading, there came a low moan from
somewhere in the back, and it sounded as if a seat had fallen
over along with whoever was sitting in it. "It's all right," I
heard an adult voice call out. The door at the back opened,
allowing a moment of brightness to break the spooky spell, and
some shadows exited. When the lights came on at the end of the
story, I noticed that one of the seats in the last row was missing
its occupant.

"Okay, kids," said the parental witch after some minor applause
for Preston, "everyone move their chairs against the walls and
make room for the games and stuff."

The games and stuff had the room in a low-grade uproar.
Masked children ruled the night, indulging their appetite for
sweet things to eat and drink, disorder for its own sake, and
high-spirited pandemonium. I stood at the periphery of the
commotion and chatted with Mr. Grosz.

"What exactly was the disturbance all about?" I asked him.
"Did one of the kids have a spell of some kind?"

He took a gulp from a plastic cup of cider and smacked his
lips offensively. "Oh, it was nothing. You see that child there
with the black-cat outfit? She seemed to have fainted. But once
we got her outside she was all right. She had on her kitty mask
all through your reading, and I think the poor thing hyperven-
tilated or something like that. Complained that she saw something in her mask and was very frightened for a while. At any
rate, you can see she's fine now, and she's even wearing her
mask again. Amazing how children can put things right out of
their minds and recover so quickly."

I agreed that it was amazing, and then asked precisely what
it was the child thought she saw in her mask. I couldn't help
being reminded of another cat earlier in the day that also saw
something that gave her a fright.

"She couldn't really explain it," replied Mr. Grosz. "It was
just something that came and went. You know how it is with

children. Yes, I daresay you *do* know, considering you've spent
your life writing about them."

I took credit for knowing how it is with children, knowing
instead that Mr. Grosz was really talking about someone else,
about *her*. Not to overdo this quaint notion of a split between
my professional and my private personas, but at the time I was
already quite self-conscious about the matter. While I was
reading the Preston book to the kids, I had suffered the uncanny
experience of having almost no recognition of my own words.
Of course, this is rather a cliché with writers, and it has happened to me many times throughout my long career. But never
so completely. They were the words of someone entirely alien
to me. They were written by some other Alice. And I'm not
her, at least not anymore.

"I do hope," I said to Mr. Grosz, "that it wasn't the story that
scared the child. I have enough angry parents on my hands as
it is."

"Oh, I'm sure it wasn't. Not that it wasn't a good scary children's story. I didn't mean to imply that, of course. But, you
know, it's that time of year. Imaginary things are supposed to
seem more real. Like your Preston. He was always a big one
for Hallowe'en, am I right?"

I said he was quite right and hoped he would not pursue the
subject. "Imaginary things" were not at all what I wanted to
talk about just then. I tried to laugh it away. And you know,
Father, for a moment it was exactly like your own laugh and
not my hereditary impersonation of it.

Much to everyone's regret, I did not stay very long at the
party. The reading had largely sobered me up, and my tolerance level was running quite low. Yes, Mr. Grosz, I promise to
do it again next year, anything you say; just let me get back to
my car and my bar.

The drive home through the suburban streets was something
of an ordeal, a trip made unnerving as well as hazardous by
pedestrian trick-or-treaters. The costumes did me no good. (The
same ghost was everywhere, a lean little wraith that I imagined
was following me home.) The masks did me no good. And those
Prestonian shadows wavering against two-story façades (why

did I have to choose *that* book?) certainly did me no good at all. Alice, the other one, could take all this madness, every nightmare her creator threw at her. That horrible Rev. Dodgson. I don't care if there is more in his books than anyone knows. I don't want to know. I wish I had never heard of him—that corrupter of little minds. I just want to forget it all. *Alice and the Disappearing Past.* Dr. Guardsman, administer your medicine in tall glasses . . . but please not looking-ones.

And now I'm safe at home with one of the tallest of those glasses resting full and faithful on my desk as I write. A lamp with a shade of Tiffany glass (circa 1922) casts its amiable light on the pages I've filled over the past few hours. (Though the hands of the clock seem locked in the same V position as when I started writing.) The lamplight shines upon the window directly in front of my desk, allowing me to see a relatively flattering reflection of myself in the black mirror of the glass. The house is soundless, and I'm a rich, retired authoress-widow.

Is there still a problem? I'm not really sure.

I remind you that I've been drinking steadily since early this afternoon. I remind you that I'm old and no stranger to the mysteries of geriatric neuroticism. I remind you that some part of me has written a series of children's books whose hero is a disciple of the bizarre. I remind you of what night this is and to what zones the imagination can fly on this hallowed eve. I need not, however, remind you that this world is stranger than we know, or at least mine seems to be, especially this past year. And I now notice that it's *very* strange—and, once again, untidy.

Exhibit One. Outside my window is an autumn moon hanging in the blackness. Now, I have to confess that I'm not up on lunar phases ("loony faces," as Preston might say), but there seems to have been a switch since I last looked out the window—the thing seems to have reversed itself. Where it used to be concaving to the right, it's now *convexing* in that direction, last quarter changed to first quarter, or something of that nature. But I doubt Nature has anything to do with it; more likely the explanation lies with Memory. So it's not the moon as such that's troubling me. The real trouble is with everything else, or at least what I can see of the suburban landscape in the street-lighted darkness. Like writing that can only be read in a mirror, the shapes outside my window—trees, houses, but thank goodness no people—now look awkward and wrong.

Exhibit Two. To the earlier list of reasons for my diminished competence, I would like to add an upcoming alcohol withdrawal. The last mouthful I guzzled from that glass on my desk tasted strangely vile, noxious to the point where I doubt I'll be having any more. I almost wrote, and now will, that the booze tasted inside out. Of course, there are certain diseases with the power to turn the flavor of one's favorite drink into that of a hellbroth. Perhaps, then, I've fallen victim to such a malady. But I remind you that though my mind may be terminally soused, it has always resided *in corpore sano.*

Exhibit Three (the last). My reflection in the window before me. Perhaps something faulty in the melt of the glass. My face. The surrounding shadows seem to be overlapping it a little at a time, like bugs attracted to something sweet. But the only thing sweet about Alice is her blood, highly sugared over the years from her drinking habit. So what is it, then? Shadows of senility? Or those starving things I read about earlier this evening come back for a repeat performance? Since when does reading a story constitute an incantation calling up its imagery before the body's eyes and not the mind's?

Something's backward here. Backward into a corner: *checkmate.*

Now, perhaps this seems like merely a cry of wolf, however sincere I may be. I can't actually say that it isn't. I can't say that what I'm hearing right now isn't some Hallowe'en trick of my besotted brain.

The giggling out in the hallway, I mean. That demonic giggling I heard at the library. Even when I concentrate, I'm still not able to tell if the sound is inside or outside my head. It's like looking at one of those toy pictures that yield two distinct scenes when tilted this way or that, but, at a certain angle, form only a merging blur of them both. Nonetheless, the laughing is there, somewhere. And the voice is so familiar.

Aaaaa heh-heh-heh-heh-heh.

Exhibit Four (the shadows again). They're all over my face in the window. Stripping away, as in the story. But there's nothing under that old mask; no child's face there, Preston. It *is* you, isn't it? I've never heard your laughter, except in my mind. Yet that's exactly how I imagined it would sound. Or has my imagination given you, too, a hand-me-down, inherited laugh?

My only fear is that it isn't you but some impostor. The moon, the clock, the drink, the window. This is all very much your style, only it's not being done in fun, is it? It's not funny at all. Stop it, Preston, or whoever you are. And who is it? Who could be doing this? I've been good. I just got old, that's all. Please stop. The shadows in the window are coming out. No, not my face. Not my little moon face.

> I can't see
>   anymore
>   I can't see.

> Help me
>   Father

DREAM OF A MANIKIN

Once upon a Wednesday afternoon a girl stepped into my office for her first session. Her name was Amy Locher. (And didn't you once tell me that long ago you had a doll with this same given name?) Under the present circumstances I don't think it too gross a violation of professional ethics to use the subject's real name in describing her case to you. Certainly there's something more than simple ethics between us, *ma chère amie*. Besides, I understood from Miss Locher that you recommended me to her. This didn't seem necessarily ominous at first; perhaps, I speculated, your relationship with the girl was such that made it awkward for you to take her on as one of your own patients. Actually it's still not clear to me, my love, just how deeply you can be implicated in the overall experience I had with the petite Miss L. So you'll have to forgive any stupidities of mine which may crudely crop up in the body of this correspondence.

My first impression of Miss Locher, as she positioned herself almost sidesaddle in a leather chair before me, was that of a tense but basically self-possessed young woman. She was outfitted, I noticed, in much the classic style you normally favor. I won't go into our first-visit preliminaries here (though we can discuss these and other matters at dinner this Saturday if only you are willing). After a brief chat we zeroed in on what Miss Locher called the "motivating factor" for consulting me. This involved, as you may or may not know, a recurring dream she had been having over the period of about a month. What will follow are the events of that dream as I have composed them from my tape of Miss Locher's September 10th session.

In the dream our subject has entered into a new life, at least to the extent that she holds down a different job from her waking one. Miss Locher had already informed me that for three years she has worked as a loan processor at a local financial firm. However, her working day in the dream finds her as a long-time employee of a fashionable clothing shop. Like those witnesses for the prosecution that the government wishes to protect with new identities, she has been outfitted by the dream with what seems to be a mostly tacit but somehow complete biography; a marvelous trick of the mind, this. It appears that one of the duties of her new job is to change the clothes of the manikins in the shop's display windows. She in fact feels as if her entire existence is slavishly given over to dressing and undressing these dummies. She is profoundly dissatisfied with her lot, and the manikins become the focal point of her animus.

Such is the general background presupposed by the dream, which now begins in proper. As our dummy dresser approaches her work, she is overwhelmed by an amorphous anxiety without a specific source. An awesome load of new clothes has arrived to adorn a display of manikins. Their unclothed bodies repel her touch because, as Miss Locher explained, they are neither warm nor cold, as only artificial bodies can be. (Note this rare awareness of temperature in a dream, albeit neutral.) After bitterly surveying the ranks of these putty-faced creatures, she says: "Time to stop dancing and get dressed, sleeping beauties." These words are spoken without spontaneity, as if ritually uttered to inaugurate each dressing session. But the dream changes before the dresser is able to put one stitch on the dummies, who stare at nothing with "anticipating" eyes.

The working day is now finished. She has returned to her small apartment, where she retires to bed . . . and has a dream. (This dream is that of the manikin dresser and not hers, she emphatically pointed out!)

The manikin dresser dreams she is in her bedroom. But what she now thinks of as her "bedroom" is to all appearances actually an archaically furnished hall with the dimensions of a small theater. The room is dimly lit by some jeweled lamps along the walls, the lights shining upon an intricately patterned carpet and various pieces of old furniture. She perceives the objects of the scene more as pure ideas than as material phenomena, for details are blurry and there are many shadows. There is something, however, which she visualizes quite clearly: one of the walls of this lofty room is missing, and beyond this great gap is a view of star-clustered blackness.

The dreamer is positioned on the other side of the room from the brink of the starry abyss. Sitting on the edge of a velvety divan, she stares and waits "without breath or heartbeat." All is silent, another odd perception to have in a dream. This silence somehow "electrifies" the dream with strange currents of force betokening an unseen demonic presence.

Then a new feeling enters the dream, one slightly more tangible. There seems to be an iciness drifting in from that starscape across the room. (Temperature again; a rare dream indeed!) Once again our dreamer experiences a premonitory dread of something unknown. Without moving from her place on that uncomfortable couch, she visually searches the room for clues to the source of her terror. Many areas are inaccessible to her sight—like a picture that has been scribbled out in places—but she sees nothing particularly frightening and is relieved for a moment. Then her trepidation begins anew when she realizes for the first time that she hasn't looked behind her, and indeed she seems physically unable to do so.

Something is back there. She feels this to be a horrible truth. She *almost* knows what the thing is, but, afflicted with some kind of oneiric aphasia, she cannot find the word for what she fears. She can only wait, hoping that sudden shock will soon bring her out of the dream, for she is now aware that "she is dreaming," thinking of herself in the third person.

The words "she is dreaming" somehow form a ubiquitous motif for the present situation: as a legend written somewhere at the bottom of the dream, as echoing voices bouncing here and there around the room, as a motto printed upon fortune cookie-like strips of paper and hidden in bureau drawers, and as a broken record repeating itself on an ancient Victrola inside the dreamer's head. Then all the words of this monotonous slogan gather from their diverse places and like an alighting flock of birds settle in the area behind the dreamer's back. There they twitter for a moment, as upon the frozen shoulders of a statue in a park. This is actually the way it seems to the dreamer, including the statue comparison. Something statuesque is approaching her. It radiates a field of dynamic tension that grows more intense the closer it comes, its shadow lengthening upon the floor. Still, she cannot turn around to see the horror behind her, for at this point she cannot move her body, which is stiff-jointed and rigid. Perhaps she can scream, she thinks, and makes an attempt to do so. But this fails, because by then there is already a firm and tepid hand that has covered her mouth from behind. The fingers on her lips feel like thick, naked crayons. Then she sees a long slim arm extending itself over her left shoulder, and a hand that is holding some filthy rags before her eyes and shaking them, "making them dance." And at that moment a dry sibilant voice whispers into her ear: "It's time to get dressed, little dolling."

She tries to look away, her eyes being the only things she can move. Now, for the first time, she notices that all around the room—in the shadowed places—are people dressed as dolls. Their forms are collapsed, their mouths opened wide. They do not look as if they are still alive. Some of them have actually become dolls, their flesh no longer supple and their eyes having lost the appearance of teary moistness. Others are at various intermediate stages between humanness and dollhood. With horror, the dreamer now becomes aware that her own mouth is opened wide and will not close.

But at last, shaking with tremors of the uncanny, she is able to turn around and face the menacing agent. The dream now reaches a shattering crescendo and she awakes. She does not, however, awake in the bed of the manikin dresser in her dream within a dream, but instead finds herself directly transported into the tangled, though real, bedcovers of her loan processor self. Not exactly sure where or who she is for a moment, her first impulse on awaking is to complete the movement she began in the dream; that is, turning around to look behind her. (The hypnopompic hallucination that followed made her feel as if she had temporarily lost her mind.) What she saw, upon pivoting about, was more than just a blank wall. For projecting out of that moon-whitened surface was the face of a female manikin. And what particularly disturbed her about this illusion (and here we go deeper into already dubious realms) was that the face didn't melt away into the background of the wall the way post-dream projections usually do. It seems, rather, that this protruding visage, in one smooth movement, *withdrew* back into the wall. Her screams summoned more than a few concerned persons from neighboring apartments. End of dream and related experiences.

Now, my darling, you can probably imagine my reaction to the above psychic yarn. Every loose skein I followed led me back to you. The character of Miss Locher's dream is strongly reminiscent, in both mood and scenario, of matters you have been exploring for some years now. I'm referring, of course, to the all-around astral ambiance of Miss Locher's dream and how eerily it relates to certain notions (very well, *theories*) that in my opinion have become altogether too central to your *oeuvre* as well as to your *vie*. Above all, I refer to those "otherworlds" you say you've detected through a combination of occult studies and depth analysis. At this juncture, allow me to digress for a brief lecture apropos of the preceding.

It's not that I object to your delving into speculative models of reality, sweetheart, but why this particular one? Why posit these "little zones," as I've heard you call them, having such hideous attributes, or should I say anti-attributes (to keep up with your theoretical lingo)? To whimsically joke about such bizarrerie with phrases like "pockets of interference" and "cosmic static" belies your talents as a thoughtful member of our profession. And the rest of it: the hyper-uncanniness, the "ontological games," the generally cosmic substance of these places, and all that other transcendent nonsense. I realize that psychology has charted some awfully weird areas in its maps of the mind, but you've gone so far into the ultra-mentational hinterlands of metaphysics that I fear you will not return (at least not with your reputation intact).

To speak of your ideas with regard to Miss Locher's dream, you can see the correlations, especially in the winding plot of her narrative. But I'll tell you when these links to your fanciful hypotheses really struck me with a hammer blow. It was just after she had related her dream to me. Now riding the saddle of her chair in the normal position, she made a few remarks obviously intended to convey the full extent of her disquiet. I'm sure she thought it *de rigueur* to tell me that after her dream episode she began entertaining doubts concerning what she really was. Loan processor? Manikin dresser? Other? Other other? Rationally, she knew her genuine, factual self. However, some "new sense of unreality" undermined her complete emotional assurance in this matter.

Surely you can see how the foregoing existential tricks fit in with those "harassments of the self," as you style such phenomena. And just what are the boundaries of the self? Is there a secret communion of seemingly separate things? How do animate and inanimate relate? Very boring, m'dear . . . zzzzz.

It all reminds me of that trite little fable of the Chinese philosopher (Chuang Tzu?) who dreamed he was a butterfly but upon waking affected not to know whether he was a man who'd dreamed he was a butterfly or a butterfly now dreaming . . . you get the idea. The question is: "Do things like butterflies dream?" Answer: an unequivocal "no," as you may be aware from the research done in this field. The issue is ended right there. Accredited studies notwithstanding—as I'm sure you would contest—suppose the dreamer is not a man or butterfly, but both . . . or neither, something else altogether. Or suppose . . . really we could go on and on like this, and we have. Possibly the most repellent concept you've developed is that which you call "divine masochism," or the doctrine of a Bigger Self terrorizing its little splinter selves, precisely that Something Else Altogether scarifying the man-butterfly with suspicions that there's a game going on over its head.

The trouble with all this, my beloved, is the way you're so adamant about its objective reality, and how you sometimes manage to infect others with your far-fetched convictions. Me, for instance. After hearing Miss Locher tell her dream story, I found myself unconsciously analyzing it much as you might have. Her multiplication of roles (including the role reversal with the manikin) really did put me in mind of some divine being that was splintering and scarring itself to relieve its cosmic ennui, as indeed a few of the well-reputed gods of world religion supposedly do. I also thought of your "divinity of the dream," that thing which is all-powerful in its own sphere. Contemplating the realm of Miss Locher's dream, I did experience a fleeting sense of that old vagary about a solipsistic dream deity commanding all it sees, all of which is only itself. And a corollary to solipsism even occurred to me: if, in any possible universe, one *always* has to allow that there are other universes that may be only dreams, then the problem becomes, as with our Chinese sleepy-head, knowing when one is actually dreaming and what form the waking self may have. And this is something one can *never* know. The fact that the overwhelming majority of thinkers reject any doctrine of solipsism more than suggests its unreality. And, after all, the feeling of dissociation from reality takes place only in a conscious state and not in dreams, wherein everything is absolutely real.

See what you've done to me! For reasons that you well know, my love, I try to give what serious consideration I can to your aberrant investigations. I can't help myself. But I don't think it right to be exerting your influence upon innocents like Miss Locher. I should tell you that I hypnotized the girl. And her unconscious testimony seems very much to incriminate you. She practically demanded the hypnosis, feeling this to be an easy way of unveiling the source of her problems. Because of her frantic insistence, I obliged her. A serendipitous discovery ensued.

She was a superior subject. In hypnosis we restricted ourselves to penetrating the mysteries of her dream. Her mesmerized rendition of it was amazingly consistent with her waking version, with the exception of one important item which I'll get to in a moment. I asked her to enlarge upon her feelings in the dream and any sense of meaning she experienced. Her responses to these questions were sometimes given in the incoherent language of the oneiric. She said some quite awful things about life and lies and "this dream of flesh." I don't think I need to go into the details of the chilling nonsense she uttered, for I've heard you say much the same in one of your "states." (Really, it's appalling the way you dwell both on and in your zones of the metaphysically flayed self.)

That little thing which Miss Locher mentioned only under

hypnosis, and which I have deferred referencing in its particulars, was a very telling piece of data. It told on you. For when my patient first described the scenes of her dream drama to me, she had forgotten—or just neglected to touch on—the presence of another character hidden in the background. This deep-cover agent was the proprietor of the clothing store, a domineering boss who was played by a certain lady psychoanalyst. Not that you were ever on stage, even in a cameo appearance. But the hypnotized Miss Locher did remark in passing on the identity of this imperious figure in the dream of her working-girl self, this information being one of the many underlying suppositions of the dream. So you, my dear, were present in Miss Locher's hypnotic statement in more than just spirit.

I found this revelation immensely helpful in coordinating the separate items of evidence against you. The nature of the said evidence, however, was such that I could not rule out the possibility of a conspiracy between you and Miss Locher. So I refrained from asking my new patient anything about her relationship with you, and I didn't inform her of what she disclosed under hypnosis. My assumption was that she was guilty until proven otherwise.

Alternatives did occur to me, though, especially when I realized Miss Locher's extraordinary susceptibility to hypnosis. Isn't it just possible, sweet love, that Miss Locher's incredible dream was brought on by one of those post-hypnotic suggestions at which you're so well practiced? I know that lab experiments in this area are sometimes eerily successful; and eeriness is, without argument, your specialty. Still another possibility involves the study of dream telepathy, in which you have no small interest. So what were you doing the night Miss Locher underwent her dream ordeal? (You weren't with me, I know that!) And how many of those eidola on my poor patient's mental screen were images projected from an outside source? These are just some of the peculiar questions which lately seem so necessary to ask.

But the answers to such questions would still only establish your means in this crime. What about your motive? On this point I need not exert my psychic resources. It seems there is nothing you won't do to impose your ideas upon common humanity—

deplorably on your patients, obnoxiously on your colleagues, and affectionately (I hope) on me. I know it must be hard for a lonely visionary like yourself to remain mute and ignored, but you've chosen such an eccentric path to follow that I fear there are few spirits brave enough to accompany you into those zones of calculated deception, at least not voluntarily.

Which brings us back to Miss Locher. By the close of our first, and only, session I still wasn't sure whether she was a willing or unwilling emissary of yours. Hence, I kept mum about anything concerning your role in this mystery tale. Nor did she happen to speak of you in any significant way, except of course unconsciously in hypnosis. At any rate, as first sessions go, this one was more arduous and time-consuming than usual, which left my new patient no less tautly wired than when we began. Not unreasonably, she asked me to prescribe for her. As Dr. Bovary tried to assuage the oppressive dreams of his wife with a prescription of valerian and camphor baths, I supplied Miss Locher with a program for serenity that included Valium and companionship (the latter of which I also recommend for us, dolling). Then we made a date for the following Wednesday at the same time. Miss Locher seemed most grateful, though not enough, according to my secretary, to pay up what she owed. And wait till you find out where she wanted us to send the bill.

The following week Miss Locher did not appear for her appointment. This did not really alarm me, for as you know many patients—armed with a script for tranquilizers and a single experience of therapy—decide they don't need any more help. But by then I had developed such a personal interest in Miss Locher's case that I was seriously disappointed at the prospect of not being able to pursue it further.

After fifteen patientless minutes had elapsed, I had my secretary call Miss Locher at the number she gave us. (With my former secretary—rest in peace—this would have been done automatically; so the new girl is not as good as you said she was, doctor. I shouldn't have let you insinuate her into my employ . . . but that's my fault, isn't it?) Maggie came into my office a few minutes later, presumably after she'd tried to reach Miss Locher. With rather cryptic impudence she suggested I dial the number myself, giving me the form containing all the information on our new patient. Then she left the room without saying another word. The nerve of that soon-to-be-unemployed girl.

I called the number, and it rang twice before someone answered. This someone was a young woman by the sound of her voice, though not our Miss Locher. And the way she answered the phone told me I had a wrong number (the right wrong number). Nevertheless, I asked if an Amy Locher was associated in any way with the place I called. But the answering voice expressed total ignorance regarding the existence of any person by that name. I thanked her and hung up.

You will have to forgive me, my lovely, if by this time I began to feel like the victim of a hoax. "Maggie," I intercommed, "how many more appointments for this afternoon?" "Just one," she immediately answered, and then without being asked said: "But I can cancel it if you'd like." I said I would like and that I intended to be out for the rest of the afternoon.

My intention was to call on Miss Locher at the, probably also phony, address on her new patient form. I had the suspicion that the address would lead to the same geographical spot as had the electronic nexus of the false phone number. Of course I could have easily verified this without leaving my office; but knowing you, sweet one, I thought that a personal visit was warranted. And I was right.

The address was a half-hour's drive away. It was in a high-class suburb on the other side of town from that high-class suburb in which I have my office. (And I wish you would move your own place of business from its present location, unless for some reason you need to be near a skid-row source that broadcasts on frequencies of chaos and squalor, which you'd probably claim.) I parked my big black car down the block from the street number I was seeking, which turned out to be located in the middle of the suburb's shopping district.

This was last Wednesday, which, if you'll recall, was a meteorologically abysmal day (an accomplishment I do *not* list among all your orchestrated connivances of my adventure). It was dim and moody most of the morning, and so prematurely dark by late afternoon that there were stars seemingly visible in the sky. A storm was imminent and the air was appropriately galvanized with a pre-deluge feeling of suspense. Display windows were softly glowing, and a jewelry store twinkled in the threatening gloom as I passed by. Of course, there's no further need to describe the atmosphere of that day, dear love. I just wanted to show how sensitive I was to a certain kind of portentous mood I know you adore, and how ripe I'd become for the staged antics to follow.

Distancewise, I only had to walk a few steps before arriving at the place purported to be the home of our Miss L. By then it was quite clear what I would find. There were no surprises so far. When I looked up at the neon-inscribed name of the shop, I heard a young woman's telephone voice whispering the words into my ear: Mademoiselle Fashions. And this is the store—n'est-ce pas?—where it seems you acquire so many of your own lovely ensembles. But I'm jumping ahead with my expectations.

What I did not expect were the sheer *lengths* to which you would go in order to fire up my sense of strange revelation. Was this, I pray, done to bring us closer in the divine bonds of unreality? Anyway, I saw what you wanted me to see, or what I thought you wanted me to see, in the window of Mlle Fashions. The thing was even dressed in the same plaid-skirted outfit that I recall Miss Locher was wearing on her only visit to my office. And I have to admit that I was taken aback when I focused on the frozen face of the manikin. Then again, perhaps I was subliminally looking for a resemblance between Miss Locher (your fellow conspirator, whether she knows it or not) and the figure in the window. You can probably guess what I noticed, or thought I noticed, about its eyes—what you would have me perceive as a watery gleam in their fixed gaze. Oh, woe is this Wednesday's child!

Unfortunately, I was unable to linger long enough to confirm positively the above perception, for a medium-intensity shower began to descend at that point. The rain sent me running to a nearby phone booth, where I had some business to conduct anyway. Retrieving the number of the clothing shop from my memory, I phoned them for the second time that afternoon. That was easy. What was not quite as easy was imitating your voice, my high-pitched love, and asking if the store's accounting department had mailed out a bill that month for my, I mean your, charge account. My impersonation of you must have been adequate, for the voice on the phone reminded me that I'd already taken care of all my recent expenditures. I, by whom I mean you, thanked the salesgirl for this information, apologizing for "our" forgetfulness, and then said good-bye. Perhaps I should have asked the girl if she was the one who helped rig up that manikin to look like Miss Locher, if indeed the situation was not the other way around, with Miss Locher following the fashion of display-window dummies. In any case, I did establish a definite link between you and the clothing shop. It seemed you might have accomplices anywhere, and to tell you the truth I was beginning to feel a bit paranoid standing in that little phone booth.

The rain was coming down even harder as I made a mad dash back to my black sedan. A bit soaked, I sat in the car for a few moments wiping off my rain-spotted glasses with a handkerchief. I said that I felt a slight case of paranoia coming on, and what follows proves it. While sitting there with my glasses off, I thought I saw something move in the rearview mirror. My visual vulnerability, combined with the claustrophobic sensation of being in a car with rain-blinded windows, together added up to a momentary but very definite panic on my part. I quickly put on my glasses and found there was no one—and no *thing*—whatever in the back seat. But the point is that I was forced to physically verify this fact in order to relieve my spasm of anxiety. You succeeded, my love, in getting me to experience a moment of self-terror. And in that moment I, too, became an accomplice in the mystical conspiracy of a treacherous universe. Brava!

You have indeed succeeded—assuming my inferences stand solid—in swaying me on a string you hold between your delicate fingers. Having confessed this much, I can now get to the *real* focus and "motivating factor" of my appeal to you. This has far less to do with A. Locher than it does with us, dearest. Please try to be sympathetic and, above all, patient.

I have not been well lately, and you know the reason why. This business with Miss Locher, far from bringing us to a more intimate understanding of each other, has only made the situation worse. Horrible nightmares now plague me on a nightly basis. Me, of all people! And they are directly due to the well-intentioned (I think) influence of you and Miss L. Let me describe one of these nightmares for you, and thereby describe them all. This will be the last dream story, I promise.

In the dream I am in my bedroom, sitting upon my unmade bed and wearing my pajamas (Oh, will you never see them?).

The room is partially illuminated by beams from a streetlight shining through the window. And it also seems to me that a galaxy of constellations, though not witnessed firsthand, are contributing their light to the scene, a vaporous glowing which unnaturally blanches the entire upstairs of the house. I have to use the bathroom and walk sleepily out to the hallway . . . where I get the shock of my life.

In the whitened hallway—I cannot say *brightened*, because it is almost as if a fluorescent powder coats everything—there are things that look like people dressed as dolls, or else dolls made up to look like people. I remember being confused about which it was. And they are lying up and down the floor, at the top of the stairway, and even upon the stairs themselves as they disappear into the darker regions below. When I emerge from the bedroom, I see their eyes shining in the white darkness, and their heads are turned in all directions. Paralyzed—yes!—with terror, I merely return a fixed gaze, wondering if my eyes are shining the same as theirs. Then one of the doll people, slouching against the wall on my left, turns its head haltingly upon a stiff little neck and looks straight at me. Worse, it talks. And its voice is a horrible parody of human speech. Even more horrible are its words when it says: "Become as we are, sweetie. Die *into* us." Suddenly I begin to feel very weak, as if my life were being drained out of me. Summoning all my willpower, I manage to rush back to my bed, which ends the dream.

After I awake, screaming, my heart pounds like a mad prisoner inside me and doesn't let up until morning. This is very disturbing, for there's truth in those studies relating nightmares to cardiac arrest. For some poor souls, that imaginary incubus squatting upon their sleeping forms can do real medical harm. And I do not want to become one of these cases.

You can help me, my precious. I know you didn't intend

things to turn out this way, but that bit of intrigue you perpetrated with the help of Miss Locher has really gotten to me. Consciously, of course, I still uphold the criticism I've already expressed about the basic absurdity of your work. Unconsciously, however, you seem to have awakened me to a stratum of abject terror. I will at least admit that your ideas form a powerful psychic metaphor, though no more than that. Which is quite enough, isn't it? It's certainly quite enough to inspire the writing of this letter, in which I plead for your attention, since I've failed to attract it in any other way. I can't go on like this! With your harrowing trickery you have possessed me down to my deepest self. Please release me from this spell, and let's begin a normal romance. However unknown may be their psychic mechanisms, it's only emotions that matter—not zones of the unreal, not a metaphysics stripped of all that is human.

In Miss Locher I believe you sent me an embodiment of your deepest convictions. But suppose I start admitting uncanny things about her? Suppose I grant that she was somehow just a dream. Suppose I allow that she was not a girl but actually a thing without a self, an unreality that, in accord with your vision of existence, dreamed it was a human being and not just a fabricated impersonation of our flesh? You would have me entertain such thoughts. You would have me think there is some mysterious affinity among the things of this world, and of other worlds. So what if there is? I don't care anymore.

Forget other selves. Forget the third (fourth, nth) person view of life in which some god or demon has individuated itself into bits and pieces of all that is. Only first and second persons matter (I and thou). And by all means forget dreams. I, for one, know I'm not a dream. I am real, Dr.——. (There, how do you like being an anonymity without foundation in this or any other universe?) So please be so kind as to acknowledge the reality of my existence.

It is now after midnight, and I dread going to sleep and having another of those nightmares. You can save me from this fate, if only you can find it in your heart to do so. But you must hurry. Time is running out for us, just as these last few waking moments are now running out for me. Tell me it is still not too late for our love. Please don't destroy everything for us. You will only hurt yourself. And despite your high-flown theory of masochism, there is really nothing divine about it. So no more playing of the inhuman visionary. Be simple, be nice. Oh, I am so tired. I must say good night, then, but not

goodbye, my foolish love. Hear me now. Sleep your singular sleep and dream of the many, the others. They are also part of you, part of us. Die into them and leave me in peace. I will come for you later, and then you can always be with me in a special corner of your own, just as my little Amy once was. This is what you've always wanted and this you shall have. Die into them, you simple soul, you silly dolling. Die with a nice bright gleam in your eyes.

THE NYCTALOPS TRILOGY

I. THE CHYMIST

Hello, Miss. Why, yes, as a matter of fact I *am* looking for some company this evening. My name is Simon, and you are . . . Rosemary. Funny, I was just daydreaming in the key of Rosicrucianism. Never mind. Please sit, and watch out for splinters on your chair, so you don't catch your dress. It appears that everything around here has come to the point of frays and splinters. But what this old place lacks in refinement of décor is amply offset by its atmosphere, don't you think? Yes, as you say, I suppose it does serve its purpose. It's a little lax as far as table service, though. I'm afraid that in the way of drinks one must procure for one's self. Thank you, I'm glad you think I have a nice way of talkin'. Now, can I get you something from the bar? All right, a beer you shall have. And do me a favor please: before I return, you will already have taken that wad of gum out of your mouth. Thank you, and I'll be back shortly with our drinks.

Here you are, Rosie, one beer from the bar. Just don't belch and we'll get along fine. I'm pleased to see you've gotten rid of your gum, though I hope you didn't swallow it. One's gut should probably remain ignorant of what it's like to accommodate bubble gum and beer in the same digestive episode. I know it's *your* gut, but I take an interest in what gets into the workings of any human vessel. That's right—*vessel.* You want me to spell it? No, I'm not making fun of you. It's just that there are certain interactions that take place when the vessel in question is the delicate system of *H. sapiens,* as opposed to a chalice in a church or a serum vial in a laboratory. Quite so, that none-too-sterile glass in your immaculate hand is a vessel, now you've got it.

My glass? Yes, you do see a lot of red in there. I like red drinks. Created this one myself. A Red Rum Ginny, I call it. White rum, gin, pale ginger ale, and, ideally, cranberry juice, though the bartender here had to substitute some maraschino solution, which has neither the rich red color nor a fraction of the tartness of your smile. Here, take a sip. If you don't like it, say so. Yes, different is the word for it, the wellspring of its interest. Even the most faithful adherence to an established mixological formula results in some difference that can be discerned in even the most banal of cocktails, not to mention other concoctions in the alcoholic formulary. You just have to cultivate the *sensitivity* to notice that difference. Ask any wine taster. And that sensitivity may be extended to every experience in our lives. Though we may think we're doing the same old thing in the same old way day in and day out, fluctuations from the norm *are* the norm. You can't step into the same river twice, as the philosopher said. Each passing moment diverts to follow its own course from the one before, often quite strangely.

I have a very keen appreciation of *diversity,* if I do say so myself. You're smiling at my emphasis. You think you know something about me, and perhaps you do. Sharp girl! But *perversity,* as you no doubt were thinking, is only one of the more ostentatious forms of the diverse. And diversions call the tune of the dance of life, even at the subatomic level.

Wow, you really guzzled down that bubbly beverage. Would you like another, or perhaps I can offer you something of my own invention? Yes, I have created other drinks. There's another red potation I've pioneered that's actually just a variation on a standard number. The Sweet and Sour Bloody Mary, made with high-test vodka, tonic water, sugar, a lemon slice, and ketchup. It does sound like a meal in itself at that. Very fortifying. No, sorry to spoil your joke, my fondness for crimson highballs does not extend to the vampire's neck-drawn nectar. Besides, I'm quite able to work during daylight hours.

Where? Well, I suppose I can tell you, *sub rosa,* that I'm

employed by a pharmaceutical company not far from here. I'm a chemist there. Yes, really. Well, it's nice the way you could see right off that I wasn't no average guy just lookin' for some fun after a hard day's work. Perceptive girl! However, I did in fact come directly here after working a little overtime. I noticed while I was at the bar counter that you were eyeing and toeing the brief-case I brought in with me and set so discreetly under the table. You guessed it, I do happen to be carrying "work stuff" in there, among other things. Spot on, my dear—it would be foolish to leave anything important out in the car in this red-light district.

Well, I wouldn't say that this part of town is simply a *pit*. It is, of course, that. But your colloquialism doesn't begin to describe the various dimensions of decrepitude in the local geography. *Decrepitude,* Ro. It has your *pit* in it and a lot more besides. I speak from experience, more than you would believe. This whole city is most certainly a pitiful corpse, while the neighborhood outside the walls of this bar has the distinction of being the with-ering heart of the deceased. And I am a devoted student of its anatomy—a pathologist, after a fashion, with an eye for necroses that others overlook.

For instance, have you ever been to that place called Speak-easy? Well, then you have some acquaintance with a bastard-ized nostalgia—the putrescence of things past. Yes, up a flight of stairs inside an old burlesque house is a high echoey hall with a leftover Deco interior of arching mirrors and chrome chandeliers. And there the giant painted silhouettes of bony flappers and gaunt Gatsbys sport about the curving ballroom walls, towering over the dance floor, their funereal elegance mocking the awkward gyrations of the living. An old dream with a new veneer. It's fascinating, you know, how an obsolete madness is sometimes adopted and stylized in an attempt to ghoulishly preserve it. These are the days of second-hand fan-tasies and out-of-date distractions.

But there are other sights in this city that I think are much more interesting. Not the least of which are those storefront temples of dubious denomination. There's one on Third and Dickerson called the Church of the True Dividing Light, not to be mistaken, I presume, with that false light which blinds so many searching eyes. Oddly enough, I've yet to see any light at all shining through the windows of this gray dwarfish building, and I always look for some sort of illumination as I ride by.

I tell you, no one worships this city as I do. Especially its witticisms of proximity, one strange thing next to another, which together add up to a greater strangeness. One of the more grotesque examples of this phenomenon occurs when you observe that a little shop whose display window features a fabulous array of prosthetic devices is right next-door to Marv's Second Hand City. Then there are those places—you've noticed them, I'm sure—that are freakishly suggestive in a variety of ways. One of them is that pink and black checkerboard box on Bender Boulevard that calls itself Bill's Bender Lounge, where a garish marquee advertises Nightly Entertainment. And if you stare at that legend long enough, the word "nightly" will begin to connote more than the interval between dusk and dawn. Soon this simple term becomes truly evocative, as if it were code for the most exotic of nocturnal entertainments. And speaking of entertainment, I should cite that establishment whose owner, no doubt an epicure of musical comedy, gave it the title of Guys and Dolls, Inc. What a genius of vulgarity, considering that this business is devoted solely to the sale and repair of manikins. Or is it really a front for a bordello of dummies? No offense intended, Rosalie.

I could go on—I still haven't mentioned Miss Wanda's Wigs or that ancient and squalid hotel that boasts "A Bath in Every Room"—but maybe you're becoming a bit bored. Yes, I can understand what you mean when you say you don't notice that stuff after a while. The mind becomes dull and complacent, I know. Sometimes I get that way myself. But it seems that just when I'm comfortably mired in complacency, some good jolt comes along.

Maybe I'm sitting in my car, waiting for a red light to change. A derelict, drunk or brain-diseased, comes up to my defenseless vehicle and pounds on my windows—with both fists, like so—and demands a cigarette. He touches his ragged lips with scissored fingers to convey his meaning, having left speech behind him long ago. A cigarette? I am a chemist, good sir, not a tobacconist. The traffic signal changes and I drive on, watching the bum's half-collapsed form shrinking in my rearview mirror. But somehow I've taken him on as a passenger, a ghostly shape sitting bleary-eyed beside me and raving about all kinds of senseless and fascinating things, the autobiography of confusion. And in a little while I'm back on the lookout once more.

Touching story, don't you— Yes, I suppose it is getting a bit late and we haven't made much progress. Your apartment? I think that would be fine. No, I had nothing else in mind as far as where we might do business. Your place is okay. Where is it, though? No kidding? That's the old Temple Towers with a new cognomen. Excellent, our ride will take us through the neighborhood in the shadow of the brewery. What floor of the building do you live on? Well, a veritable penthouse, an urban aerie. The loftier the better, I say.

Shall we go, then? My car is parked right out front.

I hope it hasn't decided to rain. Nope, it's a beautiful night. But look, that's my car where that cop is standing. Just stay calm. I certainly won't say anything if you don't. You're not, by chance, a vice officer in disguise, are you, Rosiecrantz? You wouldn't betray this unsuspecting Hamlet. A simple "no" would have been sufficient. If you use that kind of language again I'll turn you in to the authorities right now, and then we can see what sort of arrest record you've accumulated in your brilliant career. Silence, that's good. Just let me do the talking. Here goes.

Hi, officer. Yeah, that's my car. It's parked okay, isn't it? Geez, that's a relief. For a second I thought . . . my license and registration? Sure thing. Here you go. Beg pardon? Yeah, I guess I am a little far from home. But I work close by. I'm a stockbroker, here's my card. You know, I've been in the business for some time now, and I can almost tell just by the look of a guy if he's got something invested in the market. I'd bet that you have. See there, I knew I was right. Doesn't matter if you're just small-time. Hey, have you been in touch with an investment counsellor lately? Well, you should. There's a lot going on. People talk about inflation, recession, depression. Forget it. If you know where to put your finances, I mean really know, it doesn't matter if it's Friday the 13th and the streets are bloody with corporate corpses.

Smart advice is what you need. It's all anyone needs. For

example—and I tell you this just to make a point—there's an outfit in this city, not a half-mile from here in fact, by the name of Lochmyer Laboratories. They've been working on a new product and are just about ready to market it. 'Course I don't understand the whole technical end of it, but I know for sure that it's going to revolutionize the field of—what d'you call it—psychopharmaceuticals. Revolutionize it the way antidepressants did. It'll be bigger than antidepressants. You know what I mean? That's the kind of thing you've got to know.

That's right, officer, Lochmyer Laboratories. Good company all around. I own stock in it myself. What tip, hell? Hey, you don't have to thank me. Beg pardon? A tip for me? Well, now that you mention it, there probably are better neighborhoods for a man such as myself to be frequenting. You've got my promise that you *won't* be seeing me around here anymore. I appreciate that, officer. I'll remember. And you remember Loch Lab. Right, then. 'Night to you.

Wait for his car to turn the corner, Rosie, before getting in mine. We'll let the lawman maintain the illusion that his warning has set me straight with regard to the dangers of this seamy area and your seamy self. He looked at you like an old friend. Could have been trouble for both of us. You're a smart girl to have sat at my table tonight. I think my briefcase impressed him, don't you? Okay, we can get in the car now.

Yes, I did get us out of a touchy situation with that cop. But I hope when you just mentioned my *BS* apropos of that scene with the policeman, you had in mind the Bachelor of Science degree I received when I was twelve years old. This is your last warning about unclean idioms. Now roll down your window and let's air your words out of this car as we drive. And as far as my deceiving that fine officer goes—I actually didn't. No, I'm not really a stockbroker. I told you the truth about being in chemicals. And I told that mole-eyed patrolman the truth when I advised him to put his money in Lochmyer Lab, for we *are* about to market a new mind medicine that should make our investors as pleased as amphetamine addicts at an all-night coffee shop. How did I know he owned stock in the first place? That is strange, isn't it? I guess I was just lucky. This is just my lucky night—and yours too.

You don't much like the *policía,* do you, R11osa? Yes, of course I can blame you. Without them, where would all of us outlaws be? What would we have? Only a lawless paradise . . . and paradise is a bore. Violence without violation is only a noise heard by no one, the most horrendous sound in the universe. No, I realize you don't have anything to do with violence. I didn't mean to imply you did. Yes, I can drop you off back at the bar when we've finished at your apartment. Of course.

Right now let's just enjoy the ride. What do you mean "so what's to enjoy"? Can't you see we're nearing the brewery? Look, there's its beer-golden sign, advertising the alchemical quest to transmute base ingredients into liquid gold. *Alchemical,* Rosetta. And I'm not referring to that cheapjack firm of Allied Chem. Just look around at these caved-in houses, these seedy stores, each one of them a sacred site of the city, a shrine, if you will. You won't? You've seen it all a million times? A slum is a slum is a slum, eh? Always the same. *Always?*

Never.

What about when it's raining and the brown bricks of these old places start to drip and darken? And the smoke-gray sky is the smoky mirror of your soul. You give a lightning blink at a row of condemned buildings, starkly outlining them. And do they blink back at you? Or does that happen only in another type of storm, when windows are slyly browed with city-soiled clumps of snow. Was it under such conditions that you first thought of all the cold and dark places in the universe, all the clammy basements and gloomy attics of creation? Bleak locales you'd rather not think about, but at the time couldn't keep from your mind. Another time you could have. No two times are the same. No two lives are alike. We're like aliens to one another. And when you're traveling through these streets with some stranger, you have to contend with how they see things, the way you now must deal with my 20-20 visions and I with your blasé near-sightedness. Are these the same gutted houses you saw last night, or even a second ago? Or are they like the fluxing clouds that swirl above the chimneys and trees, and then pass on?

The alchemical transmutations are infinite and continuous, working all the time like slaves in the Great Laboratory. Tell me you can't perceive their work, especially in this part of the city. Especially where the glamour and sanity of former days wears a new mask of rats and rot, where an old style is transformed by time into a parody of itself which no man could foresee, where greater and greater schisms are forever developing between past shapes and future shapelessness, and finally where the evolution toward ultimate diversity can be glimpsed as if in a magic mirror.

This is, of course, the *real* alchemy, as you've probably gathered, and not that other kind which theorized that everything was struggling toward an auric perfection. Lead into gold, lower matter into higher spirit. No, it's not like that. Just the opposite, in point of fact. Please don't put that hunk of gum in your mouth. Throw it out the window, now!

As I was saying, everything is just variation without a theme. Oh, perhaps there is some unchanging ideal, some sturdy absolute. Scientifically, I suppose, we should allow for that improbability. But to reach that ideal would mean a hopeless stroll along the path to hypothetically higher worlds. And on the way our ideas become feverish and confused. What begins as a solitary truth soon proliferates like malignant cells in the body of a dream, a body whose true outline remains unknown. Perhaps, then, we should be grateful to the whims of chemistry, the caprices of circumstance, and the enigmas of personal taste for giving us such an array of strictly local realities and desires.

No, I didn't always think this freaky, as you put it. But I can tell you almost precisely when I began to see the truth of things. I was a callow freshman in college, even callower than most, given my precocious progress. One day something seemed to change in my chemistry, as I like to think of it. It was quite horrible for a while. Eventually, though, I realized that the alteration was from a false chemistry to a true one. Yes, that's when I decided to pursue the subject as my career, my calling. But that's a story in itself, and here we are now at your apartment tower.

Please don't slam the car door the way you were about to. No need to draw attention to our presence. You're right, there's really no one around to be attentive anyway. The local street vermin seem to have withdrawn into their burrows. Oops, almost forgot my briefcase. Wouldn't want to leave it unattended in this neighborhood, isn't that right? You're smiling about my brief-case, aren't you, Maryrose? You think you know something again. Well, go ahead and think that if you like. Everybody likes to think he has inside information. That policeman, for exam-ple. You could see how pleased he was to instantly become a man of knowledge, even if it's only by way of inside information about some stock on the market. Everybody wants to know what's what, *scientia arcana,* the real dope.

Maybe I do have some dope in my case. Then again, maybe it's just an empty prop, a leather vessel with a void inside. But you already know that I work for a dope company. You were thinking that, weren't you? Well, let's go up to your place and find out.

Cozy little lobby you have here. But I'm afraid the atmosphere is doing strange things to that pot of ferns over there. Of course I know they're artificial. Which only means that Nature, one of the Great Chemists, made them at one remove, that's all. Here, this elevator seems to be working, though a little noisily. After you, Lady R. The twenty-second floor if I remember right, and I always do. Uh, I believe there's to be no smoking in this eleva-tor, if you don't mind. Thank you. And here we are. I'll bet your place is down this way. See, I *am* always right. Isn't that funny? Yes, I'm coming, I'm coming.

Well, your apartment has a very nice door. No, you're wrong. There's no such thing as "just like all the others." Yours is quite different, can't you see that? And tonight your door is visibly dif-ferent from any other time you've seen it. I'm not just being egois-tical about my unique presence at your threshold this evening. Do you see what I mean? Well, I'm sorry if you feel I've been lectur-ing you all night. I was a pedagogue once, which I suppose is obvious. It's just that there are some important things I must impart to you, my little rosebud, before we're through. Okay? Now, let's go in and see what kind of view you have from up here.

Keep the ceiling light off please, so that I don't have to look at a double of this sleazy room reflected in your window. One of your dim lamps should give us all the light we need. There, that's fine. You do have a good view of the city from this height.

I think it's perfect, not too far up. I live in a mere two-story house myself and being up here makes me dizzily realize what I'm missing. From this lofty keep I could nightly look out upon the city and its constant mutations. A different city every night. Yes, Rosie, I have to say you're right—sarcastic tone and all— the city is indeed also a vessel. And it's one that obediently takes the shape of very strange contents. The Great Chemists are working out unfathomable formulae down there. Look at those lights outlining the different venues and avenues below. Look at their lines and interconnections. They're like a skeleton of something . . . the skeleton of a dream, the hidden framework ready at any moment to shift its structure to support a new shape. The Great Chemists are always dreaming new things and risking that they may wake up while doing so. Should that ever happen you can be assured there will be hell to pay.

My imagination? No, I don't think it's *vivid* at all. On the contrary, it's not nearly potent enough. My poor imaginative faculties have always needed . . . extensions. That's why I'm here with you. You're smiling again, or rather you're *smirking*. Funny word, smirk. Rather like an extraterrestrial surname. Simon Smirk. How do you think that sounds?

Yes, maybe we are wasting too much time. But of course we'll have to endure just one more delay while I rummage around in my briefcase and remove what you've been waiting for. So you hope it's good dope, eh? Well, you'll have a chance to find out, since you seem so anxious to become a vessel yourself for my chemicals. No, stay seated just where you are please. There's no reason for you to glimpse every elixir I've got in here. The only thing I have that might interest you is secured in one squat little container screwed tightly closed with a black cap . . . and here it is!

Yes, it does look like a bottle of powdered light. That's very observant. What is it? I thought you would know by now. Here, hold out your hand and you can have a closer look. Just a little mound sprinkled in the middle of your sweaty palm, about one brainful to be precise. Doesn't it look like pulverized diamonds? It glitters, yes it does. I don't blame you for thinking it might be dangerous to snort, or whatever else you imagine you're supposed to do with it. But if you watch my magic dust very closely you'll see that you don't have to do anything at all.

See, it dissolved right into you. Disappeared completely, except for a few stray grains. But don't worry about them. Calm down, the burning will soon go away. There's no point in trying to rub the drug off your hand. It's in your system now. And it certainly won't help to get excited, nor are threats of any use to you. Please remain seated in that chair.

Can you feel any effects yet? I mean besides the fact that you're no longer able to move your arms or legs. That's just the beginning of this *nightly* entertainment. The opalescent substance you've just absorbed has now made possible a very interesting relationship between us, my red red rose. The drug has rendered you fantastically sensitive to the shaping influence of a certain form of energy, namely that which is being generated by me, or rather *through* me. To put it romantically, I'm now dreaming you. That's really the only way I can explain it that you might understand. Not dreaming *about* you, like some old love song. I'm *dreaming* you. Your arms and legs don't respond to your brain's commands because I'm dreaming of someone who is as still as a statue. I hope you can appreciate how remarkable this is.

Damn! I suppose that was your attempt to scream. You really are terrified, aren't you? Just to be safe, perhaps I'd better dream of someone who hasn't anything to scream with. There, that should do it. You do look strange, though, like that. But this is only just the beginning. These minor tricks are child's play and I'm sure don't impress you in any way whatever. Soon I'll show you that I can really make an impression, once I put my mind to it.

Is there something in your eyes? Yes, I can see there is. A question. Right now you would like to ask, if only you still had the means to do so, what's to become of old Rosie? It's only fair that you should know.

We are presently coming into perfect tune with each other, my dreams and my dream girl. You are about to become the flesh and blood kaleidoscope of my imagination. In the latter stages of this procedure anything might happen. Your form will know no limits of diversity as the Great Chemists themselves take over. Soon I will put my dreaming in the hands of a prodigious insurrection of entity, and I'm sure there will be some surprises for both of us. That's one thing which never changes.

Nevertheless, there is still a problem with this process. It's not really perfect, certainly not marketable, as we say in the pill business. And wouldn't that be boring if it were perfect? What I mean to say is that under the stress of such diverse metamorphoses, the original structure of the object somehow breaks down. The consequence of this is simple—you can never be as you once were. I'm very sorry. You'll have to remain in whatever curious incarnation you take on at the dream's end. Which should rattle the wits of whoever is unfortunate enough to find you. But don't worry, you will not live long after I leave here. And by then you will have experienced god-like powers of proteation which I myself cannot hope to know, no matter how intimately I may try.

And now I think we can proceed with what has been your destiny all along. Are you ready? I am entirely ready and by degrees am giving myself over to those forces which go their own way and take us with them. Can you feel us both being swept into a tempest of transfigurations? Can you feel the fevers of this chemist? The power of my dreaming, my dreaming, my dreaming, my . . .

Now Rose of madness—BLOOM!

THE NYCTALOPS TRILOGY

II. DRINK TO ME ONLY WITH
LABYRINTHINE EYES

Everyone at the party comments on them. They ask if I had them altered in some way, suggest that I've tucked some strange crystallized lenses under my eyelids. I tell them no, that I was born with these singular optic organs. They're not from some optometrist's bag of tricks, not the result of surgical mayhem. Of course they find this hard to believe, especially when I tell them I was also born with the full powers of a master hypnotist . . . and from there I rapidly evolved, advancing into a mesmeric wilderness untrod before or since by any others of my calling. No, I wouldn't say *business* or *profession*, I would have to say *calling*. What else do you call it when you're destined from birth, marked by fate's stigmata? At this point they smile politely, saying that they really enjoyed the show and that I certainly am good at what I do. I tell them how grateful I am for the opportunity to perform for such fancy persons in such a fancy house. Unsure to what extent I'm just kidding them, they nervously twirl the stems of their champagne glasses, the beverage sparkling and the crystal twinkling under a chandelier's kaleidoscopic blaze. Despite all the beauty, power, and prestige socializing in this rather baroque room tonight, I think they know how basically ordinary they all are. They are very impressed by me and my assistant, who have been asked to mingle with the guests and amuse them in whatever way we can. One gentleman with a flushed face looks across the room at my partner in animal magnetism, guzzling his drink as he does so. "Would you like to meet her," I ask. "You bet," he replies. They all do. They all want to know you, my angel.

Earlier in the evening we presented our show to these lovely people. I instructed the host of the party to serve no alcohol before our performance, and to arrange the furniture of this overwrought room in a way that would allow everyone a perfect view of us on our little platform. He complied obediently, of course. He also conceded to my request for payment in advance. Such an agreeable man, giving in to the will of another so readily.

At the start of the show I am alone before a silent audience. All illumination is cancelled except a single spotlight which I have set up on the floor exactly two point two meters from the stage. The spotlight focuses on a pair of metronomes, their batons sweeping back and forth in perfect unison like windshield wipers in the rain: smoothly back and smoothly forth, back and forth, back and forth. And at the tip of each baton is a replica of each of my eyes swaying left and right in full view of everyone, while my voice speaks to them from a shadowy edge of the stage. First I give a brief lecture on hypnosis, its name and nature. After that I say: "Ladies and gentlemen: Please direct your attention to this glossy black cabinet. Within stands the most beautiful creature you have ever beheld. From heaven itself she has descended, a seraph of the highest order. And for your enjoyment she is already in the deepest trance. You *will* see her and be amazed." There is a dramatic pause during which my eyes fix upon the congregation before me, keeping control of them. When I look back toward the cabinet the trick door opens, seemingly of its own will.

As if with one voice, the audience emits a quiet gasp, and for a second I panic. Then there is applause, reassuring me that everything is all right, that they like the figure exhibited before them. What they see is standing upright inside the cabinet, her slender arms held absolutely still at her sides. She is wearing a tiny sequined outfit, a vulgar costume whose rampant glitter somehow transcends the cliché, rejuvenating its shoddy soul. Her eyes are two bluish gems in an alabaster setting, and her gaze seems to be fixed on infinity. After the audience has had a good look, I say: "Now, my angel, you must fall." At this signal she begins to totter within the box. Finally she teeters into a forward topple. At the last moment I reach down, collar her throat with one hand, and arrest her inflexible figure a few inches before it hits the stage. Not a lock of her golden hair is stirred out of place, and her bejeweled tiara holds tightly to her head. There is applause while I restore my long-limbed assistant to a vertical position.

Now begins the performance proper, which is an array of mesmeric stunts along with some magic. I place the somnambule's hypnotically stiffened body horizontally between two chairs and ask some behemoth from the audience to come up and sit on her. The man is only too glad to do this. Then I command the somnambule to become inhumanly limp so that I may stuff her into an impossibly small box. But she's only limber enough to fit halfway into the receptacle, I tell the audience. So I inform them that I must break her neck and other bones in order to push her whole body inside. All onlookers are on the edge of their seats, and I beg them to remain composed even though they may see some blood squeeze out the edges of the box as I close its lid. They love it when my assistant slowly rises up intact and unbloodied. (Nonetheless, like all crowds who attend events where there is, or seems to be, an element of hazard, they secretly wish to see something go wrong.) Next is the Human Voodoo Doll, wherein I stick long pins into her flesh and she doesn't wince or make a sound. We perform quite a few other routines in defiance of death and pain, afterward moving on to the memory tricks. In one of them I have everybody in the audience call out in quick succession his or her full name and birth date. Then I instruct my somnambule to repeat this information when requested at random to do so by individual audience members. She gets all the names right—and of course everyone is bowled over—but invariably the dates she gives are not in the past but in the future. Some of the days and years she mechanically speaks are relatively distant in time and some disturbingly near. I express astonishment at my somnambule's behavior, explaining to the audience that fortune-telling is not normally part of the show. I apologize for this woeful display of precognition and vow to make it up to them with a jaw-dropping finale so as to sidetrack their minds from any morbid introspection. A blare of heavenly horns would not be inappropriate at this point.

At my signal, my assistant moves to the precise center of the stage. Here she positions herself with legs outspread to form an upside-down V out of her lower body. Another signal and her arms elevate until they are stretched outward like two wings, both tensely straining to their limit. A final signal bids her nodding head to lift fully erect upon the muscle-knotted column of her neck, eyes glaring out at the audience. At the same time, the eyes out in the audience glare back at her with the same gaze. "Now," I admonish them, "there must be total silence. This means no coughing, no sniffing, no yawning, and no clearing of throats." An unreasonable directive, it would seem, but one with which they are compliant. They are silent as a grave full of buried confidences. "Ladies and gentlemen," I continue, "you are about to see something that I need not tout with a verbose preamble. My assistant is now in the deepest possible trance and every particle of her being is extremely sensitive to my will. When instructed, she will begin an astounding metamorphosis that will reveal what some of you may have conceived but never dared hope to look upon. Nothing more need be said. My dear, you may commence your change of form, code name: Seraphim."

There she stands—arms, legs, towering head—my five-pointed somnambule: a star. "Already you can see the glowing," I tell the audience. "She begins to effloresce. She begins to incandesce. And now she approaches such radiance that she almost disappears into it—kindled to the very edge of worldly existence by a supernal blaze. But there is no pain, there is anything but eyesore." No one in the audience is even squinting, of course, for the beams from her body—this labyrinth of light!—are dream beams without physical properties. "Keep watching," I shout at them, pointing to my assistant, whose costume of foil sequins has turned to a gossamer veil floating about her form. "Can you see snow-white wings sprouting beyond the horizon of her shoulders? Has not her material casing lost all carnality and transmogrified into a celestial icon? Is she not the very essence of the ethereal—the angelic luminary beneath the human beast?"

But I cannot sustain the moment. The light fades in the eyes of the audience, growing dimmer by the second, and my assistant collapses back into an earthly incarnation. I am exhausted.

What's worse, all our efforts seem to have been wasted, for the audience answers this spectacle with only perfunctory applause. I can hardly believe it, but the finale fell flat. They don't understand. They actually like all the mock-death and bogus-pain stuff better. These are what fascinate them. Bah. Double bah. Well, frolic while you can, you dullards. The show isn't over yet.

"Thank you, ladies and gentlemen," I say when the lights go up and the meager applause dies entirely. "I hope my assistant and I have not induced you into somnolence this evening. You do look a little sleepy, as if you've been lulled into a trance yourselves. Which is not such a bad feeling, is it? Sinking deep into a downy darkness, resting your souls on pillows stuffed with soft shadows. But our host informs me that things will liven up very soon. Certainly you will awake when a little chime commands you to do so. Remember, it's wake-up time when you hear the chime," I repeat. "And now I believe we can prosecute this evening's festivities."

I help my assistant down from the platform and we mix with the rest of the partiers. Drinks are served and the noise level in the room increases by several decibels. The populace of the soirée begins to coagulate into groups here and there. I separate myself from a boisterous group surrounding my assistant and me, but nobody seems to notice. They are entranced by my sequined somnambule. She dazzles them—a sun at the center of a drab galaxy, her costume catching the light of that monstrous chandelier winking with a thousand eyes. Everyone seems to be trying to gain her regard. But she just smiles, so vacant and full of grace, not even sipping the drink someone has placed in her hand. They are transfixed like lady spiders during the mating ritual. After all, didn't I tell them that my lanky hypnotizee was the perfection of beauty?

But I too have my admirers. One dark-suited bore asks me if I can help him stop smoking. Another inquires about possible ways that hypnosis could serve as a tool for his advertising business, though nothing illegal of course. I hand them each a business card with a cloud-gray pearl finish on which is printed a non-existent phone number and a phony address in a real city. As for the name: Cosimo Fanzago. What else would one expect from a performing mesmerist extraordinaire? I have other cards with names like Gaudenzio Ferrari and Johnny Tiepolo printed on them. Nobody's caught on yet. But am I not as much an artist as they were?

And while I am being accosted by people who need cures or aids for their worldliness, I am watching you, dear somnambule. Watching you waltz about this magnificent room. It is not like the other rooms in this great house. Someone really let Fancy have its wild way in here. It harkens back to a time, centuries ago, when your somnambulating predecessors did their sleep-walking act for high society. You fit in so well with the company of this manor hall of riotous rococo. It's a delight to see you make your way about the irregular circumference of this room, where the wall undulates in gentle waves and troughs, its surface sin-ewed with a maze of chinoiserie. This capacious chamber's ser-pentine configuration makes it difficult to distinguish its recesses from its protrusions. Some of the guests shift their weight wall-wards and find themselves leaning on air, stumbling sideways like comedians in an old movie. But you, my perfect sleepwalker, have no trouble. You lean at the right times and in the right places. And your eyes play beautifully to whatever camera focuses on you. Indeed, you take so many of your cues from others that one might suspect you of having no life of your own. Let's sincerely hope not!

Now I watch as a stuffed shirt in a dinner jacket invites you to be seated in a chair of blinding brocade, its flowery fabric done up in all the soft colors of a woman's cosmetics case and its dainty arms the texture of cartilage. Your high heels make subtle points in the carpet, puncturing its arabesque flights of imagina-tion. Now I watch as our host draws you over to choose a liba-tion from his well-stocked bar. He gestures with pride toward the many bottles on display, their shapes both *normale* and *baroque*. The baroquely shaped bottles are doing more interest-ing things with light and shadow than their normal brothers, and you point to one of these with a robotic finesse. He pours two drinks while you watch, and while you watch I am watching you watch. Guiding you to another part of the room, he shows you a shelf of delicate figurines, each one caught in a paralyzed

stance. He places one of them in your hand, and you angle it
every which way before your unfocused eyes, as if trying to
restore some memory that would cause you to awaken. But you
never will, not without my help.

Now he directs you to a part of the room where there is soft
music and dancing. But there are no windows in this room, only
tall smoky mirrors, and as you pass from one end to the other
you are caught between foggy looking-glasses facing their twins,
creating endless files of somnambules in a false infinity beyond
the walls. Then you dance with our host, though while he is gazing straightforwardly at you, you are gazing abstractly at the
ceiling. Oh, that ceiling! In epic contrast to the capricious volu-
tions of the rest of the room—designs tendriled to tenebrosity—
the surface above is a plane of powder blue without a hint of
flourish. In its purity it suggests a bottomless pool or a sky wiped
clean of clouds. You are dancing in eternity, my darling. And the
dance is indeed a long one, for another wants to cut in on our
gracious host and become your partner. Then another. And
another. They all want to embrace you. They are all taken in by
your dispassionate elegance, your postures and poses like frozen
roses. I am only waiting until everyone has had physical contact
with your physique so full of animal magnetism.

And while I watch and wait, I notice that we have an unexpected spectator looking down on us from above. Beyond the
wide archway at the end of the room is a staircase leading to
the second floor. And up there he is sitting, trying to glimpse
all the grown-ups, his pajama-clad legs dangling between the
Doric posts of the balustrade. I can tell he prefers the classic décor
elsewhere predominating in this house. With moderate stealth I
leave the main floor audience behind and pay a visit to the bal-
cony, which I quite ignored during my performance earlier.

After creeping up the triple-tiered stairway and sneaking
down the white-carpeted hallway, I sit beside the child. "Did
you see my little show with the lady?" I ask him. He shakes his
head in the negative, his mouth as tight as an unopened tulip.
"Can you see the lady now? You know the one I mean." I take
a shiny chrome-plated pen from the inside pocket of my coat
and point down toward the room where the party is going on.

At this distance the features of my sequined siren cannot be seen in any great detail. "Well, can you see her?" His head bobs in the affirmative. Then I whisper: "And what do you think?" His two lips open and casually reply: "She . . . she's yucky." I breathe easier now. From this height she does indeed appear merely "yucky," but you can never know what the sharp sight of children may perceive. And it is certainly not my intention tonight to make any child's eyes roll the wrong way.

"Listen closely to everything I say," I tell him in a very soft but not condescending tone, making sure the child's attention is held by my voice and by the gleaming pen on which his eyes are now focused. He is a good subject for a child, who ordinarily have wandering eyes and minds. He agrees with me that he is feeling rather tired now. "Now go back to your bed. You will fall asleep in seconds and have the most wonderful dreams. And you will not awaken until morning, *no matter what sounds you hear outside your door.* Understand?" He nods. "Very good. And for being such an agreeable young man, I'm going to make you a present of this beautiful pen of sterling silver which you will keep with you always as a reminder that nothing is what it seems to be. Do you know what I'm talking about?" His head moves up and down, and the expression on his face has the chilling appearance of deep wisdom. "All right, then. But before you return to your room, I want you to tell me if there's a back stairway by which I may leave." His finger points down the hall and to the left. "Thank you, my boy. Thank you very much. Now off to bed and to your sweet dreams." He disappears into the Piranesian darkness at the end of the hallway.

For a moment I stand staring down into that merry room below, where the crass laughter and doltish dancing of my audience has reached a climax. My fickle somnambule herself seems to be caught up in the party's web, and has forgotten all about her master. She's left me on the sidelines, a mazy wallflower. But I'm not jealous. I can understand why they've taken you away from me. They simply can't help themselves, now can they? I told them how beautiful, how perfect you were, and they can't resist you, my love.

Unfortunately they failed to appreciate the best part of you, preferring to lose themselves in the beguilements of your grosser illusions. Didn't I show our well-behaved audience an angelified version of you? And you saw their reaction. They were bored and just sat in their seats like a bunch of stiffs. Of course, what can you expect? They wanted the death stuff, the pain stuff. All that flashy junk. They wanted cartwheels of agony; somersaults through fires of doom; nosedives of vulnerable flesh into the meat grinder of life. They wanted to be *thrilled*.

And now that their merry pageant seems to have reached its peak, I think the time is right to awaken this mob from its hypnotic slumber and thrill the daylights out of them.

It is time for the chime.

There is indeed a back stairway just where the boy indicated, one which guides me to a back hallway, back rooms, and finally a back door. These backways lead me to a vast yard where a garden is silhouetted beneath the moon and a small wood sways in the distance. A thick lawn pads my footsteps as I work my way around to the fine façade of this house.

I am standing on the front porch now, between its tall columns and beneath a lamp hanging at the end of a long brazen chain. I pause for a moment, savoring each voluptuous second. The serene constellations above wink knowingly. But not even these eyes are deep enough to outgaze me, to deceive the deceiver, illude the illusionist. To tell the truth, I am a very bad mesmeric subject, unable to be drawn in by Hypnos' Heaven. For I know how easily one can be led past those shimmering gates, only to have a trap door spring open once you are inside. Then down you go! I would rather be the attendant loitering outside Mesmer's Maze than its deluded victim bumbling about within.

It is said that death is a great awakening, an emergence from the mystifications of life. Ha, I have to laugh. Death is the consummation of mortality and—to let out a big secret—only heightens mortal imperfections. Of course, it takes a great master to pry open a pair of post-mortem eyes once they are sewn tightly closed by Dr. Reaper. And even afterward there is so little these creatures are good for. As conversationalists they are incredibly feeble. The things they tell you are no more than sweet nullities. Nevertheless, they do have their uses, provided I can manage to get their awkward forms out of the mausoleum, hospital, morgue, medical school, or funeral emporium I have deviously insinuated my way into. When the mood strikes me, I recruit them for my show. Absent of any will of their own, they are exceptional at doing what they're told. However, there is one great problem: *you just can't make them beautiful.* One is not a sorcerer!

But perhaps one is a superlative mentalist, a preternaturally adept hypnotist. Then one may prompt an audience to perceive his departed subject as beautiful, to mistake her for a spell-binding, snake-eyed charmer. One *can* do this at least.

Even now I hear those high-society vulgarians still laughing, still dancing, still making a fuss over my charismatic doll of the dead. We showed them what you might be, Seraphita. Now let's show them what you really are. I have only to press this little button of a doorbell to sound the chime which will awaken them, to send the toll rolling throughout the house. Then they'll see the sepulchral wounds: your eyes recessed in their sockets, sunken into a rotting profundity—those labyrinthine depths! They'll wake up and find their nice dancing clothes all clotted with putrescent goo. And wait'll they get a sniff of that stiff. They *will* be amazed.

THE NYCTALOPS TRILOGY

III. EYE OF THE LYNX

I had been on her psychic frequency for some time, but other matters delayed our meeting in the flesh. During the frigid months of the past year I was a busy boy, and a naughty one. The relevant agencies had finally fixed on the type of companion I preferred, and warnings went out by word of mouth, or rather *lips* painted so shiny in certain shades, mostly blood red but also pall-bearer black. The underground world in which I moved was on the alert: don't talk to strangers and so on. That was not a problem, though. Such wariness just incited my impulses all the more and increased the number of "Missing Girls in Gothic Garb," as one journalistic source fatuously described my activities. Thus my meeting with her had been belated due to unscheduled distractions, or so I thought at the time. But now I was standing on the sidewalk right outside her place of business. The doorway to the crummy cinder-block building was done up, rather ineptly, like a castle with toothy merlons. I looked over at the traffic light bobbing in the winter wind that howled through every corner of that desolate part of town. It was amber going on red. I looked back at the door. It actually creaked when I opened it.

Inside I was greeted by a reception committee of girls lounging in what looked like old church pews along the walls. The narrow vestibule in which I found myself scintillated with a reddish haze that seemed not so much light as electric vapor. In the far upper corner of this entranceway a closed circuit camera was bearing down on us all, and I wondered how the camera's eye would translate that redly dyed room into the bluish hues of a security monitor. Not that it was any of my business. We might all be electronically meshed into a crazy purpurean tapestry, and that would have been just fine.

A fair-haired girl in denim slacks and leather jacket stood up and approached me. In the present light her blond locks looked more like tomato soup or greasy ketchup than fresh strawberry. She delivered a mechanical statement that began "Welcome to the House of Chains," and went on and on, spelling out various services and specific terms and finally concluding with a legal disclaimer to make sure I wasn't a member of the law enforcement community. "Definitely not," I said. "I was just reading a local tabloid and saw your ad, the one set in spiky Gothic type like a page out of an old German bible. I've come to the right place, haven't I?"

"You sure have," I thought to myself. "You sure have," echoed the blonde in the bloody moonlight that suffused that perverse establishment. "What will it be tonight?" I inwardly asked myself. "What will it be tonight?" she asked aloud. "Do you see anything you like?" we both asked me at the same time. From my expression and casual glances somewhere beyond the claustrophobic space of that tiny foyer, she could tell right away that I didn't see anything I liked. We were on the same infrared wavelength.

Both of us stood there for a moment while she took a long sip from a can of iced tea. It was then that I realized the true reason I had taken my time getting to her. I was saving this girl for last because she was such a rare exemplar of her kind. She was no dabbler in darkness and degeneracy, but a real pro. Plus the intensity and focus of her romantic nature gave off a signal that I knew I wouldn't lose. On the outside she played tough, yet I could see through that to an under-self who dreamed of persecutions and imperilments as glamorous as those of any Gothic heroine. I could have unzipped myself and taken her right on the spot. But I'm glad I waited.

She pushed a button next to an intercom on the wall behind her and turned her head to transmit some words. Their tone sounded like that of a boss giving orders to one of her underlings.

"Come and take over for me at the door," she said with

authority. What irony that she was the supervisor of the place, the head-mistress of a school for bad boys.

She turned back my way and gave me the up and down with her violet eyes. And what did those eyes tell me? They told me of her life as she lived it in fantasy: a Gothic tale of a baroness deprived of her title and inheritance by a big man with bushy eyebrows which he sometimes sprinkled with glitter. By her impoverishment, the glitter-browed man, who came out of the forest one spring while she was in retreat at a Carmelite nunnery, intended to force her into his arms. But the high-born lady would not succumb, or not until she was ready. And now she spends much of her time haunting second-hand shops, trying to reclaim her aristocratic accoutrements and various articles of her wardrobe which were dispersed by her villainous suitor. So far she's done pretty well for herself, managing to assemble many of the items she had lost as a result of the machinations of an evil-hearted malefactor who would dominate her body and soul. Her collection includes several dresses in her favorite shade of monastic black. Each of them tapers severely under the bustline, while belling out below the waist. A bib-like bodice buttons in her ribs, ascending to her neck where a strip of dark velvet is seized by a pearl brooch. At her wrist: a frail chain from which dangles a heart-shaped locket, a whirlpooling lock of golden hair inside. She wears gloves, of course, long and powdery pale. And tortuous hats from a mad milliner, with dependent veils like the fine cloth screen in a confessional. But she prefers her enveloping hoods, the ones that gather with innumerable folds at the shoulders of heavy capes lined in satin that shines like a black sun. Capes with deep pockets and generous inner pouches for secreting precious souvenirs, capes with silk strings that tie about her neck, capes with weighted hems which nonetheless flutter weightlessly in midnight gusts. She loves them dearly.

Just so is she attired when the glitter-browed villain peers in her apartment window, accursing the casement and her dreams. What can she do but shrink with terror? Soon she is only doll-size in a dark doll's costume. Quivering bones and feverish blood are the stuffings of this doll, its entrails tickled by fear's funereal plume. It flies to a corner of the room and cringes within enormous shadows, sometimes dreaming there throughout the night—of carriage wheels rioting in a lavender mist or a pearly fog, of nacreous fires twitching beyond the margins of country roads, of cliffs and stars. Then she awakes and pops a mint into her mouth from an unraveled roll on the nightstand, afterwards smoking half a cigarette before crawling out of bed and grimacing in the light of late afternoon.

"C'mon," she said with both hands in her leather pockets. And her loud heels led me out of that room where every face wore a fake blush.

"So you're going to give me the ninety-eight cent tour?" I asked my hostess. "I'm from out of town. We don't have anything like this place where I come from. I'm going to get what I pay for, right?"

She smirked at me. "Satisfaction guaranteed," she said with an arrogance meant to keep under wraps her poignantly submissive nature. She moved in a couple of indecisive directions before guiding me toward some metal steps which clanged as we descended into a blur of crimson shadows, the vicious vapor trailing us, tagging along like an insanely devoted familiar.

Surprisingly enough, there was a window in the vaguely institutional basement of the House of Chains. However, it was only a simulation made of empty panes beyond which was a painted landscape illuminated by a low-watt light bulb. Pictured were vast regions of sublime desolation towered over by mountains hulking in hazy twilight. In the distance loomed a castle that looked thoroughly foreboding. I felt a bit like a child standing before a display window at a department store model of Santa's workshop. But I can't say it didn't create a mood.

"Nice painting," I said to my companion. "Very creepy. My compliments to the artist."

"The artist is flattered," she said coldly. "But there's not much else to see down here, if that's the kind of thing you're looking for. Just a couple of rooms reserved for special clients. If you want to see something creepy, go to the end of that hall and open the door on the right."

I followed her instructions. On the door handle hung a rather large animal collar at the end of a chain leash. The chain jingled a little when I pushed open the door. The red light in the hallway barely allowed me to see inside, but there was little to see anyway except a small, empty room. Its floor was bare cement and there was straw laid down upon it. The smell was terrific.

"Well?" she asked when I returned down the hallway.

"It's something at least," I answered, winking the subtlest possible wink. We just stood for a moment gazing at each other in a light the color of fresh meat. Then she led me back upstairs.

"Where did you say you're from?" she asked as that noisy stairway amplified our footsteps into reverberant echoes that made it sound like we were traipsing through a castle hall.

"It's a real small place," I replied. "About a hundred miles outstate. It's not even on the maps."

"And you've never been to a place like this before?"

"Uh-uh, never," I lied.

"Because some customers run amok when they experience for real what they've only seen in magazines and movies, you know what I mean?"

"I won't do anything like that. I promise."

"Okay, then. Let's go."

We went.

And there was much to see on the way—a Punch and Judy panorama with characters of all kinds as well as the occasional whacking stick. Each scene flipped by like a page in a depraved storybook.

Locked doors were no obstacle for my eyes.

Behind one, where every wall of the room was painted with heavy black bars from floor to ceiling, the Queen of Pain—riding crop raised high—sat atop her human horse. The animal looked hobbled and harnessed. So it couldn't run but only lumber lamely around, with the Queen growing out of its back like a Siamese twin, her royal blood and his beast's now flowing together, tributaries from distant worlds mingling in a hybrid harmony. The creature was panting heavily as the Queen beat time upon its flanks with her stinging crop. Harder and harder she rode her steed before it finally pulled up, foaming and sweaty. Time to cool down, horsey.

Behind another door, one with a swastika painted sloppily across its front, was a scene similar to the previous. Inside, some colored lights were angled down upon the floor, where a very small man, his hunchback possibly artificial, knelt with head bowed low. His hands were lost in a pair of enormous gloves with shapeless fingers which lolled around like ten drunken jacks-in-the-box. One of the fingers was trapped beneath the pointy toe of a high boot. See the funny clown! Or rather *jester* in a jingly cap. His ringed eyes patiently gazed upwards into the darkness, attentive to the hollow voice hurling abuse from on high. The voice was playing up the disparity between its proudly booted self and the humiliated freak upon the floor, contrasting its warrior's leaping delights with the fool's dragging sack of amusements. *But couldn't the stooping hunchback's fun be beautiful too?* his eyes whispered with their elliptical mouths. *But couldn't*—Silence! Now the little fool was going to get it.

Behind still another door, which had no distinguishing marks, a single candle glowed through red glass, just barely keeping the room out of total blackness. It was hard to tell how many were in there—more than a couple, less than a horde. They were all wearing the same gear, little zippers and big zippers like silver stitches scarring their outfits. One very little one had an eyelash caught in it, I could tell that much. For the rest of it, they might as well have been human shadows that merged softly with one another, proclaiming threats of ultimate mayhem and wielding oversized straight razors. But though these glimmering blades were always potently poised, they never came down. It was only make-believe, just like everything else I had seen.

The next door, and for me the last, was at the end of an exhausting climb in what must have been a tower.

"Here's where you get your money's worth, mister," said my date for the night. "I can always tell what my clients want, even if they don't know it themselves."

"Show me your worst," I said, eyeing the undersized door before us.

The situation here was as transparent as the others. Only this time it wasn't horses, pathetic clowns, or paranoid shadows. It was, in fact, a wicked witch and her puppet slave. The clumsy little creature had apparently behaved badly and been caught in the act. Now the witch was in the process of putting him back in line, croaking about what puppets should and should not be doing with their free time. She swept across the room draped in some kind of moth-eaten cloak she had taken from a hook on the wall, her face sunken into its abundant hood. Behind her a stained-glass window shone with all the excommunicated tints of corruption. By the light of this infernal rainbow of wrinkled cellophane, she collared the puppet and chained him to a formidable-looking stone wall, which buckled aluminum-like when he collapsed against it. She angled down her hooded face and whispered into his wooden ear.

"Do you know what I do with bad little puppets like you?" she inquired. "Do you?"

The puppet trembled a bit for show, staying in character for the time being. He might even have worked up some perspiration had he been made of flesh and not wood.

"I'll tell you what I do with puppets who've been naughty," the witch continued half-sweetly. "I make them touch the fire. I burn them from the legs up."

Then, unexpectedly, the puppet smiled.

"And what will you do," the puppet asked, "with all those old dresses, gloves, veils, and capes when I'm gone? What will you do in your low-rent castle with no one to stare, his brow of glittering silver, into the windows of your dreams?"

Perhaps the puppet was perspiring after all, for his brow was now glistening with tiny flecks of starlight.

The witch stepped back and whipped off her hood, exposing the blond hair beneath it. She wanted to know how I knew about all that stuff, which she had never divulged to anyone. She accused me of peeping-tomism, of breaking and entering, and of illicit curiosity in general.

"Let me out of these chains and I'll tell you everything," I said.

"Forget it," she answered. "I'm going to get someone to throw you out of here."

"Then I'll just have to release myself." At these words, the manacles around my ankles, my wrists, and my throat opened by themselves . . . and the chains fell away. "You can't pretend," I continued, "that there isn't something familiar about me. After all we've meant to each other, after all we've done together, over and over and over. You see, I also know the desires of *my* clients, or so I might call them. Newscasters call them victims. They show their faces on television. I make them famous, though my part in their renown is a mystery to all. And mystery is what does it for you, is that not so? The thrill of not knowing what will happen next. But here it's all by the numbers. You've been cooped up in this silly place far too long. For someone like you, that can be deadly. You've always known you were special, don't deny it. You've always believed that someday—and it was always just around the corner, wasn't it?—great things were going to happen, rapturous adventures that weren't quite clear, yet when they happened would be real. As real as the velvet embrace of your favorite cape, the one with the silver chain that draws together its curtain-like wings across your bosom. As real as the tall candles you light on stormy nights. You love those storms, don't you, with their chains of raindrops whipping against your windows. All that pandemonium drives you wild. And the enthralling cruelties you imagine visited upon you in the candlelight by the man with the spangled eyebrows. How they make you swoon so helplessly.

"But now you're in danger of losing everything you really love, which is why I showed up tonight. You've got to get out of this tacky sideshow. This is for hicks, this is small time. You can do much better. I can take you places where the raging storms and brutal subjugations never end. Please, don't back away from me. There's nowhere to go and your eyes tell me you want the same things I do. If you're worried about the hardships of traveling to strange faraway places—don't! You're almost there now. Just fall into my arms, into my heart, into . . . There, that was easy, wasn't it?"

Now she was inside of me with all the others—the prize possession in my gallery of frail little dolls with souls given over to wild-wind nights and sadistic villains. How I loved to play with them.

After the assimilation, I retraced my steps up and down stairways and through corridors of scarlet darkness. "Goodnight, everybody!" I said to the girls in the reception room.

Back out on the street, I paused to make sure she was securely incarcerated within me. In the early stages there's always the possibility that a new internee will try to unzip me from inside, so to speak, and break out the front gate. She did in fact make an attempt to free herself. It wasn't serious, though. A drunk I passed on the sidewalk saw an arm shoot out at him from underneath my shirt, projecting chest-high at a perfect right angle to the rest of me. He staggered over and with a jolly vigor shook the hand reaching blindly between the bars of its cage. Then he proceeded on his way. And I proceeded on mine once I'd got her safely back inside her fabulous prison, a captive of my heart and its infinite chambers. What times we will have together, she and I and all the rest. I can do with them as I please and I am pleased to do much. But they won't have to endure my treatment forever. I'll be back on the road by first frost next year, needing more bodies to warm me. By then, the old ones will have melted like icicles in the dank bowels of my castle home. In the meantime, I'll be keeping a keen eye out for those who walk this world in glad submission to gloom.

As I strolled in good cheer from the House of Chains, the traffic light down that slummy street turned from amber to red—a portent of things to come for my new flame and me, now one in flesh as well as in dreams.

NOTES ON THE WRITING
OF HORROR: A STORY

For much too long I have been promising to formulate my views on the writing of supernatural horror tales. Yet I've continued to put off doing so. All I can say for myself is that until now I just haven't had the time. Why not? I was too busy churning out the leetle darlings. But many people, for whatever reasons, would like to be writers of horror tales and crave advice on how to go about it. I know this. Fortunately, the present moment is a convenient one for me to share my knowledge and experience regarding this special literary vocation. Well, I guess I'm ready as I'll ever be. Let's get it over with.

The way I plan to proceed is quite simple. First, I'm going to sketch out the basic plot, characters, and various other features of a short horror story. Next, I will offer suggestions on how these raw elements may be treated in a few of the major styles which horror authors have exploited over the years. If all goes well, the novice teller of terror tales will be saved much time and agony puzzling out such things for himself. At certain spots along the way I will examine specifics of technique, come to highly biased conclusions regarding intents and purposes, submit general commentary on the philosophy of horror fiction, and so forth.

At this point I would like to state that what follows is a rough draft of a story that in its finished form was meant to appear in the published works of Gerald K. Riggers (myself in literary guise if you didn't know). However, it never came to fruition. Frankly, I just couldn't bring myself to go the distance with this one. Such things happen. Perhaps farther down the line we'll analyze such cases of irreparable failure, perhaps not. Regardless, the bare elements of this narrative are still suitable for demonstrating how horror writers do what they do. Good. Here it is, then, as told in my own words.

THE STORY

A thirtyish male protagonist, let's name him Nathan, has a date with a girl whom he deeply wishes to impress. Toward this end, a minor role is to be played by an impressive new pair of trousers he intends to find and purchase. A few obstacles materialize along the way, realistic inconveniences all, before he finally manages to secure this item of apparel, and at a fair price. They are first-rate in their tailoring, this is quite evident. So far, so good. Profoundly good, to be sure, since Nathan believes that one's personal possessions should themselves possess particular qualities and pedigrees. For example, Nathan's overcoat is a handsome and well-fabricated garment he ordered from an esteemed retailer of fine clothes, his wristwatch is the superior timepiece his grandfather bequeathed to him, and his car is a distinguished but not obtrusive vehicle. For Nathan, peculiar essences inhere not only in certain possessions but also in certain places, certain happenings in time and space, and certain modes of being. In Nathan's view, every facet of one's life should shine with these essences because they are what make an individual really real. What are these essences? Over a period of time, Nathan has narrowed them down to three: something magical, something timeless, and something profound. Though the world around him is for the most part lacking in these special ingredients, he perceives his own life to contain them in fluctuating but acceptable quantities. His new trousers certainly do; and Nathan hopes, for the first time in his life, that a future romance—to be conducted with one Lorna McFickel—will too.

So far, so good. Until the night of Nathan's first date, that is.

Miss McFickel resides in a respectable suburb but, in relation to where Nathan lives, the locale of her home requires that he negotiate one of the most dangerous sectors of the city. No problem: Nathan keeps his car well maintained. If he just keeps the doors locked and windows rolled up, everything will be fine. Worst luck, broken bottles on a broken street, and a flat tire. Nathan curbs the car. He removes his grandfather's watch and locks it in the glove compartment; he takes off his overcoat, folds it up neatly, and snuggles it into the shadows beneath the dashboard. As far as the trousers are concerned, he would simply have to exercise great care while attempting to change his tire in record time, and in a part of town known as Hope's Back Door.

Now, all the while Nathan is fixing the tire, his legs feel strange. He could attribute this to the physical labor he was performing in a pair of trousers not exactly designed for such abuse. He would just have been fooling himself, though. For Nathan remembers his legs feeling strange, though less noticeably, when he tried on the trousers at home. They didn't feel that way at the clothing store. If they had, he would never have purchased them. He would also have returned them if his date with Lorna McFickel hadn't been scheduled too soon for him to find another pair of trousers as fitting as these, which turned out to be not fitting in the least once they began going strange on him. But strange how? Strange as in being a little tingly, and even then some. A little quivery. Nonsense, he's just nervous about his date with lovely Lorna. And the complications he's presently experiencing are no help.

Adding to the troubles Nathan has already had, two scraggly juveniles are now watching him change the tire. He tries to ignore them but succeeds a little too well in this. Unseen by him, one of the ostensible delinquents edges toward the car and opens the front door. Worst luck, Nathan forgot to lock it. The audacious hoodlum lays his hands on Nathan's overcoat, and then both no-goodniks disappear into a tumbledown building.

Very quickly now. Nathan chases the hooligans into what seems to be an untenanted apartment house, and he falls down some stairs leading to a sooty basement. But it's not that the stairs were rotten, no. It *is* that Nathan's legs have given out. They just won't work anymore. The tingling and quivering have now penetrated him and crippled his body from the waist down. He tries to remove his pants but they won't come off, as if they had become part of him. Something has gone horribly wrong because of those pants of his. The following is why. A few days before Nathan purchased the pants, they were returned to the store for a cash refund. The woman returning them said that her husband didn't like the way they felt, which was true. Also true was that her husband had collapsed and died from a heart attack not long after trying on the pants. In an endeavor to salvage what she could from the tragedy, the woman put her husband into a pair of old dungarees before making another move. Poor Nathan, of course, was not informed of his pants' sordid past. And when the hooligans who stole his overcoat see that he is lying helpless in the grime of that basement, they decide to take advantage of the situation and strip him of his valuables . . . starting with those expensive-looking slacks and whatever treasures they may contain. But after they relieve a protesting and paralyzed Nathan of his pants, they do not further pursue their pillaging. Not after they see Nathan's legs, which are the putrid members of a man who is decomposing. With the lower half of Nathan rapidly rotting away, the upper must also die among the countless shadows of that condemned building. And mingled with the pain and madness of his untimely demise, Nathan abhors and grieves over the thought that, for a while anyway, Miss McFickel will think he has stood her up on the first date of what was supposed to be a long line of dates destined to evolve into a magical, timeless, and profound affair of two hearts.

Incidentally, this story, had it reached its culmination, would most likely have borne the title "Romance of a Dead Man."

THE STYLES

As I've already stated, there is more than one way to write a horror story. And such a statement, true or false, is easily demonstrated. In this section we will examine the three primary techniques that authors have employed to produce tales of terror. They are: the *realistic* technique, the *traditional Gothic* technique, and the *experimental* technique. Each serves its user in different ways and realizes different ends, there's no question about that. After a little soul-searching, the prospective horror writer may awaken to the right technique for attaining his personal ends. Thus:

The realistic technique. Since the cracking dawn of consciousness, restless tongues have asked: is the world, and are its people, real? Yes, answers realistic fiction, but only when it is, and they are, normal. The supernatural, and all it represents, is profoundly abnormal, and therefore unreal. Few would argue with these conclusions. Fine. Now the highest aim of the realistic horror writer is to prove, in realistic terms, that the unreal is real. The question is: "Can this be done?" The answer is: "Of course not." One would look silly attempting such a thing. Consequently, the realistic horror writer, wielding the hollow proofs and premises of his art, must settle for merely *seeming* to smooth out the ultimate paradox. In order to achieve this effect, the supernatural realist must really know the normal world, and deeply take for granted its reality. (It helps if he himself is normal and real.) Only then can the unreal, the abnormal, the supernatural be smuggled in as a plain brown package marked Hope, Love, or Fortune Cookies, and postmarked: the Edge of the Unknown. And of the dear reader's seat. In the end, of course, the supernatural explanation of a given story depends entirely on some irrational principle which in the real, normal world looks as awkward and stupid as a rosy-cheeked farm lad in a den of reeking degenerates. (Amend this, possibly, to rosy-cheeked degenerate . . . reeking farm lads.) Nevertheless, the hoax can be pulled off with varying degrees of success. That much is obvious. Just remember to assure the reader, at certain points in the tale and by way of certain signals, that it's now all right to believe the unbelievable. Here's how Nathan's story might be told using the *realistic* technique. Fast forward.

Nathan is a normal and real character, or at least one very close to being so. Perhaps he's not as normal and real as he would like to be, but he does have his sights set on just this goal. He might even be a little too intent on it, though without passing beyond the limits of the normal and the real. We have established that Nathan has a fetish for things *"magical"* (which word should really have its own pair of quotes, given that the positive connotation our protagonist intends it to carry will be negated by the end of the narrative, when a world of bad magic comes down on Nathan's head), *"timeless"* (again the quotes, because if time runs out for anyone, it's Nathan), and *"profound."* (Hmm, this one has a knottiness about it that the others don't. "Magical" and "timeless" have a cheaply ironic connection to the incidents of the story. However, "profound" doesn't work in this way. This "essence" does have an aura about it, though, at least for this writer. For now, then, we'll let it stand.)

Nathan's search for the aforesaid qualities in his life may be somewhat uncommon, but certainly not abnormal, not unreal. (And to make him a bit more real, one could supply his overcoat, his grandfather's wristwatch, and his car with specific brand names, perhaps autobiographically borrowed from one's own closet, wrist, and garage.) The triadic formula which haunts Nathan—similar to the Latinate slogans on family coats-of-arms—also haunts the text of the tale like a song's refrain, possibly in italics as the submerged chanting of our anti-hero's under-mind, possibly not. (Try not to be too artificial; one recalls this is realism.) Nathan wants his romance with Lorna McFickel, along with everything else he considers of value in existence, to be magical, timeless, and, in some vague sense, profound. To Nathan these are attributes that are really normal and really real in a helter-skelter universe where things are ever threatening to go abnormal and unreal on one, anyone, not just him.

Okay. Now Lorna McFickel represents all the virtues of normalcy and reality. She could be played up in the *realistic* version of the story as much more normal and real than Nathan. Maybe Nathan is after all quite the neurotic; maybe he needs normal and real things too much, I don't know. (If I did, maybe I could have written the story.) Whatever, Nathan wants to win a normal, real love, but he doesn't. He loses, even before he has a chance to play. He loses badly. Why? For the answer we can appeal to a very prominent theme in horror stories: be careful what you wish for, because you will certainly get the contrary. What happened was that Nathan got greedy. He wanted something that human existence does not offer—perfection. And to highlight this reality, certain *outside* supernatural forces were brought in to teach Nathan, and the reader, a lesson. (Realistic horror stories can be very didactic.) But how can such things be? This is really what a supernatural horror story, even a realistic one, is all about. In just what way, amid all the realism of Nathan's life, does the supernatural sneak past Inspectors Normal and Real standing guard at the gate? Well, sometimes it steps softly by inches until it has crashed the party.

Now in Nathan's story the source of the supernatural is somewhere inside those mysterious trousers. They are woven of a material which he has never seen the like of; they have no label to indicate their maker; there are no others like them in the store of a different size or color. When Nathan asks the salesman about them, we introduce Exhibit One: the trousers were received as if providentially by the clothier Nathan patronizes. They were not designated to be among the batch of apparel with which they came, the salesman checks. And no one else in the store at the time can tell Nathan anything about them, which is also checked and double-checked. All of these facts make the pants a total mystery in a totally realistic way. The reader now takes the hint that there is something surpassing strange about the pants and will allow that strangeness to extend into the supernatural.

At this point the alert student may ask: but even if the trousers are acknowledged as magical, why do they have the particular effect they eventually have, causing Nathan to rot away below the waist? To answer this question we need to introduce Exhibit Two: Nathan is not the original owner of the pants. Not long before they became one of his magical, timeless, and profound possessions, they were worn by a man whose wife adhered to the rule "waste not, want not" and removed the brand new pants he was wearing when he keeled over and died. But these "facts" explain nothing, right? Of course they don't. However, they may seem to explain everything if they are revealed in the right manner. All one has to do is link up Exhibits One and Two (there may even be more) within the scheme of a realistic narrative.

For example, Nathan might find something in the trousers that leads him to deduce that he is not their original owner. Perhaps he finds a winning lottery ticket of a significant, though not too tempting, amount. Being a normally honest type of person, Nathan calls the clothes store, explains the situation, and they dig up the name and phone number of the gentleman who originally purchased those pants, and, afterward, returned them, or had them returned—the signature on the return form is hard to read (how realistic). Quite possibly the lottery ticket belonged to him. Nathan makes another phone call—not minding that the pants had a previous owner because they are so perfect for his plans—and finds out that the pants were returned not by a man, but by a woman. The very same woman who explains to Nathan that she and her husband, never mind the massive coronary, could really use the modest winnings from that lottery ticket.

By now the reader's mind is no longer on the lottery ticket, but on the revealed fact that Nathan is the owner and future wearer of a pair of pants that seems to have already killed once, and who knows how many other times—thus associating them with impermanence and decay, evils woven into the frustrating fabric of life, evils sent out under various covers (pants, pens, Christmas toys) to cut their recipients down to size because they tried to go against the ways of the world. And so when almost-real, almost-normal Nathan loses all hope of achieving full normalcy and reality, the reader knows why: wrong time, wrong pants, and wrong expectations from a life that has no sense of what we think should be normal and real.

The *realistic* technique.

It's easy. Now try it yourself.

The traditional Gothic technique. Certain kinds of people, and *a fortiori* certain kinds of writers, have always experienced the world around them in the Gothic manner, I'm almost positive. Perhaps there was even some little stump of an apeman who witnessed prehistoric lightning as it parried with prehistoric blackness in a night without rain, and felt his soul rise and fall at the same time to behold this sublime and terrifying conflict. Perhaps such displays provided inspiration for those very first imaginings that were not born of our daily life of crude survival, who knows? Could this be why all our primal mythologies are Gothic—that is, fearsome, fantastical, and inhuman? I only pose the question, you see. Perhaps the forbidding events of triple-volume shockers passed, in abstract, through the brains of hairy, waddling things as they moved around in moon-trimmed shadows during their angular migrations across lunar landscapes of craggy peaks or skeletal wastelands of jagged ice. Such ones did not doubt there was a double world of the fearsome, the fantastical, and the inhuman, for nothing needed to flaunt its reality before their eyes as long as it *felt* real to their blood. A gullible bunch of creatures, these. And to this day the fearsome, the fantastical, and the inhuman retain a firm grip upon our souls. So much goes without saying, really.

Therefore, the advantages of the *traditional Gothic* technique, even for the contemporary writer, are two. One, isolated supernatural incidents don't look as silly in a Gothic tale as they do in a realistic one, since the latter obeys the hard-knocking school of reality while the former recognizes only the University of Dreams. (Of course the entire Gothic tale itself may look silly to a given reader, but this is a matter of temperament, not technical execution.) Two, a Gothic tale gets under a reader's skin and stays there far more insistently than other kinds of stories. Of course it has to be done right, whatever you take the words *done right* to mean. Do they mean that Nathan has to function within the monumental incarceration of a castle in the mysterious fifteenth century? No, but he may function within the monumental incarceration of a castle-like skyscraper in the just-as-mysterious modern world. Do they mean that Nathan must be a brooding Gothic hero and Miss McFickel an ethereal Gothic heroine? No, but it may mean an extra dose of obsessiveness in Nathan's psychology, and Miss McFickel may seem to him less the ideal of normalcy and reality than the pure Ideal itself. Contrary to the realistic story's allegiance to the normal and the real, the world of the Gothic tale is fundamentally unreal and abnormal, harboring essences which are magical, timeless, and profound in a way the realistic Nathan never dreamed. So, to do right by a Gothic tale, let's be frank, requires that the author be a militant romantic who relates the action of his narratives in dreamy and more than usually emotive language. Hence, the well-known grandiose rhetoric of the Gothic tale, which may be understood by the sympathetic reader as not just an inflatable raft on which the imagination floats at its leisure upon waves of bombast, but also as the sails of the Gothic artist's soul filling up with the winds of ecstatic hysteria. So it's hard to tell someone how to write the Gothic tale, since one really has to be born to the task. Too bad. The most one can do is offer a pertinent example: a Gothic scene from "Romance of a Dead Man," translated from the original Italian of Geraldo Riggerini. This chapter is entitled "The Last Death of Nathan."

Through a partially shattered window, its surface streaked with a blue film of dust that thrilled the soul with a sublime sense of desolation, the diluted glow of twilight seeped down onto the basement floor where Nathan lay without hope of a saving mobility. In the dark you're not anywhere, he had thought as a child bundled beneath his bedcovers, his sight lost in night's enveloping cloak; and, in the bluish semi-luminescence of that stone cellar, Nathan was truly not anywhere where eyes could see aught but a gloomy fate. With agonizing labor, he raised himself upon one elbow, squinting through tears of confusion into the grimy azure dimness. He now appeared as would a patient who has been left alone in a doctor's surgery, anxiously looking around to see if he had been forgotten on that frigid table. If only his legs would move as they once did, if only that paralyzing pain would suddenly become cured. Where were those wretched doctors, he asked himself deliriously. Ah, there they were, standing behind the turquoise haze of the surgery lamps. "He's out of it, man," said one of them to his colleague. "We can take everything he's got on him." But after they removed Nathan's trousers, the operation was unceremoniously terminated and the patient abandoned in the blue shadows of silence. "Jesus, look at his legs," they screamed. Oh, if only he could now scream like that, Nathan thought among all the fatal chaos of his other thoughts. If only he could scream loud enough to be heard by that angelic girl, by way of apologizing for his permanent absence from their magical, timeless, and profound future, which was in fact as defunct as the two legs putrefying before his eyes. Couldn't he now emit such a scream, now that the tingling anguish of his liquefying legs was beginning to course throughout his whole being? But no. It was impossible— to scream that loudly—though he did manage, at length, to scream himself straight to death.

The *traditional Gothic* technique.

It's easy if you're right for the job. Try it yourself and see.

The experimental technique. Every story needs to be told in just the right way. And sometimes that way is puzzling to the public. In the business of storytelling there's really no such thing as experimentalism in its trial-and-error sense. A story is not an experiment, an experiment is an experiment. True. The "experimental" writer, then, is simply following the story's commands to tell it in the right way, puzzling or not. The writer is not the story, the story is the story. See?

The question we now must ask is: is Nathan's the kind of horror story that demands treatment outside the conventional realistic or Gothic techniques? Well, it may be, if only for the purpose of these "notes." Since I've pretty much given up on "Romance of a Dead Man," I guess there's no harm in giving another turn of the screw to its bare-bones narrative, even if it's in the wrong direction. Here's the way mad Dr. Riggers would experiment, blasphemously, with his man-made Nathanstein. The secret of life, my ugly Igors, is time . . . time . . . time.

The experimental version of this story could actually be told as two stories happening "simultaneously," each narrated in alternating sections which take place in parallel chronologies. One section begins with the death of Nathan and moves backward in time, while its counterpart story begins with the death of the original owner of the magical pants and moves forward. Needless to say, the facts in the case of Nathan must be juggled around so as to be comprehensible from the beginning, that is to say from the end. (Don't risk confusing your worthy readers.) The stories converge at the crossroads of the final section where the destinies of two characters also converge, this being the clothes store where Nathan purchases the fateful trousers.

On his way into the store he bumps into someone who is preoccupied with counting a handful of cash, this being the woman who has returned the trousers which have been already placed back on the rack.

"Excuse me," says Nathan.

"Look where you're going," says the woman.

Of course at this point in time we have already seen where Nathan is going and what "magical" and "profound" trouble he gets himself into as he circles in a "timeless" narrative loop.

The *experimental* technique.

It's easy. Now try it yourself.

ANOTHER STYLE

All the styles we have just examined have been simplified for the purposes of instruction, haven't they? Each is a purified example of its kind, let's not kid ourselves. In the real world of horror fiction, however, the above three techniques often get entangled with one another in hopelessly strange ways, almost to the point of rendering my previous discussion of them useless for all practical purposes. But an ulterior purpose, which I'm saving for later, may thus be better served. Before we get there, though, I'd like, briefly, to propose still another style.

The story of Nathan is one very close to my heart and I hope, in its basic trauma, to the hearts of many others. I wanted to write this horror tale in such a fashion that its readers would be distressed not by the isolated catastrophe of Nathan but by the very existence of a world where such catastrophe is possible. I wanted to forge a tale that would conjure a mournful universe independent of time, place, and persons. The characters of the story would be Death itself in the flesh, Desire in a new pair of pants, Desiderata within arm's reach, and Doom in a size to fit all.

I couldn't do it, my friends. What I took on was the writing of a story that, for *my* intents and purposes, would be consummately profound. (There, now I've given away my reason for listing this property among Nathan's three essences.) But I simply didn't have it in me to put it all together.

It's not easy, and I don't suggest that you try it yourself.

THE FINAL STYLE

Now that we are nearing the conclusion of these notes, it is time to reveal my own prejudice concerning how a horror story should be written. It is my view, and this is only an opinion, mind you, that horror has a voice proper to itself. But what is it? Is it that of an old storyteller, keeping eyes wide around the tribal campfire; is it that of a documentarian of current or historical happenings, reporting events heard-about and conversations over-heard; is it even that of a yarn-spinning god who can see the unseeable and narrate, from an omniscient perspective, a scary set of incidents for his reader's entertainment? All things considered, I contend that it is none of these voices, nor is it any of the others we have analyzed up to this point. Instead, so I say, it is a lonely voice calling out in the middle of the night. Sometimes it's muffled, like the voice of a tiny insect crying for help from inside a sealed coffin, and other times the coffin shatters, like a brittle exoskeleton, and from within rises a piercing, crystal shriek that lacerates the midnight blackness. In other words, the proper voice of horror is really that of the *personal confession*.

If you will humor me for a time, I'll try to explain the proposition that I have just advanced. Horror is not really horror unless it's *your* horror—that which you have known personally. You may not be able to get it out in a consummately profound way, but this is where true horror writing must start. And what makes it true is that the confessing narrator always has something he must urgently get off his chest and labors beneath its nightmarish weight all the while he is telling the tale. Nothing could be more obvious, I argue, except perhaps that the tale teller, ideally, should himself be a writer of horror fiction, if not by trade then at least by temperament. That really is more obvious. Better. But how can the *confessional*

technique be applied to the story we've been working with? Its
hero isn't a horror writer, at least not that I can see. Clearly
some adjustments have to be made.

As the reader may have noticed, Nathan's character can be
altered to suit a variety of literary styles. He can lean toward the
normal in one and the abnormal in another. He can be transformed from a realistic person to an experimental abstraction.
He can play any number of basic human and nonhuman roles,
representing just about anything a writer could want. Mostly,
though, I wanted Nathan, when I first conceived him and his
ordeal, to represent none other than my real life self. For behind
my pseudonymic mask of Gerald Karloff Riggers, I am none
other than Nathan Jeremy Stein.

So it's not too far-fetched that in his story Nathan should be
a horror writer who wishes to relate, via the route of supernatural fiction, the awful vicissitudes of his own experience. Perhaps he dreams of achieving Gothic glory by writing tales that
are nothing less than magical, timeless, and the other thing. He
is already an ardent consumer of the abnormal and the unreal:
a haunter of spectral marketplaces, a visitant of discount houses
of unreality, a bargain hunter in the deepest basement of the
unknown. And somehow he comes to procure his dream of
horror without even realizing what it is he's bought or with
what he has bought it. Like the other Nathan, *this* Nathan
eventually finds that what he's bought is not quite what he bar-
gained for—a pig in a poke rather than a nice pair of pants.

What? I'll explain.

In the confessional version of Nathan's horror story, the
main character must be provided with something shocking to
confess, something befitting his persona as a die-hard freak of
all things fearsome, fantastical, and inhuman. The solution is
quite obvious. Nathan will confess his realization that he is up
to his eyeballs in the aberrations of HORROR. He's had a pre-
dilection for this path since he can remember, and maybe even
earlier than that. In other words, Nathan is not a normal boy,
nor a real one.

The turning point in Nathan's biography as a man (or thing)
of horror, as in previous accounts, is an aborted fling with

Lorna McFickel. In the other versions of the story, the character known by this name is a personage of shifting significance, representing at turns the ultra-real or the super-ideal to her would-be romancer. The confessional version of "Romance of a Dead Man," however, gives her a new identity, namely that of Lorna McFickel herself, who lives across the hall from me in a Gothic castle of high-rise apartments, twin-towered and honeycombed with newly carpeted passageways. But otherwise there's not much difference between the female lead in the fictional story and her counterpart in the factual one. While the storybook Lorna will remember Nathan as the creep who spoiled her evening, who disappointed her—Real Lorna, Normal Lorna, feels exactly the same way, or rather felt, since I doubt she even thinks about the one she called *the most disgusting creature on the face of the earth.* And though these hyperbolic words were spoken in the heat of a very hot moment, I believe her attitude was sincere. Notwithstanding, I will never reveal the motivation for this outburst of hers, not even under the pain of torture. Character motivation is not important to this horror story anyway, or not nearly as important as what happens to Nathan following Lorna's revelatory rejection.

For he now finds out that his unwholesome nature is not just a fluke of psychology, and that, as a fact, supernatural influences have been governing his life all along, that he is subject only to the rule of demonic forces, which now want this expatriate from the pit of shadows back in their embracing arms. In brief, Nathan should never have been born a human being, a truth he must accept. Hard. And he knows that someday the demons will come for him.

The height of the crisis comes one evening when the horror writer's spirits are at low ebb. He has attempted to express his supernatural tragedy in a short horror story, his last, but he just can't reach a climax of suitable intensity and imagination, one that would do justice to the cosmic scale of his pain. He has failed to embody in words his semi-autobiographical sorrow, and all these games with protective names have only made it more painful. It hurts to hide his heart within pseudonyms of pseudonyms. Finally, the horror writer, while sitting at his writing desk, begins bawling all over the manuscript of his unfinished story. This goes on for quite some time, until Nathan's sole want is to seek a human oblivion in a human bed. Whatever its drawbacks, grief is a great sleeping draught to drug oneself into a noiseless, lightless paradise far from an agonizing universe. This is so.

A little later, someone is knocking, impatiently rapping really, on Nathan's apartment door. Who is it? One must answer to find out.

"Here, you forgot these," a pretty girl said to me, flinging a woolly bundle into my arms. Just as she was about to walk away, she turned and scanned the features of my face a little more scrupulously. I have sometimes impersonated other people, the odd Norman and even a Nathan or two, and that night I put on the mask once more. "I'm sorry," she said. "I thought you were Norman. This is his apartment, right across and one down the hall from mine." She pointed to show me. "Who're you?"

"I'm a friend of Norman," I answered.

"Oh, I guess I'm sorry then. Well, those're his pants I threw at you."

"Were you mending them or something?" I asked innocently, checking them as if looking for the scars of repair.

"No, he just didn't have time to put them back on the other night when I threw him out, you know what I mean? I'm moving out of this creepy dump just to get away from him, and you can tell him those words."

"Please come in from that drafty hallway and you can tell him yourself."

I smiled my smile and she, not unresponsively, smiled hers. I closed the door behind her.

"So, do you have a name?" she asked.

"Penzance," I replied. "Call me Pete."

"Well, at least you're not Harold Wackers, or whatever the name is on those lousy books of Norman's."

"I believe it's *Wickers,* H. J. Wickers."

"Anyway, you don't seem anything like Norman, or even someone who'd be a friend of his."

"I'm sure that was intended as a compliment, from what I've

gathered about you and Norman. Actually, though, I too write books not unlike those of H. J. Wickers. My apartment across town is being painted, and Norman was kind enough to take me in, even loan me his desk for a while." I manually indicated the weeped-upon object of my last remark. "In fact, Norman and I sometimes collaborate under a common pen-name, and right now we're working together on a project."

"That's nice, I'm sure," she said. "By the way. I'm Laura—"

"O'Finney," I finished. "Norman's spoken quite highly of you."

"Where is the creep, anyway?" she inquired.

"He's sleeping," I answered, lifting a finger toward the rear section of the apartment. "We've been hard at work on a new story, but I could wake him up."

The girl's face assumed a disgusted expression.

"Forget it," she said, heading for the door. Then she turned and very slowly walked a little ways back toward me. "Maybe we'll see each other again."

"Anything is possible," I assured her.

"Just do me a favor and keep Norman away from me, if you don't mind."

"I think I can do that very easily. But first you have to do something for me."

"What?"

I leaned toward her very confidentially.

"Please die, Desiderata," I whispered in her ear, while gripping her neck with both hands, cutting short a scream along with her life. Then I really went to work.

"Wake up, Norman," I shouted. I was standing at the foot of his bed, my hands positioned behind my back. "You were really dead to the world, you know that?"

A little drama took place on Norman's face in which astonishment overcame sleepiness and both were vanquished by anxiety. He had been through a lot the past couple nights, laboring over our "notes" and other things, and really needed some rest.

"Who? What do you want?" he said, quickly sitting up in bed.

"Never mind what I want. Right now we are concerned with what *you* want. Remember what you told that girl the other night? Remember what you wanted her to do that got her so upset?"

"So that's it. You're a friend of Laura. Well, you can just get the hell out of here or I'm calling the cops."

"That's what *she* said, too, remember? And then she said she wished she had *never met you.* And that was the line, wasn't it, that gave you the inspiration for our fictionalized adventure. Poor Nathan never had the chance you had. Nice work, thinking up those enchanted trousers. When the real reason—"

"Are you deaf? Get out of my apartment!" he yelled. But he calmed down somewhat when he saw that ferocity in itself had no effect on me.

"What did you expect from that girl? You did tell her that you wanted to entwine bodies with . . . what was it? Oh yes, a headless woman. Like that decapitated specter you read about in an old Gothic novel long years past. I would imagine that the illustration in that book only inflamed your fixation. I guess Laura didn't understand that in the spring a young man's fancy lightly turns to thoughts of . . . *headless apparitions.* Headless. You told her you had the whole costume back at your place, if I correctly recall. Well, my lad, I've got the answer to your prayers. How's this for headless?" I said, holding up the head from behind my back.

He didn't make a sound, though his eyes screamed madly at what he saw. I tossed the long-haired and bloody noggin in his lap. In a blink, he threw the bedcovers over it and frantically pushed the whole business onto the floor with his feet.

"The rest of the body is in the bathtub if you want to have a go at it. I'll wait."

I can't say for sure, but for a passing moment he seemed to be thinking about it. He stayed put in his bed, however, and didn't make a move or say a word for a minute or so. When he finally did speak, each syllable came out calm and smooth. It was as if one part of his mind had broken off from the rest, and it was this part that now addressed me.

"Who are you?" he asked.

"Do you really need a name, and would it do you any good? Should we call that disengaged head down there Laura or Lorna, or just plain Desiderata? And what in the name of perdition should I call you—Norman or Nathan, Harold or Gerald?"

"I thought so," he said disgustedly. Then he continued in that eerily rational voice, but very rapidly. He did not even seem to be talking to anyone in particular. "Since the thing to which I am speaking," he said, "since this thing knows what only I could know, and since it tells me what only I could tell myself, I must therefore be completely alone in this room. Perhaps I'm dreaming. Yes, dreaming. Otherwise the diagnosis is insanity. Very true. Profoundly certain. Go away now, Mr. Madness. Go away, Dr. Dream. You made your point, now let me sleep. I'm through with you."

Then he lay his head down on the pillow and closed his eyes.

"Norman," I said. "Do you always go to bed with your trousers on?"

He opened his eyes and now noticed what he had not before. He sat up again.

"Very good, Mr. Madness. These look like the real thing. But that's not possible since Laura still has them, sorry about that. Funny, they won't come off. The imaginary zipper must be stuck. I guess I'm in trouble now. I'm a dead man if there ever was one, hoo. Always make sure you know what you're buying, that's what I say. Heaven help me, please. You never know what you might be getting yourself into. Come off, damn you! Well, so when do I start to rot, Mr. Madness? Are you still there? What happened to the lights?"

The lights had gone out in the room and everything glowed with a bluish luminescence. Lightning began flashing outside the bedroom window, and thunder resounded in the midst of a rainless night. Through an aperture in the clouds shone a moon that only beings of another world can see. Puppet-shadows played upon its silvery screen.

"Rot your way back to us, you quirk of creation. Rot your way out of this world. Come home to a hell so excruciating it is bliss itself."

"Is this really happening to me? I mean, I'm doing my best, sir. But it isn't easy. Some kind of electrical charge making me all shivery down there. It feels as if I'm dissolving. Oh, it hurts, my love. Ah, ah, ah. What a way to end a miserable life, turning to mush. Can you help me, Dr. Dream?"

I could feel myself changing form, shuffling off that human suit I was wearing. Bony wings began rising out of my back, and I saw them spread gloriously in the blue mirror before me. My eyes were now jewels, hard and radiant. My jaws were a cavern of dripping silver and through my veins ran rivers of putrescent gold. He was writhing on the bed like a wounded insect, making sounds like nothing human. I swept him up and wrapped my sticky arms again and again around his trembling body. He was laughing like a child, the child of another world. And a great wrong was about to be rectified.

I signaled the windows to open onto the night, and, very slowly, they did. His childlike laughter had now turned to tears, but they would soon run dry, I knew this. At last we would be free to live magically, timelessly beyond the pull of the earth. The windows opened wide over the city below and, in a manner of speaking, the profound blackness above welcomed us.

I had never tried this before.

But when the time came, I found it all so easy.

DREAMS FOR INSOMNIACS

THE CHRISTMAS EVES OF AUNT ELISE

A TALE OF POSSESSION IN OLD GROSSE POINTE

We pronounced her name with a distinct "Z" sound—*Remember, Jack, remember*—the way some people slur Missus into Mizzuz. It was at her home in Grosse Pointe that she insisted our family, both its wealthy and its unwealthy sides, celebrate each Christmas Eve in a style that exuded the traditional, the old-fashioned, the antique. Actually, Aunt Elise constituted the wealthy side of the family all on her own. Her husband had died many years before, leaving his wife a prosperous real estate business and no children. Not surprisingly, Aunt Elise undertook the management of the firm with admirable success, perpetuating our heirless uncle's family name on "for sale" signs planted on front lawns in three states. But what was Uncle's *first* name, a young nephew or niece sometimes wondered. Or, as it was more than once put by one of us children: "Where's *Uncle* Elise?" To which the rest of us answered in unison: "He's at his ease," a response we learned from none other than our widowed aunt herself.

Aunt Elise was without husband or offspring of her own, true enough. But she loved all the ferment of big families, and every holiday season she possessed as much in blood relations as she did in her tangible and intangible assets and investments. Nevertheless, she was not the conspicuously consuming type of rich bitch. Her house was something of an Elizabethan country manor in style while remaining modest, even relatively miniature, in its mass. It fit very nicely—when it existed—into a claustrophobic cluster of trees on some corner acreage a few steps from Lake Shore Drive, profiling rather than facing the lake itself. A rather dull exterior of soot-gray stones somewhat camouflaged the old place in its woodland hideaway, until one caught sight of its diamond-paned windows and realized that a house in fact existed where before there seemed to be only shadowed vacancy.

Around Christmastime the many-faceted windows of my aunt's residence took on a candied glaze in the pink, blue, green, and other-colored lights strung about their perimeters. More often in the old days—*Remember them, Jack*—a thick December fog rolled off the not-yet-frozen lake and those kaleidoscopic windows would throw their spectrums into the softening haze. This, to my child's senses, was the image and atmosphere defining the winter holiday: a serene congregation of colors that for a time turned our everyday world into one where mysteries abounded. This was the celebration, this was the festival. Why did we leave it all behind us, leave it outside? Every Christmas Eve of my childhood, as I was guided up the winding front walk toward my aunt's house, a parent's hand in each of mine, I always stopped short, pulling Mom and Dad back like a couple of runaway horses, and for a brief, futile moment refused to go inside.

After the first Christmas Eve I can recall—chronologically my fifth—I knew what happened inside the house, and year after year there was little change either in the substance or surface details of the program. For those from large families, this scene is a little too familiar to bother describing. Perhaps even lifelong orphans are jaded to it. Still, there are others for whom depictions of unusual uncles, loveable grandparents, and a common run of cousins will always be fresh and dear; those who delight in multiple generations of characters crowding the page, who are warmed by the feel of their paper flesh. I tell you they share this temper with my Aunt Elise, and her spirit is in them.

For the duration of these Christmas assemblies, my aunt always occupied the main room of her house. This room I never saw except as a fantasy of ornamentation, a hallucinatorium in holiday dress. Right now I can only hope to portray a few of its highlights. First of all holly, both fresh and artificial, hung down from wherever it was possible to hang—the frames of paintings, the stained-wood shelves of a thousand gewgaws, even the velvety embossed pattern of the wallpaper itself, intertwining with its swirls and flourishes, if memory serves. And from the fixtures above, including a chandelier delicately sugared with tiny Italian lights, down came gardens of mistletoe. The huge fireplace blazed with a festive inferno, and before its cinder-spitting hearth was a protective screen, at either end of which stood a pair of thick brass posts. And slipped over the crown of each post was a sock-puppet Santa, its mittens outstretched in readiness to give someone a tiny, angular hug.

In the corner of the main room, the one beside the front window, a plump evergreen was somewhere hidden beneath every imaginable type of dangling, roping, or blinking decoration, as well as being dolled up with silly bows in pastel shades, satiny bows lovingly tied by human hands. The same hands also did their work on the presents beneath the tree, and year after year these seemed, like everything else in the room, to be in exactly the same place, as if the gifts of last Christmas had never been opened, quickening in me the nightmarish sense of a ritual forever reenacted without hope of escape. (Somehow I am still possessed by this same feeling of entrapment.) My own present was always at the back of that horde of packages, almost against the wall behind the tree. It was tied up with a pale purple ribbon and covered with pale blue wrapping paper upon which little bears in infants' sleeping gowns dreamed of more pale blue presents which, instead of more bears, had little boys dreaming upon them. I spent much of a given Christmas Eve sitting near this gift of mine, mostly to find refuge from the others rather than to wonder at what was inside. It was always something in the way of underwear, nightwear, or socks, never the nameless marvel which I fervently hoped to receive from my obscenely well-heeled aunt. Nobody seemed to mind that I sat on the other side of the room from where most of them congregated to talk or sing carols to the music of an ancient organ, which Aunt Elise played with her back to her audience, and to me.

Slee—eep in heav—enly peace.

"That was very good," she said without turning around. As usual, the sound of her voice led you to expect that any moment she would clear her throat of some sticky stuff which was clinging to its insides. Instead she switched off the electric organ, after which gesture some of the gathering, dismissed, left for other parts of the house.

"We didn't hear Old Jack singing with us," she said, turning to look across the room where I was seated in a large chair beside a fogged window. On that occasion I was about twenty or twenty-one, home from school for Christmas. I had drunk quite a bit of Aunt Elise's holiday punch, and felt like answering: "Who cares if you didn't hear Old Jack singing, you old bat?" But instead I simply stared her way, drunkenly taking in her visage for the family scrapbook of my memory: tight-haired head (like combed wires), calm eyes of someone in an old portrait (someone long gone), high cheekbones highly colored (less rosily than like a rash), and the prominent choppers of a horse charging out of nowhere in a dream. I had no worry about my future ability to remember these features, even though I had vowed this would be the last Christmas Eve I would view them. So I could afford to be tranquil in the face of Aunt Elise's taunts that evening. In any case, further confrontation between the two of us was aborted when some of the children began clamoring for one of their aunt's stories. "And this time a *true* story, Auntie. One that really happened."

"All right," she answered, adding that "maybe Old Jack would like to come over and sit with us."

"Too old for that, thank you. Besides, I can hear you just fine from—"

"Well," she began before I'd finished, "let me think a moment. There are so many, so *many*. Anywho, here's one of

them. This happened before any of you were born, a few winters after I moved into this neighborhood with your uncle. I
don't know if you ever noticed, but a little ways down the street
there's an empty lot where there should be, used to be, a house.
You can see it from the front window over there," she said,
pointing to the window beside my chair. I let my eyes follow
her finger out that window and through the fog witnessed the
empty lot of her story.

"There it once stood, a beautiful old house much bigger
than this one. In that house lived a very old man who never
went out and who never invited anyone to visit him, at least no
one I ever noticed. And after the old man died, what do you
think happened to the house?"

"It disappeared," answered some of the children, jumping
the gun.

"In a way, I suppose it did disappear. Actually what happened was that some men came and tore the house down brick
by brick. I think the old man who lived there must have been
very mean to want that to happen to his house after he died."

"How do you know he wanted it?" I interjected, trying to
spoil her assumption.

"What other sensible explanation is there?" Aunt Elise
answered. "Anywho," she went on, "I think that the old man
just couldn't stand the thought of anyone else living in the
house and being happy there, because surely he wasn't. But
maybe, just maybe, he had his house torn down for another
reason," said Aunt Elise, drawing out these last words to suspenseful effect. The children sitting cross-legged before her
now listened with a new intentness, while the crackling logs
seemed to start up a little more noisily in the fireplace.

"Maybe by destroying his house, making it disappear, the
old man thought he was taking it with him into the other
world. People who have lived alone for a very long time often
think and do very strange things," she emphasized, though I'm
sure no one except me thought to apply this final statement to
the storyteller herself. (*Tell everything, Jack.*) She went on:

"Now what would lead a person to such conclusions about
the old man, you may wonder? Did something strange happen

with him and his house after both of them were gone? Well, the answer is yes, something did happen. And I'm going to tell you just what it was.

"One night—a foggy winter's night like this one, oh my little children—someone came walking down this exact street and paused at the property line of the house of the old man who was now dead. This someone was a young man whom many people had seen wandering around here off and on for some years. I myself, I tell you, once confronted him and asked him what business he had with us and with our homes, because that's what he seemed most interested in. Anywho, this young man called himself an an-tee-quarian, and he said he was very interested in old things, particularly old houses. And he had a very particular interest in the house of that strange old man. A number of times he had asked him if he could look around inside, but the old man always refused. Most of the time the house was dark as though no one was home, even if someone always was.

"So you can imagine the young man's bewilderment when on that winter's night what he saw was not a dark house where it seemed no one was inside, but a place all lit up with bright Christmas lights shining through the fog. Could this be the old man's house, decorated so nice and cheerful with these lights? Yes, it could, because there was the old man himself standing at the window with a rather friendly look on his face. So, one more time, the young man thought he would try his luck and maybe get to see the inside of the old house. He rang the bell and the front door slowly opened wide. The old man didn't say anything, but merely stepped back so that his caller could come in. Finally the young antiquarian would be able to study the inside of the house to his heart's content. Along the way, in narrow halls and long-abandoned rooms, the old man stood silently beside his guest, smiling all the time."

"I can't imagine how you know this part of your *true* story," I interrupted.

"Aunt Elise *knows*," asserted one of my little cousins just to shut me up. And when my aunt cast a glance at me, it seemed for a moment that she really did know. Then she continued her true story.

"After the young man had looked all around the house, both men sat down in the deep comfortable chairs of the front parlor and talked a while. But it wasn't too long before that smile on the old man's face, that quiet little smile, began to bother his visitor in a peculiar way. At last the young man claimed he had to go, glancing down at the watch he had drawn from his pocket. And when he looked up again . . . the old man was gone. Naturally, this startled the young man, who jumped up from his chair and nervously checked the nearby rooms and hallways for his host, calling "Sir, sir," because he never found out the old man's name. And though he could have been in any number of different places, the owner of the house didn't seem to be anywhere that the young man investigated. So the anti-quarian finally decided just to leave without saying good-bye or thank you or anything like that.

"But he didn't get as far as the door when he stopped dead in his tracks because of what he saw through the front window. There seemed to be no street anymore, no street lamps or sidewalks, not even any houses, besides the one he was in, of course. There was only the fog and some horrible, tattered shapes wandering aimlessly within it. The young man could hear them crying. What was this place, and where had the old house taken him? He didn't know what to do except stare out the window. And when he saw the face reflected in the window, he thought for a second that the old man had returned and was standing behind him again, smiling his quiet smile.

"But then the young man realized that this was now his own face, and, like those terrible, ragged creatures lost in the fog, he too began to cry.

"After that night, no one around here ever saw the young man again. Well, did you like that story, children?"

I felt tired, more tired than I'd ever been in my life. I barely had the will or the strength to push myself out of the chair into which I'd sunk down so deep. How slowly I trudged past faces that seemed far off in the distance. Where was I going? Was I in want of another drink? Did I desire another dainty from the table spread with Christmas treats? What was it that was calling me away from that room?

No time seemed to have passed, but when I came to myself I was walking down a foggy street. The fog formed impenetrable white walls around me, narrow corridors leading nowhere and rooms without windows. I didn't walk very far before realizing I could go no farther. As it happened, though, I did finally see something. What I saw was a cluster of Christmas lights, their colors beaming against the fog. But what could they have signified that they should seem so horrible to me? Why did this peaceful vision of hazy wonder, which had transported the imagination of my childhood self, now strike me with such terror? These were not the colors I had loved; this could not be the house. Yet it was, for there at the window stood its owner, and the sight of her thin smiling face for some reason was not right.

Then I remembered: Aunt Elise was long dead and her house, at the instruction of her will, had been dismantled brick by brick.

"Uncle Jack, wake up," urged young voices at close range, though technically, being an only child, I was not their uncle. More accurately, I was just an elder member of the family who had nodded off in his chair. It was Christmas Eve, and I had had a little too much to drink.

"We're gonna sing carols, Uncle Jack," said the voices. Then they went away.

I went away, too, retrieving my overcoat from the bedroom where it lay buried in a communal grave under innumerable other overcoats. Everyone else was singing songs to the strumming of guitars. (I liked their metallic timbre because it was in no way reminiscent of the rich, rotting vibrations of the church organ Aunt Elise played on Christmas Eves long past.) Foregoing all rituals of departure, I slipped quietly out the back door in the kitchen.

I left that Christmas Eve get-together as if I had an appointment to keep, one of long standing whose import I never knew or had forgotten. So many things I can remember from years gone by—and easily enough because I have led such an uneventful and solitary existence—but I cannot remember what happened next that evening. My mind was not at its best, and the dream I had earlier must have carried over into one I had when I went to sleep at home, though I do not recall doing that either. The one thing I do remember, as if it happened while I was still awake and not dreaming, was standing before the door of a house that no longer existed, a door that opened in a slow, weighty sweep. Then a hand reached out and laid itself upon me. What horror I felt as I saw that great, gaping smile and heard the words: "Merry Christmas, Old Jack!"

Oh, how good it was to see the old boy when he came to me at last. He had grown old but never grew up. And finally I had him, him and his every thought, all the pretty pictures of his mind. Those weeping demons, souls forever lost, came out of the fog and took away his body. He was one of them now. But I have kept the best part, all his beautiful memories, all those lovely times we had—the children, the presents, the colors of those nights! Anywho, they are mine now. Tell us of those years, Old Jack, the years I have now taken from you—the years I can play with as I wish, like a child with his toys. Oh, how nice, how nice and lovely to be settled in a world where it's always dead with darkness and always alive with lights! And where it will always, forever after, be Christmas Eve.

THE LOST ART
OF TWILIGHT

I

I have painted it, tried to at least. Oiled it, watercolored it, smeared it upon a mirror which I positioned to rekindle the glow of the real thing. And always in the abstract. Never actual sinking suns in spring, autumn, winter skies; never a sepia light descending over the trite horizon of a lake, not even the particular lake I like to view from the great terrace of my massive old mansion. But these *Twilights* of mine were not done in the abstract merely for the sake of keeping out the riff-raff of the real world. Other painterly abstractionists may claim that nothing in life is represented by their canvases—that a streak of iodine red is just a streak of iodine red, a spattering of flat black equals a spattering of flat black. Yet sheer color, sheer rhythms of line and masses of structure, sheer composition in general meant more to me than that. The others have only *seen* their dramas of shape and shade; I—and it is impossible to insist on this too strenuously—I have *been* there. My twilight abstractions did in fact represent some reality: a zone composed of palaces of soft and sullen colors standing beside seas of scintillating pattern and beneath sadly radiant patches of sky, a zone where the observer is a formal presence, an impalpable essence, free of carnal substance—a *denizen* of the abstract. But that is just a memory to me now. What I thought would last forever was lost in the blink of an eye.

Only a few weeks ago I was sitting out on the terrace, watching the early autumn sun droop into the above-mentioned lake, talking to Aunt T. Her heels clomped with a pleasing hollowness on drab flagstones. Silver-haired, she was attired in a gray suit, a big bow flopping up to her lower chins. In her left hand was a long envelope, neatly cesareaned, and in her right hand the letter it had contained, folded in sections like a triptych.

"They want to see you," she said, gesturing with the letter. "They want to come here."

"I don't believe it," I said, and skeptically turned in my chair to watch the sunlight stretching across the extensive lawn that fronts the old pile where it seemed we had lived for centuries.

"If you would only read the letter," she insisted.

"I can't. Not if it's written in French."

"Now that's not true, to judge by those books you're always stacking in the library."

"Those happen to be art books. I just look at the pictures."

"You like pictures, André?" she asked in her best matronly ironic tone. "I have a picture for you. Here it is: they *are* going to be allowed to come here and stay with us as long as they like. There's a family of them, two children and the letter also mentions an unmarried sister. They're coming from Aix-en-Provence to visit America, and while on their trip they want to see their only living blood relation here. Do you understand this picture? They know who you are and, more to the point, where you are."

"I'm surprised they would want to, since they're the ones—"

"No, they're not. They're from your *father's* side of the family. The Duvals," she explained. "They do know all about you but say," Aunt T. here consulted the letter for a moment, "that they are *sans préjugé*."

"The generosity of such creatures freezes my blood. Twenty years ago these people do what they did to my mother, and now they have the gall, the *gall,* to say they aren't prejudiced against *me*."

Aunt T. gave me a warning hrumph to silence myself, for just then Rops appeared bearing a tray with a slender glass set upon it. I dubbed him Rops because he, as much as his artistic namesake, never failed to give me the charnel house creeps.

He cadavered across the terrace to serve Aunt T. her afternoon cocktail.

"Thank you," she said, taking the glass.

"Anything for you, sir?" he asked, now holding the tray over his chest like a silver shield.

"Ever see me have a drink, Rops?" I asked back. "Ever see me—"

"André, behave. That will be all, thank you."

Rops then lurched away in slow, bony steps.

"You can continue your rant now," said Aunt T. graciously.

"I'm through. You know how I feel," I replied and then looked away toward the lake, drinking in the dim mood of the twilight in the absence of normal refreshment.

"Yes, I do know how you feel, and you've always been wrong. You've always had these romantic ideas of how you and your mother, rest her soul, have been the victims of some monstrous injustice. But nothing is the way you like to think it is. They were not backward peasants who, we should say, *saved* your mother. They were wealthy, sophisticated members of her family. And they were not superstitious, because what they believed about your mother was the truth."

"True or not," I argued, "they believed the unbelievable— they acted on it—and that I call superstition. What reason could they possibly—"

"What *reason*? I have to say that at the time you were in no position to judge reasons, considering that we knew you only as a slight swelling inside your mother's body. I, on the other hand, was actually there. I saw the 'new friends' your mother had made, that 'aristocracy of blood,' as she called them, which I understood to signify her envy of their hereditary social status. But I don't judge her, I never have. After all, she had just lost her husband—your father was a good man and it's a shame you never knew him. And then to be carrying his child, the child of a dead man . . . She was frightened, confused, and she ran back to her family and her homeland. Who can blame her if she started acting irresponsibly. But it's a shame what happened, especially for your sake."

"You are indeed a comfort, *Auntie*," I said with now regrettable sarcasm.

"Well, you have my sympathy whether you want it or not. I think I've proven that over the years."

"Indeed you have," I agreed.

Aunt T. poured the last of her drink down her throat and a little drop she wasn't aware of dripped from the corner of her mouth, shining in the crepuscular radiance like a pearl.

"When your mother didn't come home one evening—I should say *morning*—everyone knew what had happened, but no one said anything. Contrary to your ideas about their superstitious nature, they actually could not bring themselves to believe the truth for some time."

"It was good of all of you to let me go on developing for a while, even as you were deciding how to best hunt my mother down."

"I will ignore that remark."

"I'm sure you will."

"We did not *hunt* her down, as you well know. That's another of your persecution fantasies. She came to us, now didn't she? Scratching at the windows in the night—"

"You can skip this part, I already—"

"—swelling full as the fullest moon. And that was strange, because you would actually have been considered a dangerously premature birth according to normal schedules. But when we followed your mother back to the mausoleum of the local church, where she lay during the daylight hours, she was carrying the full weight of her pregnancy. The priest was shocked to find what he had living, one might say, in his own backyard. It was actually he, and not so much any of your mother's family, who thought we should not allow you to be brought into the world. And it was his hand that released your mother from the life of her new friends. Immediately afterward, though, she began to deliver, right in the coffin in which she lay. The blood was terrible. If we did—"

"It's not necessary to—"

"—*hunt* down your mother, you should be thankful that I was among that party. I had to get you out of the country that very night, back to America. I—"

At that point she could see I was no longer paying attention to her, but was distracted by the pleasanter anecdotes of the setting sun. When she stopped talking and joined in the view, I said:

"Thank you, Aunt T., for that diverting story. I never tire of hearing it."

"I'm sorry, André, but I wanted to remind you of the truth."

"What can I say? I realize I owe you my life, such as it is."

"That's not what I mean. I mean the truth of what your mother became and what you now are."

"I am nothing. Completely harmless."

"That's why we must let the Duvals come and stay with us. To show them that the world has nothing to fear from you. I believe they need to see for themselves what you are, or rather aren't."

"You really think that's their mission?"

"I do. They could make quite a bit of trouble for us if we don't satisfy their curiosity."

I rose from my chair as the shadows of the failing twilight deepened and stood next to Aunt T. against the stone balustrade of the terrace. Leaning toward her, I said:

"Then let them come."

II

I am an offspring of the dead. I am descended from the deceased. I am the progeny of phantoms. My ancestors are the illustrious multitudes of the defunct, grand and innumerable. My lineage is longer than time. My name is written in embalming fluid in the book of death. A noble race is mine.

In the immediate family, the first to meet his maker was my own maker: he rests in the tomb of the unknown father. But while the man did manage to sire me, he breathed his last breath in this world before I drew my first. He was felled by a single stroke, his first and last. In those final moments, so I'm told, his erratic and subtle brainwaves made strange designs across the big green eye of an EEG monitor. The same doctor who told my mother that her husband was no longer among the living also informed her, on the very same day, that she was pregnant. Nor was this the only affecting coincidence in the lives of my parents. Both of them belonged to wealthy families from Aix-en-Provence in southern France. However, their first meeting took place not in the old country but in the new, at the American university they each happened to be attending. And so two neighbors crossed a cold ocean to come together in a mandatory science course. When they compared notes on their common backgrounds, they knew it was destiny at work. They fell in love with each other and with their new homeland. The couple later moved into a rich and prestigious suburb (which I will decline to mention by name or state, since I still reside there and, for reasons that will eventually become apparent, must do so discreetly). For years the couple lived in contentment, and then my immediate male forebear died just in time to miss out on fatherhood, thus becoming the appropriate parent for his son-to-be.

Offspring of the dead.

But surely, one might protest, I was born of a living mother; surely upon arrival in this world I turned and gazed into a pair of glossy maternal eyes. Not so, as I think is evident from my earlier conversation with dear Aunt T. Widowed and pregnant, my mother fled back to Aix, to the comfort of her family estate and secluded living. But more on this in a moment. Meanwhile I can no longer suppress the urge to say a few things about my ancestral hometown.

Aix-en-Provence, where I was born but never lived, has many personal, though necessarily secondhand, associations for me. However, it is not just a connection between Aix and my own life that maintains such a powerful grip on my imagination. Also intermixed with this melodrama are a few marvels exclusive to the history of that region. Separate centuries, indeed epochs, play host to these wondrous occurrences, and they likewise exist in entirely different realms of mood, worlds apart in implication. Nevertheless, from my perspective they are inseparable. The first item of "historical record" is the following: In the seventeenth century there occurred the spiritual possession by divers demons of the nuns belonging to the Ursuline convent at Aix-en-Provence. Excommunication was soon in coming for the blighted sisters, who had been seduced into assorted blasphemies by the likes of Grésil, Sonnillon, and Vérin. De Plancy's *Dictionnaire infernal* respectively characterizes these demons, in the words of an unknown translator, as "the one who glistens horribly like a rainbow of insects; the one who quivers in a horrible manner; and the one who moves with a particular creeping motion." For the curious, engravings have been made of these kinetically and chromatically weird beings, unfortunately static and in black and white. Can you believe it? What people are these—so obtuse and profound—that they could devote themselves to such nonsense? Who can fathom the science of superstition? (For, as an evil poet once scribbled, superstition is the reservoir of all truths.) This, then, is one element of the Aix of my imagination. The other is simply the birth in 1839 of Aix's most prominent citizen: Cézanne. His figure haunts the landscape of my brain, wandering about the Provençal countryside in search of his pretty pictures.

Together these two select phenomena fuse in my psyche into a single image of Aix, one as simultaneously grotesque and exquisite as a pantheon of gargoyles amid the splendor of a medieval church.

Such was the land to which my mother remigrated some decades ago, this Notre Dame world of horror and beauty. It's no wonder that she was seduced into the society of those beautiful strangers, who promised her liberation from a world of mortality where anguish had taken over, making her ripe for self-exile. I understood from Aunt T. that it all began at a summer party on the estate grounds of Ambroise and Paulette Valraux. The Enchanted Wood, as this place was known to the *hautes classes* in the vicinity. On the evening of the party, the weather was perfectly temperate. Lanterns were hung high up in the lindens, guide-lights leading to a heard-about heaven. A band played.

It was a mixed crowd at the party. And in attendance were a few persons whom nobody seemed to know, exotic strangers whose elegance was their invitation. Aunt T. did not give much thought to them at the time, and her account is rather sketchy. One of them danced with my mother, having no trouble luring the widow out of social retirement. Another with labyrinthine eyes whispered to her by the trees. Alliances were formed that night, promises made. Afterward my mother began going out on her own to assignations after sundown. Then she stopped coming home. Térèse—a personal attendant whom my mother had brought back with her from America—was hurt and confused by the cold snubs she had lately received from her mistress. My mother's family was reticent about the meaning of her recent behavior. ("And in her condition, *mon Dieu!*") Nobody knew what measures to take. Then some of the servants reported seeing a pale, pregnant woman lurking outside the house after dark.

Finally a priest was taken into the family's confidence. He suggested a course of action which no one questioned, not even Térèse. They lay in wait for my mother, righteous soul-hunters. They followed her drifting form as it returned to the mausoleum when daybreak was imminent. They removed the great stone lid of the sarcophagus and found her inside. "*Diabolique,*" one of them exclaimed. There was some question about how many times and in what places she should be impaled. In the end they pinned her heart with a single spike to the velvet bed on which she lay. But what to do about the child? What would it be like? A holy soldier of the living or a monster of the dead. (Neither, you fools!) Fortunately or unfortunately, I've never been sure which, Térèse was with them and rendered their speculations academic. Reaching into the bloody matrix, she helped me to be born.

I was now heir to the family fortune. Térèse took me back to America and made arrangements with a sympathetic and avaricious lawyer to become the trustee of my estate. This involved a little magic act with identities. It required that Térèse, for reasons of her own which I've never questioned, be promoted from my mother's adjutant to her sister. And so my Aunt T. was christened, born in the same year as I.

Naturally all this leads to the story of my life, which has no more life in it than story. It's not for the cinema, it's not for novels. It wouldn't even fill out a single lyric of modest length. It might make a piece of modern music: a slow, throbbing drone like the lethargic pumping of a premature heart. Best of all, though, would be the depiction of my life story as an abstract painting—a twilight world, indistinct around the edges and without center or focus; a bridge without banks, tunnel without openings; a crepuscular existence pure and simple. No heaven or hell, only a quiet withdrawal from life's hysteria and death's tenacious darkness. (And I tell you this: What I most love about twilight is the deceptive sense, as one looks down the dimming west, not that it is some fleeting transitional moment, but that there's actually nothing before or after it: *that that's all there is.*) My life as it was never had a beginning, but this did not mean it would be without an end, given the unforeseen factors that at length came into play. Beginnings and endings aside, I will now pick up my narrative from where I left off.

So what was the answer to those questions hastily put by the monsters who stalked my mother? Was my nature to be souled humanness or soulless vampirism? To both of these conjectures about my existential standing my response was "No." I existed between two worlds and had little claim upon the assets or liabilities of either. Neither living nor dead, unalive or undead, not having anything to do with such tedious polarities, such tiresome opposites, which as a fact are no more different from each other than a pair of imbecilic monozygotes. I said no to life and death. No, Mr. Springbud. No, Mr. Worm. Without ever saying hello or good-bye, I merely avoided their company, scorned their gaudy invitations.

Of course, in the beginning Aunt T. tried to care for me as if I were a normal child. (Incidentally, I can perfectly recall every moment of my life from birth, for my existence took the form of one seamless moment, without forgettable yesterdays or expectant tomorrows.) She tried to give me normal food, which I always regurgitated. Later she prepared for me a sort of purée of raw meat, which I ingested and digested, though it never became a habit. And I never asked her what was actually in that preparation, for Aunt T. wasn't afraid to use money, and I knew what money could buy in the way of unusual food for an unusual infant. I suppose I did become accustomed to similar nourishment while growing within my mother's womb, feeding on a potpourri of blood types contributed by the citizens of Aix. But my appetite was never very strong for physical food.

Stronger by far was my hunger for a kind of transcendental fare, a feasting of the mind and soul: the astral banquet of Art. There I fed. And I had quite a few master chefs to plan the menu. Though we lived in exile from the world, Aunt T. did not overlook my education. For purposes of appearance and legality, I have earned diplomas from some of the finest private schools in the world. (These, too, money can buy.) But my real education was even more private than that. Tutorial geniuses were well paid to visit our home, only too glad to teach an invalid child of nonetheless decided promise.

Through personal instruction I scanned the arts and sciences. Yes, I learned to quote my French poets,

> Gaunt immortality in black and gold,
> Wreathed consoler hideous to behold.
> The beautiful lie of a mother's womb,
> The pious trick—for it is the tomb!

but mostly in translation, for something kept me from ever attaining more than a beginner's facility in that foreign tongue. I did master, however, the complete grammar of the French *eye*. I could read the inner world of Redon, who was almost born an American, and his *grand isolé* paradise of black. I could effortlessly comprehend the outer world of Renoir and his associates of the era, who spoke in the language of light. And I could decipher the impossible worlds of the Surrealists— those twisted arcades where brilliant shadows are sewn to the rotting flesh of rainbows.

Among my educators, I remember in particular a man by the name of Raymond, who taught me the rudimentary skills of the artist in oils. Once I showed him a study I had done of that sacred phenomenon I witnessed each sundown. I can still see the look in his eyes, as if they beheld the rising of a curtain upon some terribly involved outrage. He abstractedly adjusted his wire-rim spectacles, wobbling them around on the bridge of his nose. His gaze shifted from the canvas to me and back again. His only comment was: "The shapes, the colors are not supposed to lose themselves that way. Something . . . no, impossible." Then he asked to be permitted use of the bathroom facilities. At first I thought this gesture was meant as a symbolic appraisal of my work. But he was quite in earnest, so all I could do was to provide directions to the nearest chamber of convenience. He walked out of the room and never came back.

Such is a thumbnail sketch of my half-toned existence: twilight after twilight after twilight. And in all that blur of time I never imagined that I would have to account for myself as one who existed beyond or between the clashing worlds of human fathers and enchanted mothers. But now I had to consider how I would explain, that is *conceal,* my unnatural mode of being from my visiting relatives. Despite the hostility I showed toward them in front of Aunt T., I actually desired that they should take a good report of me back to the real world, if only to keep it away from my own world in the future. For days prior to their arrival, I came to think of myself as a figure of invalidism living in studious isolation, a sallow-complected Schoolman laboring at recondite studies in his musty sanctum, an artist consecrated to vacuity. I anticipated they would soon have the proper image of me as all impotence and no impetus. And that would be that.

But never did I anticipate being called upon to face the almost forgotten fact of my vampiric origins—the taint beneath the paint of the family portrait.

III

The Duval family, and unmarried sister, were arriving on a night flight which we would meet at the airport. Aunt T. thought this would suit me fine, considering my tendency to sleep most of the day and arise with the setting sun. But at the last minute I suffered a seizure of stage fright. "The *crowds,*" I appealed to Aunt T. She knew that crowds were the world's most powerful talisman against me, as if it had needed any at all. She understood that I would not be able to serve on the welcoming committee, and Rops' younger brother Gerald, a good seventy-five if he was a day, drove her to the airport alone. Yes, I promised Aunt T., I would be sociable and come out to meet everyone as soon as I saw the lights of the big black car floating up our private drive.

But I wasn't and I didn't. I took to my room and drowsed before a television with the sound turned off. As the colors danced in the dark, I submitted more and more to an anti-social sleepiness. Finally I instructed Rops, by way of the estate-wide intercom, to inform Aunt T. and company that I wasn't feeling very well and needed to rest. This, I figured, would be in keeping with the façade of a harmless valetudinarian, and a perfectly normal one at that. A night-sleeper. Very good, I could hear them saying to their souls. And then, I swear, I actually turned off the television and slept real sleep in real darkness.

Yet things became less real at some point deep into the night. I must have left the intercom open, for I heard little metallic voices emanating from that little metallic square on my bedroom wall. In my state of quasi-somnolence it never occurred to me that I could simply get out of bed and make the voices go away by switching off that terrible box. And terrible it indeed seemed. The voices spoke a foreign language, but it wasn't French, as one might have suspected. It was something more foreign than that. Perhaps a cross between a madman talking in his sleep and the sonar screech of a bat. I heard the voices cluttering and chattering with each other until I fell soundly asleep once more. And their dialogue had ended before I awoke, for the first time in my life, to the bright eyes of morning.

The house was quiet. Even the servants seemed to have duties that kept them soundless and invisible. I took advantage of my wakefulness at that early hour and prowled unnoticed about the old place, figuring everyone else was still in bed. The four rooms Aunt T. had set aside for our guests all had their big paneled doors closed: a room for the mama and papa, two others close by for the kids, and a chilly chamber at the end of the hall for the maiden sister. I paused a moment outside each room and listened for the revealing songs of slumber, hoping to know my relations better by their snores and whistles and monosyllables grunted between breaths. But they made none of the usual racket. They hardly made any sounds at all, though they echoed one another in making a certain noise that seemed to issue from the same cavity. It was a kind of weird wheeze, a panting from the back of the throat, the hacking of a tubercular demon. Having had an earful of strange cacophonies the night before, I soon abandoned my eavesdropping without regret.

I spent the day in the library, whose high windows I noticed were designed to allow a maximum of natural reading light. However, I drew the curtains on them and kept to the shadows, finding morning sunshine not everything it was said to be. But it was difficult to get much reading done. Any moment I expected to hear foreign footsteps descending the double-winged staircase, crossing the black and white marble chessboard of the front hall, taking over the house. Despite these expectations, and to my increasing sense of unease, the family never appeared.

Twilight came and still no mama and papa, no sleepy-eyed son or daughter, no demure sister remarking with astonishment at the inordinate length of her beauty sleep. And no Aunt T., either. They must've had quite a time the night before, I thought. But I didn't mind being alone with the twilight. I drew back the curtains on the three west windows, each of them a canvas depicting the same scene in the sky. My private *Salon d'Automne*.

It was a rare sunset. Having sat behind opaque drapery all day, I had not realized that a storm was pushing in and that much of the sky was the precise shade of old suits of armor one finds in museums. At the same time, patches of brilliance engaged in a territorial dispute with the oncoming onyx of the storm. Light and darkness mingled in strange ways both above and below. Shadows and sunshine washed together, streaking the scene with an unearthly study of glare and gloom. Bright clouds and black folded into each other in a no-man's land of the sky. The autumn trees took on the appearance of sculptures formed in a dream, their leaden-colored trunks and branches and iron-red leaves all locked in an infinite moment, unnaturally timeless.

The gray lake slowly tossed and tumbled in a dead sleep, nudging unconsciously against its breakwall of numb stone. A vista of contradiction and ambivalence, a tragicomical haze over all. A land of perfect twilight.

I was jubilant: finally the twilight had come down to earth, and to me. I had to go out into this incomparable atmosphere, I had no choice. I left the house and walked to the lake, where I stood on the slope of stiff grass which led down to it. I gazed up through the trees at the opposing tones of the sky. I kept my hands in my pockets and touched nothing, except with my eyes.

Not until an hour or more had elapsed did I think of returning home. It was dark by then, though I don't recall the passing of the twilight into evening, for twilight suffers no flamboyant finales. There were no stars visible, the storm clouds having moved in and wrapped up the sky. They began sending out tentative drops of rain. Thunder mumbled above and I was forced back to the house, cheated once again by the night.

In the front hall I called out names in the form of questions. Aunt T.? Rops? Gerald? M. Duval? Madame? Everything was silence. Where was everyone? I wondered. They couldn't still be asleep. I passed from room to room and found no signs of occupation. A day of dust was upon all surfaces. Where were the domestics? At last I opened the double doors to the dining room. Was I late for the supper Aunt T. had planned to honor our visiting family?

It appeared so. But if Aunt T. sometimes had me consume the forbidden fruit of flesh and blood, it was never directly from the branches, never the sap taken warm from the tree of life itself. Yet here were spread the remains of just such a feast. It was the ravaged body of Aunt T., though they'd barely left enough on her bones for identification. The thick white linen was clotted like an unwrapped bandage. "Rops!" I shouted. "Gerald, somebody!" But I knew the servants were no longer in the house, that I was alone.

Not quite alone, of course. This soon became apparent to my twilight brain as it dipped its way into total darkness. I was in the company of five black shapes which stuck to the walls and soon began flowing along their surface. One of them detached

itself and moved toward me, a weightless mass which felt icy
when I tried to sweep it away and put my hand right through
the thing. Another followed, unhinging itself from a doorway
where it hung down. A third left a blanched scar upon the wallpaper where it clung like a slug, pushing itself off to join the
attack. Then came the others descending from the ceiling,
dropping onto me as I stumbled in circles and flailed my arms.
I ran from the room but the things had me closely surrounded.
They guided my flight, heading me down hallways and up
staircases. Finally they cornered me in a small room, a stuffy
little place I had not been in for years. Colored animals frolicked upon the walls, blue bears and yellow rabbits. Miniature
furniture was covered with graying sheets. I hid beneath a tiny
elevated crib with ivory bars. But they found me and closed in.

They were not driven by hunger, for they had already feasted.
They were not frenzied with a murderer's bloodlust, for they
were cautious and methodical. This was simply a family
reunion, a sentimental gathering. Now I understood how the
Duvals could afford to be *sans préjugé*. They were worse than I,
who was only a half-breed, a hybrid, a mere mulatto of the soul:
neither a blood-warm human nor a blood-drawing devil. But
they—who came from an Aix on the map—were the purebreds
of the family.

And they drained my body dry.

IV

When I regained awareness once more, it was still dark and
there was a great deal of dust in my throat. Not actually dust, of
course, but a strange dryness I had never before experienced.
And there was another new experience: hunger. I felt as if there
were a bottomless chasm within me, a great void which needed
to be filled—flooded with oceans of blood. I was one of them
now, reborn into the ravenous life of the undead. Everything I
shunned in my ambition to circumvent a birth-and-death existence I had become—just another beast with a hundred stirring
hungers. Sallow and voracious, I had joined the society of the

living dead, a contemptible participant in the worst of two worlds. André of the graveyards—a *sociable corpse*.

The five of them had each drunk from my body by way of five separate fountains. But the wounds had nearly sealed by the time I awoke in the blackness, owing to the miraculous healing capabilities of the dead. The upper floors were all in shadow now, and I made my way toward the light coming from downstairs. A hanging lamp in the hall below illuminated the carved banister at the top of the stairway, where I emerged from the darkness of the second floor, and this sight inspired in me a terrible ache of emotion I'd never known before: a feeling of loss, though of nothing I could specifically name, as if somehow the deprivation lay in my future.

As I descended the stairs I saw that they were already waiting to meet me, standing silently upon the black and white squares of the front hall. Papa the king, mama the queen, the boy a knight, the girl a dark little pawn, and a bitchy maiden bishop standing behind. And now they had my house, my castle, to complete the pieces on their side. On mine there was nothing.

"Devils," I screamed, leaning hard upon the staircase rail. "Devils," I repeated. But they appeared horribly unperturbed by my outburst. "*Diables,*" I reiterated in their own loathsome tongue.

But neither was French their true language, as I found out when they began speaking among themselves. I covered my ears, trying to smother their voices. They had a language all their own, a style of speech well-suited to dead vocal organs. The words were breathless, shapeless rattlings in the back of their throats, parched scrapings at a mausoleum portal. Arid gasps and dry gurgles were their dialects. These grating intonations were especially disturbing as they emanated from the mouths of things that had at least the form of human beings. But worst of all was my realization that I understood perfectly well what they were saying.

The boy stepped forward, pointing at me while looking back and speaking to his father. It was the opinion of this wine-eyed and rose-lipped youth that I should have suffered the same end as Aunt T. With an authoritative impatience the father told the boy that I was to serve as a sort of tour guide through this strange new land, a native who could keep them out of such difficulties as foreign visitors sometimes encounter. Besides, he concluded, *I was one of the family.* The boy was incensed and coughed out an incredibly foul characterization of his father. Exactly what he said could only be conveyed by that queer hacking patois, which suggested feelings and relationships of a nature incomprehensible outside of the world it mirrored with disgusting perfection. It was a discourse in hell on the subject of sin.

An argument ensued, and the father's composure turned to an infernal rage. He finally subdued his son with bizarre threats that have no counterparts in the language of ordinary malevolence. After the boy was silenced he turned to his aunt, seemingly for comfort. This woman of chalky cheeks and sunken eyes touched the boy's shoulder and easily drew him toward her with a single finger, guiding his body as if it were a balloon, weightless and toy-like. They spoke in sullen whispers, using a personal form of address that hinted at a long-standing and unthinkable allegiance between them.

Apparently aroused by this scene, the daughter now stepped forward and used this same mode of address as though bidding for my recognition. Her mother abruptly gagged out a single syllable at her. What she called the child might possibly be imagined, but only with reference to the most feral degenerates of the human world. Their own form of expression carried the dissonant overtones of another world altogether. Each utterance was an opera of iniquity, a chorus of savage anathemas, a psalm hissing of fetid lust.

"I will not become one of you," I *thought* I screamed at them. But the sound of my voice was already so much like theirs that the words had exactly the opposite meaning I intended. The family suddenly ceased bickering among themselves. My flare-up had consolidated them. Each mouth, cluttered with uneven teeth like a village cemetery overcrowded with battered gravestones, opened and smiled. The look on their faces told me something about my own. They could see my growing hunger, see deep down into the dusty catacomb of my throat which cried out to be anointed with bloody nourishment. They knew my weakness.

Yes, they could stay in my house. *(Famished.)*

Yes, I could make arrangements to cover up the disappearance of Aunt T. and the servants, for I am a wealthy man and know what money can buy. *(Please, my family, I'm famished.)*

Yes, they would receive sanctuary in my home for as long as they liked, which would likely be very long. *(Please, I'm famishing down to the depths of me.)*

Yes, yes, yes. I agreed to everything. It would all be taken care of. *(To the depths!)*

But first I begged them, for heaven's sake, to let me go out into the night.

Night, night, night, night. Night, night, night.

Now twilight is an alarm that rouses me to feast. And the precious import it held all through my bygone half-life is nearly gone, while the prospect of eternal life in eternal death seduces me more and more. Nevertheless, there is something in my heart that wishes them well who would put an end to my precarious immortality. I am not yet so estranged from what I was to deny them my undoing. My exsanguinations thus far are only a need, not a passion. But I know that will change. I was once the scion of an old family from an old country, but now I have new blood in my veins and mine is a country outside of time. I have been resurrected from a condition of lassitude into one of fierce survival. No longer can I retreat into a world of deliquescent sunsets, for I must go out as summoned by a craving to draw fresh blood from the night.

Night—after night—after night.

THE TROUBLES OF
DR. THOSS

When Alb Indys first heard the name of Dr. Thoss, he was flustered by his inability to locate the source from which it emanated. Right from the start, though, there seemed to be at least two voices chattering this name just within earshot, saying it over and over as if it were the central topic of some rambling discourse. Initially their words sounded as if they were being emitted by an old radio in another apartment, for Alb Indys had no such device of his own. But he finally realized that the name was being uttered, in rather hoarse tones, in the street below his window, which was set in the wall not far from the foot of his bed. After spending the night, not unusually, walking the floor or slumping wide-eyed in a stuffed chair beside the aforementioned window, he was now, at mid-afternoon, still attired in pale gray pajamas. Since morning he had kept to his bed, propped up against its tall headboard by huge pillows. Upon his lap rested a drawing book filled with thick sheets of paper, very white. A bottle of black ink was in reach on the bedside table, and a shapely black pen with a silvery nib was held tightly in his right hand. Presently Alb Indys was busily at work on a pen-and-ink rendering of the window and stuffed chair he had begun during his wakefulness the night before. That was when he overheard, however indistinctly, the voices down in the street.

Alb Indys tossed the drawing book farther down the bed, where it fell against a lump swelling in the blankets: more than likely the creation of a wadded pair of trousers or an old shirt, possibly both, given the artist's personal habits. The window of his room was partly open and, walking over to it, he discreetly pushed it out a little more. They should have been close by, those speakers whom Alb Indys wished would go on speaking. He remembered hearing one voice say, "It's going to be the end of someone's troubles," or words to that effect, with the name of Dr. Thoss figuring in the discussion. The appellation was unfamiliar to him and gave rise to feelings that had much less to do with hope, which Alb Indys tried to keep at a minimum, than it did with nervous expectancy, as of some fore-vision of the unknown. But the talking had stopped, and just as he was becoming interested in this doctor. Where were they, those interlocutors? How could they have simply vanished?

When he fully extended the bedroom window, Alb Indys saw no one on the street. He stretched forward for a better look. Strands of blond hair, almost white, fell across his face, and then by a sudden salty breeze were blown back, thin and loose. It was not a very brilliant day, not one of excess activity. A few silhouettes and shadows maneuvered in the dimness on the other side of unreflecting windows. The stones of the street, so sparkling and picturesque for those enjoying a holiday here, succumbed to dullness out of season. Alb Indys fixed on one of them which looked dislodged in the pavement, imagining he heard it working itself free, creaking around in its stony cradle. But the noise was that of metal hinges squeaking somewhere in the wind. He quickly found them, his hearing made keen by insomnia. They were attached to a wooden sign hung outside the uppermost window of an old building. The structure ascended in peaks and slants and ledges into the gray sky, until at its highest, turreted point swung the sign. Alb Indys could never clearly make out its four capital letters so far above, though he had gazed up at them a thousand times. (And how often it seemed that something gazed back at him from that high window.) But a radio station need not be a visual presence in an old resort town, only an aural landmark, a voice for vacationers signaling the "sound beside the sea."

Alb Indys closed the window and returned to his thin-lined representation of it. Though he began the picture in the middle of a sleepless night, he did not copy the constellations beyond the windowpanes, keeping the drawing unmarred by any artistic suggestion of those star-filled hours. Nothing was in the window but the pure whiteness of the page, the pale abyss of unshut eyes. After making a few more marks on the picture, completing it, he signed his work very neatly in the lower right-hand corner. This page would later be put in one of the large portfolios stacked upon a desk across the room.

What else was contained in these portfolios? Two sorts of things, two types of artwork which between them told of the nature and limits of Alb Indys's pictorial talents. The first type included such scenes as the artist had recently executed: images of his immediate surroundings, sights observable within his room. This was not his first study of the window, the subject he most often returned to and always in the same plain style. Sometimes he sat in the chair beside the window and portrayed his bed, lumpy and unmade, with occasional attention to the side table (noting each nick that blemished its original off-white surface) and the undecorated lamp which stood upon it (recording each chip that pocked its glassy smoothness). The desk-side of the room also received its fair share of treatments. The wall at that end of the room was the most tempting of the four, in itself a subtle canvas that had been painted and pitted and painted again, coated and repeatedly scraped of infinitesimal, sea-town organisms, leaving it shriveled and pasty and incurably damp. No pictures were hung to patch either this or any other wall of the room, though a tall bookcase obscured who knows what unseen worlds behind it. Transitory compositions—a flung shoe leaning toe-up against a bedpost, a dropped glove which hazard endowed with a pointing index finger—formed the remaining examples of this first type of drawing in which the artist indulged.

And the second type? Was it more interesting than the first? Perhaps, though not as far as imagination was concerned, for Alb Indys had none whatever, or at least none that he employed in a customary sense—that of evoking from within himself something that did not already exist outside him. Whenever he tried to form a picture of something, anything, in his mind, all he saw was a blank: a new page that retained the purity of its original mintage, nothingness unstained by inner conception. Once he nearly had a vision of something, a few specks flying across a fuzzy background of white snow in a white sky—and there was a garbled voice which he had not intentionally conjured. But it all fizzled out after a few seconds into a silent stretch of emptiness. This artistic handicap, however, was anything but a frustration or a disappointment to Alb Indys. He did not often test the powers of his imagination, for he somehow knew that there was as much to be lost as gained in doing so. In any case, there were many ways to make a picture, and Alb Indys had a second method, as mentioned, by which he created his artworks, one that differed markedly from his first, more conventional, idiom.

The second technique that Alb Indys put to use could be styled as a kind of artistic forgery, though it might just as well be described by the term which he himself preferred—collaboration. And who were his collaborators? In many instances, there was no way of knowing: anonymous penmen, mostly, of illustrations in very old books and periodicals. His shelves were full of them, dark and massive, their worn covers incredibly tender to the touch. French, Flemish, German, Swedish, Russian, Polish, any cultural source of published material would do as long as its pictures spoke the language of dark lines and vacant spaces. In fact, the more disparate the origins of these images, the better they served his purpose: because Alb Indys liked to take a century-old engraving of a sub-arctic landscape, studiously plagiarize its manner of depicting vast expanses of frozen whiteness, then select an equally old depiction of a church in a foreign town he had never heard of, painstakingly transport it stone by stone deep into the glacial desert, and finally, from still older pages, transcribe with all possible fidelity an unknown artist's conception of assorted devils and demons, making them dance down from the ice-mad mountains and invade the house of worship. This was the typical process and product of his work with collaborators, whose art Alb Indys plainly exploited in ways their fabricators never intended. Confiscating their images, he was moved to patch them to one another in a spirit of malicious abandon, as though to express the deranging effects worked upon him by the cruel vigilance he suffered night after night. Under his careful eye and steady hand there took place a mingling of artistic forms that together were monstrously chimerical, their disparate components tumbling out of the years to create nightmarish anatomies. For it seemed perfectly natural to Alb Indys that, like everything else, the most innocuous phenomena should eventually find their way from good dreams into bad, or from bad dreams into those that were wholly abysmal.

At the moment he was working on a new collaboration, but all he had as yet was its barest beginnings: a sickle-shaped scar of moon, a common enough image which Alb Indys wanted to remove from one black sky and fix in another where it would take on a more ominous significance. Its relocation could have provided him with a way to waste the rest of the afternoon. However, the commotion outside the window earlier had upset the pace of his day and given it a new rhythm. Almost any event could do this to an insomniac's fragile routine, so as yet there was no reason to contemplate the phenomenal. An appearance by his landlord, whether rent-hungry or merely casual, sometimes altered his course for weeks after. Before, his thoughts were of nothing, genuinely. But now old preoccupations had become stirred up and took on an edge. Was there anything special about this doctor, this Thoss? Alb Indys could not help wondering. Was he like the others, or was he a doctor who would hear, really *hear* you? Not one had yet heard him, not one had offered him a remedy worth the name.

If there was indeed a new doctor who had set up practice in the seaside town, Alb Indys could encounter none of this individual's cures, either real or pretended, by staying at home. He needed to find out some things for himself, make inquiries, get out into the world. When was the last time he had had a good meal? Perhaps that would be a way to begin, and afterward he could take it from there. One could always get acceptable food at the place right around the corner, with no reason to fear they were poisoning their patrons. Good, he thought. And once he had eaten he might have a nice walk for himself, gain some advantage from the fresh air and scenery of the town. After all, many people came here for vaguely therapeutic reasons, believing there were medicines dispensed by the very mood of the town's quaint streets and its sea-licked shores. It might even happen that his maladies would disappear of their own accord, leaving him with no need for this doctor, this Thoss.

He dressed himself in dark, heavy clothes and made sure to lock the door behind him. But he had forgotten to shut the window properly and a breeze edged in, disturbing the pages of the drawing book on his bed, fluttering them against that lump in the blankets.

At the eatery Alb Indys chose for his repast, he found a small table in a quiet, comfortable corner where he sat facing the rear wall and an unoccupied chair. Toward the front of the one-room establishment was a large blackboard that enumerated the specialties being offered. But because of his distance from the blackboard, and a certain atmospheric dimness of the place, only a single word in bold letters was easily readable. So he ordered that.

"Fish," he said when the waitress arrived.

"Fish of the day?"

"Yes," he had answered, mechanically and without a trace of the anticipation he thought he might feel.

But despite his lack of interest in daily meals, he did not regret this outing. A little lamp attached to the wall next to him, its light muffled by a grayish shade of some coarse fabric, created a nocturnal ambiance in the corner of the room where he sat. And it was not long before Alb Indys found that if he kept his gaze fixed upon a certain knotty plank in the wall just above the chair facing him, everything peripheral to his left eye's vision faded into a dark fog, while the little lamp to his right cast an island of illumination upon the table at which he was seated. This manipulation of his vision instilled in him the feeling that he was nestled in a glowing refuge somewhere in the darkness of an unknown hinterland. But he could not sustain the illusion.

The state of mild delight into which he fooled himself faded, while shapes around him sharpened.

Yet without this sharpening would he have noticed the newspaper someone had left on the seat of the other chair? Messily bunched and repeatedly creased, it was still a welcome sight to his eyes. At this point he needed something to open his mind to the world around him, something to free his awareness of the coming night wherein he would have to face the verdict that would either terminate or terribly elongate his wakefulness. He reached for the pages, then unfolded and refolded them like an arrangement of bedcovers. His eyes followed dark letters across ruddy paper, and at last his mind was out of its terrible school for a while. When the food arrived he made way for the plate, building a nest of print and pictures around it: advertisements for the town's shops and businesses, weather forecasts, happenings on the west shore, and a feature article entitled "THE REAL STORY OF DR. THOSS—Local Legend Revived." A brief note explained that the article, written some years ago, was periodically reprinted when interest in the subject seemed, for one reason or another, newly aroused. Alb Indys paused over his meal for a moment and smiled, feeling disappointed and slightly relieved at the same time. It now appeared that he had been inspired by a misunderstanding, enlivened by imaginary consultations with a legendary doctor and his fictitious cures.

Who, then? What? When and why? According to the article, Thoss might well have been a real doctor, one who lived either in the distant past or whose renown was imported, by recollection and rumor, from a distant place. A number of people associated him with the following vague but lamentable tragedy. A superb physician, and a most respected figure in his community, was psychically deranged one night by some incident of indefinite character. Afterward he continued to make use of his training in physic but in an utterly new fashion, in a different key altogether from that of his former practice. This went on for some time before, violently, he was stopped. Decapitation, drowning in the nearby sea, or both were the prevailing conclusions to the doctor's legend. Of course, the particulars vary, as do those of a second, and more widely circulated, version.

This variant Dr. Thoss was a recluse of the witch-days, less a doctor of medicine than one deeply schooled at forbidden universities of the supernatural. Or was he naturally a very wise man who was simply misunderstood? Histories of the period are unhelpful in resolving such questions. No definite misbehavior is attributed to him, except perhaps that of keeping an unpleasant little companion. The creature, according to most who know *this* Thossian legend, is said to have possessed the following traits: it was smallish, "no bigger than a man's head"; shriveled and rotting, as if with disease or decomposition; spoke in a rasping voice or in several voices at once; and moved about by means of numerous appendages of special qualities, called "miracle claws" by some. There was good reason, the article went on, to put this abbreviated marvel at the center of this legend, for the creature may not have been merely a diabolical companion of Dr. Thoss but the mysterious doctor himself. Was his tale, then, a cautionary one, illustrating what happened to those who, either from evil or benevolent motives, got "into trouble" with the supernatural? Or was Dr. Thoss *itself* intended to serve as no more than a fancied agent of spectral hideousness, a bogey for children or a spook whose yarn is spun around a campfire? Ultimately the point of the legend is unclear, the article asserted, except as a means for fascinating the imagination.

But an even greater obscurity surrounded one last morsel of lore concerning who the doctor was and what he was about. It related to the way his name had come to be employed by certain people and under certain circumstances. Not the place for a scholarly inquest into regional expressions, the article merely cited an example, one that no doubt was already familiar to many of the newspaper's readers. This particular usage was based on the idea—and the following verb must be stressed—of "*feeding* one's troubles to the sea (or 'wind') and Dr. Thoss," as if this figure—whatever its anatomical or metaphysical identity—were some kind of eater of others' suffering. A concluding note invited readers to submit whatever smatterings they could to enlarge upon this tiny daub of local color.

End of the real story of Dr. Thoss.

Alb Indys had read the article with interest and appetite,

more than he ever hoped to have, and he now pushed both the crumpled newspaper and decimated meal away from him, sitting for a moment in blurry reflection on both. The surface of the old table, jaundiced by the little lamp above it, somehow seemed to be decaying in its grain, dissolving into a putrid haze. Possibly his mind had simply wandered too far when he heard, or thought he heard, a strange utterance. And it was delivered in a distorted, dry-throated voice, as though transmitted by garbled shortwave. "Yes, my name is Thoss," the voice had said. "I am a doctor."

"Excuse me, will there be anything else you'd like to order?"

Shaken back to life, Alb Indys declined further service, paid his bill, and left. On his way out, for no defensible reason, he scrutinized every face in the room. But none of them could have said it, he assured himself.

In any case, the doctor was now exposed as only a phantasm of local superstition. Or was he? To be perfectly honest about it, Alb Indys had to credit the nonexistent healer with some part of his present well-being. How he had eaten, and every bit! True, it was not much of a day—the town was a tomb and the sky its vault—but for him a secret sun was shining somewhere, he could feel it. And there were hours remaining before it had to set, hours. He walked to the end of the street where it dipped down a hill and the sidewalk ended in a flight of old stone stairs that had curving grins sliced into them by time. He continued walking to the edge of town, and then down a narrow road which led to one of the few places he could abide outside his own room.

Alb Indys approached the old church from the graveyard side. As he closed in, he saw the great hexagonal peak, hornlike, projecting above brown-leafed trees. Surrounding the graveyard was a vertical barrier of thin black bars, with a thicker bar horizontally connecting them through the middle, spine-like. There was no gate, and the road he was on freely entered the church grounds. To his left and right were headstones and monuments. They formed a forest of memorials, clumps of crosses and groves of gravestones. Some of them were so tilted by the years that they looked as if they were about to topple over. But could one of them have just now fallen down entirely? Something was missing that seemed to have been there a moment ago. When Alb Indys reached the edge of the graveyard he turned around, surveying not only the markers themselves but also the spaces between them. And the wind was pulling at his fine pale locks.

Standing in full view of the church, Alb Indys could not resist elevating his gaze to the height of that spire which rose from the six-sided tower that crowned the edifice. This great structure— with its dark, cowl-shaped windows and broken Roman-numeral clock—was buttressed by two low-roofed transepts which squatted and slanted on either side of it. Beneath the cloud-filled sky the church was an even shade of grayish white, unblemished by shadows. And from behind the church, where pale scrubby grasses edged toward a steep descent into sand and sea, came the sound of crashing waves, which Alb Indys perceived as somehow dry and electronic.

As always, there was no one else in the church at this time of day (and with hours remaining of it). Everything was very quiet and serenely lighted. The dark-paned windows along either wall confused all time, bending dawns into twilights, suspending minutes in eternity. Alb Indys slid his unrested body into a pew at the back. His eyes were fixed on the distant apse, where everything— pillars, pictures, pulpit—was partially folded within shadows that seemed to be the creation of dark hours. But his insomnia was not at issue here, nor the pernicious rancor that derived from it. His sufferings and transgressions alike were allowed reprieve. None of the devils and demons he had inserted into a certain collaboration of his would invade *this* church and violate its solemnity. He followed the moments as they tried to move past him. Each was smothered by stillness, and he watched them die. "But trouble feeds in the wind and hides in the window," he drowsily said to himself from somewhere inside his now dreaming brain.

Suddenly everything seemed wrong and he wanted to leave. But he could not leave, because someone was speaking to him from the pulpit. Yes, a pulpit in such a large church would be equipped with a microphone that amplified normal speech. Then why not speak normally—why whisper in such confused language and so rapidly, the effect being that of a single voice multiplying itself into many? What were the voices saying now? He could not understand them, as if he were hearing them in a dream. If only he could move, just turn his head a little. And if only he could open his eyes and see what was wrong. The voices kept repeating without fading, echoing without end in what now seemed a fantastically spacious church. Then, with an effort sufficient to move the earth itself, he managed to turn his head to look out a window in the east transept. And without even opening his tightly closed eyelids, he saw what was in the window. But he suddenly awoke for an entirely different reason, because finally he understood what the voices were saying. They said they were a doctor, and their name was—

Alb Indys ran out of the church. And he kept running as if in flight from the hissing discord that now filled the seaside air, like static from a broken radio, and from what sounded like breaking waves close at his back. There was not much daylight left and he did not want to be caught in the damp and chill of an off-season evening. What misjudgments he had made that day, what mistakes, there was no question about it. An eternity of sleeplessness was to be preferred if those were the dreams sleep had in waiting.

And when Alb Indys reached his room, he was thinking about a gleaming crescent moon ready to be placed in a new scene. How thankful he was to have some project, however malicious in spirit, to fill the hours of that night. Exhausted, he threw his dark coat in a heap on the floor, then sat down on the bed to remove his shoes. He was holding the second one in his hand when he turned and, for some reason, began to contemplate that lump beneath his bedcovers. Without reasoning why, he elevated the shoe directly above this shapeless swelling, held it aloft for a few moments, then let it drop straight down. The lump collapsed with a little poof, as if it had been an old hat with no head inside. Enough of this for one day, Alb Indys thought sleepily. There was work he could be doing.

But when he picked up the drawing book from where he had earlier abandoned it on the bed, he saw that the work he intended to do had, by some miracle, already been done. Yet it had not been done rightly. He looked at the drawing of the window, the drawing he had finished off earlier that day with his meticulous signature. Was it only because he was so tired that he could not recall darkening those window panes and carving that curved scar of moon behind them? Could he have forgotten about scoring that bone-white cicatrix into the flesh of night? But he was holding that particular moon in reserve for one of his collaborations and this was *not* one of those. This belonged to that other type of drawing: in these he penned only what was enclosed within the four-walled frame of his room, never anything outside it. Then why did he ink in this night and this moon, and with the collaboration of what other artistic hand? Something was gravely wrong. If only he were not so drained by chronic insomnia, all those lost dreams swishing around in his head, perhaps he could have thought more clearly about it. His dozing brain might even have noticed another change in the picture, for something now squatted in the chair beside the window. But there was too much sleep to catch up on, and, as the sun went out in the window, Alb Indys shut his eyes languorously and lay down upon his bed.

And he very well could have slept through what would usually be one of his white nights of insomnia had it not been for a noise that wakened him. The room was moderately brightened by a blade of moon whose light came through the window. The moonlight even made visible the stuffed chair whose representation appeared in the drawing that had been meddled with. If only Alb Indys had examined the drawing more closely, he might have observed that something was crouching in that chair, that its softly packed arms had other arms overhanging them—two thin appendages that were now flexing in the room's faint luminescence. White night, white noise. As if speaking in static, a parched, crackling voice repeatedly croaked these words: *I am a doctor.* Then the roundish occupant of the chair hopped onto the bed with a single thrust, and its claws began their work, delivering the bedeviled artist to his miraculous remedy.

It was the landlord who eventually found Alb Indys, though there was considerable difficulty identifying what lay on the bed. A rumor spread throughout the seaside town about a swift-acting and terrible disease, something that one of the tourists might have brought in. But no other trouble was reported. Much later, the entire incident was confused by preposterous fabulations which had the effect of relegating it to the doubtful realm of regional legend.

MASQUERADE OF A DEAD SWORD: A TRAGEDIE

When the world uncovers some dark disguise,
Embrace the darkness with averted eyes.

PSALMS OF THE SILENT

I: FALIOL'S RESCUE

No doubt the confusions of carnival night were in some measure to blame for many unforeseen incidents. Every violation of routine order was being committed by carousing masses, their high-register songs of celebration harmonizing with a low, droning pedal point which seemed to be sustained by the night itself. Having declared their town an enemy of quiescence, the people of Soldori had taken to the streets. There they conspired against solitude and, to accompanying gyrations of squealing abandon, sabotaged monotony. Even the duke, a cautious man and one not normally given to those extravaganzas perpetrated by his counterparts in Lynnese or Daranzella, was now holding a lavish masquerade, if only as a strategic concession to his subjects. Of all the inhabitants of the Three Towns, those under the rule of the Duke of Soldori—occasionally to the duke's dismay—were the most loving of amusement. In every quarter of their usually sedate principality, frolicking merrymakers combed the night for a new paradise, and were as likely to find it in a blood-match as in a bewitching countenance. All seemed anxious, even frantic to follow blindly the entire spectrum of diversion, to dawdle about the lines between pain and pleasure, to obscure their vision of both past and future.

So three well-drunk and hog-faced men seated in a roisterous hostelry might well be excused for not recognizing Faliol, whose colors were always red and black. But this man, who had just entered the thickish gloom of that drinking house, was garbed in a craze of colors, none of them construed to a pointed effect. One might have described this outfit as a motley gone mad. Indeed, what lay beneath this fool's patchwork were the familiar blacks and reds that no other of the Three Towns—neither those who were dandies, nor those who were sword-whores, nor even those who, like Faliol himself, were both—would have dared to duplicate. But now these notorious colors were buried under a rainbow of rags which were tied about the man's arms, legs, and every other part of his person, seeming to hold him together like torn strips hurriedly applied to the storm-fractured joists of a sagging roof. Before he had closed the door of that cave-like room behind him, the draft rushing in from the street made his frayed livery come alive like a mass of tattered flags flapping in a calamitous wind.

But even had he not been cast as a tatterdemalion, there was still so much else about Faliol that was unlike his former self. His sword, a startling length of blade, bobbed about unbuckled at his left side. His dagger, whose sheath bore a mirror of polished metal (which now seemed a relic of more dandified days), was strung loosely behind his left shoulder, ready to fall at any moment. And his hair was trimmed monkishly close to the scalp, leaving little reminder of a gloriously hirsute era. But possibly the greatest alteration, the greatest problem and mystery of Faliol's travesty of his own image, was the presence on his face of a pair of spectacles. And given that these spectacles were darkly tinged, as though fashioned from some murky substance, the eyes behind them were obscured.

Still, there remained any number of signs by which a discerning scrutiny could have identified the celebrated Faliol. For as he moved toward a seat adjacent to the alcove where the booming-voiced trio was ensconced, he strode with a scornful, somehow involuntary assuredness of which no reversals of fate could completely unburden him. And his boots, though their fine black leather had gone gray with the dust of roads that a zealous equestrian such as Faliol would never have trod, still jangled with a few of those once innumerable silver links from which dangled small, agate-eyed medallions, ones identical to the onyx-eyed amulet which in other days hung from a silver chain around his lean throat.

Now, however, no medallion ornamented Faliol's chest; and since he had lost or renounced the inkish eye of onyx, he had acquired two eyes of shadowed glass. Each lens of the spectacles reflected, like twin moons, the glow of the lantern above the place where Faliol seated himself. As if unaware that he was not settled in some cloistered cell of lucubration, he removed from somewhere within his shredded clothes a small book having the words *Psalms of the Silent* inscribed upon its soft, worn cover. And the cover of the book was black, while the characters of its title were the red of autumn leaves.

"Faliol, a scholar?" someone whispered in the crowded depths of the room, while another added: "And a scholar of his own grief, so I've heard."

Faliol unfixed the tiny silver clasp and opened the book somewhere toward its middle, where a thin strip of velvet marked his place. And if there had been a miniature mirror bound in place of the book's left-hand leaf, Faliol could have seen three thuggish men gazing mutely, not to say thoughtfully, in his direction. Moreover, if there had been a second mirror set at the same angle on the book's right-hand leaf, he could also have noticed a fourth pair of eyes spying on him from the other side of the hostelry's engrimed windowpanes.

But there were only stern-looking letters written—to be precise, handwritten, in Faliol's own hand—upon the opposing leaves of the book. Thus Faliol could not have seen either of these parties who, for reasons separate or similar, were observing him. All he saw were two pale pages elegantly dappled by somber verses. Then a shadow passed across these pages, and another, and another.

The three men were now standing evenly spaced before Faliol, though he continued to read as if they were not present. He read until the lantern above was extinguished, its stump of tallow snuffed out by the middle man's grossly knuckled stumps of flesh. Clasping his book closed, Faliol replaced it within the rags around his heart and sat perfectly still. The three men seemed to watch in a trance of ugsome hilarity at this slowly and solemnly executed sequence of actions. The face at the windowpanes merely pressed closer to witness what, in its view, was a soundless scene.

Some words of insult appeared to be aimed at the man in rags by the three men standing before him. The first of them splashed some ale upon the bespectacled personage, as did the second man from his enormous tankard. Then more ale—this time expectorated—was received by the victim as the third man's contribution to what became a series of petty torments. But Faliol remained silent and as motionless as possible, thereby expressing an attitude of mind and body which seemed only to provoke further the carnival-mad souls of the three Soldorians. As the moments passed, the men waxed more cruel and their torments more inventive. Finally, they jostled a bloody-mouthed Faliol out of his seat. Two of them pinioned him against the planks of the wall, while the trio's hulking third member snatched his spectacles.

A pair of blue eyes was suddenly revealed. They firmly clenched themselves closed, then reopened as if bursting out of black depths and into the light. Faliol dropped to his knees and his mouth stretched wide to let out a strangled scream— the scream of a mute under torture. But very soon his features relaxed, while his ragged chest began pumping up and down with an even rhythm. He rose to his feet.

The one who had taken Faliol's spectacles had turned away and his clumsy fingers were fiddling with delicate silver stems, fumbling with two shadowy lenses that were more precious than he knew. Thus amused and diverted, he did not perceive that Faliol had drawn his dagger from its shoulder-sheath and was cutting away at his companions with stealth and savagery.

"Where—" he started to shout to his loutish comrades as they ran ripped and bloody from the hostelry. Then he turned about-face to feel Faliol's sword against his greasy leather doublet. He saw, he must have seen, that the blade was unclean but very sharp; and he must have felt it scrape playfully against the chain-mail vest concealed beneath his doublet's sorry cover. Soon Faliol was lowering his blade until it reached the spot where the vest's protection no longer protected. "Now put them on, that you might see," he instructed the giant who held what appeared in his hands to be tiny toy spectacles. "Put . . . them . . . on," he repeated in the toneless voice of one who was dead to all appeasement or mercy.

The giant, his lip-licking tongue visibly parched, obeyed the command. Upon doing so, his body went rigid and became as if fastened to the floor on which it stood.

Everyone in the room leaned closer to see the giant in dark spectacles, and so did the well-groomed face at the hostelry window. Most of the men laughed—drunkenly and anonymously—but a few remained silent, if they did not in fact become silent, at this sight. "And a scholar of the wildest folly, too," someone whispered. Faliol himself grinned like a demon, his eyes widening at his work. After a few moments he returned his sword to its sheath, and even so the giant held his transfixed position. Faliol put away his dagger, and the giant did not budge a hair. Trapped within himself, he stood with paralyzed arms hanging beside his enormous flanks. The giant's face was extraordinarily pale, his grizzled cheeks like two mounds of snow that had been sown with ashes. Above them, circles of glass gleamed like two black suns.

All laughter had ceased by now, and many turned away from the unwonted spectacle. The giant's meaty lips were the only part of him that moved, though very slowly and very much in the manner of a dying fish gasping in the dry air. But having seen through Faliol's spectacles, the giant was not dying in his body: only his mind was a corpse. "The wildest folly," whispered the same voice.

Gently, almost contritely, Faliol removed the spectacles from the face of the dumbstruck idol, and he waited until he was outside the hostelry before replacing them on his own.

"Good sir," called a voice from the shadows of the street. Faliol paused, but only as if considering the atmosphere of the night and not necessarily in response to a stranger who had accosted him. "Please allow me to identify myself with the name Streldone. I assume my messenger spoke with you last eve in Lynnese. How generous of you to come to Soldori to meet with me. Well, then, here is my coach," he said, "so that we need not talk in all the confusion of carnival night." And when the coach began moving down streets on the circumference of the festivities, this finely habited gentleman—though he was just barely more than a youth—continued to speak to a silent Faliol.

"I was informed you had arrived in Soldori not long before this very moment, and have been waiting for a discreet interval in which to approach you. Of course you were aware of my presence," he said, pausing to scan Faliol's expressionless face. "How unfortunate that you were forced to reveal who you are back in that sty of a drinking house. But I suppose you couldn't allow yourself to undergo much more of that treatment merely for the sake of anonymity. No harm done, I'm sure."

"And I am sure," Faliol replied in a monotone, "that three very sad men would disagree with you."

The young man laughed briefly at what he understood to be a witticism. "In any event, their kind will have their throats wrapped in the red cord sooner or later. The duke is quite severe when it comes to the lawlessness of others. Which brings me to what I require of you tonight, presuming that we need not bargain over the terms my messenger proposed to you in Lynnese. Very well," said Streldone, though obviously he had been prepared to haggle over the matter. But he left no pause which might have been filled with the second thoughts of this hired sword, who looked and acted more like one of the clockwork automatons which performed their mechanical routines high above the town square of Soldori. Thus, with a slow turn of his head and a set movement of his hand, Faliol received the jeweled pouch containing one-half his payment. Streldone promised that the other portion would follow upon the accomplishment of their night's work, as he now portrayed its reasons and aims.

It seemed there was a young woman of a noble and wealthy family, a princess in all but title whom Streldone loved and who loved him in return, accepting his proposal of marriage and cleaving to his vision of their future as two who would be one. But there was also another, who was called Wynge, though Streldone referred to him thereafter as the Sorcerer. As Streldone explained the situation, the Sorcerer had appropriated the young woman for himself. This unnatural feat was achieved, Streldone hated to say, not only through the powerful offices of the Duke of Soldori himself, but also with the willing compliance of the young woman's father. Both men, according to Streldone, had been persuaded in this affair because the Sorcerer had promised to supply them, by means of alchemical transmutations of base metals into gold and silver, with an unending source of riches to finance their wars and other undertakings of ambition. Without bothering to embellish the point, Streldone declared that he and his beloved, in their present state of separation, were two of the most wretched beings in the world and desperate for assistance in their struggle to be reunited. And that carnival night would be the last opportunity for Faliol to untangle them from the controlling strings of the Sorcerer and his compatriots.

"Do I have your attention, sir?" Streldone asked.

Faliol vouchsafed his understanding of the matter by repeating to its last detail Streldone's account of his plight.

"Well, I am glad to know that your wits are still in order, however distracted you may seem. I have heard certain rumors, you understand. In any event, tonight the Sorcerer is attending the duke's masquerade at the palace. She will be with him. Help me steal her back, so that we may both escape from Soldori, and I will fill the empty part of that pouch."

Faliol asked if Streldone had possessed the foresight to have brought along a pair of costumes to enable their entrance to the masquerade. Streldone, somewhat vainly, produced from the shadows of the coach two such costumes, one that was appropriate to a knight of the old days and the other that of a court jester of the same period. Faliol reached out for the wildly patterned costume with the jeering mask.

"But I am afraid," said Streldone, "that I intended that costume for myself. The other is more suited to allow your sword—"

"No sword will be needed," Faliol assured his nervous companion. "This will be fitting," he added, holding the hook-nosed fool's face opposite his own.

They were now traveling in the direction of the palace, and Soldori's carnival began to thicken about the wheels of Strel-done's coach. Gazing upon the nocturnal confusion, Faliol's eyes were as dark and swirled with shadows as the raving night itself.

II: THE STORY OF THE SPECTACLES

His eyes fixed and clouded as a blind man's, the mage sat before a small circular table upon which a single wax taper burned in a silver stick. Illuminated by that modest flame, the surface of the table was inlaid with esoteric symbols, a constellation of designs which reduced essential forces of existence to a few, rather picturesque, patterns. But the mage was not occupied with these. He was simply attending to someone who was raving in the shadows of a secret chamber. The hour was late and the night was without a moon. The narrow window behind the beardless, pallid face of the mage was a solid sheet of blackness that seemed to absorb the candlelight. Every so often someone would move before this window, his hands running through his thick dark hair as he spoke, or tried to speak. Occasionally he would move toward the candle flame, and a glimpse could be caught of his bold attire in blacks and reds, his shining blue eyes, his fevered face. Calmly, the mage listened to the man's wild speech.

"Not *if* I have become mad but of what my madness consists is the knowledge I seek from you. And please understand that I have no hopes, only a searing curiosity to riddle the corpse of my dead soul. As for the assertion that I have always been engaged in deeds which one might deem mad, I would be obliged to answer—Yes, countless deeds, countless mad games of flesh and steel. Having confessed that, I would also avow that these were *sanctioned* provocations of chaos, known in some form to the body of the world and even blessed by it, if the truth be spoken. But I have provoked another thing, a new madness which arrives from a world that is on the wrong side of light, a madness that is unsanctioned and without the seal of our natural selves. It is a forbidden madness, a saboteur from outside the body of known laws. And as you know, I have been the subject of its devastation.

"Since the madness began working its ruin upon me, I have become an adept of every horror which can be thought or sensed or dreamed. In my very dreams—have I not told you of them?—there are scenes of slaughter without purpose, without constraint, and without end. I have crept through dense forests not of trees but of tall pikes planted in the earth; and upon each of them a crudely formed head has been fixed. These heads all wear faces which would forever blind the one who saw them anywhere but in a dream. And they follow my movements not with earthly eyes but with shadows rolling in empty sockets. Sometimes the heads speak as I pass through their uncanny ranks, telling me things I cannot bear to hear. Nor can I shut out their words, and I listen until I have learned the horrors of each brutal head. And the voices from their lacerated mouths, so clear, so precise to my ears that every word is a bright flash in my dreaming brain, a brilliant new coin minted for the treasure house of hell. At the end of the mad dream these heads endeavor to laugh, creating a blasphemous babble which echoes throughout that terrible forest. And when I awaken, the night continues to reverberate with fading laughter.

"Yet why should I speak of waking from these dreams? For to awaken, as I once understood this miracle, means to reclaim a world of laws which for a time were lost, to rise into the light of the world as one falls into the darkness of dream. But for me there is no sense of breaking through the envelope of sleep. It seems that I remain a captive of these dreams, these visions. For when one leaves off, another begins, like a succession of connected rooms which will never lead to freedom. And for all I can know, I am even now the inhabitant of one of these rooms, and at any moment—I beg forgiveness, wise man—you may transform into a demon and begin to disembowel weeping children before my eyes and smear their entrails upon the floor so that in them you may read my future, a future without escape from those heads and from what comes after.

"For there is a citadel in which I am a prisoner and which holds within it a type of school—a school of torture. Ceremonial stranglers, their palms grooved by the red cord, stalk the corridors of this place or lie snoring in its shadows, dreaming of perfect throats. And somewhere the master carnifex, the supreme inquisitor, waits as I am taken from my cell and dragged across stone floors—until I am finally presented to this fiend with witless, rolling eyes. Then my arms, my legs, everything is shackled, and I am screaming to die while the Torture of the Question . . ."

"Enough," said the mage without raising his voice.

"Yes, enough," the madman said. "And so have I said numberless times. But there is no end, there is no hope. And this endless, hopeless torment incites me with a desire to turn its power on others, and even to dream of turning it on all. To see the world drown in oceans of agony is the only vision which now brings me any relief from my madness, from a madness which is *not of this world*."

"Though neither is it of any other world," said the mage in the same quiet voice.

"But I have also had visions of butchering the angels," replied the madman, as if to argue the irreparable nature of his mania.

"You have envisioned precisely what you have been made to envision, and nothing that has risen from your own true being. But how could you have known this, when it is the nature of what you have seen—this Anima Mundi of the oldest philosophers and alchemists—to deceive and to pose as the soul of another world, and not as the soul of the world we know? There is only one world and one soul of that world, which appears in forms of beauty or bravery or madness according to how Anima Mundi would turn you. And no ordinary devising may turn you away from what it wills. This is the power that has made you what you now are, and would unmake you for its own design. It has played with you as it would a puppet."

"Then I will make myself its destruction."

"You cannot. Your very wish to destroy it is not yours but that of the thing itself. You are not who you are. You are only what it would have you be."

"You speak as if it were a god of deceit and illusion."

"There is no other or truer way to speak of it. But no further words now," finished the mage.

He then instructed the madman to seat himself at the table of arcane designs and to wait there with eyes calmly closed. And for what remained of that moonless night the mage worked in another part of his dwelling, returning to the wretched dreamer just before dawn. In one of his hands was the product of his labors: a pair of strangely darkened spectacles, as if they had shadows sealed within them. These he fitted to the madman's face.

"Do not yet open your eyes, my unhappy friend, but heed my words. I know the visions you have known, for they are among the visions that all were born to know. There are eyes within our eyes, and when these others open all becomes confusion. The meaning of my long life consists of the endeavor to seize and settle these visions, until my natural eyes themselves have altered in accordance with my purpose. Now, for what reason I cannot say, Anima Mundi has revealed itself to you in its most essential aspect—that of *chaos at feast*. Having seen the face behind all its others, your life can never again be as you have known it. All the pleasures of the past are now defiled, all your hopes violated beyond hope. There are things which only madmen fear because only madmen may truly conceive of them. Your world is presently black with the scars of madness, but you must make it blacker still in order to find any solace. You have seen both too much and not enough. Through the shadow-fogged lenses of these spectacles, you will be blinded so that you may see with greater sight. Through their darkly clouded glass Anima Mundi will diffuse into nothingness before you. What would murder another man's mind will bring yours peace.

"Henceforth, all things will be in your eyes a distant play of shadows that fretfully strive to engage you, ghosts that clamor to pass themselves as actualities, masks that desperately flit about to conceal the stillness of the void behind them. Henceforth, I say, all things will be reduced in your eyes to their inconsequential essence. And all that once shined for you—the steel, the stars, the eyes of another—will lose its luster and take its place among the other shadows. All will be dulled in the power of your vision, which will give you the ability to see that the greatest power, the only power, is to care for nothing.

"Please know that this is the only means by which I may help you. You have been made ready to receive this salvation by your very torments. Though we cannot overthrow the hold that Anima Mundi has on the others of this earth, we must still try as we can. For as long as the soul of the world has its way, it will grieve all in whom it lives. But it will not live in you on the condition you obey one simple rule: You must never be without these spectacles or your furies will return to you. There, now you may open your eyes."

Faliol sat very still for some time, an ease of heart within him as he gazed through the spectacles. At first he did not notice that one of the mage's own eyes was closed, covered by a sagging eyelid. When at last he saw this and perceived the sacrifice, he said, "And how may I serve you, wise man?"

Beyond the window at the back of the two figures, something seemed to be at watch. Neither man took note of the image, which was so obscure as to be nearly invisible. Some would call it a face, yet its features were translucent such that not even the sharpest eye could read them clearly. Nor could any eye outside that room where Faliol and the mage sat quietly conversing suffer to behold such a vision.

III: ANIMA MUNDI

While the revelers in the streets of Soldori remedied their discontents by throwing off the everyday face of orthodoxy, those attending the masquerade at the duke's palace found their deliverance by donning other faces, other bodies, and perhaps other souls. The anonymity of that night—no unmasking was expected to be held—enabled a multitude of sins against taste, from the most subtle to the most grotesque indiscretions. The society of the court had transformed itself into a race of gods or monsters, competing at once with the brightest and highest of stars and the strangest of the world's lower creatures. Many would undoubtedly spend the succeeding days or weeks in darkened rooms behind closed doors, so that the effects their disguises had wrought on their bodies might be known to none. For a few rare spirits, this by necessity would be their last appearance in the eyes of the court before a final seclusion. All were quite clearly arrayed as if something unparalleled, and possibly conclusive, was to occur that night. Musicians played in several of the palace's most sumptuous and shimmering halls, glittering glasses were filled by fountains of unnaturally colored wine, and maskers swarmed about like living gargoyles freed from the cathedral's stone. All, or nearly all, were straining for some unheard-of antic, suffering the pleasures of expectancy.

But as the hours passed, hopes dissolved. The duke—in essence a simple man, even a dull one—took no initiative to unloose the abundant possibilities of the masquerade; and, as if instinctively aware of these perilous directions, he restrained the efforts of others to pursue them and thereby digress in a wayward manner from the night's steadily unwinding course. No petitioning could sway him. He allowed several odd witticisms to pass unacknowledged, and he feigned that certain dubious suggestions and proposals were abstruse to his mind. Unnourished by any source within the duke's character, every attempt at innovation curled at its colorful edges and died. The initial strangeness of the masked gathering went stale. Voices began to sound as though they were transacting business of some tedious sort, and even the sight of a jester, albeit one with darkness within the eyes of his mask, offered no special merriment to this sullen assembly.

Accompanying the jester, who made no lively movements, was a knight out of armor, dressed in radiant blues and golds, a crusader's cross emblazoned upon his chest, and over his face a white silk mask of blandly noble expression. The odd duo progressed from room to room of the palace, as if they were negotiating a thick wood in search of something or someone. The knight was manifestly nervous, his hand too obviously ready to go for the sword at his side, his head patrolling with skittish alertness the bizarre world around him. The jester, on the other hand, was altogether composed and methodical, and with excellent reason: he knew, as the knight did not, that their purpose was not a difficult one, as they would enjoy the complicity of Wynge himself, whom the knight had called the Sorcerer but whom the jester knew to be the wise man mage in disguise. With this advantage, Faliol might easily assist the knight in escaping Soldori. Not that such heroics were any longer of concern to Faliol, who was merely serving the mage in a machination to break the duke. The alchemical transformation that the ruler desired would indeed take place, though not precisely as promised. What reserves of wealth the duke and his sorcerous conspirator possessed would tonight undergo, per the plan of the mage, a *reverse* alchemy that would leave them paupers. And then his work would be done in Soldori, such as he could accomplish what he set out to do.

The knight and the jester now paused at the arched entrance to the last, and most intimate, of the masquerade's many rooms. Pulling at the knight's golden sleeve, the jester angled his pointed, sneering muzzle toward a costumed pair in the far corner. The indicated figures were appareled as monarchs of the old days, a king and queen in ancient robes and stoles and many-horned crowns.

"How can you be sure they are the ones?" whispered the knight to the buffoon at his side.

"Approach and take her hand. You will be sure. But say nothing until you have led yourselves back through these rooms and to freedom."

"But the king might well be the Sorcerer in disguise," objected the knight. "He could have us both executed."

"Do as I tell you, though I cannot tell you all. You will see me greet the king and caper about as his jester. Believe me when I say that he is no sorcerer, only one who does what he can in this world against powers that can never be undone. And he has been working for your cause even before you knew of its troubles. Trust me that all will be well."

"I do trust you," said the knight, as he furtively stuffed a jeweled pouch twice the size of the first into the belt of the jester, though Faliol cared nothing for the copious reward.

The two characters separated and merged with the murmuring crowd. The jester arrived first at their destination. From a distance he seemed to speak a few words into the king's ear and then suddenly leaped back to play the fool before him, hopping about wildly. The knight bowed before the queen and then without ostentation led her away to other rooms. Though her mask covered the expression beneath it, the manner in which she placed her hand upon the knight's appeared to reveal her knowledge of his identity. After they had gone, the jester ceased his antics and stood close to the statue-like king.

"I shall watch the duke's men around us, who may have been watching you, wise man."

"And I shall see that our two little babes find their way through the forest," replied the mock-monarch, who abruptly strode off.

But that was not part of your design, thought Faliol. And neither was the king's roguish voice that of the solemn mage. The dark eyes of the jester's mask followed the movements of the impostor until he became lost in the throng. Faliol had just started in pursuit when a strange commotion in another part of the palace educed much talk on all sides.

It seemed that something unheard-of had finally occurred, though it did not gladden any of those who had hoped for a unique happening on that carnival night.

The disturbance originated in the centermost of that labyrinth of capacious rooms composing the arena of the masquerade. To the surrounding as well as the more peripheral rooms, including the one in which Faliol was now caught by the crushing crowd, there first traveled what sounded like cries of amusement. These quickly transformed, however, into ambiguous outbursts of surprise unto the edge of shock. Finally, the uproar took on the character of intense horror—all voices in alarm and confusion. Tidings passed rapidly, though less and less reliably, from mouth to mouth, room to room. Something terrible had happened, something which had begun, or was initially perceived, as a fabulous hoax. No one knew exactly how it was possible, but there suddenly appeared an outlandish spectacle in the midst of the most congested room of that night's affair. The matter of the event was that two participants in the masque, without being spied by those around them, had donned costumes which went far beyond the most gruesome seen beforehand at the palace gathering. Among some persons, word circulated about semblances most closely akin to giant leeches or worms, for they did not walk upright but writhed along the floor as if absent of bones. Others heard that these prodigies of disguise possessed countless tiny legs, and thus more properly resembled centipedes of some type. Still others averred that what was now in their company were not masqueraders but things inhuman in nature, having many-taloned claws, reptilian tails, serpent faces, and an overall composition of fantastical beasts which could not be dissembled by man nor woman. But whatever may have constituted the true substance and form of these beings, at some stage they affected the crowd with a panic past all reckoning. And however subsequent actions were construed to transpire, the consequence was that these bizarre intruders were hacked and torn and trampled owing to an unreasoning revulsion for their aspect, or many aspects.

Tragically, once the massacre was accomplished, it was not the slaughtered remains of two uncanny monsters that the masqueraders, their masks removed, looked down upon. Instead, it was two of their own—a knight and queen of the old days—whose blood was spreading across the ornate designs of the palace floor. Their bodies, which they had feared would be lastingly parted, were now all but indistinguishable from each other.

Throwing off his jester's face, Faliol worked himself near enough to the scene to view the horror with his own shaded eyes. A tragedy, yes, but not such that would return Faliol to his furies. For the image he saw immediately took its place among the seamless and unending flow of hellish eidola which constituted Anima Mundi and which, in his vision, was a monotonous tapestry of the terrible ceaselessly unfurling itself in the faintest shades of gray. Thus, the appalling tableau was neither more nor less sinister in his sight than any other which the world might show him.

"Look again, Fa-fa-faliol," said a voice at his back, as a forceful boot propelled him toward the carnage.

But why was everything painted with such brilliance now, when a moment ago it was all so insipid? Why did every piece of mutilated flesh pulse with color? And why was Faliol wholly benumbed by these red-smeared forms and their unhappy fate? He had been charged to save them and he could do . . . nothing.

His thoughts were now careening wildly through crimson corridors within him, madly seeking solutions but falling at every turn into blind corners and flailing in vain against something immovable, impossible. He pressed his hands over his face, hoping to blind himself to the scene. But everything remained invincibly there before his eyes—everything save his spectacles.

Now the duke's voice broke the brief lull of the dazed and incredulous assembly. The enraged sovereign shouted orders, demanded answers. How justified had proved his misgivings concerning the masquerade. He had long known that something of this nature might occur, and had done what he could to prevent its coming to pass. On the spot, he outlawed all future occasions of this kind and called for arrests and interrogations, the Torture of the Question to be liberally implemented. Exodus was instantaneous—the palace became a chaos of fleeing freaks.

"Faliol!" called a voice that sounded too clear, within all the confusion, to have its origin outside his own mind. "I have what you're looking for. They're with me now, right here in my hand, not lost forever."

When Faliol turned around, he saw the masked king standing some distance away, unmolested by the frantic mob. The king was holding out the spectacles as if they were the dangling head of a conquered foe. Fighting his way toward the unknown persecutor, Faliol would chase him down and reclaim sanity, though not before he had barbarously dispatched the fiend. Yet he could not catch up to this figure which led him through all the rooms where the masquerade once flourished, and then deeper into the palace. At the end of a long silent corridor, the gaudy, flapping train of a royal robe disappeared through a doorway. Faliol followed the shape and at last entered a dim chamber with a single window, before which stood the mummer who taunted him. The spectacles were still held by the velvet fingers of a tightly gloved hand. Watching as the dark lenses flashed in the candlelight, Faliol's eyes burned as much with questions as with madness.

"Where is the mage?" he demanded.

"The mage is no more."

"Then tell me who are you before I send you to hell?"

"You know who I am. But say I'm a sorcerer if that is well with you."

"And you killed the mage as you did the others."

"The others? How could you have not heard that rattling pantomime, all those swords and swift feet? Did you not hear that there was a pair of leviathan leeches, or something in that way, menacing the guests? True, I had a hand in the illusion, but my hand contained no gouging blade. A shambles, you saw it with your own eyes."

"In their fate you saw your own future. Even a sorcerer may be killed."

"Agreed, though I think not by your hand."

"Who are you to have destroyed the mage?"

"In fact, he destroyed himself—a heroic act, I'm sure. And he did it before *my* own eyes, as if in spite. As for myself, I confess that I am disappointed to be so far beneath your recognition. We have met previously, please remember. But it was many years past, and I suppose you became forgetful as well as dim-sighted once you put those pieces of glass over your eyes. You see why the mage had to be stopped. He ruined you as a madman, as *my* madman.

"But you might recall that you had another career before the madness took you, did you not? Buh-buh-brave Faliol. Do you not remember how you were made as such? Do you not wish to remember that you were Faliol the dandy before we met on the road that day? It was I—in my role as a charm seller—who outfitted you with that onyx-eyed amulet which you once wore around your neck. It was that bauble which made you the skillful mercenary you once were, and that you loved to be.

"And how everyone else loved you that way: to see a weakling become a man of strength and of steel is the stuff of public comment, of legend, and of diversion in general. And how much more do they love to witness the reverse of this process: to see the mighty laid low, the lord of the sword made mad. This was the little drama I had planned. You were supposed to be *my* madman, Faliol, not the imperturbable fool of that magician. You were supposed to be a real lost soul of torments in red and black, not a pathetic monk chanting silent psalms in pale breaths. Do you not understand? It was Wynge who ruined you, who undid all my schemes for your tragic and colorful history. Because of him I was forced to change my plans, which are many and touch the lives of all. Yes, it was your mage, who had wrested his soul from me and believed he could do the same for you. Blame him for the slaughter of those innocents and for what you are about to suffer. You know my ways. We are not strangers."

"No, demon horror, we are not. You are indeed the foul thing the wise man described to me, all the dark powers which we cannot understand but only hate."

"Poor Faliol. How wrong you are to contend that the one who stands before you is hated, whatever few enemies I may have. Do you hear those rhapsodic voices in the streets below? They are not filled with hate. Even when I excruciate them, they make excuses for me. They could not possibly hold a greater love for what gives them all they have, however little it may sometimes come to. But I would never go so far that they would turn against their own perpetuity. Only as they live do I live on. And the exceptional destinies of heroes and magicians, of kings and queens, saints and martyrs—these have special roles to perform in my scheme. From the highest to the lowest, they are all my children, and through their eyes I see my own glory."

"You see but your own foulness."

"No, the foulness is yours alone to lay eyes on, my dear Faliol. For those enamored of their continuance, no foulness exists. You have worn these spectacles too long and, to my disappointment, still see too much. You have seen me as others have not, if that pleases you, and for that you must come to an end. This is a privileged doom for those such as yourself. A type of consolation."

"You have said enough."

"To be sure. My time is precious. And yet I have not said what I came here to say, or rather to ask. You know the question, do not deny it, Faliol. The one you dreamed in those mad dreams I sent you. The torture of the question you dreaded to hear asked, and dreaded more to have answered."

"Demon!"

"What is the face of the soul of the world?"

"No, it is not a face . . . it is only—"

"Yes, there is a face, Faliol. And you will see it," said the masked figure as it peeled away its mask. "But why have you hidden your eyes that way, Faliol? And why have you fallen to your knees? Do you not appreciate the vision I have shown you? Could you ever have imagined that your existence would lead you into the presence of such a sight? Your spectacles cannot save you now. They are only so much glinting glass—hark to my grinding them underfoot upon the cool marble of the floor. No more spectacles, Faliol. And I think, too, no more Faliol. Can you understand what I am telling you now, jester? Well, what have you to say? Nothing? How black your madness must be to make you so rude. How black. But see, even if you will not, how I have provided these escorts to show you the way back to the carnival, which is where a buffoon belongs. And be sure that you make my legions of admirers laugh, or I will punish you. Yes, I can still punish you, Faliol. A living man can always be punished, so remember to be good. I will be watching. I am always watching. Farewell, then, fool."

A glazen-eyed guard on either side of him, Faliol was dragged from the duke's palace and given to the crowd which still rioted in the streets of Soldori. And the crowd embraced the mad jester, hoisting his jingling form upon their shoulders, shaking him like a toy as they carried him along. In its scheme to strangle silence forever, Soldori's unruly populace bellowed a robust refrain to Faliol's sickly moans. Into an onyx-black night his eyes gazed and his mind vanished.

But there must have been some moment, however brief, in which Faliol regained his old enlightenment and which allowed him to accomplish such a crucial and triumphant action. Was it solely by his own sleeping strength, fleetingly aroused, that he attained his greatest prize? If not, then what power could have enabled his trembling hands to reach so deeply into those haggard sockets, and with a gesture brave and sure dig out the

awful seeds of his suffering? However it was done, the deed
was done well. For as Faliol perished his face was flushed with
a crimson glory.

And the crowd fell silent, and a new kind of confusion spread
among them—those heads which were always watching—when
it was found that what they were bearing through the streets of
Soldori was only Faliol's victorious corpse.

DR. VOKE AND MR. VEECH

There is a stairway. It climbs crooked up the side of total darkness. Yet its outlines are visible, like a scribble of lightning engraved upon a black sky. And though standing unsupported, it does not fall. Nor does it end its jagged ascent until it has reached the obscure loft where Voke, the recluse, has cloistered himself.

Someone named Veech is now mounting the stairway, which seems to trouble him somehow. Though the angular scaffolding as a whole seems secure enough, Veech appears hesitant to place his full weight on the individual steps. A victim of vague misgivings, he ascends in weird mincing movements. Every so often he looks back over his shoulder at the stairs he has just placed his weight upon, for they feel to him more like soft clay than solid material and perhaps he is expecting to see the imprints of his soles on their surface. But the stairs are unchanged.

Veech is wearing a long, brightly colored coat, and the splinters on the railing of the stairway sometimes snag his bulky sleeves. They also snag his bony hands, but Veech is more exasperated by the destruction of expensive cloth than injuries to his undear flesh. While climbing, he sucks at a small puncture in his forefinger to keep from staining his coat with blood. At the seventeenth stair above the seventeenth, and last, landing—Veech trips. The long tails of the coat become tangled between his legs and there is a ripping sound as he falls. At the end of his patience, Veech removes the coat and flings it over the side of the stairway into the black abyss. Shabby clothes hang loosely upon his thin body.

At the top of the stairs there is only a single door. With widely splayed fingers, Veech pushes it open. Behind the door is Voke's loft, which appears to be a cross between a playroom and a place of torture.

The darkness and silence of the great room are somewhat compromised by noisy jets of blue-green light flickering spasmodically along the walls. But for the most part the room lies buried in shadows. Even its exact height is uncertain, since above the convulsive illumination almost nothing can be seen by even the sharpest pair of eyes, never mind Veech's squinting little slits. Some of the lower beams of the crisscrossing rafters are visible, but the ceiling is entirely obscured, if in fact Voke's sanctum has been provided with one.

Somewhere above the gritty floor, more than a few life-size dolls hang suspended by wires which glisten like wetted strands of a spider web. But none of the dolls is seen in whole. The long-beaked profile of one juts into the light; the shiny satin legs of another find their way out of the upper dimness; a beautifully pale hand glows in the distance; while much closer the better part of a harlequin dangles into view, cut off at the neck by blackness. Indeed, much of the inventory of this vast room appears only as parts and pieces of objects which manage to push their way out of the smothering dark. Upon the floor, a long low box thrusts partway into the scene, showing off its reinforced edges of bright metal strips plugged with heavy bolts. Pointed and strangely shaped instruments bloom out of the loam of shadows. They are crusted with age. A great wheel appears at quarter-phase in the room's dimness. Other sections, appendages, and gear-works of curious machines also complicate this immense gallery.

As Veech progresses through the half-light, he is suddenly halted by a metal arm with a soft black handle. He backs off and continues to walk about the chamber, grinding sawdust, sand, perhaps pulverized stars underfoot. The dismembered limbs of dolls and puppets are strewn about everywhere. Posters, signs, billboards, and leaflets of various sorts are scattered around like playing cards, their bright words disarranged into nonsense. Countless other objects, devices, and leftover goods stock the room, more than one could possibly take notice of.

But they are all, in some way, like those which have been described. One wonders, then, how they could add up to such an atmosphere of . . . isn't *repose* the word? Yes, but a certain kind of repose: the repose of ruin.

"Hello," Veech calls out. "Doctor, are you here?"

Within the darkness ahead there suddenly appears a tall rectangle, like a ticket-seller's booth at a carnival. The lower part is composed of wood and the upper part of glass. Its interior is lit up by an oily red glare. Slumped forward on its seat inside the booth, as if asleep, is a well-dressed dummy: nicely fitting black jacket and vest with bright silver buttons, a white high-collar shirt with silver cufflinks, and a billowing cravat which displays a pattern of moons and stars. Because his head is forwardly inclined, the dummy's only feature of note is the black sheen of its painted hair.

Veech approaches the booth a little cautiously. He seems to be most interested in the figure within. Through a semi-circular opening in the glass, Veech slides his hand into the booth, apparently with the intention of giving the dummy's arm a shake. But before his own arm creeps very far toward its goal, several things occur in succession: the dummy casually lifts its head and opens its eyes . . . it reaches out and places its wooden hand on Veech's hand of flesh . . . and its jaw drops open to dispense a mechanical laugh—yah-ha-ha-ha-ha, yah-ha-ha-ha-ha.

Wresting his hand away from the dummy, Veech staggers backward a few steps. The dummy continues to give forth its mocking laughter, which flaps its way into every niche of the loft and flies back as peculiar echoes. The dummy's face is vacant and handsome; its eyes roll like mad marbles. Then, from out of the shadows behind the dummy's booth, steps someone who is every bit as thin as Veech, though much taller. His outfit is not unlike the dummy's, but his clothes hang on him, and what there is left of his sparse hair falls like torn rags across his bone-white scalp.

"Did you ever wonder, Mr. Veech," Voke begins, parading slowly toward his guest while holding one side of his coat like the train of a gown. "I say, did you ever wonder what it is that makes the animation of a wooden dummy so terrible to see, not to mention to hear? Listen to it, I mean really listen. Ya-ha-ha-ha-ha: a series of sounds that becomes excruciatingly eloquent when uttered by the Ticket Man. They are a species of poetry that sings what should not be sung, that speaks what should not be spoken. But what in the world is it laughing about? Nothing, it would seem. No clear motives or impulses make the dummy laugh, and yet it does!

"'But what is this laughter for?' you might well ponder. It seems to be for your ears alone, doesn't it? It seems to be directed at every part of your being. It seems . . . knowing. And it is knowing, but in another way from what you suppose, in another direction entirely. It is not you the dummy knows— it is only itself. The question is not: 'What is the laughter for,' not at all. The question is: 'Where does it come from?' This in fact is what inspires your apprehension. While the dummy does terrorize you, his terror is actually greater than yours.

"Think of it: *wood waking up.* I can't put it any clearer than that. And let's not forget about the painted hair and lips, the glassy eyes. These, too, are aroused from a sleep that should never have been broken; these, too, are now part of a tingling network of dummy-nerves, alive and aware in a way we cannot begin to imagine. This is something too painful for tears and so the dummy laughs in your face, trying to give vent to a horror that was no part of his old home of wood and paint and glass. But this horror is the very essence of its new home—our world, Mr. Veech. This is what is so terrible about the laughing Ticket Man. Go to sleep now, dummy. There, he has gone back to his lifeless slumber. Be glad I didn't make one that screams, Mr. Veech. And be gladder still that the dummy, after all, is just a device. Am I getting through to you, Mr. Veech?"

"Yes," says Veech, who seems not to have heard a word of Voke's monologue.

"Well, to what do I owe your presence here today? It is day, isn't it, or very close to it?"

"It is," Veech replies.

"Good, I like to keep abreast of things. What's your latest?"

Voke inquires while sauntering slowly about the clutter of his loft.

Veech leans back against a vague mound of indefinable objects and stares at the floor. He sounds drowsy. "I wouldn't have come here, but I didn't know what else to do. How can I tell you? The past days and nights, especially the nights, like icy hells. I suppose I should say that there is someone—"

"Whom you have taken a liking to," Voke finishes.

"Yes, but then there is someone else—"

"Who is somehow an obstacle, someone who has made your nights so frosty. This seems very straightforward. Tell me, what is her name, the first someone?"

"Prena," answers Veech after some hesitation.

"And his, the second."

"Lamm. But why do you need their names to help me?"

"Their names, like your name, and mine for that matter, are of no actual importance. I was just maintaining a polite interest in your predicament, nothing more. As for helping you, that assumes I have some mastery over this situation."

"But I thought," stammers Veech, "the loft, your devices, you seem to have a certain . . . knowledge."

"Like the dummy's knowledge? You shouldn't have depended on it. Now you just have one more disappointment to contend with. One more pain. But listen, can't you just stick it out? In time you will forget all about this Prena. Why become involved in that madness. It's something to consider."

"I can't help myself, doctor," says Veech in a plaintive voice.

"I understand, but first hear me out. I hate to see you like this, Mr. Veech. Believe me, I know whereof I speak. I was not always as you see me. But you know what they say: *Body and soul are both undone when two by two they become as one.* Or perhaps I made that up. My memory is blissfully bad. In any event, let me give you one final nugget of advice: forsake the world and cling to the shadows."

"I am my own shadow," Veech replies.

"Yes, I can see that. Then all I can say at this point is that you've been warned. So let us speak hypothetically for a moment. Are you familiar with the Street of Wavering Peaks?

I know it has a more common name, but I like to call it that because of all those tall, slanting houses."

Veech nods to indicate that he, too, knows the street.

"Well—and I promise nothing, remember, I make no pledges or vows—but if you can somehow manage to bring both of your friends through that street tonight, I think there might be a solution to your problem, if you really want one. Do you mind what form the solution takes?"

"I just want your help, doctor. I'm in your hands."

"You really are serious, aren't you?"

Veech says nothing in reply. Voke shrugs and gradually fades back to his point of origin within the deepest shadows of the room. The red light in the booth of the Ticket Man also fades like a setting sun, until the only color left in the room is the ultramarine of the flames burning on the walls. Veech folds his hands and gazes into the upper reaches of the loft, as if he can already see the slender rooftops hovering over the Street of Wavering Peaks.

By night, the façades of each edifice on either side of this narrow street seem to be fused together, as if they are bonded by shadows to one another. Aside from their foundations and a few floors with shuttered windows, they are all roof. Splendidly they rise into the night, often reaching fantastic altitudes. At angles they sway a little against the sky, undulating at their pinnacles like tall trees in a gentle wind.

Tonight the sky is a swamp of murky clouds glowing in the false fire of the moon. From the direction of the street's arched entranceway, three approaching figures are preceded by three elongated shadows. One walks ahead, leading the way but lacking the proper gestures of knowledge and authority. Behind are the shapes of a man and a woman, side by side with only a slice of evening's soft radiance between them.

Toward the end of the street, the leading figure stops and the other two catch up with him. They are now all three standing outside the loftiest of the street's peaked buildings. This one appears to serve as a place of business, since there is a sign hanging above its door. Muddled by shadows, it swings ever so slightly in the wind, squeaking softly. On either of its sides there is a painted picture of the goods or services sold there: a pair of tongs, or something similar, laying crosswise upon what is perhaps a poker, or some other lengthy implement. But the business is closed for the night and the shutters are secured. A round attic window high above seems to be no more than an empty socket, though from ground level—where the three figures have assumed the tentative postures of somnambulists—it is difficult to tell exactly what things are like up there. And now a fog begins to cut off their gaze from the upper regions of the Street of Wavering Peaks.

Veech looks vaguely distressed, apparently unsure just how much longer they should loiter in this place. Not being privy to what is supposed to occur, if anything, what action should he take? All he can do at the moment is stall. But soon enough everything is brought to a swift conclusion.

One moment Veech is drowsily conversing with his two companions, both of them looking sternly suspicious at this point; the next moment it is as if they are two puppets who have been whisked upwards on invisible strings, into the fog and out of sight. It all happens so suddenly that they do not make a sound, though a little later there are faint, hollow screams from high above. Veech has fallen to his knees and is covering his face with both his hands.

Two went up, but only one comes down—a single form suspended an arm's length above the stone-paved street and twisting a bit, as if at the end of a hangman's rope. Veech uncovers his eyes and looks at the thing. Yes, there is only one, but this one has too many . . . there is too much of everything on this body. Two faces sharing a single head, two mouths that have fallen silent forever with parted lips. The thing continues to dangle in the air even after Veech has completely collapsed on the Street of Wavering Peaks.

Voke's next meeting with Veech is as unexpected as the last. There is a disturbance in the loft, and the recluse lugs his bones out of the shadows to investigate. What he sees is Veech and the Ticket Man both screaming with laughter. Their cachinnations stir up the stagnant air of the loft. They are two maniac twins crying and cackling with a single voice.

"What's going on here, Mr. Veech?" demands Voke.

Veech ignores him and continues his riotous duet with the dummy. Even after Voke touches the booth and says "Go to sleep, dummy," Veech still giggles all by himself, as if he, too, is an automaton without command over his own actions. Voke knocks Veech to the floor, which seems to hit the right mechanism to shut off his voice. At least he is quiet for a few moments. Then he looks up and scowls at Voke.

"Why did you have to do that to them?" he asks with a deeply stricken reproachfulness. His voice is rough from all that laughter. It sounds like grating machinery.

"I'm not going to pretend I don't know what you're talking about. I have heard about what happened, not that I should care. But you can't hold me responsible, Mr. Veech. I never leave my loft, you know that. However, you're perfectly free to go, if you go now. Haven't you caused me enough trouble!"

"Why did it have to happen like that?" Veech protests.

"How should I know? You said you didn't mind what form the solution to your problem took. Besides, I think it all worked out for the best. Those two were making a fool of you, Mr. Veech. They wanted each other and now they have each other. Two by two they have become as one, while you are free to move on to your next disaster. Wait one moment, I know what's bothering you," says Voke with sudden enlightenment. "You're distressed because it all ended up with *their* demise and not yours. Death is always the best thing, Mr. Veech, but who would have thought you could appreciate such a view? I've underestimated you, no doubt about it. My apologies."

"No," screams Veech, shivering like a sick animal. Voke now becomes excited.

"No? Noooo? What is the matter with you? Why do you set me up for these disappointments? I've had quite enough without your adding to the heap. Take a lesson from the Ticket Man here. Do you see him whining? No, he is silent, he is still. A dummy's silence is the most soothing silence of all, and his stillness is the perfect stillness of the unborn. He could be making a fuss, but he isn't. And it is precisely his lack of action, his unfulfilled nature that makes him the ideal companion, my only true friend it seems. Dead-wood, I adore you. Look at how his hands rest upon his lap in empty prayer. Look at the noble bearing of his collapsed and powerless limbs. Look at his numb lips muttering nothing, and look at those eyes—how they gaze on and on forever!"

Voke takes a closer look at the dummy's eyes, and his own begin to lower with dark intentness. He leans his head against the booth for the closest possible scrutiny, his hands adhering to the glass as if by the force of some powerful suction. Finally, Voke sees that the dummy's eyes have changed. They are now dripping little drops of blood which roll slowly down shiny cheeks.

Voke pulls himself away from the booth and turns to Veech.

"You've been *tampering* with him!" he bellows as best he can.

Veech blinks a few leftover tears of berserk laughter out of his eyes, and his lips form a smile. "I didn't do a thing," he whispers mockingly. "Don't blame me for your troubles!"

Voke seems to be momentarily paralyzed with outrage, though his face is twisted by a thousand thoughts of action. Veech apparently is aware of the danger and his eyes search throughout the room, possibly for a means of escape or for a weapon to use against his antagonist. He fixes on something and begins to move toward it in a crouch.

"Where do you think you're going?" says Voke, now liberated from the disabling effects of his rage.

Veech is trying to reach something on the floor that is the approximate shape and size of a coffin. Only part of the long black box sticks out of the shadows into the bluish-green irradiance of the loft. A thick strip of burnished silver edges the object and is secured to it with heavy bolts.

"Get away from there," shouts Voke as Veech stoops over the box, fingering its lid.

But before he can open it, before he can make another move, Voke makes his.

"I've done my best for you, Mr. Veech, and you've given me nothing but grief. I've tried to deliver you from the fate of your friends . . . but now I deliver you *to* it."

At these words, Veech's body begins to rise in a puppet's hunch, then soars up into the tenebrous rafters and beyond, transported by unseen wires. His arms and legs twitch uncontrollably during the elevation, and his screams . . . fade.

But Voke pays no attention to his victim's progress. His baggy clothes fluttering, he rushes to the object so recently threatened with violation and drags it toward an open spot on the floor. The light from the walls shines on the coffin's silky black surface. Voke is on his knees before the long box, tenderly testing its security with his fingertips. As if each accumulated moment of deliberation were a blasphemy, he suddenly lifts back the lid.

Laid out inside is a young woman whose beauty has been unnaturally perpetuated by a fanatic of her form. Voke gazes for some time at the corpse. Then he whispers to her who cannot hear him: "Always the best thing, my dear. Always the best thing."

He is still kneeling before the coffin as his features begin to undergo the ravages of various, obviously conflicting, phases of feeling. Eyes, mouth, the whole facial structure is called upon to perform gruesome acrobatics of expression. Ultimately, the strain of Voke's inner turmoil resolves itself in a fit of convulsive laughter: the liberating laughter of an antic derangement. By the powers of his idiotic hilarity, Voke rises to his feet and begins to caper about, wildly dancing to absent music with an invisible partner. Hopping and bouncing and bobbing, he seems to be overtaken by a bout of seizures, while his laughter turns into a hoarse cacophony. Through complete absence of mind, or perhaps because he has momentarily gained possession of himself, Voke makes his way out of the loft and is now laughing into the dark abyss beyond the precarious railing at the top of the crooked stairway. His final laugh seems to stick in his throat as over the railing he falls without a sound.

Thus the screams you now hear are not those of the plummeting Voke or the hapless Veech, both of them gone into what dark regions none can say. Nor are they the last echoes of Prena and Lamm's cries of horror. These screams, the ones from beyond the doorway at the top of the stairs, belong only to a helpless dummy who now feels warm drops of blood sliding down his lacquered cheeks. For the Ticket Man has been left—alone and alive—in the shadows of an abandoned loft. And his eyes are rolling like mad marbles.

PROFESSOR NOBODY'S LITTLE LECTURES ON SUPERNATURAL HORROR

THE EYES THAT NEVER BLINK

Mist on a lake, fog in thick woods, a golden light shining on wet stones—such sights make it all very easy. Something lives in the lake, rustles through the woods, inhabits the stones or the earth beneath them. Whatever it may be, this *something* lies just out of sight, but not out of vision for the eyes that never blink. In the right surroundings our entire being is made of eyes that dilate to witness the haunting of the universe. But really, do the right surroundings have to be so obvious in their spectral atmosphere?

Take a cramped waiting room, for instance. Everything there seems so well-anchored in normalcy. Others around you talk ever so quietly; the old clock on the wall is sweeping aside the seconds with its thin red finger; the window blinds deliver slices of light from the outside world and shuffle them with shadows. Yet at any time and in any place, our bunkers of banality may begin to rumble. You see, even in a stronghold of our fellow beings we may be subject to abnormal fears that would land us in an asylum if we voiced them to another. Did we just feel some presence that does not belong among us? Do our eyes see something in a corner of that room in which we wait for we know not what?

Just a little doubt slipped into the mind, a little trickle of suspicion in the bloodstream, and all those eyes of ours, one by one, open up to the world and see its horror. Then: no belief or body of laws will guard you; no friend, no counselor, no appointed personage will save you; no locked door will protect you; no private office will hide you. Not even the solar brilliance of a summer day will harbor you from horror. For horror eats the light and digests it into darkness.

ON MORBIDITY

Isolation, mental strain, emotional exertions, visionary infatuations, well-executed fevers, repudiations of well-being: only a few of the many exercises practiced by that specimen we shall call the "morbid man." And our subject of supernatural horror is a vital part of his program. Retreating from a world of health and sanity, or at least one that daily invests in such commodities, the morbid man seeks the shadows behind the scenes of life. He backs himself into a corner alive with cool drafts and fragrant with centuries of must. It is in that corner that he builds a world of ruins out of the battered stones of his imagination, a rancid world rife with things smelling of the crypt.

But this world is not all a romantic sanctum for the dark in spirit. So let us condemn it for a moment, this deep-end of dejection. Though there is no name for what might be called the morbid man's "sin," it still seems in violation of some deeply ingrained morality. The morbid man does not appear to be doing himself or others any good. And while we all know that melancholic moping and lugubrious ruminating are quite palatable as side-dishes of existence, he has turned them into a house specialty! Ultimately, however, he may meet this charge of wrongdoing with a simple "What of it?"

Now, such a response assumes morbidity to be a certain class of vice, one to be pursued without apology, and one whose advantages and disadvantages must be enjoyed or endured *outside the law*. But as a sower of vice, if only in his own soul, the morbid man incurs the following censure: that he is a symptom or a cause of decay within both individual and collective spheres of being. And decay, like every other process of becoming, hurts everybody. "Good!" shouts the morbid man. "No good!" counters the crowd. Both positions betray dubious origins: one in resentment, the other in fear. And when the moral debate on this issue eventually reaches an impasse or becomes too tangled for truth, then psychological polemics can begin. Later on we will find other angles from which this problem may be attacked, enough to keep us occupied for the rest of our lives.

Meanwhile, the morbid man keeps putting his *time on earth* to no good use, until in the end—amidst mad winds, wan moonlight, and pasty specters—he uses his exactly like everyone else uses theirs: all up.

PESSIMISM AND SUPERNATURAL HORROR—LECTURE ONE

Madness, chaos, bone-deep mayhem, devastation of innumerable souls—while we scream and perish, History licks a finger and turns the page. Fiction, unable to compete with the world for vividness of pain and lasting effects of fear, compensates in its own way. How? By inventing more bizarre means to outrageous ends. Among these means, of course, is the supernatural. In transforming natural ordeals into supernatural ones, we find the strength to affirm and deny their horror simultaneously, to savor and suffer them at the same time.

So it is that supernatural horror is the product of a profoundly divided species of being. It is not the pastime of even our closest relations in the wholly natural world: we gained it, as part of our gloomy inheritance, when we became what we are. Once awareness of the human predicament was achieved, we immediately took off in two directions, splitting ourselves down the middle. One half became dedicated to apologetics, even celebration, of our new toy of consciousness. The other half condemned and occasionally launched direct assaults on this "gift."

Supernatural horror was one of the ways we found that would allow us to live with our double selves. By its employ, we discovered how to take all the things that victimize us in our natural lives and turn them into the very stuff of demonic delight in our fantasy lives. In story and song, we could entertain ourselves with the worst we could think of, overwriting real pains with ones that were unreal and harmless to our species. We can also do this trick without trespassing onto the property of supernatural horror, but then we risk running into miseries that are too close to home. While horror may make us squirm or quake, it will not make us cry at the pity of things. The vampire may symbolize our horror of both life and death, but none of us has ever been uprooted by a symbol. The zombie may conceptualize our sickness of the flesh and its appetites, but no one has ever been sickened to death by a concept. By means of supernatural horror we may pull our own strings of fate without collapsing—natural-born puppets whose lips are painted with our own blood.

PESSIMISM AND SUPERNATURAL HORROR—LECTURE TWO

Dead bodies that walk in the night, living bodies suddenly possessed by new owners and deadly aspirations, bodies without sensible form, and a body of unnatural laws in accordance with which tortures and executions are meted out—some examples of the logic of supernatural horror. It is a logic founded on fear, a logic whose sole principle states: "Existence equals nightmare." Unless life is a dream, nothing makes sense. For as a reality, it is a rank failure. A few more examples: a trusting soul catches the night in a bad mood and must pay a dreadful price; another opens the wrong door, sees something he should not have, and suffers the consequences; still another walks down an unfamiliar street . . . and is *lost* forever.

That we all deserve punishment by horror is as mystifying as it is undeniable. To be an accomplice, however involuntarily, in a reasonless non-reality is cause enough for the harshest sentencing. But we have been trained so well to accept the "order" of an unreal world that we do not rebel against it. How could we? Where pain and pleasure form a corrupt alliance against us, paradise and hell are merely different divisions in the same monstrous bureaucracy. And between these two poles exists everything we know or can ever know. It is not even possible to imagine a utopia, earthly or otherwise, that can stand up under the mildest criticism. But one must take into account the shocking fact that we live on a world that *spins*. After considering this truth, nothing should come as a surprise.

Still, on rare occasions we do overcome hopelessness or velleity and make mutinous demands to live in a real world, one that is at least episodically ordered to our advantage. But perhaps it is only a demon of some kind that moves us to such idle insubordination, the more so to aggravate our condition in the unreal. After all, is it not wondrous that we are allowed to be both witnesses and victims of the sepulchral pomp of wasting tissue? And one thing we know is real: horror. It is so real, in fact, that we cannot be sure it could not exist without us. Yes, it needs our imaginations and our consciousness, but it does not ask or require our consent to use them. Indeed, horror operates with complete autonomy. Generating ontological havoc, it is mephitic foam upon which our lives merely float. And, all said, we must face up to it: horror is more real than we are.

SARDONIC HARMONY

Compassion for human hurt, a humble sense of our impermanence, an absolute valuation of justice—all of our so-called virtues only trouble us and serve to bolster, not assuage, horror. In addition, these qualities are our least vital, the least in line with life. More often than not, they stand in the way of one's rise in the welter of this world, which found its pace long ago and has not deviated from it since. The putative affirmations of life— each of them based on the propaganda of Tomorrow: reproduction, revolution in its widest sense, piety in any form you can name—are only affirmations of our desires. And, in fact, these affirmations affirm nothing but our penchant for self-torment, our mania to preserve a demented innocence in the face of gruesome facts.

By means of supernatural horror we may evade, if momentarily, the horrific reprisals of affirmation. Every one of us, having been stolen from nonexistence, opens his eyes on the world and looks down the road at a few convulsions and a final obliteration. What a weird scenario. So why affirm anything, why make a pathetic virtue of a terrible necessity? We are destined to a fool's fate that deserves to be mocked. And since there is no one else around to do the mocking, we will take on the job. So let us indulge in cruel pleasures against ourselves and our pretensions, let us delight in the Cosmic Macabre. At least we may send up a few bitter laughs into the cobwebbed corners of this crusty old universe.

Supernatural horror, in all its eerie constructions, enables a reader to taste treats inconsistent with his personal welfare. Admittedly, this is not a practice likely to find universal favor. True macabrists are as rare as poets and form a secret society by the bad-standing of their memberships elsewhere, some of their outside affiliations having been cancelled as early as birth. But those who have gotten a good whiff of other worlds and sampled a cuisine marginal to stable existence will not be able to stay themselves from the uncanny feast of horrors that has been laid out for them. They will loiter in moonlight, eyeing the entranceways to cemeteries, waiting for some propitious moment to crash the gates and see what is inside.

Once and for all, let us speak the paradox aloud: "We have been force-fed for so long the shudders of a thousand graveyards that at last, seeking a macabre redemption, a salvation by horror, we willingly consume the terrors of the tomb . . . and find them to our liking."

DREAMS FOR THE DEAD

DR. LOCRIAN'S ASYLUM

Years passed and no one in our town, no one I could name, allotted a single word to that great ruin which marred the evenness of the horizon. Nor was mention made of the gated patch of ground closer to the town's edge. Even in days more remote, few things were said about these sites. Perhaps someone would propose tearing down the old asylum and razing the burial ground where no inmate had been interred for a generation or more; and perhaps a few others, swept along by the moment, would nod their heart's assent. But the resolution always remained poorly formed, very soon losing its shape entirely, its impetus dying a gentle death in the gentle old streets of our town.

Then how can I explain that sudden turn of events, that overnight conversion which set our steps toward that hulking and decayed structure, trampling its burial ground along the way? In answer, I put forward the existence of a secret movement, one conducted in the souls of the town's citizens, and in their dreams. Conceived thus, the mysterious conversion loses some of its mystery. One need only accept that we were all haunted by the same revenant, that certain images began to establish themselves deep within each of us and became part of our hidden lives. Finally, we resolved that we could no longer live as we had been.

When the idea of taking action first arose, the residents of the humble west end of town were the most zealous and impatient.

For it was they who had suffered the severest unease, living as they did in close view of the wild plots and crooked headstones of that crowded strip of earth where mad minds had come to be shut away for eternity. But all of us were equally burdened by the asylum itself, which seemed to be visible from every corner of town—from the high rooms of the old hotel, from the quiet rooms of our houses, from streets obscured by morning mist or twilight haze, and from my own shop whenever I looked out its front window. To make things worse, the setting sun would each day slip out of sight behind the asylum, thus committing our town to a premature darkness in the long shadow of that massive edifice.

Yet more disturbing than our view of the asylum was the idiotic gaze that it seemed to cast back at us. Throughout the years, some persons actually claimed to have seen mad-eyed and immobile figures staring out from the asylum's windows on nights when the moon shone with unusual brightness and the sky appeared to contain more than its usual share of stars. Though few people spoke of such experiences, almost everyone had seen other sights at the asylum that no one could deny. And what strange things were brought to mind because of them; all over town vague scenes were inwardly envisioned.

As children, most of us had paid a visit at some time to that forbidden place, and later we carried with us memories of our somber adventures. Over time we came to compare what we experienced, compiling this knowledge of the asylum until it became unseemly to augment it further.

By all accounts that old institution was a chamber of horrors, if not in its entirety then at least in certain isolated corners. It was not simply that a particular room attracted notice for its atmosphere of desolation: gray walls pocked like sponges, the floor filthied by the years entering freely through broken windows, and a shallow bed sunken after supporting so many nights of futile tears and screaming. There was something more.

Perhaps one of the walls to such a room would have built into it a sliding panel that could be opened only from the other side. And next to that room would be another room that was unfurnished and seemed never to have been occupied. But leaning against one wall of this other room, directly below the sliding panel, would be some long wooden sticks; and mounted at the ends of these sticks would be horrible little puppets.

Another room might be completely bare, yet its walls would be covered with pale fragments of weird funereal scenes. By removing some loose floorboards at the center of the room, one would discover several feet of earth piled upon an old, empty coffin.

Then there was a very special room—a room I had visited myself—that was located on the uppermost floor of the asylum. In the ceiling of that room was a great skylight. And positioned under that opening upon the heavens, fixed securely in place, there stood a long table with thick straps hanging from its sides.

Other rooms of a strange type have been struck from my memory, though I know they existed and may have dreamed of them. But none of these was singled out for comment during the actual dismantling of the asylum, when most of us were busy heaving the debris of decades through great breaches we had made in the building's outer walls, while some distance away the rest of the town witnessed the wrecking in a state of watchful silence. Among this group was Mr. Harkness Locrian, a thin and large-eyed old gentleman whose silence was not like that of the others.

Perhaps we expected Mr. Locrian to voice opposition to our project, but he did not do so. Though no one to my knowledge suspected him of preserving any morbid sentiment for the old asylum, it was difficult to forget that his grandfather had been the director of the Shire County Sanitarium during its declining years and that his father had closed down the place under circumstances that remained an obscure episode in the town's history. If we spoke very little about the asylum and its burial ground, Mr. Locrian spoke of them not at all. This reticence, no doubt, served only to strengthen in our minds the intangible bond which seemed to exist between him and the awful ruin that sealed the horizon. Even I, who knew the old man better than anyone else in the town, regarded him with a degree of circumspection. Outwardly, of course, I was courteous to him, even friendly; he was, after all, the oldest and most reliable patron of my business. And not long after the demolition of the asylum was concluded, and the last of its former residents' remains had been exhumed and hastily cremated, Mr. Locrian paid me a visit.

At the very moment he entered the shop, I was examining some volumes of curiosa which had just arrived for him by special order. But even if I had grown jaded to such coincidences following years of dealing in books, which have a quality about them that seems to breed events of this nature, there was something unpleasant about this particular freak of timing.

"Afternoon," I said. "You know, I was just looking over—"

"So I see."

Mr. Locrian approached the counter where tiers of books left very little open space. As he glanced at these new arrivals— hardly interested, it seemed—he slowly unbuttoned his overcoat, a bulky thing which made his head appear somewhat small for his body. How easily I can envision him on that day. And even now his voice sounds clear in my memory, a voice that was far too quiet for the old man's harshly brilliant eyes. After a few moments he turned and casually began to wander about the shop, as if seeking out others who might be secluded among its stacks. He rounded a corner and momentarily left my view. "So at last it's done," he said. "Something of a feat, I would say. A deed worthy of record."

"I suppose it is," I replied, watching as Mr. Locrian traversed the rear aisle of the shop, appearing and disappearing as he passed by several rows of shelves.

"Without doubt it is," he said, proceeding straight down the aisle in front of me. Finally reaching the counter behind which I stood, he placed his hands upon it, leaned forward, and said: "But what has been achieved, what has really changed?"

The tone of voice in which he posed this question was both sardonic and morose, carrying undesirable connotations that echoed in all the remote places where truth had been shut up and abandoned like a howling imbecile. Nonetheless, I held to the lie.

"If you mean that there's very little difference now, I would have to agree. Only the removal of an eyesore. That was all we intended to do. Simply that."

Then I tried to draw his attention to the books that had arrived for him that day. But I was coldly interrupted when he said: "We must be walking different streets, Mr. Crane, and seeing quite different faces, hearing different voices in this town." He paused, as if waiting for me to contradict him. His face took on a sly look. "Tell me, Mr. Crane, did you ever hear those stories about the sanitarium? What some people saw in its windows? Perhaps you yourself were one of them."

I said nothing, which he might have accepted as a confirmation that I was one of those people. He continued:

"And isn't there now the same sense of consternation, here in this town, as those stories inspired in anyone who heard them? Can you admit that the days and nights are much worse now than they were before? Of course, you may tell me that it's just the moodiness of the season, the chill, the dour afternoons you observe through your shop window. On my way here, I actually heard some people saying such things. They also said other things which they didn't think I could hear. Somehow everyone seems to know about these books of mine, Mr. Crane."

He did not look at me while delivering this last remark, but began to pace slowly between one end of the counter and the other.

"I'm sorry, Mr. Locrian, if you feel that I've violated some trust. I never imagined it would mean anything."

He paused in his pacing and now gazed at me with an expression of almost paternal forgiveness.

"Of course," he said. "But things are now very different, will you allow that?"

"Yes," I finally conceded.

"But no one is exactly sure in what way things are different."

"No," I agreed.

"Did you know that my grandfather, *Doctor* Harkness Locrian, was buried in that cemetery you ravaged?"

Feeling a sudden surprise and embarrassment, I replied:

"I'm sure if you had said something." But he ignored my words as if I had said nothing at all, or at least nothing that would deter him from imposing his confidences on me.

"Is this safe to sit in?" he asked, pointing to an old chair by the front window. And beyond the window, unobstructed, the pale autumn sun was sinking down.

"Yes, help yourself," I said, noticing some passersby who had noticed Mr. Locrian and looked oddly at him.

"My grandfather," Mr. Locrian continued, "felt at home with his lunatics. You may be startled to hear such a thing. Though the house that is now mine was once his, he did not spend any time there, not even to sleep. It was only after they closed down the sanitarium that he actually became a resident of his own home, which by then had become the residence where I lived with my parents, who now had charge of the old man.

"My grandfather passed his final years in a small upstairs room overlooking the outskirts of town, and I recall seeing him day after day gazing through his window at the sanitarium."

"I had no idea," I interjected. "That seems rather—"

"Please, before you are led to think that his was merely a sentimental attachment, however perverse, let me say that it was no such thing. His feelings with respect to the sanitarium were in fact quite incredible by reason of the manner in which he had used his authority at that place. I found out about this when I was still very young, but not so young that I could not understand the profound conflict that existed between my father and grandfather. I disregarded my parents' admonitions that I not spend too much time with the old man, succumbing to the mystery of his presence. And one afternoon he revealed himself.

"He was gazing through the window and never once turned to face me. But after we had sat in silence for some time, he started to whisper something. 'They questioned,' he said. 'They accused. They complained that no one in that place ever became well.' Then he smiled and began to elaborate. 'What things had they seen,' he hissed, 'to give them such . . . wisdom? They did not look into the faces,' no, he did not say 'faces' but 'eyes.' Yes, he said, '. . . did not look into the *eyes* of those beings, the eyes that reflected the lifeless beauty of the silent, staring universe itself.'

"Those were his words. And then he talked about the voices of the patients under his care. He whispered, and I quote, that 'the wonderful music of those voices spoke the supreme delirium of the planets as they go round and round like bright puppets dancing in the blackness.' In the wandering words of those lunatics, he told me, the ancient mysteries were restored.

"Like all true mysteriarchs," Mr. Locrian went on, "my grandfather aspired to a knowledge that was unspoken and unspeakable. And every volume of the strange library he left to his heirs attests to this aspiration. As you know, I have added to this collection in my own way, as did my father. But our reasons were not those of the old doctor. At his sanitarium, Dr. Locrian had done something very strange, something that perhaps only he possessed both the knowledge and the impulse to do. It was not until many years later that my father attempted to explain everything to me, as I now am attempting to explain it to you.

"I have said that my grandfather was and always had been a mysteriarch, never a philanthropist of the mind, not a restorer of wounded psyches. In no way did he take a therapeutic approach with the inmates at the sanitarium. He did not view them as souls that were possessed, either by demons or by their own painful histories, but as beings who held a strange alliance with other orders of existence, who contained within themselves a particle of something eternal, a golden speck of magic which he thought might be enlarged. Thus, his ambition led him not to relieve his patients' madness, but to *exasperate* it— to let it breathe with a life of its own. And this he did in certain ways that wholly eradicated what human attributes remained in these people. But sometimes that peculiar magic he saw in their eyes would seem to fade, and then he would institute his 'proper treatment,' which consisted of putting them through a battery of hellish ordeals intended to loosen their attachment to the world of humanity and to project them further into the realm of the 'silent, staring universe' where the insanity of the infinite might work a rather paradoxical cure. The result was something as pathetic as a puppet and as exalted as the stars, something at once dead and never dying, a thing utterly without destiny and thus imperishable, forever consigned to that abysmal vacuity which is the essence of all that is immortal. And somehow, in his last days, my grandfather used this same procedure on himself, reaching into spaces beyond death.

"I know this to be true, because one night late into my childhood, I awoke and witnessed the proof. Leaving my bed, I walked down the hallway toward the closed door of my grandfather's room. Stopping in front of that door, I turned its cold handle and peeked timidly into the room, where I saw my grandfather sitting before the window in the moonlight. My curiosity must have overcome my horror, for I actually spoke to this specter. 'What are you doing here, Grandfather?' I asked. And without turning away from the window, he replied: 'We are doing just what you see.' Of course, what I saw was an old man who belonged in his grave, but who was now staring out his window across to the windows of the sanitarium, where others who were not human stared back.

"When I fearfully alerted my parents to what I had seen, I was stunned that my father responded not with disbelief but with anger. I had disobeyed his warnings about my grandfather's room. Then he revealed the truth just as I now reveal it to you, and year after year he reiterated and expanded upon this enigmatic learning: why that room must always be kept shut and why the sanitarium must never be disturbed. You may not be aware that an earlier effort to destroy the sanitarium was aborted through my father's intervention. He was far more attached than I could ever be to this town, which ceased to have a future long ago. How long has it been since a new building was erected here? This place would have crumbled in time. The natural course of things would have dismantled it, just as the asylum would have disappeared had it been left alone. But when all of you rose up and marched toward the old ruin, I felt no impulse to interfere. You have brought it on yourselves," he complacently ended.

"And what is it we have done?" I asked in a cold voice, now suppressing a mysterious outrage.

"You are only trying to preserve what remains of your mind's peace. You know that something is very wrong in this town, that you should never have done what you did. But still you cannot draw any conclusion from what I have told you."

"With all respect, Mr. Locrian, how can you expect me to believe what you've told me?"

He laughed weakly. "Actually, I don't. But in time you will come to know. And then I will tell you more things, things you will not be able to keep yourself from believing."

As he pushed himself up from the chair by the window, I asked: "Why tell me anything? Why did you come here today?"

"Why? Because I thought that perhaps my books had arrived. And also because everything is finished now. The others," he shrugged, ". . . hopeless. You are the only one who could understand. Not now, but in time."

And now I do understand what the old man told me as I never could on that autumn day some forty years ago.

It was toward the end of that same sullen day, in the course of a bleak twilight, that they began to appear. Like figures quietly emerging from the depths of memory, they struggled in the shadows and slowly became visible. But even if the transition had been subtle, insidiously graduated, it did not long go unnoticed. By nightfall they were distractingly conspicuous throughout the town, always framed in some high window of the structures they occupied: the living quarters above the shops in the heart of the town, the highest story of the old hotel, the empty towers of civic buildings, the lofty turrets and grand gables of the most distinguished houses, and the attics of the humblest homes.

Their forms were as softly lustrous as the autumn constellations in the black sky above, their faces glowing with the same fixed expression of placid vacuity. And the habiliments of these apparitions were grotesquely suited to their surroundings. Buried many years before in antiquated clothes of a formal cut, they seemed to belong to the dying town in a manner its living members could not emulate. For the streets of the town now lost what life was left in them and became the dark corridors of a museum where these waxen nightmares had been put on exhibition.

In daylight, when viewed at street level, the figures in the windows took on a dull wooden appearance. Somehow that was less maddening. It was then that some of us ventured into those high rooms. But nothing was ever found on the other side of what were now *their* windows—nothing save a tenant-less room which no light would illuminate and which sooner or later drove us away in seizures of uncanny dread. By night, when it seemed we could hear them erratically tapping on the floors above us, their presence in our homes drove us out into the streets. Day and night we became sleepless vagrants, strangers in our own town. As I remember, we eventually ceased to recognize one another. But one name, one face was still known to all—that of Mr. Harkness Locrian, whose gaze haunted every one of us.

It was undoubtedly in his house that the fire began which consumed every corner of the town. There were attempts made to oppose its path, but they were half-hearted and soon abandoned. For the most part we stood in silence, vacantly staring as the flames burned their way up to the high windows where spectral figures posed like portraits in their frames.

Ultimately these demons were exorcised, their windows left empty. But only after the town had been annulled by the holocaust.

Nothing more than charred wreckage remained. Afterward it got around that one of our citizens perished in the conflagration, though none of us inquired into the exact circumstances under which old Mr. Locrian met his fiery death.

No effort was made by anyone to recover the town we had lost. When the first snow fell that year, it fell upon unclaimed ruins. But now, after the passing of so many years, it is not the ashen rubble of that town which haunts each of my hours; it is that one great ruin in whose shadow my mind has been interned.

And if they have kept me in this room because I speak to a charred face that appears at my window, then let them protect this same room from violations after I am gone. For Mr. Locrian has been true to his promise; he has told me of certain things when I was ready to hear them. And he has other things to tell me, secrets surpassing all insanity. Commending me to an absolute cure, he will have immured another soul within the black and boundless walls of that eternal asylum where stars dance forever like bright puppets in the silent, staring void.

THE SECT OF THE IDIOT

The primal chaos, Lord of All . . . the blind idiot god—
Azathoth.

—NECRONOMICON

The extraordinary is a province of the solitary soul. Lost the
very moment the crowd comes into view, it remains within the
great hollows of dreams, an infinitely secluded place that pre-
pares itself for your arrival, and for mine. Extraordinary joy,
extraordinary pain—the fearful poles of a world that both
menaces and surpasses this one. It is a miraculous hell towards
which one unknowingly wanders. And its gate, in my case,
was an old town whose allegiance to the unreal inspired my
soul with a holy madness long before my body had come to
dwell in that incomparable place.

Soon after arriving in the town—whose identity, along with
my own, it is best not to bring to light—I was settled in a high
room overlooking the ideal of my dreams through diamond
panes. How many times had I already lingered in mind before
these windows and roamed in reverie the streets I now gazed
upon below.

I discovered an infinite stillness on foggy mornings, miracles of silence on indolent afternoons, and the strangely flickering tableau of neverending nights. A sense of serene enclosure
was conveyed by every aspect of the old town. There were balconies, railed porches, and jutting upper stories of shops and
houses that created intermittent arcades over sidewalks. Colossal roofs overhung entire streets and transformed them into

the corridors of a single structure containing an uncanny multitude of rooms. And these fantastic crowns were echoed below by lesser roofs that drooped above windows like half-closed eyelids and turned each narrow doorway into a magician's cabinet harboring deceptive depths of shadow.

It is difficult to explain, then, how the old town also conveyed an impression of endlessness, of proliferating unseen dimensions, at the same time that it served as the very image of a claustrophobe's nightmare. Even the nights above the great roofs of the town seemed merely the uppermost level of an earthbound estate, at most an old attic in which the stars were useless heirlooms and the moon a dusty trunk of dreams. And this paradox was precisely the source of the town's enchantment. I imagined the heavens themselves as part of an essentially interior decor. By day: heaps of clouds like dust balls floated across the empty rooms of the sky. By night: a fluorescent map of the cosmos was painted upon a great black ceiling. How I ached to live forever in this province of medieval autumns and mute winters, serving out my sentence of life among all the visible and invisible wonders I had only dreamed about from so far away.

But no existence, however visionary, is without its trials and traps.

After only a few days in the old town, I had been made acutely sensitive by the solitude of the place and by the solitary manner of my life. Late one afternoon I was relaxing in a chair beside those kaleidoscopic windows when there was a knock at the door. It was only the faintest of knocks, but so unanticipated was this elementary event, and so developed was my sensitivity, that it seemed like some unwonted upheaval of atmospheric forces, a kind of cataclysm of empty space, an earthquake in the invisible. Hesitantly I walked across the room and stood before the door, which was only a simple brown slab without molding around its frame. I opened it.

"Oh," said the little man waiting in the hallway outside. He had neatly groomed silver hair and strikingly clear eyes. "This is embarrassing. I must have been given the wrong address. The hand-writing on this note is such chaos." He looked at the crumpled piece of paper in his hand. "Ha! Never mind, I'll go back and check."

However, the man did not immediately leave the scene of his embarrassment; instead, he pushed himself upwards on the points of his tiny shoes and stared over my shoulder into my room. His entire body, compact as it was in stature, seemed to be in a state of concentrated excitement. Finally he said, "Beautiful view from your room," and he smiled a very tight little smile.

"Yes, it is," I replied, glancing back into the room and not really knowing what to think. When I turned around the man was gone.

For a few startled moments I did not move. Then I stepped into the hallway and gazed up and down its dim length. It was not very wide, nor did it extend a great distance before turning a windowless corner. All the doors to the other rooms were closed, and not the slightest noise emerged from any of them. At last I heard what sounded like footsteps descending flights of stairs on the floors below, faintly echoing through the silence, speaking the quiet language of old rooming houses. I felt relieved and returned to my room.

The rest of the day was uneventful, though somewhat colored by a whole spectrum of imaginings. And that night I experienced a very strange dream, the culmination, it seemed, of both my lifetime of dreaming and of my dreamlike sojourn in the old town. Certainly my view of the town was thereafter dramatically transformed. And yet, despite the nature of the dream, this change was not immediately for the worse.

In the dream I occupied a small dark room, a high room whose windows looked out on a maze of streets which unraveled beneath an abyss of stars. But though the stars were spread across a great reaching blackness, the streets below were bathed in a stale gray dimness which suggested neither night nor day nor any natural phase between them. Gazing out the window, I was sure that cryptic proceedings were taking place in sequestered corners of this scene, vague observances that were at odds with accepted reality. I also felt there was special cause for me to fret over certain things that were happening in one of the other high rooms of the town, a particular room whose location was nevertheless outside my cognizance. Something told me that what was taking place there was specifically devised to affect my existence in a profound manner. At the same time I did not feel myself to be of any consequence in this or any other universe. I was nothing more than an unseen speck lost in the convolutions of strange schemes. And it was this very remoteness from the designs of my dream universe, this feeling of fantastic homelessness amid an alien order of being, that was the source of anxieties I had never before experienced. I was no more than an irrelevant parcel of living tissue caught in a place I should not be, threatened with being snared in some great dredging net of doom, an incidental shred of flesh pulled out of its element of light and into an icy blackness. In the dream nothing supported my existence, which I felt at any moment might be horribly altered or simply ended. In the most far-reaching import of the phrase, my life was of *no matter*.

But still I could not keep my attention from straying into that other room, sensing what elaborate plots were evolving there and what they might mean for my existence. I thought I could see indistinct figures occupying that spacious chamber, a place furnished with only a few chairs of odd design and commanding a dizzying view of the starry blackness. The great round moon of the dream created sufficient illumination for the night's purposes, painting the walls of the mysterious room a deep aquatic blue; the stars, unneeded and ornamental, presided as lesser lamps over this gathering and its nocturnal offices.

As I observed this scene—though not "bodily" present, as is the way with dreams—it became my conviction that certain rooms offered a marvelous solitude for such functions or festivities. Their atmosphere, that intangible quality which exists apart from its composing elements of shape and shade, was of a dreamy cast, a state in which time and space had become deranged. A few moments in these rooms might count as centuries or millennia, and their tiniest niche might encompass a universe. Simultaneously, this atmosphere seemed no different from that of the old rooms, the high and lonely rooms, I had known in waking life, even if *this* room appeared to border on the voids of astronomy and its windows opened onto the infinite outside. Then I began speculating that if the room itself was not one of a unique species, perhaps it was the occupants that had introduced its singular element.

Though each of them was completely draped in a massive cloak, the places in which the material of these garments pushed out and folded inwards as it descended to the floor, along with the unnatural contrivance of the chairs whereupon these creatures were situated, betrayed a peculiarity of formation that held me in a state of both paralyzed terror and spellbound curiosity. What were these beings that their robes should adumbrate such unaccountable configurations? With their tall, angular chairs arranged in a circle, they appeared to be leaning in every direction, like unsettled monoliths. It was as if they were assuming postures that were mysteriously symbolic, locking themselves in patterns hostile to mundane analysis. Above all it was their heads, or at least their topmost segments, that were skewed most radically as they inclined toward one another, nodding in ways heretical to terrestrial anatomy. And it was from this part of their structures that there came forth a soft buzzing noise which seemed to serve them as speech.

But the dream offered another detail which possibly related to the mode of communication among these whispering figures who sat in stagnant moonlight. For projecting out of the bulky sleeves dangling at each figure's side were delicate appendages that appeared to be withered, wilted claws bearing numerous talons that tapered off into drooping tentacles. And all of these stringy digits seemed to be working together with lively and unceasing agitation.

At first sight of these gruesome gestures I felt myself about to awaken, to carry back into the world a sense of terrible enlightenment without sure meaning or possibility of expression in any language except the whispered vows of this eerie sect. But I remained longer in this dream, far longer than was natural. I witnessed further the fidgeting of those shriveled claws, a hyperactive gesticulating which seemed to communicate an intolerable knowledge, some ultimate disclosure concerning the order of things. Such movements suggested an array of repulsive analogies: the spinning legs of spiders, the greedy rubbing of a fly's spindly feelers, the darting tongues of snakes. But my cumulative sensation in the dream was only partially involved with what I would call the *triumph of the grotesque*. This sensation— in keeping with the style of certain dreams—was complicated and exact, allowing no ambiguities or confusions to comfort the dreamer. And what was imparted to my witnessing mind was the vision of a world in a trance—a hypnotized parade of beings sleepwalking to the odious manipulations of their whispering masters, those hooded freaks *who were themselves among the hypnotized*. For there was a power superseding theirs, a power which they served and from which they merely emanated, something which was beyond the universal hypnosis by virtue of its very mindlessness, its awesome idiocy. These cloaked masters, in turn, partook in some measure of godhood, passively presiding as enlightened zombies over the multitudes of the entranced, that frenetic domain of the human.

And it was at this place in my dream that I came to believe that there obtained a terrible intimacy between myself and those whispering effigies of chaos whose existence I dreaded for its very remoteness from mine. Had these beings, for some grim purpose comprehensible only to themselves, allowed me to intrude upon their infernal wisdom? Or was my access to such putrid arcana merely the outcome of some fluke in the universe of atoms, a chance intersection among the demonic elements of which all creation is composed? But the truth was notwithstanding in the face of these insanities; whether by calculation or accident, I was the victim of the unknown. And I succumbed to an ecstatic horror at this insight.

On waking, it seemed that I had carried back with me a tiny, jewel-like particle of this horrific ecstasy, and, by some alchemy of association, this darkly crystalline substance infused its magic into my image of the old town.

Though I formerly believed myself to be the consummate knower of the town's secrets, the following day was one of unforeseen discovery. The streets that I looked upon that motionless morning were filled with new secrets and seemed to lead me to the very essence of the extraordinary. A previously unknown element appeared to have emerged in the composition of the town, one that must have been hidden within its most obscure quarters. I mean to say that while these quaint, archaic façades still put on all the appearance of a dreamlike repose, there presently existed, in my sight, evil stirrings beneath this surface. The town had more wonders than I knew, a cache of unwonted offerings stored out of sight. Yet somehow this formula of deception, of corruption in disguise, served to intensify the town's most attractive aspects: a wealth of unsuspected sensations was now provoked by a few slanting rooftops, a low doorway, or a narrow backstreet. And the mist spreading evenly through the town early that morning was luminous with dreams.

The whole day I wandered in a fevered exaltation throughout the old town, seeing it as if for the first time. I scarcely stopped a moment to rest, and I am sure I did not pause to eat. By late afternoon I might also have been suffering from a strain on my nerves, for I had spent many hours nurturing a rare state of mind in which the purest euphoria was invaded and enriched by currents of fear. Each time I rounded a street-corner or turned my head to catch some beckoning sight, dark tremors were inspired by the hybrid spectacle I witnessed—splendid scenes broken with malign shadows, the lurid and the lovely forever lost in each other's embrace. And when I passed under the arch of an old street and gazed up at the towering structure before me, I was nearly overwhelmed.

My recognition of the place was immediate, though I had never viewed it from my present perspective. Suddenly it seemed I was no longer outside in the street and staring upwards, but was looking down from the room just beneath that peaked roof. It was the highest room on the street, and no window from any of the other houses could see into it. The building itself, like some of those surrounding it, seemed to be empty, perhaps abandoned. I assessed several ways by which I could force entry, but none of these methods was needed: the front door, contrary to my initial observation, was slightly ajar.

The place was indeed abandoned, stripped of wall-hangings

and fixtures, its desolate, tunnel-like hallways visible only in the sickly light that shone through unwashed, curtainless windows. Identical windows also appeared on the landing of each section of the staircase that climbed up through the central part of the edifice like a crooked spine. I stood in a near cataleptic awe of the world I had wandered into, this decayed paradise. It was a venue of strange atmospherics of infinite melancholy and unease, the everlasting residue of some cosmic misfortune. I ascended the stairs of the building with a solemn, mechanical intentness, stopping only when I had reached the top and found the door to a certain room.

And even at the time, I asked myself: could I have entered this room with such unhesitant resolve if I truly expected to find something extraordinary within it? Was it ever my intention to confront the madness of the universe, or at least my own? I had to confess that though I had accepted the benefits of my dreams and fancies, I did not profoundly believe in them. At the deepest level I was their doubter, a thorough skeptic who had indulged a too-free imagination, and perhaps a self-made lunatic.

To all appearances the room was unoccupied. I noted this fact without the disappointment born of real expectancy, but also with a strange relief. Then, as my eyes adjusted to the artificial twilight of the room, I saw the circle of chairs.

They were as strange as I had dreamed, more closely resembling devices of torture than any type of practical or decorative object. Their tall backs were slightly bowed and covered with a coarse hide unlike anything I had ever beheld; their arms were like blades and each had four semicircular grooves cut into them that were spaced evenly across their length; and below were six jointed legs jutting outwards, a feature which transformed each piece into some crablike thing with the apparent ability to scuttle across the floor. If, for a stunned moment, I felt the idiotic desire to install myself in one of these bizarre thrones, this impulse was extinguished upon my observing that the seat of each chair, which at first appeared to be composed of a smooth and solid cube of black glass, was in fact only an open cubicle filled with a murky liquid which quivered strangely when I passed my hand over its surface. As I did this I could feel my entire arm tingle in a way which sent me stumbling backward to the door of that horrible room and which made me loathe every atom of flesh gripping the bones of that limb.

I turned around to exit but was stopped by a figure standing in the doorway. Though I had previously met the man, he now seemed to be someone quite different, someone openly sinister rather than merely enigmatic. When he had disturbed me the day before, I could not have suspected his alliances. His manner had been idiosyncratic but very polite, and he had offered no reason to question his sanity. Now he appeared to be no more that a malignant puppet of madness. From the twisted stance he assumed in the doorway to the vicious and imbecilic expression that possessed the features of his face, he was a thing of strange degeneracy. Before I could back away from him, he took my trembling hand. "Thank you for coming to visit," he said in a voice that was a parody of his former politeness. He pulled me close to him; his eyelids lowered and his mouth widely grinned, as if he were enjoying a pleasant breeze on a warm day.

Then he said to me: "They want you with them on their return. They want their chosen ones."

Nothing can describe what I felt on hearing these words which could only have meaning in a nightmare. Their implications were a quintessence of hellish delirium, and at that instant all the world's wonder suddenly turned to dread. I tried to free myself from the madman's grasp, shouting at him to let go of my hand. "*Your* hand?" he shouted back at me. Then he began to repeat the phrase over and over, laughing as if some sardonic joke had reached a conclusion within the depths of his lunacy. In his foul merriment he weakened, and I escaped. As I rapidly descended the many stairs of the old building, his laughter pursued me as hollow reverberations that echoed far beyond the shadowy spaces of that place.

And that freakish, echoing laughter remained with me as I wandered dazed in darkness, trying to flee my own thoughts and sensations. Gradually the terrible sounds that filled my brain subsided, but they were soon replaced by a new terror—

the whispering of strangers whom I passed on the streets of the old town. And no matter how low they spoke or how quickly they silenced one another with embarrassed throat-clearings or reproving looks, their words reached my ears in fragments that I was able to reconstruct because of their frequent repetition. The most common terms were *deformity* and *disfigurement*. If I had not been so distraught I might have approached these persons with a semblance of civility, cleared my own throat, and said, "I beg your pardon, but I could not help overhearing . . . And what exactly did you mean, if I may ask, when you said . . ." But I discovered for myself what those words meant—*how terrible, poor man*—when I returned to my room and stood before the mirror on the wall, holding my head in balance with a supporting hand on either side.

For only one of those hands was mine.

The other belonged to them.

Life is a nightmare that leaves its mark upon you in order to prove that it is, in fact, real. And to suffer a solitary madness seems the joy of paradise when compared to the extraordinary condition in which one's own madness merely emulates that of the world. I have been lured away by dreams; all is nonsense now.

Let me write, while I still am able, that the transformation has not limited itself. I now find it difficult to continue this manuscript with either hand. These twitching tentacles are not suited for writing in a human manner, and I am losing the will to push my pen across this page. While I have put myself at a great distance from the old town, its influence is undiminished. In these matters there is a terrifying freedom from the recognized laws of space and time. New laws of entity have come to their work as I look helplessly on.

In the interest of others, I have taken precautions to conceal my identity and the precise location of a horror which cannot be helped. Yet I have also taken pains to reveal, as if with malicious intent, the existence and nature of those same horrors. Be that as it may, neither my motives nor my actions matter in the least. They are both well known to the things that whisper in the highest room of an old town. They know what I write and why I am writing it. Perhaps they are even guiding my pen by means of a hand that is an extension of their own. And if I ever wished to see what lay beneath those dark robes, I will soon be able to satisfy this curiosity with only a glance in my mirror.

I must return to the old town, for now my home can be nowhere else. But my manner of passage to that place cannot be the same, and when I enter again that world of dreams it will be by way of a threshold which no human being has ever crossed . . . nor ever shall.

THE GREATER
FESTIVAL OF MASKS

There are only a few houses in the part of town where Noss begins his excursion. Nonetheless, they are spaced in such a way that suggests there had once been a greater number of them that filled out the landscape, like a garden that seems sparse merely because certain growths have withered and others have not yet been planted to replace them. It even occurs to Noss that these hypothetical houses, counterfactual at present, may at some point change places with those which now exist, in order to bestow on the visible a well-earned repose within nullity. For by then they will have served their purpose as features that gave the town an identity. And now is just the season for so many things to pass into emptiness and make way for other entities and modes of being. Such are the declining days of the festival, when the old and the new, the real and the imaginary, truth and deception, all join in the masquerade.

But even at this stage of the festival some have yet to take a large enough interest in tradition to visit one of the shops of costumes and masks. Until recently Noss was among this group. Finally, though, he has decided to visit an establishment whose shelves spill over with costumes and masks, even at this late stage of the festival.

In the course of his little journey, Noss keeps watch as buildings become more numerous, enough to make a street, many narrow streets, a town. He also observes manifold indications of the festival season. These are sometimes baffling, sometimes blatant in nature. For instance, not a few doors have been left ajar, even throughout the night, as if to challenge callers or intruders to discover what waits within. And dim lights are left to burn in empty rooms, or rooms that appear empty if one does not approach their windows with an incautious curiosity and look inside. Less dire are those piles of filthy rags deposited in the middle of certain streets, shredded rags that are easily disturbed by the wind and twist gaily about. At every turn, it seems, Noss comes upon some gesture of festive abandonment: a hat, all style mangled out of it, has been jammed into the space where a board is missing in a high fence; a poster stuck to a crumbling wall has been diagonally torn in half, leaving a scrap of face fluttering at its edges; and into strange pathways of caprice revelers will go, but to have *shorn* themselves just anywhere, to have littered the shadows of doorways and alleys with wiry clippings and tumbling fluff. Reliquiae of the hatless, the faceless, the impetuously groomed. As Noss walks on, he takes only a desultory interest in the sportive occasion he is witnessing for the first time since he settled in this place.

But he becomes more interested as he approaches the center of town, where the houses, the shops, the fences, the walls are more, much more . . . close. There seems barely enough space for a few stars to squeeze their bristling light between the roofs and towers above, and the outsized moon—not a familiar face in this neighborhood—must suffer to be seen only as a fuzzy anonymous glow mirrored in silvery windows. The streets are more tightly strung here, and a single one may have several names compressed into it from end to end. Some of the names may be credited less to deliberate planning, or even the quirks of local history, than to an apparent need for the superfluous. Perhaps a similar need may explain why the buildings in this district exhibit so many pointless embellishments: doors which are elaborately decorated yet will not budge in their frames; massive shutters covering blank walls behind them; enticing balconies, well-railed and promising in their views, but without any means of entrance; stairways that enter dark niches . . . and a dead end. These structural adornments are mysterious indulgences in an area so pressed for room that even shadows must be shared. And so must other things. Backyards, for example, where a few fires still burn, the last of the festival pyres. For in this part of town the season is still at its peak, or at least the signs of its termination have yet to appear. Perhaps celebrants hereabouts are still nudging each other provocatively, still engaging in preposterous escapades they would not ordinarily dare to imagine, and, in general, indulging themselves as if there were no tomorrow. Here the festival is not dead. For the delirium of this celebration does not radiate out from the center of things, but seeps inward from remote margins. Thus, the festival may have begun in an isolated hovel at the edge of town, if not in some forlorn residence in the woods beyond. In any case, its agitations have now reached the heart of this dim region where Noss is about to visit one of the many shops of costumes and masks.

A steep stairway leads him to a shrunken platform of a porch, and a thin door puts him inside the shop whose shelves indeed spill over with costumes and masks. To Noss, these shelves also seem reticent in a way hard to pinpoint, stuffed into silence by wardrobes and faces of dreams. Warily, he pulls at a mask that is over-hanging a high shelf. A heap of them fall down on his head. Backing away from the avalanche of false faces, he looks at the sardonically grinning one in his hand.

"Brilliant choice," says the shopkeeper, who steps out from behind a counter at the back of the shop. "Put it on and let's see. Yes, my gracious, this is excellent. You see how your entire face is well-covered, from the hairline to just beneath the chin and no farther. And at the sides it clings snugly. It doesn't pinch, am I right?" The mask nods in agreement. "Good, that's how it should be. Your ears are unobstructed—you have very nice ones, by the way—in case someone calls out to you while your face is concealed by the mask. It is comfortable, yet secure enough to stay put and not fall off in the heat of activity. You'll see, after a while you won't even know you're wearing it! The holes for the eyes, nostrils, and mouth are perfectly placed for your features. No natural function is inhibited, that is a must. And it looks so good on you, especially up close, though I'm sure also at a distance. Go stand over there in the moonlight. Yes, it was made for you, what do you say? I'm sorry, what?"

Noss walks back toward the shopkeeper and removes the mask. "I said all right. I suppose I'll take this one."

"Fine, as if there were any question about it. Now let me show you some of the other ones, just a few steps this way."

The shopkeeper pulls something down from a high shelf and places it in his customer's hands. What Noss now holds is another mask, but one that somehow seems to be . . . impractical. While the first mask he chose possessed every virtue of conformity to its wearer's face, this mask is neglectful of such advantages. Its surface is uneven, with bulges and depressions which appear unaccommodating at best, and possibly pain-inflicting. And it is so much heavier than the one he picked himself.

"No," says Noss, handing back the mask, "I believe the other will do."

The shopkeeper looks as if he is at a loss for words. He stares at Noss for many moments before saying: "May I ask a personal question? Have you lived, how shall I say this, *here* all your life?"

The shopkeeper is now gesturing beyond the thick glass of the shop's windows. Noss shakes his head in reply.

"Well, then there's no rush. Don't make any hasty decisions. Stay around the shop and think it over, there's still time. In fact, it would be a favor to me. I have to go out for a while, you see, and if you could keep an eye on things I would greatly appreciate it. You'll do it, then? Good. And don't worry," he says, taking a large hat from a peg that poked out of the wall, "I'll be back in no time, no time at all. If someone pays us a visit, just do what you can for them," he shouts before closing the front door behind him.

Now alone, Noss takes a closer look at the shelves stocked with the other kind of mask the shopkeeper had shown him. How different they were from what he conceived a mask should be. Every one of them shared the same impracticalities of shape and weight, as well as having some very oddly placed apertures for ventilation, and too many of them. Outlandish indeed! Noss gives these new masks back to the shelves from which they came, and he holds on tightly to the one that the shopkeeper had said was so perfect for him, so practical in every way. After a vaguely exploratory amble about the shop, Noss finds a stool behind the counter and there falls asleep.

It seems only a few moments later that he is awakened by some sound or other. Collecting his wits, he gazes around looking for its source. Then the sound returns, a soft thudding at the rear of the shop. Hopping down from the stool, Noss passes through a narrow doorway, descends a brief flight of stairs, passes through another doorway, ascends another brief flight of stairs, walks down a short and very low hallway, and eventually arrives at the shop's back door. It rumbles again once or twice.

"Just do what you can for them," Noss remembers. But he looks uneasy.

"Why don't you come around the front?" he shouts through the door. There is no reply, however, only a request.

"Please bring out five of those masks to us. We're just across the yard at the back of the shop. There's a fence. And a fire on the other side. That's where we are now. Well, can you do this or not?"

Noss leans his head into the shadows by the wall: one side of his face is now in darkness while the other is indistinct, blurred by a strange glare which is only an impostor of true light. "Give me a moment, I'll meet you there," he finally replies. "Did you hear me?"

There is no response from the other side. Noss opens the door a little and peers out into the backyard of the shop. What he sees is a patch of scruffy ground surrounded by the tall wooden slabs of a fence. On the other side of the fence is a fire, though not a large one, just as the voice said. But whatever signs of pranksterism Noss perceives or is able to fabricate to himself, there is no defying the traditions of the festival, even if one can claim to have merely adopted this town and its seasonal practices, however *rare* they may be. For innocence and excuses are not harmonious with the spirit of this fabulously infrequent occasion. Compliantly, then, Noss retrieves the masks and brings them to the rear door of the shop. Cautiously, he steps out.

When he reaches the far end of the yard—a much greater distance from the shop than it had seemed—he sees a reddish glow of fire through the cracks in the fence, which has a door leaning loose on its hinges and only a hole for a handle. Setting on the ground the masks he is carrying, Noss squats down and peers through the hole. On the other side of the fence is a dark yard exactly like the one on his side, save for the fire burning there. Gathered around the blaze are several figures—five, perhaps four—with hunched shoulders and spines curving toward the light of the flames. They are all wearing masks which at first seem securely fitted to their faces. But one by one these masks appear to loosen and slip down, as if each is losing hold upon its wearer. Finally, one of the figures pulls his mask off completely and tosses it into the fire, where it curls and shrinks into a wad of bubbling blackness. The others follow this action when their time comes. Relieved of their masks, the figures resume their shrugging stance. But the light of the fire now shines on four, yes four, smooth and faceless faces.

"These are the wrong ones, you little idiot," says someone whom he had not noticed standing in the shadows. And Noss can only stare dumbly as a hand snatches up the masks and draws them into the darkness. "We have no more use for *these*!" the voice shouts.

Noss runs in retreat toward the shop, the five masks striking his narrow back and falling face-up on the ground. For he has gained a glimpse of the speaker in the shadows and now understands why *those* masks are no good to them now.

Once inside the shop, Noss leans upon the counter to catch his breath. Then he looks up and sees that the shopkeeper has returned.

"There were some masks I brought out to the fence. They were the wrong ones," he says to the shopkeeper.

"No trouble at all," the other replies. "I'll see that the right ones are delivered. Don't worry, there's still time. And how about you, then?"

"Me?"

"And the masks, I mean."

"Oh, I'm sorry to have bothered you in the first place. It's not at all what I thought. That is, maybe I should just—"

"Nonsense! You can't leave now. Give me your trust, and I'll take care of everything. I want you to go to a place where they know how to handle cases like this. You're not the only one who is a little frightened tonight. It's right around the corner, this—no, *that* way, and across the street. It's a tall gray building, but it hasn't been there very long so watch you don't miss it. And you have to go down some stairs around the side. Now will you please follow my advice?"

Noss nods obediently.

"Good, you won't be sorry. Now go straight there. Don't stop for anyone or anything. And here, don't forget these," the shopkeeper reminds Noss, handing him a pair of masks that are not a match. "Good luck!"

Though there doesn't seem to be anyone or anything to stop for, Noss does stop once or twice and dead in his tracks, as if someone behind him has just called his name. Then he thoughtfully caresses his chin and smooth cheeks. He also touches other parts of his face, frantically, before proceeding toward the tall gray building. By the time he reaches the stairway at the side, he cannot keep his hands off himself. Finally Noss puts on one of the masks, this being the semblance that was sized so well for him. But somehow it no longer fits as it once did. It keeps slipping as he descends the stairs, which look worn down by countless footsteps, bowed in the middle by the tonnage of time. Yet Noss remembers the shopkeeper saying that this place had not been here very long.

The room at the bottom, which Noss now enters, looks very old and is very quiet. At this late stage of the festival it is crowded with occupants who do nothing but sit silently in the shadows, with a face here and there reflecting the dull light. These faces are horribly simple, falling far short of countenances exhibiting familiar articulations. But gradually they are assuming features, though not those they once had. And the developments in progress, if the ear listens closely, are not entirely silent. Perhaps this is how a garden might sound if it could be heard growing in the dead of night. But here, on this night, the only sound is the soft creaking of new faces breaking through old flesh. And they are sprouting very nicely. With a torpid solemnity, Noss now removes the mask he is wearing and tosses it away. It falls to the floor and lies there sardonically grinning, fixed in an expression that, in days to come, many will find strange and wonder at.

For the old festival has ended so that a greater festival may begin. And of the old time nothing will be said, because nothing will be known. But the masks of that departed era, forgotten in a world that has no tolerance for monotony, will find something to remember. And perhaps they will speak of those days as they loiter on the threshold of doors that do not open, or in the darkness at the summit of stairways leading nowhere.

THE MUSIC OF THE MOON

With considerable interest, and some disquiet, I listened while a small, pale man named Tressor told of his remarkable experience, his mild voice barely breaking the quiet of a moonlit room. It seems he was one of those who could not rest and, as a poor substitute for unconsciousness, habitually took to the streets in search of what our city has to offer by way of diversion. There are nightspots, of course, where one may pass the hours until daybreak. But their entertainments soon grow stale for the perpetually sleepless, who in any event have no use for a crowd that is wide-awake *by choice*. Nevertheless, there are certain individuals, and Tressor was one of them, to whom our city may disclose its nocturnal mysteries. In the absence of dreams that preserve the balance of the ordinary world, who would not be on the lookout for beguilements to replace them?

Indeed, there are enchantments that nearly make amends for one's stolen slumber. To gaze up and glimpse some unusual shape loping across steep roofs with a bewildering agility might well be compensation for many nights of sleepless hell. Or to hear sinister whispers in one of our narrow streets, and to follow them through the night without ever being able to close in on them, yet without their ever fading in the slightest degree—this very well might relieve the wearing effects of an awful wakefulness. And what if these incidents remain inconclusive, if they are left as merely enticing episodes, undocumented and underdeveloped? May they not still serve their purpose? And how many has our city *saved* in this manner, staying their hands from the knife, the rope, or the poison vial? Yet if there is any truth to what I believe has happened to Tressor, he just may have become lost in an exploit of uncommon decisiveness.

I should say that when Tressor told me his story, I believed it to be an exaggeration, an embellished version of one of his nightlong adventures. It seems that during one of his blank nights of insomnia, he had wandered into the older section of town where the activity is as unreserved as it is constant throughout the night. As I have previously stated, Tressor was among those who was not averse to whatever obscure caper our city might extend to him. Thus, he gave more than modest scrutiny to a character standing by the steps of a rotten old building, noting that this man seemed to be loitering to no special purpose, his hands buried in the pockets of his overcoat and his eyes gazing upon the passersby with a look of profound patience. The building outside of which he stood was itself a rather plain structure, one notable only for its windows, the way some faces are distinctive solely by virtue of an interesting pair of eyes. These windows were not the slender rectangles of most of the other buildings along the street, but were half-circles divided into several slice-shaped panes. And in the moonlight they seemed to shine in a particularly striking way, though possibly this was merely an effect of contrast to the surrounding area, where a few clean pieces of glass will inevitably draw attention to themselves. I cannot say for certain which may be upheld as the explanation.

In any case, Tressor was passing by this building, the one with those windows, when the man standing by the steps shoved something at him, leaving it in his grasp. And as he did so, he looked straight and deep into poor Tressor's eyes, which the insomniac was quick to lower and fix upon the object in his hand. What had been given to him was a small sheet of paper, and further down the street Tressor paused by a lamp post to read the thin lines of tiny letters. Printed in black ink on one side of a coarse, rather gummy grade of pulp, the handbill announced an evening's entertainment later that same night at the building he had just passed. Tressor looked back at the man who had handed him this announcement, but he was no longer standing in his place. For a moment this seemed very odd, for despite his casual, even restful appearance of waiting for no one and for nothing, this man did seem to have been somehow attached to that particular spot outside the building. Now his sudden absence caused Tressor to feel . . . confused, which is to say, captivated.

Once again Tressor scanned the page in his hand, absent-mindedly rubbing it between his thumb and fingers. It did have a strange texture, like ashes mixed with grease. Soon, however, he began to feel that he was giving the matter too much thought; and, as he resumed his insomniac peregrinations, he flung the sheet aside. But before it reached the pavement, the handbill was snatched out of the air by someone walking very swiftly in the opposite direction. Glancing back, Tressor found it difficult to tell which of the other pedestrians had retrieved the paper. He then continued on his way.

Later that night, he returned to the building whose windows were shining half-circles. Entering through the front door, which was unlocked and unattended, he proceeded down silent, empty hallways. Along the walls were lamps in the form of dimly glowing spheres. Turning a corner, Tressor was suddenly faced with a black abyss, within which an unlighted stairway began to emerge as his eyes grew accustomed to the greater dark. After some hesitation he went up the stairs, playing a brittle music upon the old planks. From the first landing of the stairway he could see the soft lights above, and rather than turning back he ascended toward them. The second floor, however, much resembled the first, as did the third and all the succeeding floors. Reaching the heights of the building, Tressor began to roam around once again, even opening some of the doors.

But most of the rooms behind these doors were dark and empty, and the moonlight that shone through the perfectly clear windows fell upon bare, dust-covered floors and unadorned walls. Tressor was about to turn around and head back outside when he spotted at the end of the last hallway a door with a faint yellow aura leaking out at its edges. He walked up to this door, which was slightly opened, and cautiously pushed it back.

Peering into the room, Tressor saw the yellowish globe of light which hung from the ceiling. Scanning slowly down the walls, he spied small, shadowlike things moving in corners and along the floor molding—the consequences of inept housekeeping, he concluded. Then he saw something by the far wall which made him withdraw back into the hallway. What he had glimpsed were four strangely contoured figures, the tallest of which was nearly his height, while the smallest was half his size. Once out in the hallway, though, he found these images had become clearer in his mind. He now felt almost sure of their true nature, though I have to confess that I could not imagine what they might have been until he spoke the key word: "cases."

Venturing back into the room, Tressor stood before the closed cases which in all likelihood belonged to a quartet of musicians. They looked very old and were bound like books in some murky cloth. Tressor ran his fingers along this material, then before long began fingering the tarnished metal latches of the violin case. But he suddenly stopped when he saw a group of shadows rising on the wall in front of him.

"Why have you come in here?" asked a voice which sounded both exhausted and malicious.

"I saw the light," answered Tressor without turning around, still crouching over the violin case. Somehow the sound of his own voice echoing in that empty room disturbed him more than that of his interrogator, though he could not at the moment say why this was. He counted four shadows on the wall, three of them tall and trim, and the fourth somewhat smaller but with an enormous, misshapen head.

"Stand up," ordered the same voice as before.

Tressor stood up.

"Turn around."

Tressor slowly turned around. And he was relieved to see standing before him three rather ordinary-looking men and a woman whose head was enveloped by pale, ragged clouds of hair. Moreover, among the men was the one who had given Tressor the handbill earlier that night. But he now seemed to be much taller than he had been outside in the street.

"You handed me the paper," Tressor reminded the man as if trying to revive an old friendship. And again his voice sounded queer to him as it reverberated in that empty room.

The tall man looked to his companions, surveying each of the other three faces in turn, as though reading some silent message in their expressionless features. Then he removed a piece of paper from inside his coat.

"You mean this," he said to Tressor.

"Yes, that's it."

They all smiled gently at him, and the tall man said, "Then you're in the wrong place. You should be one floor up. But the main stairway won't take you to it. There's another, smaller flight of stairs in the back hallway. You should be able to see it. Are your eyes good?"

"Yes."

"Good as they look?" asked one of the other men.

"I can see very well, if that's what you mean."

"Yes, that's exactly what we mean," said the woman.

Then the four of them stepped back to make a path for Tressor, two on either side of him, and he started to walk from the room.

"There are already some people upstairs for the concert," said the tall man as Tressor reached the door. "We will be up shortly—to play!"

"Yes . . . yes . . . yes," muttered the others as they began fumbling with the dark cases containing their instruments.

"*Their* voices," thought Tressor, "not my voice."

As Tressor later explained it to me, the voices of the musicians, unlike his own, made no echoes of any kind in the empty room. Undeterred by the implications of this sonic abnormality, Tressor went to find the stairway, which at first looked like an empty shaft of blackness in the corner of the back hall. Guided by the flimsy railing that twisted in a spiral, he reached the uppermost level of the old building. Here the hallways were much narrower than those below, tight passages lit by spherical lamps caked with dust and hung at irregular intervals. There were also fewer doors, each of which was barely more than a cutout in the wall around it and thus quite difficult to discern, more easily found by touch it would seem than by sight. But Tressor's eyes were very good, as he claimed, and he soon found the entrance to a room where a number of people were already gathered, just as the musicians had said.

I can imagine that it was not easy for Tressor to decide whether or not to go through with what he had started that night. If the inability to sleep sometimes leads a sufferer into strange or perilous consolations, Tressor still retained enough of a daylight way of thought to make a compromise. He did not enter the room where he saw people slumped down in seats scattered about, the black silhouettes of human heads visible only in the moonlight which poured through the pristine glass of those particular windows. Instead, he hid in the shadows farther down the hallway. And when the musicians arrived upstairs, burdened with their instruments, they filed into the moonlit room without suspecting Tressor's presence outside. The door closed behind them with a hardly audible click.

For a few moments there was only silence, a purer silence than Tressor had ever known, like the silence of a dark, lifeless world. Then sound began to enter the silence, but so inconspicuously that Tressor could not tell when the absolute silence had ended and an embellished silence had begun. Sound became music, slow music in the soft darkness, music somewhat muffled as it passed through the intervening door. At first there was only a single note wavering in a universe of darkness, compelling those who heard it to an understanding of its subtle voice. This lone note carried an abundance of distinct overtones, and a few beats later a second note produced the same effect; then another note, and another, each of them mingling to create an incalculable proliferation of slightly dissonant harmonies. There was now more music than could possibly be contained by that earlier silence, expansive as it may have seemed. Soon there was no space remaining for silence, or perhaps music and silence became confused, indistinguishable from each other, as colors may merge into whiteness. And at last, for Tressor, that interminable sequence of wakeful nights, each a mirror to the one before it and the one to follow, was finally broken.

When Tressor awoke, the light of a quiet gray dawn filled the narrow hallway where he lay hunched between peeling walls. Recalling in a moment the events of the previous night, he pushed himself to his feet and began walking toward the room whose door was still closed. He put his ear up to the rough wood but heard no sounds on the other side. In his mind a memory of wonderful music rose up and then quickly faded. As before, the music sounded muffled to him, diminished in its power because he had been too fearful to enter the room where the music was played. But he entered it now.

And he was bemused to see the audience still in their seats, which were all facing four empty chairs and four abandoned instruments of varying size. The musicians themselves were nowhere in sight.

The spectators were all dressed in white hooded robes woven of some gauzy material, almost like ragged shrouds wrapped tightly around them. They were very quiet and very still, perhaps sleeping that profound sleep from which Tressor had just risen. But there was something about this congregation that filled Tressor with a strange fear, strange because he also sensed that they were completely helpless, and yet content to be so—hypnotics in ecstasy. As his eyes became sharper in the grayish twilight of the room, the robes worn by these paralyzed figures began to look more and more like bandages of some kind, a heavy white netting which bound them securely. "But they were not bandages, or robes, or shrouds," Tressor finally told me. "They were webs, thick layers of webs which I first thought covered everyone's entire body."

But this was only how it appeared to Tressor from his perspective behind the mummified audience. For as he moved along the outer edge of the terrible gathering, progressing toward the four empty chairs at the front of the room, he saw that each stringy white cocoon was woven to expose the face of its inhabitant. He also saw that the expressions on these faces were very similar. They might almost have been described as serene, Tressor told me, if only those faces had been whole.

But none of them seemed to have any eyes. The crowd was faced in the same direction to witness a spectacle it could no longer see, gazing at nothing with bleeding sockets. All save one of them, as Tressor finally discovered.

At the end of a rather chaotic row of chairs in the back of the room, one member of the audience stirred in his seat. As Tressor slowly approached this figure, with vague thoughts of rescue in his mind, he noticed that its eyelids were shut. Without delaying for an instant, he began tearing at the webs which imprisoned the victim, speaking words of hope as he worked at the horrible mesh. But then the closed eyelids of the bound figure popped open and looked around, ultimately focusing on Tressor.

"You're the only one," said Tressor, laboring at the webby bonds.

"Shhhh," said the other, "I'm waiting."

Tressor paused in confusion, his fingers tangled with a gruesome stuff which felt sticky and abrasive, intolerably strange to touch.

"They might return," insisted Tressor, even though he was not entirely sure whom he meant by "they."

"They *will* return," answered the other's soft but excited voice. "With the moon they will return with their wonderful music."

Appalled by this enigma, Tressor began to back away. And I suspect that from within a number of those hollow sockets, four of them to be exact, the tiny eyes of strange creatures were watching him as he fled that horrible room.

Afterward Tressor visited me night after night to tell me about the music, until it seemed I could almost hear it myself and could tell his story as my own. Soon he talked only about the music, as he recalled hearing it somewhat dulled by a closed door. When he tried to imagine what it would be like to have heard the music, as he phrased it, "in the flesh," it was obvious that he had forgotten the fate of those who did hear it in this way. His voice became more and more faint as the music grew louder and clearer in his mind. Then one night Tressor stopped coming to visit me.

Now it seems I am the one who cannot sleep, especially when I see the moon hovering above our city—the moon all fat and pale, glaring down on us from within its gauzy webs of clouds. How can I rest beneath its enchanting gaze? And how can I keep myself from straying into a certain section of town as night after night I wander strange streets alone?

THE JOURNAL OF
J.P. DRAPEAU

INTRODUCTION

It was late and we had been drinking. My friend, a poet who can become very excitable at times, looked across the table at me. Then he revived a pet grievance of his as though I had not heard it all before.

"Where is the writer," he began, "who is unstained by any habits of the human, who is the ideal of everything alien to living, and whose eccentricity, in its darkest phase, turns in on itself to form increasingly more complex patterns of strangeness? Where is the writer who has lived out his entire life in a prodigious dream that began on his day of birth, if not long before? Where is the writer from some molding backwater of the earth—the city of Bruges itself, that withered place which some dreamer has described as 'a corpse of the Middle Ages that sings to itself from innumerable bell-towers and lays bony bridges across the black veins of its old canals.'

"But perhaps our writer's home would have to be an even older, more decaying Bruges in some farther, more obscure Flanders . . . the one envisioned by Bruegel and by Ensor. Where is the writer who was begotten by two passionate masks in the course of those macabre festivities called *kermesse*? Who was abandoned to develop in his own way, left to a lonely evolution in shadowed streets and beside sluggish canals. Who was formed by the dreams around him as much as those within him, and who had satiated himself with recondite learning. Where is this

writer, the one whose entangled hallucinations could be accom-
modated only by the most intimate of diaries? And this diary,
this journal of the most unnecessary man who ever lived, would
be a record of the most questionable experiences ever known,
and the most beautiful."

"Of course, there is no such writer," I replied. "But there's
always Drapeau. Out of anyone I could name, he most nearly
meets, if I may say, those rather *severe* prerequisites of yours.
Living the whole of his life in Bruges, keeping those notebooks
of his, and he—"

But my friend the poet only moaned in despair:
"Drapeau, always Drapeau."

EXCERPTS FROM THE JOURNAL

April 31, 189—

I have noticed that certain experiences are left to languish in
the corners of life, passed by like waifs on the street, as if they
should be dissuaded from circulating too freely among legiti-
mate persons. Since childhood, for example, not one day has
passed in which I have failed to hear the *music of graveyards*. It
sounds everywhere I go—a resonant chorus that fills the air and
sometimes drowns out the voices of those who still live. And yet,
to my knowledge, never has another soul on earth made mention
of this ubiquitous singing, which vibrates even in the currents of
our blood. Is the circulation of upright society so poor that it
cannot carry these dead notes? It must be a mere trickle!

December 24, 189—

Two tiny corpses, one male and the other female, rattle around
that enormous closet in my bedroom. Though deceased, still
they are quick enough to hide themselves whenever I need to
enter the closet to retrieve something. I keep various odds and
ends in there, stuffed into trunks or baskets and piled all over
the place. I can't even see the floor or the walls any longer, and

only if I hold a light high over my head can I study the layers of cobwebs floating about near the ceiling. After I close the door of the closet, its two miniature inhabitants resume their activities. Their voices are only faint squeaks which during the day hardly bother me at all. But sometimes I am kept awake far into the night by those interminable conversations of theirs.

May 31, 189—

After tossing about for most of the night, I went out for a walk. I had not gone far when I became spectator to a sad scene. Some yards ahead of me on the street, an old man was being forcibly led from a house by two other men who were quite large. They had him in restraints and were delivering him to a waiting vehicle. Laughing hysterically, the man was apparently destined for the asylum. As the scuffling trio reached the street, the eyes of the laughing man met my own. Suddenly he stopped laughing. Then, in a burst of resistance, he broke free of his escorts and ran right up to me.

"Never speak out," he said frantically, almost weeping. "Never say a word about the things you know. I can tell by the look in your eyes."

"But I am just an ordinary person," I said, seeing that his captors were approaching.

"Swear!" he demanded. "Or they will have us all."

By then, however, his pursuers had caught up with him. As they dragged him off he began laughing just as before, and the peals of his laughter, in the early morning quiet, were soon devoured by the pealing of church bells. It was at that moment that I decided to heed the old man's warning and disguise certain perceptions of mine in the language of whimsy. Or leave them out altogether from these pages on the chance that someone might find them while I am still alive.

August 1, 189—

As a child I maintained some very strange notions. For instance, I used to believe that during the night, while I slept, demons removed parts of my body and played games with them, hiding my arms and legs, rolling my head across the floor. Of course I abandoned this belief as soon as I entered school, but it was not until much later that I discovered the truth about it. After assimilating many facts from various sources and allowing them to mingle in my mind, I was prepared for the realization. It happened one night as I was crossing a bridge that stretched over a narrow canal. (This was in a part of town fairly distant from where I live.) Pausing for a moment, as I routinely do when crossing one of these bridges, I gazed not down into the dark waters of the canal, but upwards into the night sky. It was those stars, I knew that now. Certain of them had been promised specific parts of my body. In the darkest hours of the night, when one is unusually sensitive to such things, I could— and still can, though just barely—feel the force of these stars tugging away at various points, eager for the moment of my death when each of them might carry off that part of me which is theirs by right. Of course a child would misinterpret this experience. And how often I have found that every superstition has its basis in truth.

October 9, 189—

Last night I visited one of the little theaters that operate here-abouts and stood at the back for a while. Onstage was a magi-cian, his shiny black hair parted straight down the middle, with full prestidigitorial regalia about him: a long box to his left (moons and stars), a tall box to his right (oriental designs), and before him a low table covered with a red velvet cloth lit-tered with diverse objects. The audience, a full house, cheered wildly after each trick he performed. At one point the magician divided the various sections of his assistant into separate boxes which he then proceeded to move to distant areas of the stage, while the dismembered hands and feet continued to wiggle about and the decapitated head laughed with a piercing inten-sity. The audience was at great pains to express its amusement. "Isn't it incredible!" exclaimed a man standing beside me. "If you say so," I replied, and then headed for the exit, realizing that for me such things only provoke my rage against a world that applauds trumped-up illusions while denying or demeaning those that create the very lives they are living. No *real* illusion will ever gain their favor, or even their attention. They would rather be bound inside a heavy chest wrapped with chains and thrown into the deepest waters. As would I.

November 1, 189—

From the earliest days of human life there have existed persons, almost all of us in fact, who hold that the visible world is only a mere mote in the totality of being. Everything we witness is thereby translated into an indicator of an unseen order of being that expresses itself by means of the gross materials we perceive with our senses. Hence, it may seem that a tree is not a tree but a signpost to another realm, a spectral thing full of strange suggestion; that a house is not a house but a threshold by which we may pass into another home, one more suited to our nameless yearnings; that an empty street at twilight may intimate another side of existence, one that complements this side of things and consoles us for its imperfections.

But is there really another world that overshadows ours? Who can say, and why should we care? We might just as truly claim that worlds which seem resistant to our sensory detection are but parasites of the only mystery there is—our own lives. That we benefit by our unknowingness is not an uncommon idea. It is also not a welcome notion to those who would believe our destiny to be presided over by invisible powers. This is the suspicion we must never attempt to verify: that the whole of creation might best be pictured as an untenanted room filled with the echoes of nothingness. Why should this condition, this intimation of the unreal, be insufficient for our spiritual requirements?

January 1, 189—

There is a solitary truth which, whether for good or ill I don't know, cannot be expressed on this earth. This is very strange, since everything—outward scenes as much as inward ones—

suggests this truth and like some fantastic game of charades is always trying to coax the secret into the open. The eyes of certain crudely fashioned dolls are especially suggestive. And distant laughter. In rare moments I feel myself very close to setting it down in my journal, just as I would any other revelation. It would only be a few sentences, I'm sure. But whenever I feel them beginning to take shape in my mind, the page before me will not welcome my pen. Afterward I become fatigued with my failure and suffer headaches that may last for days. At these times I also tend to see odd things reflected in windows. Even after a full week has passed I may continue to wake up in the middle of the night, the semidarkness of my room faintly reverberant with a voice that cries out to me from nowhere.

March 30, 190—

Out of sheer inattentiveness I had stared at my reflection in the mirror a little too deeply. I should say that this mirror has been hanging in my room for more years, I would guess, than I have been on this earth. It's no surprise, then, that sooner or later it would get the edge on me. Up to a certain point there were no problems to speak of: there were only my eyes, my nose, my mouth, and that was that. But then it began to seem that those eyes were regarding me, rather than I them; that that mouth was about to speak of things outside of my knowledge. Finally, I realized that an entirely different creature was hiding behind my face, making it wholly unrecognizable to me. Let me say that I spent considerable time reshaping my reflection into what it should be.

Later, when I was out walking, I stopped dead on the street. Ahead of me, standing beneath a lamp hanging from an old wall, was the outline of a figure of my general size and proportions. He was looking the other way but very stiffly and very tense, as if waiting anxiously for the precise moment when he would suddenly twist about-face. If that should happen, I knew what I would see: my eyes, my nose, my mouth, and behind those features a being strange beyond all description. I retraced my steps back home and went immediately to bed.

But I couldn't sleep. All night long a greenish glow radiated from the mirror in triumph.

No Date

I had just finished a book in which there is an old town strung with placid meandering canals. I closed the book and went over to the window. This is an old town, if medieval may be thought old, strung with placid meandering canals. The town depicted in the book is often enwrapped in mist. This town is often enwrapped in mist. The book's town has close crumbling houses, odd arching bridges, innumerable church towers, and narrow twisting streets that end in queer little courtyards. So has this one, needless to say. And the infinitely hollow bells in that book, tolling the arrival of each lambent morning and sullen twilight, is the same as your sounding bells, my adorable little town. Thus, I pass easily between one town and the other, pleasantly confusing them.

Oh my storybook town, how privileged I have been to suffer a few brief chapters in your sumptuous history of decay. I have studied your most obscure passages and found them as dark as the waters of your canals.

My town, my storybook, myself—how long we have held on! But it seems we will have to make up for this endurance and each, in our turn, must disappear. Every brick of yours, every bone of mine, every word in our book . . . everything gone forever. Everything, perhaps, except the sound of those bells haunting an empty mist through an eternal twilight.

VASTARIEN

Within the blackness of his sleep a few lights began to glow like candles in a cloistered cell. Their illumination was unsteady and dim, issuing from no definite source. Nonetheless, he now discovered many shapes beneath the shadows: tall buildings whose rooftops nodded groundward, wide buildings whose façades followed the curve of a street, dark buildings whose windows and doorways tilted like badly hung paintings. And even if he found himself unable to fix his own location in this scene, he knew where his dreams had delivered him once more.

Even as the warped structures multiplied in his vision, crowding the lost distance, he possessed a sense of intimacy with each of them, a special knowledge of the spaces inside them and of the streets which coiled themselves around their mass. Once again he knew the depths of their foundations, where an obscure life seemed to establish itself, a sequestered civilization of echoes flourishing among groaning walls. Yet upon his probing more extensively into such interiors, certain difficulties presented themselves: stairways that wandered off-course into useless places; caged elevators that urged unwanted stops on their passengers; thin ladders ascending into a maze of shafts and conduits, the dark valves and arteries of a petrified and monstrous organism.

And he knew that every corner of this corroded world was prolific with choices, even if they had to be made blindly in a place where clear consequences and a hierarchy of possibilities were lacking. For there might be a room whose decor exuded a desolate serenity which at first attracts the visitor, who then discovers certain figures enveloped in plush furniture, figures that do not move or speak but only stare; and, concluding that these weary manikins have exercised a bizarre indulgence in repose, the visitor must ponder the alternatives: to linger or to leave?

Eluding the claustral enchantments of such rooms, his gaze now roamed the streets of this dream and scanned the altitudes beyond high sloping roofs. The stars seemed to be no more than silvery cinders which showered up from the mouths of great chimneys and clung to something dark and dense heaving above, a material presence that slouched and slumped, nearly lowering over the horizon. It appeared to him that certain high towers nearly breached this sagging blackness, stretching themselves nightward to attain the farthest possible remove from the world below. And toward the peak of one of the highest towers he spied vague silhouettes that moved hectically in a bright window, twisting and leaning upon the glass like shadow-puppets in the fever of some mad dispute.

Through the mazy streets his vision slowly glided, as if carried along by a sluggish draft. Darkened windows reflected the beams of grotesquely configured streetlamps, and lighted windows betrayed strange scenes which were left behind long before their full mystery could overwhelm the dreaming traveler. Wandering into thoroughfares more remote, he soared past cluttered gardens and crooked gates, drifted alongside a fence of rotted palings that seemed to teeter into an abyss, and floated over bridges that arched above the purling waters of black canals.

Near a certain streetcorner, a place of supernatural clarity and stillness, he saw two figures standing beneath the crystalline glaze of a lantern ensconced high upon a wall of carved stone. Their shadows were perfect columns of blackness upon the livid pavement; their faces were a pair of faded masks concealing profound schemes. And they appeared to have lives of their own, with no awareness of their dreaming observer, who wished only to live with these specters and know *their* dreams, to remain in this place that owed nothing to corporeal existence.

Never, it seemed, could he be forced to abandon this domain of wayward wonders. *Never.*

Victor Keirion awoke with a brief convulsion of his limbs, as if he had been chaotically scrambling to break his fall from an imaginary height. For a moment he held his eyes closed, hoping to preserve the dissipating euphoria of the dream. Finally he blinked once or twice. Moonlight through a curtainless window allowed him the image of his outstretched arms and his somewhat twisted hands. Releasing his awkward hold on the edge of the sheeted mattress, he rolled onto his back. Then he groped around until his fingers found the cord dangling from the light above the bed. A small, barely furnished room appeared.

He pushed himself up and reached toward the painted metal nightstand. Through the spaces between his fingers he saw the pale gray binding of a book and some of the dark letters tooled upon its cover: V, S, R, N. Suddenly he withdrew his hand without touching the book, for the magical intoxication of the dream had died, and he feared that he would not be able to revive it.

Freeing himself from coarse bedcovers, he planted his feet on the cold floor, elbows resting on his legs and hands loosely folded. His hair and eyes were pale and his complexion rather grayish, suggesting the color of certain clouds or that of long confinement. The only window in the room was just a few steps away, but he kept himself from approaching it, from even glancing in its direction. He knew exactly what he would see at that time of night: tall buildings, wide buildings, dark buildings, a scattering of stars and lights, and some lethargic movement in the streets below.

In so many ways the city outside the window was a semblance of that other place, which now seemed impossibly far off and inaccessible. But the likeness was evident only to his inner vision, only in the recollected images he formed when his eyes were closed or out of focus. It would be difficult to conceive of a creature for whom *this* world—its bare form seen with open eyes—represented a coveted paradise.

Now standing before the window, his hands deep in the pockets of a papery bathrobe, he saw that something was missing from the view, some crucial property that was denied to the stars above and the streets below, some unearthly essence needed to save them. Though unspoken, the word *unearthly* reverberated in the room. In that place and at that hour, the paradoxical absence, the missing quality, became clear to him: it was the element of unreality, or perhaps of a reality so saturated with its own presence that it had made a leap into the unreal.

Such was the secret sanctuary of Victor Keirion, a votary of that wretched sect of souls who believe that the only value of this world lies in its power—at certain times—to suggest another. Nevertheless, the place he now surveyed through the high window could never be anything but the most gauzy phantom of that other place, nothing save a shadowy mimic of the anatomy of that great dream. And though there were indeed times when one might be deceived, isolated moments when a gift for disguise triumphed, the impersonation could never be perfect or lasting. No true challenge to the rich unreality of Vastarien, where every formation suggested a thousand others, every sound disseminated everlasting echoes, every word founded a world. No horror, no joy was the equal of the abysmally vibrant sensations known in this place that was elsewhere, this spellbinding retreat where all experiences were interwoven to compose fantastic textures of feeling, a fine and dark tracery of limitless patterns. For everything in the unreal points to the infinite, and everything in Vastarien was unreal, unbounded by the strictures of existing. Even its most humble aspects proclaimed this truth: was there anything or anywhere in tedious actuality that could conjure the abundant and strange imaginings in the dream?

Then, as he focused his eyes upon a distant part of the city, he recalled the place that had opened the door to his long-sought abode of exquisite disfigurations.

Nothing of what lay within was intimated by its modest entranceway: a rectangle of smudged glass within another rectangle of scuffed wood, a battered thing lodged within a brick wall at the bottom of a stairway leading down from a crumbling street. And it pushed easily inward, merely a delicate formality between the underground shop and the outside world. Inside was an open room of vaguely circular shape that seemed more like the lobby of an old hotel than a bookstore. The circumference of the room was composed of crowded shelves whose separate sections were joined to one another to create a polygon of eleven sides, with a long desk standing where a twelfth would have been. Beyond the desk stood more bookshelves, their considerable length leading into shadows. At the furthest point from this part of the shop, Victor Keirion began his circuit of the shelves, which appeared so promising in their array of ruddy bindings, like remnants of a luxuriant autumn.

Very soon, however, he felt betrayed as the mystique of the Librairie de Grimoires was stripped away to reveal, in his eyes, a sideshow of charlatanry. For this disillusionment he had only himself to blame. It was his own fault that he continually subjected himself to the discrepancy between what he hoped to find and what he actually found in such establishments. In truth, there was little basis for his belief that there existed some arcana of a different kind altogether from that tendered by the books before him, all of which were sodden with an obscene reality. The other worlds portrayed in these books served only as annexes of this one; they were impostors of the authentic unreality which was the only redemption for Victor Keirion. And it was this *terminal* point that he sought, not those guidebooks of the "way" to useless destinations, heavens or hells that were mere pretexts for circumnavigating the real and reveling in it. For he dreamed of shadowed volumes that preached no earthly catechisms but delineated only a tenebrous liturgy of the spectral and rites of salvation by way of meticulous derangement. His absolute: to dwell among the ruins of reality.

And it seemed to surpass all probability that there existed no bibliographic representation of this dream, no elaboration of this vision in a delirious bible that would be the blight of all others—a scripture that would begin with portents of apocalypse and end with the wreck of all creation.

He had, in fact, come upon passages in certain books that approached this ideal, hinting to the reader—almost admonishing him—that the pages before his eyes were about to offer a

view from the abyss and cast a wavering light on desolate hallucinations. *To become the wind in the dead of winter and howl
the undoing of all that would abide in warmth and light.* So
might begin an enticing verse in a volume of esoterica. But soon
the bemazed visionary would falter, retracting the promised
flight to emaciated landscapes of unbeing, perhaps offering an
apologetics for this lapse into the unreal. The work would then
take up the timeworn theme, disclosing its true purpose in bela-
boring the most futile and profane of all ambitions: the dream
of attaining some untainted good, with mystic knowledge as its
drudge. The vision of a disastrous enlightenment was conjured
up in passing and then cast aside. What remained was invariably a metaphysics as systematically trivial and debased as the
world it purported to transcend, a manual outlining the path to
some hypothetical state of pure glory. What remained *lost* was
the revelation that nothing ever known has ended in glory; that
all which ends does so in exhaustion, confusion, and debris.

All the same, a book that contained even a deceitful gesture
toward Victor Keirion's truly eccentric absolute might indeed
serve his purpose. Directing the attention of a bookseller to
selected contents of such books, he would say: "I have an interest in a certain subject area, perhaps you will see . . . that is, I
wonder, do you know of other, what should I say, *sources* that
you would be able to recommend to assist me in my research,
by which I mean . . ."

Sometimes he was referred to another bookseller or to the
owner of a private collection. Occasionally it happened that
he had been ludicrously misunderstood when he found himself on the fringe of a society devoted to some strictly demonic
enterprise.

The very bookshop in which Victor Keirion was now browsing represented only the most recent digression in a search
without progress. But he had learned to be cautious and would
try to waste as little time as possible in determining whether
or not there was anything for him here. Thus, he intently
flipped through the pages of one book after another.

Absorbed as he was in perusing so much verbiage, he was

startled when someone with a voice like that of a child spoke to him.

"Have you seen our friend?" asked a nearby voice, startling him somewhat. Victor Keirion turned to face the stranger. The man was rather small and wore a black overcoat; his hair was also black and fell loosely across his forehead. Besides his general appearance, there was also something about his presence that made one think of a crow, a scavenging creature in wait. "Has he come out of his sanctum?" the man asked, gesturing toward the empty desk and the dark area behind it.

"I'm sorry, I haven't seen anyone," Keirion replied. "I only now noticed you."

"I can't help being quiet. Look at these little feet," the man said, indicating his highly polished pair of black shoes. Without thinking, Keirion looked down; then, feeling duped, he looked up again at the smiling stranger.

"You look very bored," said the human crow.

"I'm sorry?"

"Never mind. I can see that I'm bothering you." Then the man walked away, his coat flapping slightly, and began scanning some distant bookshelves. "I've never seen you in here before," he said from across the room.

"I've never been in here before," Keirion answered.

"Have you ever read this?" the stranger asked, pulling down a book and holding up its wordless black cover.

"Never," Keirion replied without so much as glancing at the book. Somehow this seemed the best action to take with this character, who appeared to be foreign in some indefinable way.

"Well, you must be looking for something special," continued the other man, replacing the black book on its shelf. "And I know what that's like, when you're looking for something very special. Have you ever heard of a book, an extremely special book, that is not . . . yes, that is not *about* something, but actually is that something?"

For the first time the obnoxious stranger had managed to intrigue Keirion rather than annoy him. "That sounds . . ." he started to say, but then the other man exclaimed:

"There he is, there he is. Excuse me."

It seemed that the proprietor—that mutual friend—had finally made his appearance and was now standing behind the desk, looking toward his two customers. "My friend," said the crowman as he stepped with outstretched hand over to the smoothly bald and softly fat gentleman. The two of them shook hands. For a few moments they chatted quietly, much too quietly for Victor Keirion to hear what they were saying. Then the crowman was invited behind the desk, and—led by the corpulent bookseller—made his way into the darkness at the back of the shop. In a distant corner of that darkness the brilliant rectangle of a doorway suddenly flashed into outline, admitting through its frame a large, two-headed shadow.

Left alone among the worthless volumes of that shop, Victor Keirion felt the sad frustration of the uninvited, the abandoned. More than ever he had become infected with hopes and curiosities of an indeterminable kind. And he soon found it impossible to remain outside that radiant little room the other two had entered, and at whose door he presently stood in silence.

The room was a cramped cubicle within which stood another cubicle formed by free-standing bookcases, creating four very narrow aisleways in the space between them. From the doorway he could not see how the inner cubicle might be entered, but he heard the voices of the others whispering within. Stepping quietly, he began making his way along the perimeter of the room, his eyes surveying a wealth of odd-looking volumes.

Immediately he sensed that something of a special nature awaited his discovery, and the evidence for this intuition began to build. Each book that he examined served as a clue in this delirious investigation, a cryptic sign which engaged his powers of interpretation and imparted the faith to proceed. Many of the works were written in foreign languages he did not read; some appeared to be composed in ciphers based on familiar characters and others seemed to be transcribed in a wholly artificial cryptography. But in every one of these books he found an oblique guidance, some feature of more or less indirect significance: a strangeness in the typeface, pages and bindings of uncommon texture, abstract diagrams suggesting no orthodox ritual or occult system. Even greater anticipation was inspired by certain illustrated plates, mysterious drawings and engravings that depicted scenes and situations unlike anything he could name. And such works as *Cynothoglys* or *The Noctuary of Tine* conveyed schemes so bizarre, so remote from known texts and treatises of the esoteric tradition, that he felt assured of the sense of his quest.

The whispering grew louder, though no more distinct, as he edged around a corner of that inner cubicle and anxiously noted the opening at its far end. At the same time he was distracted, for no apparent reason, by a small grayish volume leaning within a gap created by oversized tomes on either side. The little book had been set upon the highest shelf, making it necessary for him to stretch himself, as if on an upright torture rack, to reach it. Trying not to give away his presence by the sounds of his pain, he finally secured the ashen-colored object—as pale as his own coloring—between the tips of his first two fingers. Mutely he strained to slide it quietly from its place. This act accomplished, he slowly shrunk down to his original stature and looked into the book's brittle pages.

It seemed to be a chronicle of strange dreams. Yet somehow the passages he examined were less a recollection of unruled visions than a tangible incarnation of them, not mere rhetoric but the thing itself, just as the crow-man had described. The use of language in the book was arrantly unnatural and the book's author unknown. Indeed, the text conveyed the impression of speaking for itself and speaking only to itself, its words being like shadows that were cast by no forms outside the book. But though this volume appeared to be composed in a vernacular of mysteries, its words did inspire a sure understanding and created in their reader a visceral apprehension of the phenomenon to which the characters cut into the front of the book gave name. Passing his right forefinger across these gnarled letters, which appeared to be deeply engraved into the volume's stiffly bound surface, Victor Keirion could not feel their physicality. It was as if he intuited the word they spelled out: *Vastarien*. Could this book be a kind of invocation of a world in waiting of genesis? And was it a world at all? Rather the unreal essence of one, all natural elements purged from it by an ineffable process of extraction, all days distilled into dreams and nights into nightmares. Each passage he entered in the book both enchanted and appalled him with images and incidents so freakish and chaotic that his usual sense of these terms disintegrated along with everything else. Rampant oddity seemed to be the rule of the realm, while imperfection was the paradoxical source of idealities—miracles of aberrance and marvels of miscreation. There was horror, undoubtedly. But it was a horror uncompromised by any feeling of lost joy or a thwarted searching for the good. Instead, there was proffered a deliverance by damnation. And if Vastarien was a nightmare, it was a nightmare transformed in spirit by the utter absence of refuge: nightmare made normal.

"I'm sorry, I didn't see that you had drifted in here," said the bookseller in a high thin voice. He had just emerged from the inner chamber of the room and was standing with arms folded across his wide chest. "Please don't touch anything. And may I take that from you?" The right arm of the bookseller reached out, then returned to its former place when the man with the pale eyes did not relinquish the merchandise.

"I think I would like to purchase it," said Keirion. "I'm sure I would, if . . ."

"Of course, if the price is reasonable," finished the bookseller. "But who knows, you might not be able to appreciate how valuable these books can be. The one in your hands," he said, removing a little pad and pencil from inside his jacket and scribbling briefly. He ripped off the top sheet and held it up for the would-be buyer to see, then confidently put away all writing materials, as if that would be the end of it.

"But there must be some latitude for bargaining," Keirion protested.

"I'm afraid not," answered the bookseller. "Not with something that is the only one of its kind, as are many of these volumes. Yet the book you are holding, that single copy . . ."

A hand touched the bookseller's shoulder and seemed to

switch off his voice. Then the crow-man stepped into the aisle-way, his eyes fixed upon the object under discussion, and asked: "Don't you find that the book is somewhat . . . difficult?"

"Difficult," repeated Keirion. "I'm not sure . . . If you mean that the language is strange, I would have to agree, but—"

"No," interjected the bookseller, "that's not what he means at all."

"Excuse us for a moment," said the crow-man.

Then both men went back into the inner room, where they whispered for some time. When the whispering ceased, the bookseller came forth and announced that there had been a mistake. The book, while something of a curiosity, was worth a good deal less than the price earlier quoted. The revised evaluation, while still costly, was within the means of this particular buyer, who agreed at once to pay it.

Thus began Victor Keirion's preoccupation with a certain book and a certain hallucinated world, though to make a distinction between these two phenomena ultimately seemed an error. The book, indeed, did not merely describe that strange world but, in some obscure fashion, was a true composition of the thing itself, its very form incarnate.

Each day thereafter he studied the hypnotic episodes of the little book; each night, as he dreamed, he carried out shapeless expeditions into its fantastic topography. To all appearances it seemed he had discovered the summit or abyss of the unreal, that utopia of exhaustion, confusion, and debris where reality ends and where one may dwell among its ruins. And it was not long before he found it necessary to revisit that twelve-sided shop, intending to question the obese bookseller on the matter of the book and unintentionally learning the truth of how it came to be sold.

When he arrived at the bookstore, sometime in the middle of a grayish afternoon, Victor Keirion was surprised to find that the door, which had opened so freely on his previous visit, was now firmly locked. It would not even rattle in its frame when he nervously pushed and pulled on the handle. Since the interior of the store was lighted, he took a coin from his pocket and began tapping on the glass. Finally, someone came forward from the shadows of the back room.

"Closed," the bookseller pantomimed on the other side of the glass.

"But—" Keirion argued, pointing to his wristwatch.

"Nevertheless," the wide man shouted. Then, after scrutinizing the disappointed patron, the bookseller unlocked the door and opened it far enough to carry on a brief conversation. "And what is it I can do for you? I'm closed, so you'll have to come some other time if—"

"I only wanted to ask you something. Do you remember the book that I bought from you some days ago?"

"Yes, I remember," replied the bookseller, as if quite prepared for the question. "And let me say that I was quite impressed, as of course was . . . the other man."

"Impressed?" Keirion repeated.

"Ecstatic is more the word in his case," continued the bookseller. "He said to me, 'The book has found its reader,' and what could I do but agree with him?"

"I'm afraid I don't understand," said Keirion.

The bookseller blinked and said nothing. After a few moments he reluctantly explained: "I was hoping that by now you would understand. He hasn't contacted you? The man who was in here that day?"

"No, why should he?"

The bookseller blinked again and said: "Well, I suppose there's no reason for you to stand out there. It's getting very cold, don't you feel it? Please come in." As Victor Keirion entered, the bookseller stuck his head outside, looking up the stairs that led down to his shop and scanning as much of the street above as he could see. Then he closed the door and pulled Keirion a little to one side of it, whispering: "There's just one thing I would like to tell you. I made no mistake the other day about the price of that book. And it was that price which was paid by the other man, minus the small amount that you contributed. I didn't cheat anyone, least of all *him*. He would have been happy to pay even more to get that book into your hands. And though I'm not exactly sure of his reasons, I think you should know that."

"But why didn't he simply purchase the book for himself?" asked Keirion.

The bookseller seemed confused. "It was of no use to him. Perhaps it would have been better if you hadn't given yourself away when he asked you about the book. How much you knew."

"But I don't know anything, apart from what I've read in the book itself. I came here to look into its provenance."

"Its provenance? You're the one who should be telling me about that. I didn't even know I had that book on my shelves. I tried to price it out of your hands, but I should have expected that *he* wouldn't allow that. I'm not asking anything of you, don't misunderstand. I've already violated every precept of discretion in this matter. This is such an exceptional case, though. Very impressive, if in fact you are the reader of that book."

Realizing that, at best, he had been led into a dialogue of mystification, and possibly one of lies, Victor Keirion had no regrets when the bookseller held the door open for him to leave.

But before long he learned why the bookseller had been so impressed with him, and why the crow-like stranger had been so generous: the bestower of the book who was blind to its mysteries. In due course he learned that the stranger had given only so that he might possess the thing he could gain in no other way, that he was reading the book with borrowed eyes and stealing its secrets from the soul of its rightful reader. At last it became clear what was happening to him, and how his strange nights of dreaming were being affected *from inside*.

This phenomenon was not immediately apparent, though. For several more nights, as the outlines of Vastarien slowly pushed through the obscurity of his sleep, a vast terrain emerged from its own profound slumber and loomed forth from a place without coordinates or dimension. And as the oddly angled monuments became manifest once again, they seemed to expand and soar high above, coaxing his sight toward them. Progressively the scene acquired nuance and articulation; steadily the creation became dense and intricate within its black womb. The streets were sinuous entrails winding through that dark body, and each edifice was the jutting bone of a skeleton hung with a thin musculature of shadows.

But little by little, Victor Keirion began noticing that something was in the course of change during his dreams. The world of Vasterien seemed more and more to be losing its consistency, its *suchness*. Then one night, just as his vision reached out to embrace fully the mysterious and jagged form of a given dream, it all appeared to pull away, abandoning him on the edge of a dreamless void. The treasured eidolon was receding, shrinking into the distance. Now all he could see was a single street bordered by two converging rows of buildings. And at the opposite end of that street, rising up taller than the buildings themselves, stood a great figure in silhouette. This colossus made no movement or sound but nonetheless increasingly dominated the horizon where the single remaining street seemed to end. From this position the towering shadow was absorbing all other shapes into its own, which gradually gained in stature as the dreamscape withdrew and diminished. And the outline of this titanic figure appeared to be that of a man, yet it was also that of a dark and devouring bird.

Though Victor Keirion managed to awake before the scavenger had thoroughly consumed what was not its own, there was no assurance that he would always be able to do so and that the dream would not pass into the hands of another. And so he conceived and executed the act that was necessary to keep possession of what he had desired for so long.

Vastarien, he whispered as he stood in the shadows and moonlight of that bare little room, where a monolithic metal door prevented his escape. Within that door a small square of thick glass was implanted so that he might be watched by day and by night. And there was an unbending web of heavy wire covering the window which overlooked the city that was *not* Vastarien. *Never,* chanted a voice which might have been his own. Then more insistently: *I told him that. I told him. Never, never, never.*

When the door opened and some men in uniforms entered the room, they found Victor Keirion screaming to the raucous limits of his voice and trying to scale the thick metal mesh veiling the window, as if he were dragging himself along some unlikely route of liberation. Of course, they pulled him to the floor; and they stretched him out upon the bed, where his wrists and ankles were tightly strapped. Then through the doorway strode a nurse who carried a slender syringe crowned with a silvery needle.

During the injection he continued to scream words which everyone in the room had heard before, each outburst developing the theme of his unjust confinement: how the man he had murdered was using him in a horrible way, a way impossible to explain or make credible. The man could not read the book—there, *that* book—and was stealing the dreams which the book had spawned. *Stealing my dreams,* he mumbled softly as the drug began to take effect. *Stealing my . . .*

The stewards of Victor Keirion's incarceration remained around his bed for a few moments, silently staring at its restrained occupant. Then one of them pointed to the book and initiated a conversation now familiar to them all.

"What should we do with it? It's been taken away enough times already, but then there's always another that appears."

"And there's no point to it. Look at these pages—nothing, nothing written anywhere."

"So why does he sit reading them for hours? He does nothing else."

"I think it's time we told someone in authority."

"Of course, we could do that, but what exactly would we say? That a certain inmate should be forbidden from reading a certain book? That he becomes violent?"

"And then they'll ask why we can't keep the book away from him or him from the book. What should we say to that?"

"There would be nothing we could say. Can you imagine what lunatics we would seem? As soon as we opened our mouths, that would be it for all of us."

"And when someone asks what the book means to him, or even what its name is . . . what would be our answer?"

As if in response to this question, a word was uttered by the criminally insane creature bound to the bed. But none of them could understand the meaning of what he had said. They were part of a world of overbearing and yet deficient realities. They were shackled for life to their own bodies, while he was now in a place that owed nothing to corporeal existence.

And never, it truly seemed, could he be forced to abandon this domain of wayward wonders. *Never.*

Grimscribe

His Lives and Works

To my brother Bob

INTRODUCTION

His name is . . .

Will it ever come to me? There is a grand lapse of memory that may be the only thing to save us from ultimate horror. Perhaps they know the truth who preach the passing of one life into another, vowing that between a certain death and a certain birth there is an interval in which an old name is forgotten before a new one is learned. And to remember the name of a former life is to begin the backward slide into that great blackness in which all names have their source, becoming incarnate in a succession of bodies like numberless verses of an infinite scripture.

To find that you have had so many names is to lose claim to any one of them. To gain the memory of so many lives is to lose them all.

So he keeps his name secret, his many names. He hides each one from all the others, so that they will not become lost among themselves. Protecting his life from all his lives, from the memory of so many lives, he hides behind the mask of anonymity.

But even if I cannot know his name, I have always known his voice. That is one thing he can never disguise, even if it sounds like many different voices. I know his voice when I hear it speak, because it is always speaking of terrible secrets. It speaks of the most grotesque mysteries and encounters, sometimes with despair, sometimes with delight, and sometimes with a spirit not possible to define. What crime or curse has kept him turning upon this same wheel of terror, spinning out his tales which always tell of the strangeness and horror of things? When will he make an end to his telling?

He has told us so many things, and he will tell us more. Yet he will never tell his name. Not before the very end of his old life, and not after the beginning of each new one. Not until time itself has erased every name and taken away every life.

But until then, everyone needs a name. Everyone must be called something. So what can we say is the name of everyone?

Our name is GRIMSCRIBE.

This is our voice.

THE VOICE OF
THE DAMNED

THE LAST FEAST
OF HARLEQUIN

My interest in the town of Mirocaw was first aroused when I heard that an annual festival was held there which, among its other elements of pageantry, featured the participation of clowns. A former colleague of mine, who is now attached to the anthropology department of a distant university, had read one of my recent articles ("The Clown Figure in American Media," *Journal of Popular Culture*), and wrote to me that he vaguely remembered reading about or being told of a town somewhere in the state that held a kind of "Fool's Feast" every year, thinking that this might be pertinent to my peculiar line of study. It was, of course, more pertinent than he had reason to think, both to my academic aims in this area and to my personal pursuits.

Aside from my teaching, I had for some years been engaged in various anthropological projects with the primary ambition of articulating the significance of the clown figure in diverse cultural contexts. Every year for the past twenty years I have attended the pre-Lenten festivals that are held in various places throughout the southern United States. Every year I learned something more concerning the esoterics of celebration. In these studies I was an eager participant—along with playing my part as an anthropologist, I also took a place behind the clownish mask myself. And I cherished this role as I did nothing else in my life. To me the title of Clown has always carried connotations of a noble sort. I was an adroit jester, strangely enough, and had always taken pride in the skills I worked so diligently to develop.

I wrote to the State Department of Recreation, indicating what information I desired and exposing an enthusiastic urgency which came naturally to me on this topic. Many weeks later I received a tan envelope imprinted with a government logo. Inside was a pamphlet that catalogued all of the various seasonal festivities of which the state was officially aware, and I noted in passing that there were as many in late autumn and winter as in the warmer seasons. A letter inserted within the pamphlet explained to me that, according to their voluminous records, no festivals held in the town of Mirocaw had been officially registered. Their files, nonetheless, could be placed at my disposal if I should wish to research this or similar matters in connection with some definite project. At the time this offer was made I was already laboring under so many professional and personal burdens that, with a weary hand, I simply deposited the envelope and its contents in a drawer, never to be consulted again.

Some months later, however, I made an impulsive digression from my responsibilities and, rather haphazardly, took up the Mirocaw project. This happened as I was driving north one afternoon in late summer with the intention of examining some journals in the holdings of a library at another university. Once out of the city limits the scenery changed to sunny fields and farms, diverting my thoughts from the signs that I passed along the highway. Nevertheless, the subconscious scholar in me must have been regarding these with studious care. The name of a town loomed into my vision. Instantly the scholar retrieved certain records from some deep mental drawer, and I was faced with making a few hasty calculations as to whether there was enough time and motivation for an investigative side trip. But the exit sign was even hastier in making its appearance, and I soon found myself leaving the highway, recalling the road sign's promise that the town was no more than seven miles east.

These seven miles included several confusing turns, the forced taking of a temporarily alternate route, and a destination not even visible until a steep rise had been fully ascended. On the descent another helpful sign informed me that I was within the city limits of Mirocaw. Some scattered houses on the outskirts of the town were the first structures I encountered. Beyond them the numerical highway became Townshend Street, the main avenue of Mirocaw.

The town impressed me as being much larger once I was within its limits than it had appeared from the prominence just outside. I saw that the general hilliness of the surrounding countryside was also an internal feature of Mirocaw. Here, though, the effect was different. The parts of the town did not look as if they adhered very well to one another. This condition might be blamed on the irregular topography of the town. Behind some of the old stores in the business district, steeply roofed houses had been erected on a sudden incline, their peaks appearing at an extraordinary elevation above the lower buildings. And because the foundations of these houses could not be glimpsed, they conveyed the illusion of being either precariously suspended in air, threatening to topple down, or else constructed with an unnatural loftiness in relation to their width and mass. This situation also created a weird distortion of perspective. The two levels of structures overlapped each other without giving a sense of depth, so that the houses, because of their higher elevation and nearness to the foreground buildings, did not appear diminished in size as background objects should. Consequently, a look of flatness, as in a photograph, predominated in this area. Indeed, Mirocaw could be compared to an album of old snapshots, particularly ones in which the camera had been upset in the process of photography, causing the pictures to develop on an angle: a cone-roofed turret, like a pointed hat jauntily askew, peeked over the houses on a neighboring street; a billboard displaying a group of grinning vegetables tipped its contents slightly westward; cars parked along steep curbs seemed to be flying skyward in the glare-distorted windows of a five-and-ten; people leaned lethargically as they trod up and down sidewalks; and on that sunny day a clock tower, which at first I mistook for a church steeple, cast a long shadow that seemed to extend an impossible distance and wander into unlikely places in its progress across the town. I should say that perhaps the disharmonies of Mirocaw are more acutely affecting my imagination in retrospect than they were on that first day, when I was primarily concerned with locating the city hall or some other center of information.

I pulled around a corner and parked. Sliding over to the other side of the seat, I rolled down the window and called to a passerby: "Excuse me, sir." The man, who was shabbily dressed and very old, paused for a moment without approaching the car. Though he had apparently responded to my call, his vacant expression did not betray the least awareness of my presence, and for a moment I thought it just a coincidence that he halted on the sidewalk at the same time I addressed him. His eyes were focused somewhere beyond me with a weary and imbecilic gaze. After a few moments he continued on his way and I said nothing to call him back, even though at the last second his face began to appear dimly familiar. Someone else finally came along who was able to direct me to the Mirocaw City Hall and Community Center.

The city hall turned out to be the building with the clock tower. Inside I stood at a counter behind which some people were working at desks and walking up and down a back hallway. On one wall was a poster for the state lottery: a jack-in-the-box with both hands grasping green bills. After a few moments, a tall, middle-aged woman came over to the counter.

"Can I help you?" she asked in a neutral, bureaucratic voice.

I explained that I had heard about the festival—saying nothing about being a nosy academic—and asked if she could provide me with further information or direct me to someone who could.

"Do you mean the one held in the winter?" she asked.

"How many of them are there?"

"Just that one."

"I suppose, then, that that's the one I mean." I smiled as if sharing a joke with her.

Without another word, she walked off into the back hallway. While she was absent I exchanged glances with several of the people behind the counter who periodically looked up from their work.

"There you are," she said when she returned, handing me a piece of paper that looked like the product of a cheap copy machine. *Please Come to the Fun,* it said in large letters. *Parades,* it went on, *Street Masquerade, Bands, The Winter Raffle,* and *The Coronation of the Winter Queen.* The page continued with the mention of a number of miscellaneous festivities. I read the words again. There was something about that imploring little "please" at the top of the announcement that made the whole affair seem like a charity function.

"When is it held? It doesn't say when the festival takes place."

"Most people already know that." She abruptly snatched the page from my hands and wrote something at the bottom. When she gave it back to me, I saw "Dec. 19-21" written in blue-green ink. I was immediately struck by an odd sense of scheduling on the part of the festival committee. There was, of course, solid anthropological and historical precedent for holding festivities around the winter solstice, but the timing of this particular event did not seem entirely practical.

"If you don't mind my asking, don't these days somewhat conflict with the regular holiday season? I mean, most people have enough going on at that time."

"It's just tradition," she said, as if invoking some venerable ancestry behind her words.

"That's very interesting," I said as much to myself as to her.

"Is there anything else?" she asked.

"Yes. Could you tell me if this festival has anything to do with clowns? I see there's something about a masquerade."

"Yes, of course there are some people in . . . costumes. I've never been in that position myself . . . that is, yes, there are clowns of a sort."

At that point my interest was definitely aroused, but I was not sure how much further I wanted to pursue it. I thanked the woman for her help and asked the best means of access to the highway, not anxious to retrace the labyrinthine route by which

I had entered the town. I walked back to my car with a whole flurry of half-formed questions, and as many vague and conflicting answers, cluttering my mind.

The directions the woman gave me necessitated passing through the south end of Mirocaw. There were not many people moving about in this section of town. Those that I did see, shuffling lethargically down a block of battered storefronts, exhibited the same sort of forlorn expression and manner as the old man from whom I had asked directions earlier. I must have been traversing a central artery of this area, for on either side stretched street after street of poorly tended yards and houses bowed with age and indifference. When I came to a stop at a streetcorner, one of the citizens of this slum passed in front of my car. This lean, morose, and epicene person turned my way and sneered outrageously with a taut little mouth, yet seemed to be looking at no one in particular. After progressing a few streets farther, I came to a road that led back to the highway. I felt detectably more comfortable as soon as I found myself traveling once again through the expanses of sun-drenched farmlands.

I reached the library with more than enough time for my research, and so I decided to make a scholarly detour to see what material I could find that might illuminate the winter festival held in Mirocaw. The library, one of the oldest in the state, included in its holdings the entire run of the Mirocaw *Courier*. I thought this would be an excellent place to start. I soon found, however, that there was no handy way to research information from this newspaper, and I did not want to engage in a blind search for articles concerning a specific subject.

I next turned to the more organized resources of the newspapers for the larger cities located in the same county, which incidentally shares its name with Mirocaw. I uncovered very little about the town, and almost nothing concerning its festival, except in one general article on annual events in the area that erroneously attributed to Mirocaw a "large Middle-Eastern community" which every spring hosted a kind of ethnic jamboree. From what I had already observed, and from what I subsequently learned, the citizens of Mirocaw were solidly Midwestern-American, the probable descendants in a direct line from some enterprising pack of New Englanders of the last century. There was one brief item devoted to a Mirocavian event, but this merely turned out to be an obituary notice for an old woman who had quietly taken her life around Christmastime. Thus, I returned home that day all but empty-handed on the subject of Mirocaw.

However, it was not long afterward that I received another letter from the former colleague of mine who had first led me to seek out Mirocaw and its festival. As it happened, he rediscovered the article that caused him to stir my interest in a local "Fool's Feast." This article had its sole appearance in an obscure festschrift of anthropology studies published in Amsterdam twenty years before. Most of these papers were in Dutch, a few in German, and only one was in English: "The Last Feast of Harlequin: Preliminary Notes on a Local Festival." It was exciting, of course, finally to be able to read this study, but even more exciting was the name of its author: Dr. Raymond Thoss.

2.

Before proceeding any further, I should mention something about Thoss, and inevitably about myself. Over two decades ago, at my alma mater in Cambridge, Mass., Thoss was a professor of mine. Long before playing a role in the events I am about to describe, he was already one of the most important figures in my life. A striking personality, he inevitably influenced everyone who came in contact with him. I remember his lectures on social anthropology, how he turned that dim room into a brilliant and profound circus of learning. He moved in an uncannily brisk manner. When he swept his arm around to indicate some common term on the blackboard behind him, one felt he was presenting nothing less than an item of fantastic qualities and secret value. When he replaced his hand in the pocket of his old jacket this fleeting magic was once again stored away in its well-worn pouch, to be retrieved at the sorcerer's discretion. We sensed he was teaching us more than we could possibly learn, and that he himself was in possession of greater and deeper knowledge than he could possibly impart. On one occasion I summoned up the audacity to offer an interpretation—which was somewhat opposed to his own—regarding the tribal clowns of the Hopi Indians. I implied that personal experience as an amateur clown and special devotion to this study provided me with an insight possibly more valuable than his own. It was then he disclosed, casually and very obiter dicta, that he had actually acted in the role of one of these masked tribal fools and had celebrated with them the dance of the *kachinas*. In revealing these facts, however, he somehow managed not to add to the humiliation I had already inflicted upon myself. And for this I was grateful to him.

Thoss's activities were such that he sometimes became the object of gossip or romanticized speculation. He was a fieldworker par excellence, and his ability to insinuate himself into exotic cultures and situations, thereby gaining insights where other anthropologists merely collected data, was renowned. At various times in his career there had been rumors of his having "gone native" à la the Frank Hamilton Cushing legend. There were hints, which were not always irresponsible or cheaply glamorized, that he was involved in projects of a freakish sort, many of which focused on New England. It is a fact that he spent six months posing as a mental patient at an institution in western Massachusetts, gathering information on the "culture" of the psychically disturbed. When his book *Winter Solstice: The Longest Night of a Society* was published, the general opinion was that it was disappointingly subjective and impressionistic, and that, aside from a few moving but "poetically obscure" observations, there was nothing at all to give it value. Those who defended Thoss claimed he was a kind of superanthropologist: while much of his work emphasized his own mind and feelings, his experience had in fact penetrated to a rich core of hard data which he had yet to disclose in objective discourse. As a student of Thoss, I tended to support this latter estimation of him. For a variety of tenable and untenable reasons, I believed Thoss capable of unearthing hitherto inaccessible strata of human existence. So it was gratifying at first that this article entitled "The Last Feast of Harlequin" seemed to uphold the Thoss mystique, and in an area I personally found captivating.

Much of the content of the article I did not immediately comprehend, given its author's characteristic and often strategic obscurities. On first reading, the most interesting aspect of this brief study—the "notes" encompassed only twenty pages—was the general mood of the piece. Thoss's eccentricities were definitely present in these pages, but only as a struggling inner force which was definitely contained—incarcerated, I might say—by the somber rhythmic movements of his prose and by some gloomy references he occasionally called upon. Two references in particular shared a common theme. One was a quotation from Poe's "The Conqueror Worm," which Thoss employed as a rather sensational epigraph. The point of the epigraph, however, was nowhere echoed in the text of the article save in another passing reference. Thoss brought up the well-known genesis of the modern Christmas celebration, which of course descends from the Roman Saturnalia. Then, making it clear he had not yet observed the Mirocaw festival and had only gathered its nature from various informants, he established that it too contained many, even more overt, elements of the Saturnalia. Next he made what seemed to me a trivial and purely linguistic observation, one that had less to do with his main course of argument than it did with the equally peripheral Poe epigraph. He briefly mentioned that an early sect of the Syrian Gnostics called themselves "Saturnians" and believed, among other religious heresies, that mankind was created by angels who were in turn created by the Supreme Unknown. The angels, however, did not possess the power to make their creation an erect being and for a time it crawled upon the earth like a worm. Eventually, the Creator remedied this grotesque state of affairs. At the time I supposed that the symbolic correspondences of mankind's origins and ultimate condition being associated with worms, combined with a year-end festival recognizing the winter death of the earth, was the gist of this Thossian "insight," a poetic but scientifically valueless observation.

Other observations he made on the Mirocaw festival were

also strictly etic; in other words, they were based on second-hand sources, hearsay testimony. Even at that juncture, however, I felt Thoss knew more than he disclosed; and, as I later discovered, he had indeed included information on certain aspects of Mirocaw suggesting he was already in possession of several keys which for the moment he was keeping securely in his own pocket. By then I, too, possessed a most revealing morsel of knowledge. A note to the "Harlequin" article apprised the reader that the piece was only a fragment in rude form of a more wide-ranging work in preparation. This work was never seen by the world. My former professor had not published anything since his withdrawal from academic circulation some twenty years ago. Now I suspected where he had gone.

For the man I had stopped on the streets of Mirocaw and from whom I tried to obtain directions, the man with the disconcertingly lethargic gaze, had very much resembled a superannuated version of Dr. Raymond Thoss.

3.

And now I have a confession to make. Despite my reasons for being enthusiastic about Mirocaw and its mysteries, especially its relationship to both Thoss and my own deepest concerns as a scholar—I contemplated the days ahead of me with no more than a feeling of frigid numbness and often with a sense of profound depression. Yet I had no reason to be surprised at this emotional state, which had little relevance to the outward events in my life but was determined by inward conditions that worked according to their own, quite enigmatic, seasons and cycles. For many years, at least since my university days, I have suffered from this dark malady, this recurrent despondency in which I would become buried when it came time for the earth to grow cold and bare and the skies heavy with shadows. Nevertheless, I pursued my plans, though somewhat mechanically, to visit Mirocaw during its festival days, for I superstitiously hoped that this activity might diminish the weight of my seasonal despair.

In Mirocaw would be parades and parties and the opportunity to play the clown once again.

For weeks in advance I practiced my art, even perfecting a new feat of juggling magic, which was my special forte in foolery. I had my costumes cleaned, purchased fresh makeup, and was ready. I received permission from the university to cancel some of my classes prior to the holiday, explaining the nature of my project and the necessity of arriving in the town a few days before the festival began, in order to do some preliminary research, establish informants, and so on. Actually, my plan was to postpone any formal inquiry until after the festival and to involve myself beforehand as much as possible in its activities. I would, of course, keep a journal during this time.

There was one resource I did want to consult, however. Specifically, I returned to that outstate library to examine those issues of the Mirocaw *Courier* dating from December two decades ago. One story in particular confirmed a point Thoss made in the "Harlequin" article, though the event it chronicled must have taken place after Thoss had written his study.

The *Courier* story appeared two weeks after the festival had ended for that year and was concerned with the disappearance of a woman named Elizabeth Beadle, the wife of Samuel Beadle, a hotel owner in Mirocaw. The county authorities speculated that this was another instance of the "holiday suicides" which seemed to occur with inordinate seasonal regularity in the Mirocaw region. Thoss documented this phenomenon in his "Harlequin" article, though I suspect that today these deaths would be neatly categorized under the heading "seasonal affective disorder." In any case, the authorities searched a half-frozen lake near the outskirts of Mirocaw where they had found many successful suicides in years past. This year, however, no body was discovered. Alongside the article was a picture of Elizabeth Beadle. Even in the grainy microfilm reproduction one could detect a certain vibrancy and vitality in Mrs. Beadle's face. That a hypothesis of "holiday suicide" should be so readily posited to explain her disappearance seemed strange and in some way unjust.

Thoss, in his brief article, wrote that every year changes occurred of a moral or spiritual cast which seemed to affect Mirocaw along with the usual winter metamorphosis. He was not precise about its origin or nature but stated, in typically mystifying fashion, that the effect of this "subseason" on the town was conspicuously negative. In addition to the number of suicides actually accomplished during this time, there was also a rise in treatment of "hypochondriacal" conditions, which was how the medical men of twenty years past characterized these cases in discussions with Thoss. This state of affairs would gradually worsen and finally reach a climax during the days scheduled for the Mirocaw festival. Thoss speculated that given the secretive nature of small towns, the situation was probably even more intensely pronounced than casual investigation could reveal.

The connection between the festival and this insidious sub-seasonal climate in Mirocaw was a point on which Thoss did not come to any rigid conclusions. He did write, nevertheless, that these two "climatic aspects" had had a parallel existence in the town's history as far back as available records could document. A late nineteenth-century history of Mirocaw County speaks of the town by its original name of New Colstead, and castigates the townspeople for holding a "ribald and soulless feast" to the exclusion of normal Christmas observances. (Thoss comments that the historian had mistakenly fused two distinct aspects of the season, their actual relationship being essentially antagonistic.) The "Harlequin" article did not trace the festival to its earliest appearance (this may not have been possible), though Thoss emphasized the New England origins of Mirocaw's founders. The festival, therefore, was one imported from this region and could reasonably be extended at least a century; that is, if it had not been brought over from the Old World, in which case its roots would become indefinite until further research could be done. Surely Thoss's allusion to the Syrian Gnostics suggested the latter possibility could not entirely be ruled out.

But it seemed to be the festival's link to New England that

nourished Thoss's speculations. He wrote of this patch of geography as if it were an acceptable place to end the search. For him, the very words "New England" seemed to be stripped of all traditional connotations and had come to imply nothing less than a gateway to all lands, both known and suspected, and even to ages beyond the civilized history of the region. Having been educated partly in New England, I could somewhat understand this sentimental exaggeration, for indeed there are places that seem archaic beyond chronological measure, appearing to transcend relative standards of time and achieving a kind of absolute antiquity which cannot be logically fathomed. But how this vague suggestion related to a small town in the Midwest I could not imagine. Thoss himself observed that the residents of Mirocaw did not betray any mysteriously primitive consciousness. On the contrary, they appeared superficially unaware of the genesis of their winter merrymaking. That such a tradition had endured through the years, however, even eclipsing the conventional Christmas holiday, revealed a profound awareness of the festival's meaning and function.

I cannot deny that what I had learned about the Mirocaw festival inspired me with a trite sense of fate, especially given the involvement of such an important figure from my past as Thoss. It was the first time in my academic career that I knew myself to be better suited than anyone else to discern the true meaning of scattered data, even if I could only attribute this special authority to chance circumstances.

Nevertheless, as I sat in that library on a morning in mid-December I doubted for a moment the wisdom of setting out for Mirocaw rather than returning home, where the more familiar *rite de passage* of winter depression awaited me. My original scheme was to avoid the cyclical blues the season held for me, but it seemed this was also a part of the history of Mirocaw, only on a much larger scale. My emotional instability, however, was exactly what qualified me most for the particular fieldwork ahead, though I did not take pride or consolation in the fact. And to retreat would have been to deny myself an opportunity that might never offer itself again. In retrospect, there seems to have been no fortuitous resolution to the decision I had to make. As it happened, I went ahead to the town.

4.

Just past noon, on December 18, I started driving toward Mirocaw. A blur of dull, earthen-colored scenery extended in every direction. The snowfalls of late autumn had been sparse, and only a few white patches appeared in the harvested fields along the highway. The clouds were gray and abundant. Passing by a stretch of forest, I noticed the black, ragged clumps of abandoned nests clinging to the twisted mesh of bare branches. I thought I saw black birds skittering over the road ahead, but they were only dead leaves and they flew into the air as I drove by.

I approached Mirocaw from the south, entering the town from the direction I had left it on my visit the previous summer. This took me once again through that part of town which seemed to exist on the wrong side of some great invisible barrier dividing the desirable sections of Mirocaw from the undesirable. As lurid as this district had appeared to me under the summer sun, in the thin light of that winter afternoon it degenerated into a pale phantom of itself. The frail stores and starved-looking houses suggested a borderline region between the material and nonmaterial worlds, with one sardonically wearing the mask of the other. I saw a few gaunt pedestrians who turned as I passed by, though seemingly not *because* I passed by, making my way up to the main street of Mirocaw.

Driving up the steep rise of Townshend Street, I found the sights there comparatively welcoming. The rolling avenues of the town were in readiness for the festival. Streetlights had their poles raveled with evergreen, the fresh boughs proudly conspicuous in a barren season. On the doors of many of the businesses on Townshend were holly wreaths, equally green but observably plastic. However, although there was nothing unusual in this traditional greenery of the season, it soon became apparent to me that Mirocaw had quite abandoned itself to this particular symbol of Yuletide. It was garishly in evidence everywhere. The windows of stores and houses were framed in green lights, green streamers hung down from storefront awnings, and the beacons of the Red Rooster Bar were peacock green floodlights. I supposed the residents of Mirocaw desired these decorations, but the effect was one of excess. An eerie emerald haze permeated the town, and faces looked slightly reptilian.

At the time I assumed that the prodigious evergreen, holly wreaths, and colored lights (if only of a single color) demonstrated an emphasis on the vegetable symbols of the Nordic Yuletide, which would inevitably be muddled into the winter festival of any northern country just as they had been adopted for the Christmas season. In his "Harlequin" article Thoss wrote of the pagan aspect of Mirocaw's festival, likening it to the ritual of a fertility cult, with probable connections to chthonic divinities at sometime in the past. But Thoss had mistaken, as I had, what was only part of the festival's significance for the whole.

The hotel at which I had made reservations was located on Townshend. It was an old building of brown brick, with an arched doorway and a pathetic coping intended to convey an impression of neoclassicism. I found a parking space in front and left my suitcases in the car.

When I first entered the hotel lobby it was empty. I thought perhaps the Mirocaw festival would have attracted enough visitors to at least bolster the business of its only hotel, but it seemed I was mistaken. Tapping a little bell, I leaned on the desk and turned to look at a small, traditionally decorated Christmas tree on a table near the entranceway. It was complete with shiny, egg-fragile bulbs; miniature candy canes; flat, laughing Santas with arms wide; a star on top nodding awkwardly against the delicate shoulder of an upper branch; and colored lights that bloomed out of flower-shaped sockets. For some reason this seemed to me a sorry little piece.

"May I help you?" said a young woman arriving from a room adjacent to the lobby.

I must have been staring rather intently at her, for she looked away and seemed quite uneasy. I could hardly imagine what to say to her or how to explain what I was thinking. In person she immediately radiated a chilling brilliance of manner and expression. But if this woman had not committed suicide twenty years before, as the newspaper article had suggested, neither had she aged in that time.

"Sarah," called a masculine voice from the invisible heights of a stairway. A tall, middle-aged man came down the steps. "I thought you were in your room," said the man, whom I took to be Samuel Beadle. Sarah, not Elizabeth, Beadle glanced sideways in my direction to indicate to her father that she was conducting the business of the hotel. Beadle apologized to me, and then excused the two of them for a moment while they went off to one side to continue their exchange.

I smiled and pretended everything was normal, while trying to remain within earshot of their conversation. They spoke in tones that suggested their conflict was a familiar one: Beadle's overprotective concern with his daughter's whereabouts and Sarah's frustrated understanding of certain restrictions placed upon her. The conversation ended, and Sarah ascended the stairs, turning for a moment to give me a facial pantomime of apology for the unprofessional scene that had just taken place.

"Now, sir, what can I do for you?" Beadle asked, almost demanded.

"Yes, I have a reservation. Actually, I'm a day early, if that doesn't present a problem." I gave the hotel the benefit of the doubt that its business might have been secretly flourishing.

"No problem at all, sir," he said, presenting me with the registration form, and then a brass-colored key dangling from a plastic disc bearing the number 44.

"Luggage?"

"Yes, it's in my car."

"I'll give you a hand with that."

While Beadle was settling me in my fourth-floor room it seemed an opportune moment to broach the subject of the festival, the holiday suicides, and perhaps, depending upon his reaction, the fate of his wife. I needed a respondent who had lived in the town for a good many years and who could enlighten me about the attitude of Mirocavians toward their season of sea-green lights.

"This is just fine," I said about the clean but somber room. "Nice view. I can see the bright green lights of Mirocaw just fine from up here. Is the town usually all decked out like this? For the festival, I mean."

"Yes, sir, for the festival," he replied mechanically.

"I imagine you'll probably be getting quite a few of us out-of-towners in the next couple days."

"Could be. Is there anything else?"

"Yes, there is. I wonder if you could tell me something about the festivities."

"Such as . . ."

"Well, you know, the clowns and so forth."

"Only clowns here are the ones that're . . . well, picked out, I suppose you would say."

"I don't understand."

"Excuse me, sir. I'm very busy right now. Is there anything else?"

I could think of nothing at the moment to perpetuate our conversation. Beadle wished me a good stay and left.

I unpacked my suitcases. In addition to regular clothing I had also brought along some of the items from my clown's wardrobe. Beadle's comment that the clowns of Mirocaw were "picked out" left me wondering exactly what purpose these street masqueraders served in the festival. The clown figure has had so many meanings in different times and cultures. The jolly, well-loved joker familiar to most people is actually but one aspect of this protean creature. Madmen, hunchbacks, amputees, and other abnormals were once considered natural clowns; they were elected to fulfill a comic role which could allow others to see them as ludicrous rather than as terrible reminders of the forces of disorder in the world. But sometimes a cheerless jester was required to draw attention to this same disorder, as in the case of King Lear's morbid and honest fool, who of course was eventually hanged, and so much for his clownish wisdom. Clowns have often had ambiguous and sometimes contradictory roles to play.

Thus, I knew enough not to brashly jump into costume and cry out, "Here I am again!"

That first day in Mirocaw I did not stray far from the hotel. I read and rested for a few hours and then ate at a nearby diner. Through the window beside my table I watched the winter night turn the soft green glow of the town into a harsh and almost totally new color as it contrasted with the darkness. The streets of Mirocaw seemed to me unusually busy for a small town at evening. Yet it was not the kind of activity one normally sees before an approaching Christmas holiday. This was not a crowd of bustling shoppers loaded with bright bags of presents. Their arms were empty, their hands shoved deep in their pockets against the cold, which nevertheless had not driven them to the solitude of their presumably warm houses. I watched them enter and exit store after store without buying anything. Many merchants remained open late, and even the places that were closed had left their neon signs illuminated. The faces that passed the window of the diner were possibly just stiffened by the cold, I thought; frozen into deep frowns and nothing else. In the same window I saw the reflection of my own face. It was not the face of an adept clown; it was slack and flabby and at that moment seemed the face of someone less than alive. Outside was the town of Mirocaw, its streets dipping and rising with a lunatic severity, its citizens packing the sidewalks, its heart bathed in green: as promising a field of professional and personal challenge as I had ever encountered—and I was bored to the point of dread. I hurried back to my hotel room.

"Mirocaw has another coldness within its cold," I wrote in my journal that night. "Another set of buildings and streets that exists behind the visible town's façade like a world of disgraceful back alleys." I went on like this for about a page, across which I finally engraved a big "X." Then I went to bed.

In the morning I left my car at the hotel and walked toward the main business district a few blocks away. Mingling with the good people of Mirocaw seemed like the proper thing to do at that point in my scientific sojourn. But as I began laboriously walking up Townshend (the sidewalks were cramped with wandering pedestrians), a glimpse of someone suddenly replaced my haphazard plan with a more specific and immediate one. Through the crowd and about fifteen paces ahead was my goal.

"Dr. Thoss," I called.

His head almost seemed to turn and look back in response to my shout, but I could not be certain. I pushed past several warmly wrapped bodies and green-scarved necks, only to find that the object of my pursuit appeared to be maintaining the same distance from me, though I did not know if this was being done deliberately or not. At the next corner, the dark-coated Thoss abruptly turned right onto a steep street which led downward directly toward the dilapidated south end of Mirocaw. When I reached the corner I looked down the sidewalk and could see him very clearly from above. I also saw how he managed to stay so far ahead of me in a mob that had impeded my own progress. For some reason the people on the sidewalk made room so that he could move past them easily, without the usual jostling of bodies. It was not a dramatic physical avoidance, though it seemed nonetheless intentional. Fighting the tight fabric of the throng, I continued to follow Thoss, losing and regaining sight of him.

By the time I reached the bottom of the sloping street the crowd had thinned out considerably, and after walking a block or so farther I found myself practically a lone pedestrian pacing behind a distant figure that I hoped was still Thoss. He was now walking quite swiftly and in a way that seemed to acknowledge my pursuit of him, though really it felt as if he were leading me as much as I was chasing him. I called his name a few more times at a volume he could not have failed to hear, assuming that deafness was not one of the changes to have come over him; he was, after all, not a young man, or even a middle-aged one any longer.

Thoss suddenly crossed in the middle of the street. He walked a few more steps and entered a signless brick building between a liquor store and a repair shop of some kind. In the "Harlequin" article Thoss had mentioned that the people living in this section of Mirocaw maintained their own businesses, and that these were patronized almost exclusively by residents of the area. I could well believe this statement when I looked at these little sheds of commerce, for they had the same badly weathered appearance as their clientele. The formidable shoddiness of these buildings notwithstanding, I followed Thoss into the plain brick shell of what had been, or possibly still was, a diner.

Inside it was unusually dark. Even before my eyes made the adjustment I sensed that this was not a thriving restaurant cozily cluttered with chairs and tables—as was the establishment where I had eaten the night before—but a place with only a few disarranged furnishings, and very cold. It seemed colder, in fact, than the winter streets outside.

"Dr. Thoss?" I called toward a table near the center of the long room. Perhaps four or five were sitting around the table, with some others blending into the dimness behind them. Scattered across the tabletop were some books and loose papers. Seated there was an old man indicating something in the pages before him, but it was not Thoss. Beside him were two youths whose wholesome features distinguished them from the grim weariness of the others. I approached the table and they all looked up at me. None of them showed a glimmer of emotion except the two boys, who exchanged worried and guilt-ridden glances with each other, as if they had just been discovered in some shameful act. They both suddenly burst from the table and ran into the dark background, where a light appeared briefly as they exited by a back door.

"I'm sorry," I said diffidently. "I thought I saw someone I knew come in here."

They said nothing. Out of a back room others began to emerge, no doubt interested in the source of the commotion. In a few moments the room was crowded with these tramp-like figures, all of them gazing emptily in the dimness. I was not at this point frightened of them; at least I was not afraid they would do me any physical harm. Actually, I felt as if it was quite within my power to pummel them easily into submission, their mousy faces almost inviting a succession of firm blows. But there were so many of them.

They slid slowly toward me in a wormy mass. Their eyes seemed empty and unfocused, and I wondered a moment if they were even aware of my presence. Nevertheless, I was the center upon which their lethargic shuffling converged, their shoes scuffing softly along the bare floor. I began to deliver a number of hasty inanities as they continued to press toward me, their weak and unexpectedly odorless bodies nudging against mine. (I understood now why the people along the sidewalks seemed instinctively to avoid Thoss.) Unseen legs became entangled with my own; I staggered and then regained my balance. This sudden movement aroused me from a kind of mesmeric daze into which I must have fallen without being aware of it. I had intended to leave that dreary place long before events had reached such a juncture, but for some reason I could not focus my intentions strongly enough to cause myself to act. My mind had been drifting farther away as these abject things approached. In a sudden surge of panic I pushed through their soft ranks and was outside.

The open air revived me to my former alertness, and I immediately started pacing swiftly up the hill. I was no longer sure that I had not simply imagined what had seemed, and at the same time did not seem, like a perilous moment. Had their movements been directed toward a harmful assault, or were they trying merely to intimidate me? As I reached the green-glazed main street of Mirocaw I really could not determine what had just happened.

The sidewalks were still jammed with a multitude of pedestrians, who now seemed more lively than they had been only a short time before. There was a kind of vitality that could only be attributed to the imminent festivities. A group of young men had begun celebrating prematurely and strode noisily across the street at midpoint, obviously intoxicated. From the laughter and joking among the still sober citizens I gathered that, mardi-gras style, public drunkenness was within the traditions of this winter festival. I looked for anything to indicate the beginnings of the Street Masquerade, but saw nothing: no brightly garbed harlequins or snow-white pierrots. Were the ceremonies even now in preparation for the coronation of the Winter Queen? "The Winter Queen," I wrote in my journal. "Figure of fertility invested with symbolic powers of revival and prosperity. Elected in the manner of a high school prom queen. Check for possible consort figure in the form of a representative from the underworld."

In the pre-darkness hours of December 19 I sat in my hotel room and wrote and thought and organized. I did not feel too badly, all things considered. The holiday excitement which was steadily rising in the streets below my window was definitely infecting me. I forced myself to take a short nap in anticipation of a long night. When I awoke, Mirocaw's annual feast was in full motion.

5.

Practically bounding from my bed to the sounds of bustling and carousing outside, I went to the window and looked out over the town. It seemed all the lights of Mirocaw were shining, save in that section down the hill which became part of the black void of winter. And now the town's greenish tinge was even more pronounced, spreading everywhere like a great green rainbow that had melted from the sky and endured, phosphorescent, into the night. In the streets was the brightness of an artificial spring. The byways of Mirocaw vibrated with activity: on a nearby corner a brass band blared; marauding cars blew their horns and were sometimes mounted by laughing pedestrians; a man emerged from the Red Rooster Bar, threw up his arms, and crowed. I looked closely at the individual celebrants, searching for the vestments of clowns. Soon, delightedly, I saw them. The costume was red and white, with matching cap, and the face painted a noble alabaster. It almost seemed to be a clownish incarnation of that white-bearded and black-booted Christmas fool.

This particular fool, however, was not receiving the affection and respect usually accorded to a Santa Claus. My poor fellow-clown was in the middle of a circle of revelers who were pushing him back and forth from one to the other. The object of this abuse seemed to accept it somewhat willingly, but this little game nevertheless appeared to have humiliation as its purpose. "Only clowns here are the ones that're picked out," echoed Beadle's voice in my memory. "Picked on" seemed closer to the truth.

Packing myself in some heavy clothes, I went out into the green gleaming streets. Not far from the hotel I was stumbled into by a character with a wide blue and red grin and bright baggy clothes. Actually he had been shoved in my direction by some young men outside a drugstore. He lost his footing on the slick sidewalk and tumbled down into a bank of snow along the street.

"See the freak," said an obese and drunken fellow. "See the freak fall."

My first response was anger, and then fear as I saw two others flanking the fat drunk. They walked toward me and I tensed myself for a confrontation.

"This is a disgrace," one said, the neck of a wine bottle held loosely in his left hand.

But it was not to me they were speaking; it was to the clown. His three persecutors helped him up with a sudden jerk and then splashed wine in his face. They ignored me altogether.

"Let him loose," the fat one said. "Crawl away, freak. Oh, he flies!"

The clown trotted off, becoming lost in the throng.

"Wait a minute," I said to the rowdy trio, who had started lumbering away. I quickly decided that it would probably be futile to ask them to explain what I had just witnessed, especially amid the noise and confusion of the festivities. In my best jovial fashion I proposed we all go someplace where I could buy them each a drink. They had no objection and in a short while we were all squeezed around a table in the Red Rooster.

Soon after we were served, I told them that I was from out of town and asked if they could explain some things I did not understand about their festival.

"I don't think there's anything *to* understand," the fat one said. "It's just what you see."

I asked him about the people dressed as clowns.

"Them? They're the freaks. It's their turn this year. Everyone takes their turn. Next year it might be mine. Or *yours,*" he said, pointing at one of his friends across the table. "And when we find out which one you are—"

"You're not smart enough," said the defiant potential freak.

This was an important point: the fact that individuals who played the clowns remained, or at least attempted to remain, anonymous. This arrangement would help remove inhibitions a resident of Mirocaw might have about abusing his own neighbor or even a family relation. From what I later observed, the extent of this abuse did not go beyond a kind of playful roughhousing. And even so, it was only the occasional group of rowdies who actually took advantage of this aspect of the festival, the majority of the citizens very much content to stay on the sidelines.

As far as being able to illuminate the meaning of this custom, my three young friends were quite useless. To them it was just amusement, as I imagine it was to the majority of Mirocavians. This was understandable. I suppose the average person would not be able to explain exactly how the profoundly familiar Christmas holiday came to be celebrated in its present form.

I left the bar alone and not unaffected by the drinks I had consumed there. Outside, the general merrymaking continued. Loud music emanated from several quarters. Mirocaw had fully transformed itself from a sedate small town to an enclave of Saturnalia within the dark immensity of a winter night. But Saturn is also the planetary symbol of melancholy and sterility, a clash of opposites contained within that single word. And as I wandered half-drunkenly down the street, I discovered that there was a conflict within the winter festival itself. This discovery indeed appeared to be that secret key which Thoss withheld in his study of the town. Oddly enough, it was through my unfamiliarity with the outward nature of the festival that I came to know its true nature.

I was mingling with the crowd on the street, warmly enjoying the confusion around me, when I saw a strangely designed creature lingering on the corner up ahead. It was one of the Mirocaw clowns. Its clothes were shabby and nondescript, almost in the style of a tramp-type clown, but not humorously exaggerated enough. The face, though, made up for the lackluster costume. I had never seen such a strange conception for a clown's countenance. The figure stood beneath a dim streetlight, and when it turned its head my way I felt a sense of recognition. The thin, smooth, and pale head; the wide eyes; the oval-shaped features resembling nothing so much as the skull-faced, screaming creature in that famous painting (memory fails me). This clownish imitation rivaled the original in summoning an effect of stricken horror and despair. It had an inhuman likeness more proper to something under the earth than upon it.

From the first moment I saw this creature, I thought of those inhabitants of the ghetto down the hill. There was the same nauseating passivity and languor in its bearing. Perhaps if I had not been drinking earlier I would not have been bold enough to take the action I did. I decided to join in one of the upstanding traditions of the winter festival, for it annoyed me to see this morbid impostor of a clown standing up. When I reached the corner I laughingly pushed myself into the creature—"Whoops!"—who stumbled backward and ended up on the sidewalk. I laughed again and looked around for approval from my fellow merrymakers in the vicinity. No one, however, seemed to appreciate or even acknowledge what I had done. They did not laugh with me or point with amusement, but only passed by, perhaps walking a little faster until they were some distance from this streetcorner incident. I realized instantly I had violated some tacit rule of behavior, though I had thought my action well within the common practice. The idea occurred to me that I might even be apprehended and prosecuted for what in any other circumstances was certainly a criminal act. I turned around to help the clown back to his feet, hoping to somehow redeem my offense, but the creature was gone. Solemnly I walked away from the scene of my inadvertent crime and sought other streets away from its witnesses.

Along the various back avenues of Mirocaw I wandered, pausing exhaustedly at one point to sit at the counter of a small sandwich shop that was packed with customers. I ordered a cup of coffee to revive my inebriated system. Warming my hands around the cup and sipping slowly from it, I watched the people outside as they passed the front window. It was well after midnight but the thick flow of passersby gave no indication that anyone was going home early. A carnival of profiles filed past the window and I was content simply to sit back and observe, until finally one of these faces made me start. It was that frightful little clown I had roughed up earlier. But although its face was familiar in its ghastly aspect, there was something different about it. And I wondered that there should be two hideous freaks.

Quickly paying the man at the counter, I dashed out to get a second glimpse of the clown, who was now nowhere to be seen. I wondered how it could have made its way so easily out of sight, unless the dense crowd along the sidewalk had instinctively allowed this creature to pass unhindered through its massive ranks, as it did for Thoss. In the process of searching for this particular freak, I discovered that interspersed among the celebrating populace of Mirocaw, which included the sanctioned festival clowns, there was not one or two, but a considerable number of these pale, wraithlike creatures. And they all drifted along the streets unmolested by even the rowdiest of revelers. I now understood one of the taboos of the festival. These other clowns were not to be disturbed and should even be avoided, much as were the residents of the slum at the edge of town. Nevertheless, I felt instinctively that the two groups of clowns were somehow identified with each other, even if the ghetto clowns were not welcome at Mirocaw's winter festival. Indeed, they might legitimately be regarded as part of the community and celebrating the season in their own way. To all appearances, this group of melancholy mummers constituted nothing less than an entirely independent festival—a festival within a festival.

Returning to my room, I entered my suppositions into the journal I was keeping for this venture. The following are excerpts:

There is a superstitiousness displayed by the residents of Mirocaw with regard to these people from the slum section, particularly as they lately appear in those dreadful faces signifying

their own festival. What is the relationship between these simul-
taneous celebrations? Did one precede the other? If so, which?
My opinion at this point—and I claim no conclusiveness for it—
is that Mirocaw's winter festival is the later manifestation, that
it appeared after the festival of those depressingly pallid clowns,
in order to cover it up or mitigate its effect. The holiday suicides
come to mind, and the "subclimate" Thoss wrote about, as well
as the disappearance of Elizabeth Beadle twenty years ago, and
my encounter this very day with the pariah clan existing outside
yet within the community. Of my own experience with this emo-
tionally deleterious subseason I would rather not speak at this
time. Still not able to say whether or not my usual winter melancholy is the cause. On the general subject of mental health, I
must consider Thoss's book about his stay in a psychiatric hospital (in western Massachusetts, almost sure of that. Check on
this book and Mirocaw's New England roots). The winter solstice is tomorrow, albeit sometime past midnight. It is, of course,
the day of the year on which night hours surpass daylight hours
by the greatest margin. Note what this has to do with the suicides and a rise in psychic disorder. Recalling Thoss's list of documented suicides in his article, there seemed to be a recurrence
of specific family names, as there very likely might be for any
kind of data collected in a small town. Among these names was
a Beadle or two. Perhaps, then, there is a hereditary basis for the
suicides which has nothing to do with Thoss's mystical subclimate, which is a colorful idea to be sure and one that seems fitting for this town of various outward and inward aspects, but is
not a conception that can be substantiated.

One thing that seems certain, however, is the division of Mirocaw into two very distinct types of citizenry, resulting in two
festivals and the appearance of similar clowns—a term now
used in an extremely loose sense. But there is a connection, and
I believe I have some idea of what it is. I said before that the normal residents of the town regard those from the ghetto, and
especially their clown figures, with superstition. Yet it's more
than that: there is fear, perhaps hatred—the particular kind of
hatred resulting from some powerful and irrational memory. What

threatens Mirocaw I think I can very well understand. I recall the incident earlier today in that vacant diner. "Vacant" is the appropriate word here. The congregation of that half-lit room formed less a presence than an absence, even considering the oppressive number of them. Those eyes that did not or could not focus on anything, the pining lassitude of their faces, the lazy march of their feet. I was spiritually drained when I ran out of there. I then understood why these people and their activities are avoided.

I cannot question the wisdom of those ancestral Mirocavians who began the tradition of the winter festival and gave the town a pretext for celebration and social intercourse at a time when the consequences of brooding isolation are most severe, those longest and darkest days of the solstice. A mood of Christmas joviality obviously would not be sufficient to counter the menace of this season. But even so, there are still the suicides of individuals who are somehow cut off, I imagine, from the vitalizing activities of the festival.

It is the nature of this insidious subseason that seems to determine the outward forms of Mirocaw's winter festival: the optimistic greenery in a period of gray dormancy; the fertile promise of the Winter Queen; and, most interesting to my mind, the clowns—the bright clowns of Mirocaw who are treated so badly. They appear to serve as surrogate figures for those dark-eyed mummers of the slums. Since the latter are feared for some power or influence they possess, they may still be symbolically confronted and conquered through their counterparts, who are elected for precisely this function. If I am right about this, I wonder to what extent there is a conscious awareness among the town's populace of this indirect show of aggression. Those three young men I spoke with tonight did not seem to possess much insight beyond seeing that there was a certain amount of robust fun in the festival's tradition. For that matter, how much awareness is there on the *other side* of these two antagonistic festivals? Too horrible to think of such a thing, but I must wonder if, for all their apparent aimlessness, those inhabitants of the ghetto are not the only ones who know what they are about. No denying that behind those inhumanly limp expressions there seems to be a kind of obnoxious intelligence.

As I wobbled from street to street tonight, watching those oval-mouthed clowns, I could not help feeling that all the merrymaking in Mirocaw was somehow allowed only by their sufferance. This I hope is no more than a fanciful Thossian intuition, the sort of idea that is curious and thought-provoking without ever seeming to gain the benefit of confirmation. I know my mind is not entirely lucid, but I feel that it may be possible to penetrate Mirocaw's many complexities and illuminate the hidden side of the festival season. In particular I must look for the significance of the other festival. Is it also some kind of fertility celebration? From what I have seen, the tenor of this "celebrating" sub-group is one of anti-fertility, if anything. How have they managed to keep from dying out completely over the years? How do they maintain their numbers?

But I was too tired to formulate any more of my sodden speculations. Falling onto my bed, I soon became lost in dreams of streets and faces.

6.

I was, of course, slightly hung over when I woke up late the next morning. The festival was still going strong, and blaring music outside roused me from a nightmare. It was a parade. A number of floats proceeded down Townshend, a familiar color predominating. There were theme floats of pilgrims and Indians, cowboys and Indians, and clowns of an orthodox type. In the middle of it all was the Winter Queen herself, freezing atop an icy throne. She waved in all directions. I even imagined she waved up at my dark window. In the first few groggy moments of wakefulness I had no sympathy with my excitation of the previous night. But I discovered that my former enthusiasm had merely lain dormant, and soon returned with an even greater intensity. Never before had my mind and senses been so active during this usually inert time of year. At home I would have been playing lugubrious old records and looking out the window quite a bit. I was terribly grateful in a completely abstract way for my commitment to a meaningful mania. And I was eager to get to work after I had had some breakfast at the coffee shop.

When I got back to my room I discovered the door was unlocked. And there was something written on the dresser mirror. The writing was red and greasy, as if done with a clown's make-up pencil—my own, I realized. I read the legend, or rather I should say *riddle,* several times: "What buries itself before it is dead?" I looked at it for quite a while, very shaken at how vulnerable my holiday fortifications were. Was this supposed to be a warning of some kind? A threat to the effect that if I persisted in a certain course I would end up prematurely interred? I would have to be careful, I told myself. My resolution was to let nothing deter me from the inspired strategy I had conceived for myself. I wiped the mirror clean, for it was now needed for other purposes.

I spent the rest of the day devising a very special costume and the appropriate face to go with it. I easily shabbied up my overcoat with a torn pocket or two and a complete set of stains. Combined with blue jeans and a pair of rather scuffed-up shoes, I had a passable costume for a derelict. The face, however, was more difficult, for I had to experiment from memory. Conjuring a mental image of the shrieking pierrot in that painting (*The Scream,* I now recall), helped me quite a bit. At nightfall I exited the hotel by the back stairway.

It was strange to walk down the crowded street in this gruesome disguise. Though I thought I would feel conspicuous, the actual experience was very close, I imagined, to one of complete invisibility. No one looked at me as I strolled by, or as they strolled by, or as we strolled by each other. I was a phantom—perhaps the ghost of festivals past, or those yet to come.

I had no clear idea where my disguise would take me that night, only vague expectations of gaining the confidence of my fellow specters and possibly in some way coming to know their secrets. For a while I would simply wander around in that lackadaisical manner I had learned from them, following their lead in any way they might indicate. And for the most part this meant doing almost nothing and doing it silently. If I passed one of my kind on the sidewalk there was no speaking, no exchange of knowing looks, no recognition at all that I was aware of. We were there on the streets of Mirocaw to create a presence and nothing more. At least this is how I came to feel about it. As I drifted along with my bodiless invisibility, I felt myself more and more becoming an empty, floating shape, seeing without being seen and walking without the interference of those grosser creatures who shared my world. It was not an experience completely without interest and even enjoyment. The clown's shibboleth of "Here we are again" took on a new meaning for me as I felt myself a novitiate of a more rarefied order of harlequinry. And very soon the opportunity to make further progress along this path presented itself.

Going the opposite direction, down the street, a pickup truck slowly passed, gently parting a sea of zigging and zagging celebrants. The cargo in the back of this truck was curious, for it was made up entirely of my fellow sectarians. At the end of the block the truck stopped and another of them boarded it over the back gate. One block down I saw still another get on. Then the truck made a U-turn at an intersection and headed in my direction.

I stood at the curb as I had seen the others do. I was not sure the truck would pick me up, thinking that somehow they knew I was an impostor. The truck did, however, slow down, almost coming to a stop when it reached me. The others were crowded on the floor of the truck bed. Most of them were just staring at nothing with the usual indifference I had come to expect from their kind. But a few actually glanced at me with some anticipation. For a second I hesitated, not sure I wanted to pursue this ruse any further. At the last moment, though, some impulse sent me climbing up the back of the truck and squeezing myself in among the others.

There were only a few more to pick up before the truck headed for the outskirts of Mirocaw and beyond. At first I tried to maintain a clear orientation with respect to the town. But as we took turn after turn through the darkness of narrow country roads, I found myself unable to preserve any sense of direction. The majority of the others in the back of the truck exhibited no apparent awareness of their fellow passengers. Guardedly, I looked from face to ghostly face. A few of them spoke in short whispered phrases to others close by. I could not make out what they were saying but the tone of their voices was one of innocent normalcy, as if they were not of the hardened slum-herd of Mirocaw. Perhaps, I thought, these were thrill-seekers who had disguised themselves as I had done, or, more likely, initiates of some kind. Possibly they had received prior instructions at such meetings as I had stumbled onto the day before. It was also likely that among this crew were those very boys I had frightened into a precipitate exit from that old diner.

The truck was now speeding along a fairly open stretch of country, heading toward those higher hills that surrounded the now distant town of Mirocaw. The icy wind whipped around us, and I could not keep myself from trembling with cold. This definitely betrayed me as one of the newcomers among the group, for the two bodies that pressed against mine were rigidly still and even seemed to be radiating a frigidity of their own. I glanced ahead at the darkness into which we were rapidly progressing.

We had left all open country behind us now, and the road was enclosed by thick woods. The mass of bodies in the truck leaned into one another as we began traveling up a steep incline. Above us, at the top of the hill, were lights shining somewhere within the woods. When the road leveled off, the truck made an abrupt turn, steering into what looked like a great ditch. There was an unpaved path, however, upon which the truck proceeded toward the glowing in the near distance.

This glowing became brighter and sharper as we approached it, flickering upon the trees and revealing stark detail where there had formerly been only smooth darkness. As the truck pulled into a clearing and came to a stop, I saw a loose assembly of figures, many of which held lanterns that beamed with a dazzling and frosty light. I stood up in the back of the truck to unboard as the others were doing. Glancing around from that height I saw approximately thirty more of those cadaverous clowns milling about. One of my fellow passengers spied me lingering in the truck and in a strangely high-pitched whisper told me to hurry, explaining something about the "apex of darkness." I thought again about this solstice night; it was technically the longest period of darkness of the year, even if not by a very significant margin from many other winter nights. Its true significance, though, was related to considerations having little to do with either statistics or the calendar.

I went over to the place where the others were forming into a tighter crowd, which betrayed a sense of expectancy in the subtle gestures and expressions of its individual members. Glances were now exchanged, the hand of one lightly touched the shoulder of another, and a pair of circled eyes gazed over to where two figures were setting their lanterns on the ground about six feet apart. The illumination of these lanterns revealed an opening in the earth. Eventually the awareness of everyone was focused on this roundish pit, and as if by prearranged signal we all began huddling around it. The only sounds were those of the wind and our own movements as we crushed frozen leaves and sticks underfoot.

Finally, when we had all surrounded this gaping hole, the first one jumped in, leaving our sight for a moment but then reappearing to take hold of a lantern which another handed him from above. The miniature abyss filled with light, and I could see it was no more than six feet deep. One of its walls opened into the mouth of a tunnel. The figure holding the lantern stooped a little and disappeared into the passage.

Each of us, in turn, dropped into the darkness of this pit, and every fifth one took a lantern. I kept to the back of the group, for whatever subterranean activities were going to take place, I was sure I wanted to be on their periphery. When only about ten of us remained on the ground above, I maneuvered to let four of them precede me so that I might receive a lantern. This was exactly how it worked out, for after I had leaped to the bottom of the hole a light was ritually handed down to me. Turning about-face, I quickly entered the passageway. At that point I shook so with cold that I was neither curious nor afraid, grateful for the shelter.

I entered a long, gently sloping tunnel, just high enough for me to stand upright. It was considerably warmer down there than outside in the cold darkness of the woods. After a few moments I had sufficiently thawed out so that my concerns shifted from those of physical comfort to a sudden and justified preoccupation with my survival. As I walked I held my lantern close to the sides of the tunnel. They were relatively smooth as if the passage had not been made by manual digging but had been burrowed by something which left behind a clue to its dimensions in the tunnel's size and shape. This delirious idea came to me when I recalled the message that had been left on my hotel room mirror: "What buries itself before it is dead?"

I had to hurry along to keep up with those uncanny spelunkers who preceded me. The lanterns ahead bobbed with every step of their bearers, the lumbering procession seeming less and less real the farther we marched into that snug little tunnel. At some point I noticed the line ahead of me growing shorter. The processioners were emptying out into a cavernous chamber where I, too, soon arrived. This area was about thirty feet in height, its other dimensions approximating those of a large ballroom. Gazing into the distance above made me uncomfortably aware of how far we had descended into the earth. Unlike the smooth sides of the tunnel, the walls of this cavern looked jagged and irregular, as though they had been gnawed at. The earth had been removed, I assumed, either through the tunnel from which we had emerged, or else by way of one of the many other black openings that I saw around the edges of the chamber, for possibly they too led back to the surface.

But the structure of this chamber occupied my mind a great deal less than did its occupants. There to meet us on the floor of the great cavern was what must have been the entire slum population of Mirocaw, and more, all with the same eerily wide-eyed and oval-mouthed faces. They formed a circle around an altar-like object which had some kind of dark, leathery covering draped over it. Upon the altar, another covering of the same material concealed a lumpy form beneath. And behind this form, looking down upon the altar, was the only figure whose face was not greased with makeup.

He wore a long snowy robe that was the same color as the wispy hair berimming his head. His arms were calmly at his sides. He made no movement. The man I once believed would penetrate great secrets stood before us with the same professorial bearing that had impressed me so many years ago, yet now I felt nothing but dread at the thought of what revelations lay pocketed within the abysmal folds of his magisterial attire. Had I really come here to challenge such a formidable figure? The name by which I knew him seemed itself insufficient to designate one of his stature. Rather I should name him by his other incarnations: god of all wisdom, scribe of all sacred books, father of all magicians, thrice great and more—rather I should call him *Thoth*.

He raised his cupped hands to his congregation and the ceremony was underway.

It was all very simple. The entire assembly, which had remained speechless until this moment, broke into the most horrendous high-pitched singing that can be imagined. It was a choir of sorrow, lament, and mortification. The cavern rang with the dissonant, whining chorus. My voice, too, was added to the congregation's, trying to blend with their maimed music. But my singing could not imitate theirs, having a huskiness at odds with the keening ululation of that company. To keep from exposing myself as an intruder I continued to mouth their words without sound. These words were a revelation of the moody malignancy which until then I had no more than sensed whenever in the presence of these figures. They were singing to the "unborn in paradise," to the "pure unlived lives." They sang a dirge for existence, for all its vital forms and seasons. Their ideal was a melancholy half-existence consecrated to all the many shapes of death and dissolution. A sea of thin, bloodless faces trembled and screamed their antipathy to being itself. And the robed, guiding figure at the heart of all this—elevated over the course of twenty years to the status of high priest—was the man from whom I had taken so many of my own life's principles. It would be useless to describe what I felt at that moment and a waste of the time I need to describe the events which followed.

The singing abruptly stopped and the towering white-haired figure began to speak. He was welcoming those of the new generation—twenty winters had passed since the "Pure Ones" had expanded their ranks. The word "pure" in this setting was a violence to what sense and composure I still retained, for nothing could have been more foul than what was to come. Thoss— and I employ this defunct identity only as a convenience—closed his sermon and drew closer to the dark-skinned altar. Then, with all the flourish of his former life, he drew back the topmost covering. Beneath it was a limp-limbed effigy, a collapsed puppet sprawled upon the slab. I was standing toward the rear of the congregation and attempted to keep as close to the exit passage as I could. Thus, I did not see everything as clearly as I might have.

Thoss looked down upon the crooked, doll-like form and then out at the gathering. I even imagined that he made knowing eye-contact with me. He spread his arms and a stream of continuous and unintelligible words flowed from his moaning mouth. The congregation began to stir, not greatly but perceptibly. Until that moment there was a limit to what I believed was the evil of these people. They were, after all, only that. They were merely morbid souls with beliefs that were eccentric to the healthy social order around them. If there was anything I had learned in all my years as an anthropologist it was that the world is infinitely rich in phenomena that society as we know it (whoever "we" might be) would regard as strange, even to the point where the concept of strangeness itself had little meaning for me. But with the scene I then witnessed, my conscience vaulted into a realm from which it will never return.

For now was the transformation scene, the culmination of every harlequinade.

It began slowly. There was increasing movement among those on the far side of the chamber from where I stood. Someone had fallen to the floor and the others in the area backed away. The voice at the altar continued its chanting. I tried to gain a better view but there were too many of them around me.

Through the mass of obstructing bodies I caught only glimpses of what was taking place.

The one who had swooned to the floor of the chamber seemed to be losing all former shape and proportion. I thought it was a clown's trick. They were clowns, were they not? I myself could make four white balls transform into four black balls as I juggled them. And this was not my most astonishing feat of clownish magic. And is there not always a sleight-of-hand inherent in all ceremonies, often dependent on the transported delusions of the celebrants? This was a good show, I thought, and giggled to myself. The transformation scene of Harlequin throwing off his fool's façade. O God, Harlequin, do not move like that! Harlequin, where are your arms? And your legs have melted together and begun squirming upon the floor. What horrible, mouthing umbilicus is that where your face should be? *What is it that buries itself before it is dead?* The almighty serpent of wisdom—the Conqueror Worm.

It now started happening all around the chamber. Individual members of the congregation would gaze emptily—caught for a moment in a frozen trance—and then collapse to the floor to begin the sickening metamorphosis. This happened with ever-increasing frequency the louder and more frantically Thoss chanted his insane prayer or curse. Then there began a writhing movement toward the altar, and Thoss welcomed the things as they curled their way to the altar-top. I knew now what lax figure lay upon it.

This was Kora and Persephone, the daughter of Ceres and the Winter Queen: the child abducted into the underworld of death. Except this child had no supernatural mother to save her, no living mother at all. For the sacrifice I witnessed was an echo of one that had occurred twenty years before, the carnival feast of the preceding generation—O *carne vale!* Now both mother and daughter had become victims of this subterranean sabbat. I finally realized this truth when the figure stirred upon the altar, lifted its head of icy beauty, and screamed at the sight of mute mouths closing around her.

I ran from the chamber into the tunnel. (There was nothing else that could be done, I have obsessively told myself.) Some of the others who had not yet changed began to pursue me. They would have caught up to me, I have no doubt, for I fell only a few yards into the passage. And for a moment I imagined that I too was about to undergo a transformation. Anything seemed possible now. When I heard the approaching footsteps of my pursuers I was sure there was nothing left for me but the worst finale a human being can suffer—the death known to those whom the gods have first made mad. Perhaps I would even be forced to take a place on the altar among the gory remnants of the Winter Queen. But the footsteps behind me ceased and retreated. They had received an order in the voice of their high priest. I too heard the order, though I wish I had not, for until then I had imagined that Thoss did not remember who I was. It was that voice which taught me otherwise.

For the moment I was free to leave. I struggled to my feet and, having broken my lantern in the fall, retraced my way back through cloacal blackness.

Everything seemed to happen very quickly once I emerged from the tunnel and climbed up from the pit. I wiped the reeking greasepaint from my face as I ran through the woods and back to the road. A passing car stopped, though I gave it no other choice except to run me down.

"Thank you for stopping."

"What the hell are you doing out here?" the driver asked.

I caught my breath. "It was a joke. The festival. Friends thought it would be funny. Please drive on."

My ride let me off about a mile out of town, and from there I could find my way. It was the same route I traveled when I first visited Mirocaw the summer before. I stood for a while at the summit of that high hill just outside the city limits, looking down upon the busy little hamlet. The intensity of the festival had not abated. I walked toward the welcoming glow of green and slipped through the festivities unnoticed.

When I reached the hotel I was glad to see that no one was about. Given that I was so obviously a wreck, I feared meeting anyone who might ask what had happened to me. The hotel desk was unattended, so I was spared having to speak with

Beadle. Indeed, there was an atmosphere of abandonment throughout the place that I found ominous yet did not pause to contemplate.

I trod up the stairs to my room. Locking the door behind me, I then collapsed upon the bed and was soon enshrouded by a merciful blackness.

7.

When I awoke the next morning I saw from my window that the town and surrounding countryside had been visited during the night by a heavy snowfall, one which was entirely unpredicted. A few leftover flakes were still lighting on the now deserted streets of Mirocaw, and buried beneath the drifts below were the last vestiges of revelry and celebration. The festival was over. Everyone had retired to their homes.

And this was exactly my own intention. Any action on my part concerning what I had seen the night before would have to wait until I was away from the town. I am still not sure it will do the slightest good to speak up like this. Any accusations I have made with respect to the slum populace of Mirocaw are eminently subject to dismissal, perhaps as a hoax or a festival hallucination. And thereafter this document will take its place alongside the works of Raymond Thoss.

With packed suitcases in both hands I walked up to the front desk to check out. The man behind the desk was not Samuel Beadle, and he had to fumble around to find my bill.

"Here we are. Everything all right?"

"Fine," I answered in a dead voice. "Is Mr. Beadle around?"

"No, I'm afraid he's not back yet. Been out all night looking for his daughter. She's a very popular girl, being the Winter Queen and all that nonsense. Probably find she was at a party somewhere."

A little noise came out of my throat.

I threw my suitcases in the back seat of my car and got behind the wheel. On that morning nothing I could recall seemed real to me. The snow was falling and I watched it through my windshield, slow and silent and entrancing. I started up my car, routinely glancing in my rear view mirror. What I saw there is now vividly framed in my mind, as it was framed in the back window of my car when I turned to verify its reality.

In the middle of the street behind me, standing ankle-deep in snow, were Thoss and another figure. When I looked closely at the other I recognized him as one of the boys whom I surprised in that diner. But he had now taken on a listless resemblance to his new family. Both he and Thoss stared at me, making no attempt to forestall my departure. Thoss knew that this was unnecessary.

I had to carry the image of those two dark figures in my mind as I drove back home. And only now has the full gravity of my experience descended upon me. So far I have claimed illness in order to avoid my teaching schedule. To face the normal flow of life as I had formerly known it would be impossible. I am now very much under the influence of a season and a climate far colder and more barren than all the winters in human memory. And mentally retracing past events does not seem to have helped. If anything, I now feel myself sinking deeper into a velvety white abyss.

At certain times I could almost dissolve entirely into this inner realm of purity and emptiness, the paradise of the unborn. I remember how I was momentarily overtaken by a feeling I had never known when in disguise I drifted through the streets of Mirocaw, untouched by the drunken, noisy forms around me: untouchable. It was the feeling that I had been liberated from the *weight of life*. But I recoil at this seductive nostalgia, for it mocks my existence as mere foolery, a bright clown's mask behind which I have sought to hide my darkness. I realize what is happening and what I do not want to be true, though Thoss proclaimed it was. I recall his command to those others as I lay helplessly prone in the tunnel. They could have apprehended me, but Thoss, my old master, called them back. His voice echoed throughout that cavern, and it now reverberates within the psychic chambers of my memory.

"He is one of us," it said. "He has *always* been one of us."

It is this voice which now fills my dreams and my days and my long winter nights. I have seen you, Dr. Thoss, through the snow outside my window. Soon I will celebrate, alone, that last feast which will kill your words, only to prove how well I have learned their truth.

TO THE MEMORY OF H. P. LOVECRAFT

THE SPECTACLES IN
THE DRAWER

Last year at this time, perhaps on this very day, Plomb visited me at my home. He always seemed to know when I had returned from my habitual traveling and always appeared uninvited on my doorstep. Although my former residence was pathetically run-down, Plomb seemed to regard it as a kind of palace of wonders, and he would gaze at its high ceilings and antiquated fixtures as if he saw some new glamour in them on each of his visits. That day—a dim one, I think—he did not fail to do the same. Then we settled into one of the spacious though sparsely furnished rooms of my house.

"And how were your travels?" he asked, as if only in the spirit of polite conversation. I could see by his smile—an emulation of my own, no doubt—that he was glad to be back in my house and in my company. I smiled too and stood up. Plomb, of course, stood up along with me, almost simultaneously with my own movements.

"Shall we go then?" I said. *What a pest,* I thought.

Our footsteps tapped a moderate time on the hard wooden floor leading to the stairway. We ascended to the second floor, which I left almost entirely empty, and then up a narrower stairway to the third floor. Although I had led him along this route several times before, I could see from his wandering eyes that, for him, every crack in the walls, every cobweb fluttering in the corners above, every stale draft of the house composed a suspenseful prelude to our destination. At the end of the

third-floor hall there was a small wooden stairway, no more
than a ladder, that led to an old storeroom where I kept certain
things which I collected.

It was not by any means a spacious room, and its enclosed
atmosphere was *thickened,* as Plomb would have emphasized,
by its claustrophobic arrangement of tall cabinets, ceiling-high
shelves, and various trunks and crates. This is simply how matters worked out over a period of time. In any case, Plomb seemed
to favor this state of affairs. "Ah, the room of secret mystery," he
said. "The chamber where all your hermetical prodigies are
cached away."

These treasures and marvels, as Plomb called them, were, I
suppose, remarkable from a certain point of view. Plomb loved
to go through my collection of curiosities, gathering together a
lapful of exotic objects and settling down on the dusty sofa at
the center of the room. But it was the new items, whenever I
returned from one of my protracted tours, that always took pre-
cedence in Plomb's hierarchy of fascination. Thus, I immediately
brought out the double-handled dagger with the single blade of
polished stone. At first sight of the ceremonial object, Plomb held
out the flat palms of his hands, and I placed this queer device
upon its rightful altar. "Who could have made such a thing?" he
asked, though rhetorically. He expected no answer to his questions and possibly did not really desire any. And of course I
offered no more elaborate an explanation than a simple smile.
But how quickly, I noticed on this occasion, the magic of that
first token of my "tantalizing arcana," as he would say, lost its
initial surge of attraction. How fast that glistening fog, which
surrounded only Plomb, dispersed to unveil a tedious clarity. I
had to move faster.

"Here," I said, my arm searching the shadows of an open
wardrobe. "This should be worn when you handle that sacrificial artifact." And I threw the robe about his shoulders, engulf-
ing his smallish frame with a cyclone of strange patterns and
colors. He admired himself in the mirror attached inside the
door of the wardrobe. "Look at the robe in the mirror," he
practically shouted. "The designs are all turned around. How

much stranger, how much better." While he stood there glaring at himself, I relieved him of the dagger before he had a chance to do something careless. This left his hands free to raise themselves up to the dust-caked ceiling of the room, and to the dark gods of his imagination. Gripping each handle of the dagger, I suddenly elevated it above his head, where I held it poised. In a few moments he started to giggle, and then fell into spasms of sardonic hilarity. He stumbled over to the old sofa and collapsed upon its soft cushions. I followed, but when I reached his prostrate form it was not the pale-blue blade that I brought down upon his chest—it was simply a book, one of many I had put before him. His peaked legs created a lectern on which he rested the huge volume, propping it securely as he began turning the stiff, crackling pages. The sound seemed to absorb him as much as the sight of a language he could not even name let alone comprehend.

"The lost grimoire of the Abbot of Tine," he giggled. "Transcribed in the language of—"

"A wild guess," I interjected. "And a wrong one."

"Then the forbidden *Psalms of the Silent*. The book without an author."

"Without an author who ever lived in this world, if you will recall what I told you about it. But you're very wide of the mark."

"Well, suppose you give me a hint," he said with an impatience that surprised me.

"But wouldn't you prefer to speculate on its secrets?" I suggested. Some moments of precarious silence passed.

"I suppose I would," he finally answered. Then I watched him gorge his eyes on the inscrutable script of the ancient volume.

In truth, the mysteries of this Sacred Writ were among the most genuine of their kind, for it had never been my intention to dupe my disciple, as he justly thought of himself, with false secrets. But the secrets of such a book are not perpetual. Once they are known, they become relegated to a lesser sphere, which is that of the knower. Having lost the prestige they once enjoyed, these former secrets now function as tools in the excavation of still deeper ones which, in turn, will suffer the same corrosive fate. And this is the fate of all the secrets of the universe. Eventually the seeker of a recondite knowledge may conclude—either through insight or sheer exhaustion—that this ruthless process is never-ending, that the mortification of one mystery after another has no terminus beyond that of the seeker's own extinction. And how many still remain susceptible to the search? How many pursue it to the end of their days with undying hope of some ultimate revelation? Better not to think in precise terms just how few the faithful are. More to the present point, it seems that Plomb belonged to their infinitesimal number. And it was my intention to reduce that number by one.

The plan was simple: to feed Plomb's hunger for mysterious sensations to the point of nausea . . . and beyond. The only thing to survive would be a gutful of shame and regret for a defunct passion.

As Plomb lay upon the sofa, ogling that stupid book, I moved toward a large cabinet whose several doors were composed of a tarnished metal grillwork framed by dark wood. I opened one of these doors and exposed a number of shelves cluttered with books and odd objects. Upon one shelf, resting there as its sole occupant, was a very white box. It was no larger, as I mentally envision it, than a modest jewelry case. There were no markings on the box, except the fingerprints, or rather thumbprints, smearing its smooth white surface at its opposing edges and halfway along its length. There were no handles or embellishments of any kind; not even, at first sight, the thinnest of seams to indicate the level at which the lower part of the box met the upper part, or perhaps give away the existence of a drawer. I smiled a little at the mock intrigue of the object, then gripped it from either side, gently, and placed my thumbs precisely over the fresh, greasy prints. I applied pressure with each thumb, and a shallow drawer popped open at the front of the box. As hoped, Plomb had been watching me as I went through these motions.

"What do you have there?" he asked.

"Patience, Plomb. You will see," I answered while delicately removing two sparkling items from the drawer: one a small and silvery knife which very much resembled a razor-sharp letter opener, and the other a pair of old-fashioned wire-rimmed spectacles.

Plomb laid aside the now-boring book and sat up straight against the arm of the sofa. I sat down beside him and opened up the spectacles so that the stems were pointing toward his face. When he leaned forward, I slipped them on. "They're only plain glass," he said with a definite tone of disappointment. "Or a very weak prescription." His eyes rolled about as he attempted to scrutinize what rested upon his own face. Without saying a word, I held up the little knife in front of him until he finally took notice of it. "Ahhhh," he said, smiling. "There's more to it." "Of course there is," I said, gently twirling the steely blade before his fascinated eyes. "If you would, I need you to hold out the palm of your hand. It doesn't matter which one. Good, just like that. Don't worry, you won't even feel this. There," I said after making a tiny cut. "Now," I instructed him, "keep watching that thin red trickle.

"Your eyes are now fused with those fantastic lenses, and your sight is one with its object. And what exactly is that object? Obviously it is everything that fascinates, everything that has power over your gaze and your dreams. You cannot even conceive the wish to look away. And even if there are no simple images to see, nonetheless there is a vision of some kind, an infinite and overwhelming scene expanding before you. And the vastness of this scene is such that even the dazzling diffusion of all the known universes cannot convey *these* prodigies. Everything is so brilliant, so great, and so alive. Landscapes without end are rolling with a life unknown to mortal eyes. Unimaginable diversity of form and motion, design and dimension, with each detail perfectly crystalline, from the mammoth shapes lurching in outline against endless horizons to the minutest cilia wriggling in an obscure oceanic niche. And even this is only a mere fragment of all that there is to see and to know. There are labyrinthine astronomies mingling together and yielding instantaneous evolutions, constant transformations of both appearance and essence. You feel yourself to be a witness to the most cryptic phenomena that exist or ever could exist. And yet, somehow concealed in the shadows of what you can see is something that is not yet visible, something that is beating like a thunderous pulse and promises still greater visions. All else is merely its membrane enclosing the ultimate thing waiting to be born, preparing for the cataclysm which will be both the beginning and the end. To behold the prelude to this event is an experience of unbearable anticipation, so that ecstasy and dread merge into a new emotion, one corresponding perfectly to the exposure of the ultimate source of all manifestation. The next instant, it seems, will bring with it a revolution of the total substance of things. As the seconds keep passing, the experience grows more fascinating without fulfilling its portents, without extinguishing itself in revelation. And although the visions remain active inside you, deep in your blood—you now awake."

Pushing himself up from the sofa, Plomb staggered forward a few steps and wiped his bloodied palm on the front of his shirt, as if to wipe away the visions he had seen. He shook his head vigorously once or twice, but the spectacles remained secure.

"Is everything all right?" I asked him.

Plomb appeared to be dazzled in the worst way. Behind the spectacles his eyes gazed dumbly, and his mouth gaped with countless unspoken words. However, when I said, "Perhaps I should remove these for you," his hand rose toward mine, as if to prevent me from doing so. But his effort was half-hearted. Folding their wire stems one across the other, I replaced them back in their box. Plomb now watched me, as if I were performing some ritual of great moment. He seemed to be still composing himself from his experience.

"Well?" I asked.

"Dreadful," he answered. "But . . ."

"But?"

"What I mean is—where did they come from?"

"Can't you imagine that for yourself?" I countered. And for a moment it seemed that in this case, too, he desired some simple answer, contrary to his most hardened habits. Then he smiled rather deviously and threw himself down upon the sofa. His eyes glazed over as he fabricated an anecdote to his fancy.

"I can see you," he said, "at an occultist auction in a disreputable quarter of a foreign city. The box is carried forward, the spectacles taken out. They were made several generations ago by a man who was at once a student of the Gnostics and a master of optometry. His ambition: to construct a pair of artificial eyes that would allow him to bypass the obstacle of physical appearances and glimpse a far-off realm of secret truth whose gateway is within the depths of our own blood."

"Remarkable," I replied. "Your speculation is so close to truth itself that the details are not worth mentioning for the mere sake of vulgar accuracy."

In fact, the spectacles belonged to a lot of antiquarian rubbish I once bought blindly, and the box was of unknown, or rather unremembered, origin—just something I had lying around in my attic room. And the knife, a magician's prop for efficiently slicing up paper money and silk ties.

I carried the box containing both spectacles and knife over to Plomb, holding it just beyond his reach. I said, "Can you imagine the dangers involved, the possible nightmare of possessing such 'artificial eyes'?" He nodded gravely in agreement. "And you can imagine the restraint the possessor of such a gruesome contrivance must practice." His eyes were all comprehension, and he was sucking a little at his slightly lacerated palm. "Then nothing would please me more than to pass the ownership of this miraculous artifact on to you, my dear Plomb. I'm sure you will hold it in wonder as no one else could."

And it was exactly this wonder that it was my malicious aim to undermine, or rather to expand until it ripped itself apart. For I could no longer endure the sight of it.

As Plomb once again stood at the door of my home, holding his precious gift with a child's awkward embrace, I could not resist asking him the question.

"By the way, Plomb, have you ever been hypnotized?"

"No," he said. "Why do you ask?"

"Curiosity," I replied. "You know how I am. Well, good night."

Then I closed the door behind the most willing subject in the world, hoping it would be some time before he returned. "If ever," I said aloud, and the words echoed in the hollows of my home.

2.

But it was not long afterward that Plomb and I had our next confrontation, though the circumstances were accidental. Late one afternoon, as it happens, I was browsing through a shop that dealt in second-hand merchandise of the most pathetic sort. The place was positively littered with tossed-off oddments and pure trash: rusty scales that once would have given your weight for a penny, cockeyed bookcases, broken toys, old furniture, standing ashtrays late of some hotel lobby, and a hodge-podge of items that seemed entirely inscrutable in their origin and purpose. For me, however, such desolate bazaars offered more diversion and consolation than the most exotic market-places, which so often made good on their strange promises that mystery itself ceased to have meaning. But my second-hand seller made no promises and inspired no dreams, leaving all that to those more ambitious hucksters who trafficked in such stock in trade. And I had left that search behind me, as previously explained. What the mystical rarities of this earth were for Plomb, the most used-up and dismal commodities had become for me. Now I could ask no more of a given gray afternoon than to find myself in an establishment that had nothing to sell but the charm of disenchantment.

By coincidence, that particular afternoon in the second-hand shop brought me, if only in an indirect manner, together with Plomb. The visual transaction took place in a tilting mirror that stood near the shop's back wall, one of the many mirrors that seemed to constitute a specialty of the place. I had squatted down before this relic and wiped my bare hand across its dusty surface. And there, hidden beneath the dust, was the face of Plomb, who must have just entered the shop and was standing a room's length away. While he seemed to recognize immediately the reverse side of me, his expression betrayed the hope that I had not seen him. There was shock as well as shame upon that face, and something else besides. And if Plomb had approached me, what could I have said to him? Perhaps I would have mentioned that he did not look very well or that it appeared he had been the victim of an accident. But how could he explain what had happened to him except to reveal the truth that we both knew and neither would speak? Fortunately, this scene was to remain in its hypothetical state, because a moment later he was out the door.

I cautiously approached the front window of the shop in time to see Plomb hurrying off into the dull, unreflecting day, his right hand held up to his face. "It was only my intention to cure him," I mumbled to myself. I had not considered that he was incurable, nor that things would have developed in the way they did.

3.

After that day I wondered, eventually to the point of obsession, what kind of hell had claimed poor Plomb for its own. I knew only that I had provided him with a type of toy: the subliminal ability to feast his eyes on an imaginary universe in a droplet of his own blood. The possibility that he would desire to magnify this experience, or indeed that he would be capable of such a feat, had not seriously occurred to me. Obviously, however, this had become the case. I now had to ask myself how much farther Plomb's situation could be extended. The answer, though I could not guess it at the time, was presented to me in a dream.

And it seemed fitting that the dream had its setting in that old attic storeroom of my house, which Plomb once prized above all other rooms in the world. I was sitting in a chair, a huge and enveloping chair which in reality does not exist but in the dream directly faces the sofa. No thoughts or feelings troubled me, and I had only the faintest sense that someone else was in the room. But I could not see who it was, because everything appeared so dim in outline, blurry and grayish. There seemed to be some movement in the region of the sofa, as if the enormous cushions themselves had become lethargically restless. Unable to fathom the source of this movement, I touched my hand to my temple in thought. This was how I discovered that I was wearing a pair of spectacles with circular lenses connected to wiry stems. I thought to myself: "If I remove these spectacles I will be able to see more clearly." But a voice told me not to remove them, and I recognized that voice. Then something moved, a man-shaped shadow upon the sofa. A climate of dull horror began to invade my surroundings. "Go away, Plomb. You have nothing to show me," I said. But the voice disagreed with me in sinister whispers that made no sense yet seemed filled with meaning. I would indeed be shown things, these whispers seemed to be saying. Already I was being shown things, astonishing things—mysteries and marvels beyond anything I had ever suspected. And suddenly all my feelings, as I gazed through the spectacles, were proof of that garbled pronouncement. They were feelings of a peculiar nature which, to my knowledge, one experiences only in dreams: sensations of infinite expansiveness and ineffable meaning that have no place elsewhere in our lives. But although these astronomical emotions suggested wonders of incredible magnitude and character, I saw nothing through those magic lenses except this: the obscure shape in the shadows before me as its outline grew clearer and clearer to my eyes. Gradually I came to view what appeared to be a mutilated carcass, something of a terrible rawness, a torn and flayed thing whose every laceration could be seen with microscopic precision. The only thing of color in my grayish surroundings, it twitched and quivered like a gory heart exposed beneath the body of the dream. And it made a sound like hellish giggling. Then it said, "I am back from my trip," as if mocking me.

It was this simple statement that inspired my efforts to tear the spectacles from my face, even though they now seemed to be part of my flesh. I gripped them with both hands and flung them against the wall, where they shattered. Somehow this served to exorcise my tormented companion, who faded back into the grayness. Then I looked at the wall and saw that it was running red where the spectacles had struck. And the broken lenses that lay upon the floor were bleeding.

To experience such a dream as this on a single occasion might very well be the stuff of a haunting, lifelong memory, something that perhaps might even be cherished for its unfathomable depths of feeling. But to suffer over and over this same nightmare, as I soon found was my fate, leads one to seek nothing so much as a way to kill the dream, to expose all its secrets and reduce it to fragments that can be forgotten.

In my search for this deliverance, I first looked to the sheltering shadows of my home, the sobering shadows which at other times had granted me a cold and stagnant peace. I tried to argue myself free of my nightly excursions, to discourse these visions away, lecturing the walls *contra* the prodigies of a mysterious world. "Since any form of existence," I muttered, "since any form of existence is by definition a conflict of forces, or it is nothing at all, what can it possibly matter if these skirmishes take place in a world of marvels or one of mud? The difference between the two is not worth mentioning, or none. Such distinctions are the work of only the crudest and most limited perspectives, the sense of mystery and wonder foremost among them. Even the most esoteric ecstasy, when it comes down to it, requires the prop of vulgar pain in order to stand up as an experience. Having acknowledged the truth, however provisional, and the reality, if subject to mutation, of all that is most strange in the universe—whether known, unknown, or merely suspected—one must conclude that such marvels change nothing in our existence. The gallery of human sensations that existed in prehistory is identical to the one that faces each life today, that will continue to face each new life as it enters this world . . . and then looks beyond it."

Thus I attempted to reason my way back to self-possession. But no measure of my former serenity was forthcoming. On the contrary, my days as well as my nights were now poisoned by an obsession with Plomb. Why had I given him those spectacles! More to the point, why did I allow him to retain them? It was time to take back my gift, to confiscate those little bits of glass and twisted metal that were now harrowing the wrong mind. And since I had succeeded too well in keeping him away from my door, I would have to be the one to approach his.

4.

But it was not Plomb who answered the rotting door of that house which stood at the street's end and beside a broad expanse of empty field. It was not Plomb who asked if I was a newspaper journalist or a policeman before closing that gouged and filthy door in my face when I replied that I was neither of those. Pounding on the door, which seemed about to crumble under my fist, I summoned the sunken-eyed man a second time to ask if this in fact was Mr. Plomb's address. I had never visited him at his home, that hopeless little box in which he lived and slept and dreamed.

"Was he a relative?"

"No," I answered.

"Then what? You're not here to collect a bill, because if that's the case . . ."

For the sake of simplicity I interjected that I was a friend of Mr. Plomb.

"Then how is it you don't know?"

For the sake of my curiosity I said that I had been away on a trip, as I often was, and had my own reasons for notifying Mr. Plomb of my return.

"Then you don't know anything," he stated flatly.

"Exactly," I replied.

"It was even in the newspaper. And they asked me about him."

"Plomb," I confirmed.

"That's right," he said, as if he had suddenly become the custodian of a secret knowledge.

Then he waved me into the house and led me through its ugly, airless interior to a small storage room at the back. He reached along the wall inside the room, as if he wanted to avoid entering it, and switched on the light.

Immediately I understood why the hollow-faced man preferred not to go into that room, for Plomb had renovated this space in a very strange way. Each wall, as well as the ceiling and floor, was a mosaic of mirrors, a shocking galaxy of redundant reflections. And each mirror was splattered across its surface, as if someone had swung brushfuls of paint from various points throughout the room, spreading dark stars across a silvery firmament. In his attempt to exhaust or exaggerate the visions to which he had apparently become enslaved, Plomb had done nothing less than multiplied these visions into infinity, creating oceans of his own blood and enabling himself to see with countless eyes. Entranced by such aspiration, I gazed at the mirrors in speechless wonder. Among them was that tilting mirror I remembered looking into not so long ago.

The landlord, who did not follow me into the room, said something about suicide and a body ripped raw. This news was of course unnecessary as I stood overwhelmed at Plomb's ingenuity. It was some time before I could look away from that gallery of glass and gore. Only afterward did I fully realize that I would never be rid of the horrible Plomb. He had broken through all the mirrors, projected himself into the eternity beyond them.

And even when I abandoned my home, with its hideous attic storeroom, Plomb still followed me in my dreams. He now travels with me to the ends of the earth, initiating me night after night into his unspeakable wonders. I can only hope that we will not meet in another place, one where the mysteries are always new and dreams never end. Oh, Plomb, will you not stay in that box where they have put your self-riven body?

FLOWERS OF THE ABYSS

I must whisper my words in the wind, knowing somehow that they will reach you who sent me here. Let this misadventure, like the first rank scent of autumn, be carried back to you, my good people. For it was you who decided where I would go, you who wished I come here and to him. And I agreed, because the fear that filled your voices and lined your faces was so much greater than your words could explain. I feared your fear of him: the one whose name we did not know, the one who lived far from town in that ruined house which long ago had seen the passing of the family Van Livenn. "What a tragedy," we all agreed. "And they kept that beautiful garden for so long. But he . . . he doesn't seem much interested in such things."

I was chosen to unravel his secrets and find what malice or indifference the new owner harbored toward our town. I should be the one, you said. Was I not the teacher of the town's child-citizens, the one who had knowledge that you had not and who might therefore see deeper into the mystery of our man? That was what you said, in the shadows of our church where we met that night; but what you thought, I could not help but sense, was that *he* has no children of his own, no one, and so many of his hours are spent walking through those same woods in which lives the stranger. It would seem quite natural if I happened to pass the old Van Livenn house, if I happened to stop and perhaps beg a glass of water for a thirsty walker of the woods. But these simple actions, even then, seemed an extraordinary adventure, though none of us confessed to this feeling. Nothing to fear, you said. And so I was chosen to go alone to that house which had fallen into such disrepair.

You have seen the house and how, approaching it from the road that leads out of town, it sprouts suddenly into view—a pale flower amid the dark summer trees, now a ghostly flower at autumn. At first this is how it appeared to my eyes. (Yes, my eyes, think about them, good people: dream about them.) But as I neared the house, its grayish planks, bowed and buckled and oddly spotted, turned the pallid lily to a pulpy toadstool. Surely the house has played this trick on some of you, and all of you have seen it at one time or another: its roof of rippling shingles shaped like scales from some great fish, sea-green and sparkling in the autumn sun; its two attic gables with paned windows that come to a point like the tip of a tear; its sepulcher-shaped doorway at the top of rotted wooden stairs. And as I stood among the shadows outside that door, I heard hundreds of raindrops running up the steps behind me, as the air went cold and the skies gained shadows of their own. The light rain spotted the empty, ashen plot nearby the house, watering the barren ground where that remarkable garden had blossomed in the time of the Van Livenns. What better excuse for my imposing upon the present owner of this house? Shelter me, stranger, from the icy autumn storm, and from a fragrance damp and decayed.

He responded promptly to my rapping, without suspicious movements of the ragged curtains, and I entered his dark home. There was no need for explanation; he had already seen me walking ahead of the clouds, though I had not seen him: his lanky limbs like vaguely twisted branches; his lazy expressionless face; the colorless rags which are easier to see as tattered wrappings than as parts of even the poorest wardrobe. But his voice, that is something none of you has ever heard. Although shaken at how gentle and musical it sounded, I was even less prepared for the sense of great distances created by the echo of his hollow words.

"It was just such a day as this when I saw you for the first time walking in the woods," he said, looking out at the rain. "But you did not come near to the house. I wondered if you ever would."

His words put me at ease, for our introduction to each other appeared to have already been made. I removed my coat, which he took and placed on a very small wooden chair beside the front door. Extending a long crooked arm and wide hand toward the interior, he formally welcomed me into his home.

But somehow he himself did not seem at home there. It was as if the Van Livenn family had left all their worldly goods behind them for the use of the next occupant of their house, which would not be peculiar, tragedy considered. Nothing seemed to belong to him, though there was little enough in that house to be possessed by anyone. Apart from the two old chairs in which we sat down and the tiny misshapen table between them, the few other objects I could see appeared to have been brought together only by accident or default, a sign of the last days of the Van Livenns. A huge trunk lying in the corner, its great tarnished lock sprung open and its heavy straps falling loosely to the floor, would have looked much less sullen buried away in an attic or a cellar. And that miniature chair by the door, with an identical twin fallen on its back near the opposite wall, belonged in a child's room. Standing by the shuttered window, a tall bookcase seemed proper enough, if only those cracked pots, bent boots, and other paraphernalia foreign to bookcases had not been stuffed among its battered volumes. A large bedroom bureau stood against one wall, but that would have seemed misplaced in any room: the hollows of its absent drawers were deeply webbed with disuse. All of these things seemed to me wracked with the history of degeneration and death chronicled in our memory of the Van Livenns. But let that rest for now, lest I forget to tell of the thick, dreamy smell that permeated that room, inspiring the sense that malodorous gardens of misshapen growths were budding in the dust and dirty corners everywhere around me.

The only light in the house was provided by two lamps that burned on either side of a mantle over the fireplace. Behind each of these lamps was an oval mirror in an ornate frame, and the reflected light of their quivering wicks threw our shadows onto the wide bare wall at our backs. And while the two of us were sitting still and silent, I saw those other two fidgeting upon the wall, as if wind-blown or perhaps undergoing some subtle torture.

"I have something for you to drink," he said. "I know how far it is to walk from the town."

And I did not have to feign my thirst, good people, for it was such that I wanted to swallow the storm, which I could hear beyond the door and the walls but could only see as a brilliance occasionally flashing behind the curtains or shining needle-bright between the dull slats of the shutters.

In the absence of my host, I directed my eyes to the treasures of his house and made them my own. But there was something I had not yet seen, somehow I felt this. Then again, I was sent to spy and so everything around me appeared suspicious. Can you see now what I failed to see then? Can you see it coming into focus through my eyes? Can you peek into those cobwebbed corners or scan the titles of those tilting books? Yes; but can you now, in the maddest dream of your lives, peer into places that have no corners and bear no names? This is what I tried to do: to see beyond the ghoulish remnants of the Van Livenns; to see beyond the haunted stage upon which I had made my entrance. And so I had to turn corners inside-out with my eyes and to read the third side of a book's page, seeking in futility to gaze at what I could then touch with none of my senses. It remained something shapeless and nameless, dampish and submerged, something swampy and abysmal which opposed the pure cold of the autumn storm outside.

When my host returned, he carried with him a dusty green bottle and a sparkling glass, both of which he set upon that little table between our chairs. I took up the bottle and it felt warm in my hand. Expecting some thickish dark liquid to gush from the bottle's neck, I was surprised to see only the purest liquid flowing into the glass. I drank and for a few moments was removed to a world of frozen light that lived within the cool and limpid water.

In the meantime, the blank-faced man had placed something else upon the table. It was a small music box made of some dark wood which looked as if it had the hardness of a jewel and was florid with strange designs that were at once distinct and impossible to focalize. "I found this while rummaging about this place," the stranger said. Then slowly he drew back the cover of the box and sat back in his chair. I held both hands around that cold glass and listened to the still colder music. The crisp little notes that arose from the box were like stars of sound coming out in the twilight shadows and silence of the house. The storm had ended, leaving the world outside muffled by wetness. Within those closed rooms, which might now have been transported to the brink of a chasm or deep inside the earth, the music glimmered like infinitesimal flakes of light in that barren décor of dead days. Neither of us appeared to be breathing, and even the shadows behind our chairs were charmed with enchanted immobility. Everything held for a moment to allow the wandering music from the box to pass on toward some sublimely terrible destination. I tried to follow it—through the yellowish haze of the room and deep into the darkness that pressed against the walls, and then deeper into the darkness between the walls, then through the walls and into the unbordered spaces where those silvery tones ascended and quivered like a swarm of insects. There was still beauty in this vision, however tinged it was with the sinister. Even at that point I felt I could lose myself in the vastness spreading about me, a tenebrous expanse rich with unknown exploits. But then something began stirring, irrupting like a disease, poking its horribly colored head through the cool blackness . . . and chasing me back to my body.

"So what did you think? It was getting bad toward the end, wasn't it? I closed the box before it got worse. Would you say I was correct in my action?"

"Yes," I said, my voice trembling.

"I could see it on your face. My purpose wasn't to harm you. I just wanted to show you something—to give you a glimpse."

I drank the rest of the water, then set the glass I was still holding on the table. Settling down a bit, I said, "And what was it that you showed me?"

"The madness of things," he said. And he pronounced these words calmly, precisely, while staring into my eyes to see how I would react.

Of course, I had to hear more. After all, that was why I was there, was it not? Can you hear me in your dreams, my friends?

"The madness of things," I reiterated, trying to draw more from him. "I'm afraid I don't understand."

"Nor do I. But that is all I can say about it. Those are the only words I can use. The only ones that apply. Once I delighted in them. As a young student in philosophy I used to say to myself, 'I am going to learn the madness of things.' This was something I felt I needed to know—that I needed to *confront*. If I could face the madness of things, I thought, then I would have nothing more to fear. I could live in the universe without feeling I was coming apart, without feeling I would explode with the madness of things that to my mind formed the very foundation of existence. I wanted to tear off the veil and see things as they are, not to blind myself to them."

"And did you succeed?" I asked, not caring in the least if I were listening to a lunatic, so fascinated was I by what he had to say. Though I could hardly grasp his words, I knew there was something in them that was not alien to me, and for some moments I was distracted by their implications. For who among us has not experienced something that could be called *the madness of things?* Even if we do not use those exact words, we must at sometime in our lives have had a sense of their meaning. We must have touched, or been touched, by that derangement which the stranger thought to be the foundation of existence. If nothing else, my good people, we have all known the fate of the Van Livenns. It would not be unusual if we pondered in the solitude of our minds what we call their "tragedy" and wondered at this world of ours.

"Succeeded?" said the stranger, bringing me back to myself. "Oh, yes. Only too well I would say. I succeeded in tearing myself loose from all my fears, and even from the world itself. Now I am a vagabond of the universe, a drifter among spaces where the madness of things has no limits. One day, after years of study and practice, I gave myself over to whatever awaited me. But I cannot say where I go or why I go there. Everything is so much chaos in my existence. Somehow, though, I always come back to this world, as if I were some creature that returns on occasion to its home ground. These places at which I arrive seem to draw me to them, as if they have been prepared, even invaded before me. For there are always things, little items, that are just what I would expect. That music box, for instance. I looked around until I found something of that sort. By its designs I could see it had been *touched* by the madness of things, and so could you, I noticed. What havoc it must have caused for those unready for such phenomena. What happened in this house? I can only wonder."

And so the tragedy of the Van Livenns was illuminated. Which of them had come across the music box where it must have lain hidden for who knows how long? Over time, they must have all become its victims. The condition of the house and its grounds—that was the first sign. And then the shouting we began to hear from inside that made us stay away. What did it all mean? It was almost a year before there were no longer any sounds or any movement behind the shutters of the house. Soon after, the five bodies were found, some of them dead longer than others. None of them whole. All of them savaged beyond what was human. We wanted to think it was a stranger, but could not do so for long. Not after an inspection was conducted, and the conclusion drawn that they had gone after one another over at least a month's time. They said that old man Van Livenn must have been the last of them. His body was a mess of hacked pieces, but he must have done it himself, judging by the axe that was still gripped in his dead hand.

"Excuse me," said the stranger, once again arousing me from a state of distraction. He was now standing by the shuttered window, peering through a row of slats he had pulled open. With a slow movement of his hand, he beckoned me to join him, surreptitiously it seemed. "Look. Can you see them?"

Through the slats of the shuttered window I could see something outside, just where the Van Livenns had once cultivated their much-admired garden in bygone days. But what I saw was like the designs on the music box—intricate yet indistinct.

"They almost look like flowers, don't they? So brightly colored as they shine in the night. And yet when I first came upon them—not in this body, of course—almost everything was dark. But it wasn't dark as a house is sometimes dark or as the woods are dark because of thick trees keeping out the light. It was dark only because there was *nothing to keep out the darkness*. How do I know this? I know because I could see with more than my eyes—I could see with the darkness itself. With the darkness I saw the darkness. It was immensity without end around me—unbroken expansion, dark horizon meeting dark horizon. And there were also things within the darkness, and I believe within my own form, so that if I reached out to touch them across a universe of darkness, I also reached deep inside of myself, such as I was. Yet all I could feel were those things, the flowers. To touch them was like touching light and colors and a thousand kinds of bristling and growing shapes. In all that darkness which let me see with itself, these things squirmed, a wormy mass that was trying to make itself part of me. I must have brought them here when I came to this place. After I took this shape, they abandoned me and burrowed into that ground over there. They broke through the earth that same night, and I thought they would come after me. But somehow the situation had changed. I think they like being where they are now. You can see yourself how they twist about, almost happily."

After these words he fell silent for a moment. It was a dark night, the skies still blanketed by the clouds that earlier had brought the rain. The lamps upon the mantle shone with a piercing light that cut shadows out of the cloth of blackness around us. Why, good people, was I so astonished that this phantom before me could walk across the room and actually lift one of the lamps, then carry it toward the back hallway of the house? He paused, turned, and gestured for me to follow.

"Now you will see them better for the darkness. That is, if you would see the *true* madness."

Oh, my friends, please do not despise me for the choice I made this night. Remember it was you who sent me, for I was the one who belonged least to our town.

Quietly we walked from the house, as if we were two children sneaking away for a night in the woods. The lamplight skimmed across the wet grass behind the house and then paused where the yard ended and the woods began, fragrant and wind-blown. The light moved to the left and I moved with it, toward that area where a garden once grew.

"Look at them wriggling in the light," he said when the first rays fell on a convulsing tangle of shapes, like the radiant entrails of hell. But the shapes quickly disappeared into the darkness and out of view, pulling themselves from the rain-softened soil. "They retreat from this light. And you see how they return to their places when the light is withdrawn."

They closed in again like parted waters rushing to remerge. But these were corrupt waters whose currents had congealed and diversified into creaturely forms strung with sticky and pumping veins, hung with working mouths.

"Move the light as close as you can to the garden," I said.

He stepped to the very edge, as I stepped farther still toward that retreating flood of slimy tendrils, those aberrations of the abyss. When I was deep into their mesh, I whispered behind me: "Don't lose the light, or they will cover again the ground I am standing on. I can see them so well. The *true* madness. I have confronted it without fear."

"No," said the stranger. "You are not prepared. Come back to the light before the candle blows out."

But I did not listen to him, or to the wind that rose up. It came down from the trees and swept across the garden, throwing it into darkness.

And the wind now carries my words to you, good people. I cannot be there to guide you, but you know now what must be done, both to this horrible house and to its garden that was brought into this world by one who doomed himself to wander other worlds. Please, one last word to stir your sleep. I remember screaming to the stranger:

They are drawing me into themselves. My eyes can see everything in the darkness. I am not who I am. Can you hear me? Can you hear my words?

"I just had the most terrible dream," whispered one of the many who were awakening in the dark bedrooms of the town.

"It was not a dream. Can you hear the others outside?"

A night-gowned figure rose from the bed and moved as a silhouette to the window. Down in the street was a crowd carrying lights and rapping on doors for those still dreaming to join them. Their lamps and lanterns bobbed in the darkness, and the fires of their torches flickered madly. Clusters of flame shot up into the night.

The people of the town said not a word to one another, but they knew where they were going and what they would do to free their fellow citizen, my own self, from his tragedy. And though their eyes saw nothing but the wild destruction that lay ahead, buried like a forgotten dream within each one of them was a perfect picture of other eyes and of the unspeakable shapes in which they were now embedded. But do not let your fires burn out while you go about your work. Do not let them take you, too, into their unearthly realm. Come, then, and close my eyes. Murder the beings into which they have been drawn. Then shutter your minds as well as you can to the abyss that is home to the madness of things.

NETHESCURIAL

THE IDOL AND THE ISLAND

I have uncovered a rather wonderful manuscript, *the letter begin*. It was an entirely fortuitous find, made during my day's dreary labors among some of the older and more decomposed remains entombed in the library archives. If I am any judge of antique documents, and of course I am, these brittle pages date back to the closing decades of the last century. (A more precise estimate of age will follow, along with a photocopy which I fear will not do justice to the delicate, crinkly script, nor to the greenish black discoloration the ink has taken on over the years.) Unfortunately there is no indication of authorship either within the manuscript itself or in the numerous and tedious papers whose company it has been keeping, none of which seem related to the item under discussion. And what an item it is—a real storybook stranger in a crowd of documentary types, and probably destined to remain unknown.

I am almost certain that this invention, though at times it seems to pose as a letter or journal entry, has never appeared in common print. Given the bizarre nature of its content, I would surely have known of it before now. Although it is an untitled "statement" of sorts, the opening lines were more than enough to cause me to put everything else aside and seclude myself in a corner of the library stacks for the rest of the afternoon.

So it begins: "Amid the rooms of our houses and beyond their walls—beneath dark waters and across moonlit skies— below earth mound and above mountain peak—in northern leaf and southern flower—inside each star and the voids between them—within blood and bone—throughout all souls and spirits—upon the watchful winds of this and the several worlds—behind the faces of the living and the dead . . ." And there it trails off, a quoted fragment of some more ancient text. But this is certainly not the last we will hear of this rambling refrain!

As it happens, the above string of phrases is cited by the narrator in reference to a certain *presence,* more properly an omnipresence, which he encounters on an obscure island located at some unspecified northern latitude. Briefly, he has been summoned to this island, which appears on a local map under the name of Nethescurial, in order to rendezvous with another man, an archaeologist who is designated only as Dr. N— and who will come to know the narrator of the manuscript by the self-admitted alias of "Bartholomew Gray."

Dr. N—, it seems, has been occupying himself upon that barren, remote, and otherwise uninhabited isle with some peculiar antiquarian rummagings. As Mr. Gray sails toward the island he observes the murky skies above him and the murky waters below. His prose style is somewhat plain for my taste, but it serves well enough once he approaches the island and takes surprisingly scrupulous notice of its eerie aspect: contorted rock formations; pointed pines and spruces of gigantic stature and uncanny movements; the masklike countenance of sea-facing cliffs; and a sickly, stagnant fog clinging to the landscape like a fungus.

From the moment Mr. Gray begins describing the island, a sudden glamour enters into his account—that sinister enchantment which derives from a profound evil that is kept at just the right distance from us so that we may experience both our love and our fear of it in one sweeping sensation. Too close and we may be reminded of an omnipresent evil in the living world, and threatened with having our sleeping sense of doom awakened into full vigor. Too far away and we become even more incurious and complacent than is our usual state, and ultimately exasperated when an imaginary evil is so poorly evoked that it fails to offer the faintest echo of its real and all-pervasive counterpart. Of course, any number of locales may serve as the setting to reveal ominous truths; evil, beloved and menacing evil, may show itself anywhere precisely because it is everywhere and is as stunningly set off by a foil of sunshine and flowers as it is by darkness and dead leaves. A purely private quirk, nevertheless, sometimes allows the purest essence of life's malignity to be aroused only by sites such as the lonely island of Nethescurial, where the real and the unreal swirl freely and madly about in the same fog.

It seems that in this place, this far-flung realm, Dr. N— has discovered an ancient and long-sought artifact, a marginal but astonishing entry in that unspeakably voluminous journal of creation. Soon after landfall, Mr. Gray finds himself verifying the truth of the archaeologist's claims: that the island has been strangely molded in all its parts, and within its shores every manifestation of plant or mineral or anything whatever appears to have fallen at the mercy of some shaping force of demonic temperament, a genius loci which has sculpted its nightmares out of the atoms of the local earth. Closer inspection of this insular spot on the map serves to deepen the sense of evil enchantment that had been lightly sketched earlier in the manuscript. But I refrain from further quotation (it is getting late and I want to wrap up this letter before bedtime) in order to cut straight through the epidermis of this tale and penetrate to its very bones and viscera. Indeed, the manuscript does seem to have an anatomy of its own, its dark green holography rippling over it like veins, and I regret that my paraphrase may not deliver it alive. Enough!

Mr. Gray makes his way inland, lugging along with him a fat little traveling bag. In a clearing he comes upon a large but unadorned, almost primitive house which stands against the backdrop of the island's wartlike hills and tumorous trees. The outside of the house is encrusted with the motley and leprous stones so abundant in the surrounding landscape. The inside of the house, which the visitor sees upon opening the unlocked door, is spacious as a cathedral but far less ornamented. The walls are white and smoothly surfaced; they also seem to taper inward, pyramid-like, as they rise from floor to lofty ceiling. There are no windows, and numerous oil lamps scattered about fill the interior of the house with a sacral glow.

A figure descends a long staircase, crosses the great distance of the room, and solemnly greets his guest. At first wary of each other, they eventually achieve a degree of mutual ease and finally get down to their true business.

Thus far one can see that the drama enacted is a familiar one: the stage is rigidly traditional and the performers upon it are caught up in its style. For these actors are not so much people as they are puppets from the old shows, the ones that have told the same story for centuries, the ones that can still be very strange to us. Traipsing through the same old foggy scene, seeking the same old isolated house, the puppets in these plays always find everything new and unknown, because they have no memories to speak of and can hardly recall making these stilted motions countless times in the past. They struggle through the same gestures, repeat the same lines, although in rare moments they may feel a dim suspicion that this has all happened before. How like they are to the human race itself! This is what makes them our perfect representatives—this and the fact that they are hand carved in the image of maniacal victims who seek to share the secrets of their individual torments as their strings are manipulated by the same master.

The secrets which these two Punchinellos share are rather deviously presented by the author of this confession (for upon consideration this is the genre to which it truly belongs). Indeed, Mr. Gray, or whatever his name might be, appears to know much more than he is telling, especially with respect to his colleague the archaeologist. Nevertheless, he records what Dr. N— knows and, more importantly, what this avid excavator has found buried on the island. The thing is only a fragment of an object dating from antiquity. Known to be part of a religious idol, it is difficult to say which part. It is a twisted piece of a puzzle, one suggesting that the figure as a whole is wickedly repulsive in its design. The fragment is also darkened with the verdigris of centuries, causing its substance to resemble something like decomposing jade.

And were the other pieces of this idol also to be found on the same island? The answer is no. The idol seems to have been shattered ages ago, and each broken part of it buried in some remote place so that its entirety might not easily be joined together again. Although it was a mere representation, the effigy itself was the focus of a great power. The members of the ancient sect which was formed to worship this power seem to have been pantheists of a sort, believing that all created things— appearances to the contrary—are of a single, unified, and transcendent *stuff,* an emanation of a central creative force. Hence the ritual chant which runs "amid the rooms of our houses," et cetera, and alludes to the all-present nature of this deity—a most primal and pervasive type of god, one that falls into the category of "gods who eclipse all others," territorialist divinities whose claim to the creation purportedly supersedes that of their rivals. (The words of the famous chant, by the way, are the only ones to come down to us from the ancient cult and appeared for the first time in an ethnographical, quasi-esoteric work entitled *Illuminations of the Ancient World,* which was published in the latter part of the nineteenth century, around the same time, I would guess, as this manuscript I am rushing to summarize was written.) At some point in their career as worshipers of the "Great One God," a shadow fell upon the sect. It appears that one day it was revealed to them, in a manner both obscure and hideous, that the power to which they bowed was essentially evil in character and that their religious mode of pantheism was in truth a kind of *pandemonism.* But this revelation was not a surprise to all of the sectarians, since there seems to have been an internecine struggle which ended in slaughter. In any case, the anti-demonists prevailed, and they immediately rechristened their ex-deity to reflect its newly discovered essence in evil. And the name by which they henceforth called it was Nethescurial.

A nice turn of affairs: this obscure island openly advertises itself as the home of the idol of Nethescurial. Of course, the island is only one of several to which the pieces of the vandalized totem were scattered. The original members of the sect who had treacherously turned against their god knew that the power concentrated in the effigy could not be destroyed, and so they decided to parcel it out to isolated corners of the earth where it could do the least harm. But would they have brought attention to this fact by allowing these widely disseminated burial plots to bear the name of the pandemoniacal god? This is doubtful, just as it is equally unlikely that it was they who built those crude houses, temples of a fashion, to mark the spot where a particular shard of the old idol might be located by others.

Thus, Dr. N— is forced to postulate a survival of the demonist faction of the sect, a cult that had devoted itself to searching out those places which had been transformed by the presence of the idol and might thus be known by their gruesome features. This quest would require a great deal of time and effort for its completion, given the global reaches where those splinters of evil might be tucked away. Known as the "seeking," it also involved the enlistment of outsiders, who in latter days were often researchers into the ways of bygone cultures, though they remained ignorant that the cause they served was still a living one. Dr. N— therefore warns his "colleague, Mr. Gray," that they may be in danger from those who carried on the effort to reassemble the idol and revive its power. The very presence of that great and crude house on the island certainly proved that the cult was already aware of the location of *this* fragment of the idol. In fact, the mysterious Mr. Gray, not unexpectedly, is actually a member of the cult in its modern incarnation; furthermore, he has brought with him to the island—bulky traveling bag, you know—all the other pieces of the idol, which have been recovered through centuries of seeking. Now he only needs the one piece discovered by Dr. N— to make the idol whole again for the first time in a couple millennia.

But he also needs the archaeologist himself as a kind of sacrifice to Nethescurial, a ceremony which takes place later the same night in the upper part of the house. If I may telescope the ending for brevity's sake, the sacrificial ritual holds some horrific surprises for Mr. Gray (these people seem never to realize what they are getting themselves into), who soon repents of his evil practices and is driven to smash the idol to pieces once more. Making his escape from that weird island, he throws these pieces overboard, sowing the cold gray waters with the scraps of an incredible power. Later, fearing an obscure threat to his existence (perhaps the reprisal of his fellow cultists), he composes an account of a horror which is both his own and that of the whole human race.

   End of manuscript.*

Now, despite my penchant for such wild yarns as I have just attempted to describe, I am not oblivious to their shortcomings. For one thing, whatever emotional impact the narrative may have lost in the foregoing précis, it certainly gained in coherence. The incidents in the manuscript are clumsily developed; important details lack proper emphasis; and impossible things are thrown at the reader without any real effort at persuasion of their veracity. I do admire the fantastic principle at the core of this piece. The nature of that pandemoniac entity is very intriguing. Imagine all of creation as a mere mask for the foulest evil, an absolute evil whose reality is mitigated only by our blindness to it, an evil at the heart of things, existing "inside each star and the voids between them—within blood and bone—through all souls and spirits," and so forth. There is even a reference in the manuscript that suggests an analogy between Nethescurial and that beautiful myth of the Australian aborigines known as the Alchera (the Dreamtime, or Dreaming), a super-reality which is the source of all we see in the world around us. (And this reference will be useful in dating the manuscript, since it was toward the end of the last century that Australian anthropologists made the aboriginal cosmology known to the general public.) Imagine the universe as the dream, the feverish nightmare of a demonic demiurge. O Supreme Nethescurial!

   The problem is that such supernatural inventions are indeed quite difficult to imagine. So often they fail to materialize in the mind, to take on a mental texture, and thus remain unfelt as anything but an abstract monster of metaphysics—an elegant or awkward schematic that cannot rise from the paper to touch us. Of course, we do need to keep a certain distance from such specters as Nethescurial, and this is usually secured

---

*Except for the concluding lines, which reveal the somewhat extravagant, but not entirely uninteresting, conclusion of the narrator himself.

through the medium of words as such, which ensnare all kinds of menacing creatures before they can tear us body and soul. (And yet the words of this particular manuscript seem rather weak in this regard, possibly because they are only the drab green scratchings of a human hand and not the heavy mesh of black type.) But we do want to get close enough to feel the foul breath of these beasts, or to see them as prehistoric leviathans circling about the tiny island on which we have taken refuge. Even if we are incapable of a sincere belief in ancient cults and their unheard of idols, even if these pseudonymous adventurers and archaeologists appear to be mere shadows on a wall, and even if strange houses on remote islands are of shaky construction, there may still be a power in these things that threatens us like a bad dream. And this power emanates not so much from within the tale as it does from somewhere *behind* it, some place of infinite darkness and ubiquitous malignity in which we may walk unaware.

But never mind these night thoughts; it's only to bed that *I* will walk after closing this letter.

POSTSCRIPT

Later the same night.

Several hours have passed since I set down the above description and analysis of that manuscript. How naive those words of mine now sound to me. And yet they are still true enough, from a certain perspective. But that perspective was a privileged one which, at least for the moment, I do not enjoy. The distance between me and a devastating evil has lessened considerably. I no longer find it so difficult to imagine the horrors delineated in that manuscript, for I have known them in the most intimate way. What a fool I seem to myself for playing with such visions. How easily a simple dream can destroy one's sense of safety, if only for a few turbulent hours. Certainly I have experienced all this before, but never as acutely as tonight.

I had not been asleep for long but apparently long enough. At the start of the dream I was sitting at a desk in a very dark room. It also seemed to me that the room was very large, though I could see little of it beyond the area of the desktop, at either end of which glowed a lamp of some kind. Spread out before me were many papers varying in size. These I knew to be maps of one sort or another, and I was studying them each in turn. I had become quite absorbed in their chartings, which now dominated the dream to the exclusion of all other images. Each of them focused on some concatenation of islands without reference to larger, more familiar land masses. A powerful impression of remoteness and seclusion was conveyed by these irregular daubs of earth fixed in bodies of water that were unnamed. But although the location of the islands was not specific, somehow I was sure that those for whom the maps were meant already had this knowledge. Nevertheless, this secrecy was only superficial, for no esoteric key was required to seek out the greater geography of which these maps were an exaggerated detail: they were all distinguished by some known language in which the islands were named, different languages for different maps. Yet upon closer view (indeed, I felt as if I were actually journeying among those exotic fragments of land, tiny pieces of shattered mystery), I saw that every map had one thing in common: within each group of islands, whatever language was used to name them, there was always one called Nethescurial. It was as if all over the world this terrible name had been insinuated into diverse locales as the only one suitable for a certain island. Of course there were variant cognate forms and spellings, sometimes transliterations, of the word. (How precisely I saw them!) Still, with the strange conviction that may overcome a dreamer, I knew these places had all been claimed in the name of Nethescurial and that they bore the unique sign of something which had been buried there—the pieces of that dismembered idol.

And with this thought, the dream reshaped itself. The maps dissolved into a kind of mist; the desk before me became something else, an altar of coarse stone, and the two lamps upon it flared up to reveal a strange object now positioned between them. So many visions in the dream were piercingly clear, but this dark object was not. My impression was that it was conglomerate in

form, suggesting a monstrous whole. At the same time these outlines which alluded to both man and beast, flower and insect,
reptiles, stones, and countless things I could not even name, all
seemed to be changing, mingling in a thousand ways that prevented any sensible image of the idol.

With the upsurge in illumination offered by the lamps, I
could see that the room was truly of unusual dimensions. The
four enormous walls slanted toward one another and joined at
a point high above the floor, giving the space around me the
shape of a perfect pyramid. But I now saw things from an oddly
remote perspective: the altar with its idol stood in the middle of
the room and I was some distance away, or perhaps not even in
the scene. Then, from a dark corner or secret door, there
emerged a file of figures walking slowly toward the altar and
finally congregating in a half-circle before it. I could see that
they were all quite skeletal in shape, for each of them was iden-
tically dressed in a black material which clung tightly to their
bodies and made them look like skinny shadows. They seemed
to be actually bound in blackness from head to foot, with only
their faces exposed. But they were not, in fact, faces—they
were pale, expressionless, and identical masks. The masks were
without openings and bestowed upon their wearers a terrible
anonymity, an ancient anonymity. Behind these smooth and
barely contoured faces were spirits beyond all hope or consolation except in the evil to which they would willingly abandon
themselves. Yet this abandonment was a highly selective process, a ceremony of the chosen.

One of the white-faced shadows stepped forward from the
group, seemingly drawn forth into the proximity of the idol.
The figure stood motionless, while from within its dark body
something began to drift out like luminous smoke. It floated,
swirling gently, toward the idol and there was absorbed. And I
knew—for was this not my own dream?—that the idol and its
sacrifice were becoming one within each other. This spectacle
continued until nothing of the glowing, ectoplasmic haze
remained to be extracted, and the figure—now shrunken to
the size of a marionette—collapsed. But soon it was being
lifted, rather tenderly, by another from the group who placed

the dwarfish form upon the altar and, taking up a knife, carved deep into the body, making no sound. Then something oozed upon the altar, something thick and oily and strangely colored, darkly colored though not with any of the shades of blood. Although the strangeness of this color was more an idea than a matter of vision, it began to fill the dream and to determine the final stage of its development.

Quite abruptly, that closed, cavernous room dissolved into a stretch of land that was cluttered with a bric-a-brac topography whose crazed shapes were of that single and sinister color, as if everything were covered with an ancient, darkened mold. It was a landscape that might once have been of stone and earth and trees (such was my impression) but had been transformed entirely into something like petrified lichen. Spreading before me, twisting in the way of wrought iron tracery or great over-grown gardens of writhing coral, was an intricate latticework whose surface was overrun with a chaos of little carvings, scabby designs that suggested a world of demonic faces and forms. And their complexion was so much like all else I have described that I felt there was nowhere I could turn, not even to my own flesh, to escape its aspect. It was then I sensed that peculiar panic welling up within me that often precedes one's emergence from a nightmare. Yet before I broke free of my dream, I beheld one further occurrence of the ubiquitous color of that island. As if to heighten the horror of my oneiric visions, it was also the color of the inkish waters washing upon the island's shores and trending into the far distance.

As I wrote a few pages ago, I have been awake for some hours now. What I did not mention was the state in which I found myself after waking. Throughout the dream, and particularly in those last moments when I positively identified that foul place, there was an unseen *presence,* something I could feel was circulating within all things and unifying them in an infinitely extensive body of evil. I suppose it is nothing unusual that I continued to be under this visionary spell even after I left my bed. I tried to invoke the gods of the ordinary world—calling them with the whistle of a coffee pot and praying before their icon of the electric light—but they were too weak to deliver me from that other whose name I can no longer bring myself to write. It seemed to be in possession of my house, of every common object inside and the whole of the dark world outside. Yes—lurking among the watchful winds of this and the several worlds. Everything seemed to be a manifestation of this evil and to my eyes was taking on its aspect. I could feel it also emerging in myself, growing stronger behind this living face that I am afraid to confront in the mirror.

Nevertheless, these dream-induced illusions now seem to be abating, perhaps driven off by my writing about them. Like someone who has had too much to drink the night before and swears off liquor for life, I have forsworn any further indulgence in weird reading matter. No doubt this is only a temporary vow, and soon enough my old habits will return. But certainly not before morning!

THE PUPPETS IN THE PARK

Some days later, and quite late at night.

Well, it seems this letter has mutated into a chronicle of my adventures Nethescurialian. See, I can now write that unique nomen with ease; furthermore, I feel almost no apprehension in stepping up my mirror. Soon I may even be able to sleep in the way I once did, without visionary intrusions of any kind. No denying that my experiences of late have tipped the scales of the strange. I found myself just walking restlessly about—impossible to work, you know—and always carrying with me this heavy dread in my solar plexus, as if I had feasted at a banquet of fear and the meal would not digest. Most strange, since I have been loath to take nourishment during this time. How could I ingest even the least morsel when everything looked the way it did? Hard enough to touch a doorknob or a pair of shoes, even with the protection of gloves. I could feel every damn thing squirming, not excluding my own flesh. And I could also see what was squirming beneath every surface, my vision penetrating through the usual armor of objects and discerning the same gushing *stuff* inside whatever I looked upon. It was that dark color from the dream, I could identify it clearly now. Dark and greenish. How could I possibly feed myself? How could I even bring myself to settle very long in one spot? So I kept on the move. And I tried not to look too closely at how everything, *everything* was crawling within itself and making all kinds of shapes inside there, making all kinds of faces at me. (Yet it was really all the same face, everything gorged with that same creeping stuff.) There were also sounds that I heard, voices speaking vague words, voices that came not from the mouths of the people I passed on the street but from the very bottom of their brains, garbled whisperings at first and then so clear, so eloquent.

This rising wave of chaos reached its culmination tonight and then came crashing down. But my timely maneuvering, I trust, has put everything right again.

Here, now, are the terminal events of this nightmare as they occurred. (And how I wish I were not speaking figuratively, that I was in fact only in the world of dreams or back in the pages of books and old manuscripts.) This conclusion had its beginning in the park, a place that is actually some distance from my home, so far had I wandered. It was already late at night, but I was still walking about, treading the narrow asphalt path that winds through that island of grass and trees in the middle of the city. (And somehow it seemed I had already walked in this same place on this same night, that this had all happened to me before.) The path was lit by globes of light balanced upon slim metal poles; another glowing orb was set in the great blackness above. Off the path the grass was darkened by shadows, and the trees swishing overhead were the same color of muddied green.

After walking some indefinite time along some indefinite route, I came upon a clearing where an audience had assembled for a late-night entertainment. Strings of colored lights had been hung around the perimeter of this area and rows of benches had been set up. The people seated on these benches were all watching a tall, illuminated booth. It was the kind of booth used for puppet shows, with wild designs painted across the lower part and a curtained opening at the top. The curtains were now drawn back and two clownish creatures were twisting about in a glary light which emanated from inside the booth. They leaned and squawked and awkwardly batted each other with soft paddles they were hugging in their little arms. Suddenly they froze at the height of their battle; slowly they turned about and faced the audience. It seemed the puppets were looking directly at the place I was standing behind the last row of benches. Their misshapen heads tilted, and their glassy eyes stared straight into mine.

Then I noticed that the others were doing the same: all of them had turned around on the benches and, with expressionless faces and dead puppet eyes, held me to the spot. Although their mouths didn't move, they were not silent. But the voices I heard were far more numerous than was the gathering before me. These were the voices I had been hearing as they chanted confused words in the depths of everyone's thoughts, fathoms below the level of their awareness. The words still sounded hushed and slow, monotonous phrases mingling like the sequences of a fugue. But now I could understand these words, even as more voices picked up the chant at different points and overlapped one another, saying, "Amid the rooms of our houses—across moonlit skies—throughout all souls and spirits—behind the faces of the living and the dead."

I find it impossible to say how long it was before I was able to move, before I backed up toward the path, all those multitudinous voices chanting everywhere around me and all those many-colored lights bobbing in the wind-blown trees. Yet it now seemed to be only a single voice I heard, and a single color I saw, as I found my way home, stumbling through the greenish darkness of the night.

I knew what needed to be done. Gathering up some old boards from my basement, I piled them into the fireplace and opened the flue. As soon as they were burning brightly, I added one more thing to the fire: a manuscript whose ink was of a certain color. Blessed with a saving vision, I could now see whose signature was on that manuscript, whose hand had really written those pages and had been hiding in them for a hundred years. The author of that narrative had broken up the idol and drowned it in deep waters, but the stain of its ancient patina had stayed upon him. It had invaded the author's crabbed script of blackish green and survived there, waiting to crawl into another lost soul who failed to see what dark places he was wandering into. How I knew this to be true! And has this not been proved by the color of the smoke that rose from the burning manuscript, and keeps rising from it?

I am writing these words as I sit before the fireplace. The flames have gone out but still the smoke from the charred paper hovers within the hearth, refusing to ascend the chimney and disperse itself into the night. Perhaps the chimney has become blocked. Yes, this must be the case, this must be true. Those other things are lies, illusions. That mold-colored smoke has not taken on the shape of the idol, the shape that cannot be seen steadily and whole but keeps turning out so many arms and heads, so many eyes, then pulls them back in and brings them out again in other configurations. That shape is not drawing something out of me and putting something else in its place, something that seems to be bleeding into the words as I write. And my pen is not growing bigger in my hand, nor is my hand growing smaller, smaller . . .

See, there is no shape in the fireplace. The smoke is gone, gone up the chimney and out into the sky. And there is nothing in the sky, nothing I can see through the window. There is the moon, of course, high and round. But no shadow falls across the moon, no churning chaos of smoke that chokes the frail order of the earth. It is not a squirming, creeping, smearing shape I see upon the moon, not the shape of a great deformed crab scuttling out of the black oceans of infinity and invading the island of the moon, crawling with its innumerable bodies upon all the spinning islands of space. That shape is not the cancerous totality of all creatures, not the oozing ichor that flows within all things. *Nethescurial is not the secret name of the creation.* It is not amid the rooms of our houses and beyond their walls—beneath dark waters and across moonlit skies—below earth mound and above mountain peak—in northern leaf and southern flower—inside each star and the voids between them—within blood and bone—throughout all souls and spirits—upon the watchful winds of this and the several worlds—behind the faces of the living and the dead.

I am not dying in a nightmare.

THE VOICE OF THE DEMON

THE DREAMING IN NORTOWN

There are those who require witnesses to their doom. Not content with a solitary perdition, they seek an audience worthy of the spectacle—a mind to remember the stages of their downfall or perhaps only a mirror to multiply their abject glory. Of course, other motives may figure in this scheme, ones far too tenuous and strange for mortal reminiscence. Yet there exists a memoir of dreams in which I may recollect an erstwhile acquaintance whose name I shall give as Jack Quinn. For it was he who sensed my peculiar powers of sympathy and, employing a rather contrary stratagem, engaged them. This all began, according to my perspective, late one night in the decaying and spacious apartment which Quinn and I shared and which was located in that city—or, more precisely, in a certain region *within* it—where we attended the same university.

I was asleep. In the darkness a voice was calling me away from my ill-mapped world of dreams. Then something heavy weighed down the edge of the mattress and a slightly infernal aroma filled the room, an acrid combination of tobacco and autumn nights. A small red glow wandered in an arc toward the apex of the seated figure and there glowed even brighter, faintly lighting the lower part of a face. Quinn was smiling, the

cigar in his mouth smoking in the darkness. He remained silent
for a moment and crossed his legs beneath his long threadbare
overcoat, an ancient thing that was wrapped loosely around
him like a skin about to be sloughed. So many pungent Octo-
bers were collected in that coat. It is the events of this month
that I am remembering.

I assumed he was drunk, or perhaps still in the remote
heights or depths of the artificial paradise he had been exploring that night. When Quinn finally spoke, it was definitely
with the stumbling words of a returning explorer, a stuporous
and vaguely awed voice. But he seemed more than simply
drug-entranced.

He had attended a meeting, he said, speaking the word in an
odd way which seemed to expand its significance. Of course
there were others at this gathering, people who to me remained
simply "those others." It was a kind of philosophical society,
he told me. The group sounded colorful enough: midnight
assemblies, the probable use of drugs, and participants in the
grip of strange mystical ecstasies.

I got out of bed and switched on the light. Quinn was a chaotic sight, his clothes more crumpled than usual, his face
flushed, and his long red hair intricately tangled.

"And exactly where did you go tonight?" I asked with the
measure of true curiosity he seemed to be seeking. I had the
distinct idea that Quinn's activities of that evening had
occurred in the vicinity of Nortown (another pseudonym, of
course, as are all the names in this narrative), where the apartment we shared was located. I asked him if they had.

"And perhaps in other places," he answered, laughing a little
to himself as he meditated upon the gray end of his cigar. "But
you might not understand. Excuse me, I have to go to bed."

"As you wish," I replied, leaving aside all complaints about
this nocturnal intrusion. He puffed on his cigar and went to
his room, closing the door behind him.

This, then, was the beginning of Quinn's ultimate phase of
esoteric development. And until the final night, I actually saw
very little of him during that most decisive episode of his life.
We were pursuing different courses of study in our graduate

school days—I in anthropology and he in . . . it troubles me
to say I was never entirely sure of his academic program. In
any case, our respective timetables seldom intersected. Nonetheless, Quinn's daily movements, at least the few I was aware
of, did invite curiosity. There was a general tenor of chaos that
I perceived in his behavior, a quality which may or may not
make for good company but which always offers promise of
the extraordinary.

He continued to come in quite late at night, always entering
the apartment with what seemed a contrived noisiness. After
that first night he did not overtly confide his activities to me.
The door to his room would close, and immediately afterward
I would hear him collapse on the old springs of his mattress. It
seemed he did not undress for bed, perhaps never even removed
the overcoat which was becoming shabbier and more crumpled day by day. My sleep temporarily shattered, I passed this
wakeful time by eavesdropping on the noises in the next room.
There was a strange catalogue of sounds which either I had
never noticed before or which were somehow different from
the usual nightly din: low moans emanating from the most
shadowy chasms of dream; sudden intakes of breath like the
suction of a startled gasp; and abrupt snarls and snorts of a
bestial timbre. The whole rhythm of his sleep betrayed expressions of unknown turmoil. And sometimes he would violate
the calm darkness of the night with a series of staccato groans
followed by a brief vocal siren that made me bolt up suddenly
in my bed. This alarming sound surely carried the entire audible spectrum of nightmare-inspired terror . . . but there were
also mingling overtones of awe and ecstasy, a willing submission to some unknown ordeal.

"Have you finally died and gone to hell?" I shouted one
night through his bedroom door. The sound was still ringing
in my ears.

"Go back to sleep," he answered, his low-pitched voice still
speaking from the deeper registers of somnolence. The smell
of a freshly lit cigar then filtered out of his bedroom.

After these late-night disturbances, I would sometimes sit up
to watch the dun colors of dawn stirring in the distance outside

my eastern window. And as the weeks went by that October, the carnival of noise going on in the next room began to work its strange influence upon my own sleep. Soon Quinn was not the only one in the apartment having nightmares, as I was inundated by a flood of eidetic horrors that left only a vague residue upon waking.

It was throughout the day that fleeting scenes of nightmare would suddenly appear to my mind, brief and vivid, as though I had mistakenly opened a strange door somewhere and, after inadvertently seeing something I should not have, quickly closed it once again with a reverberating slam. Eventually, however, my dream-censor himself fell asleep, and I recalled in total the elusive materials of one of those night-visions, which returned to me painted in scenes of garishly vibrant colors.

The dream took place at a small public library in Nortown where I sometimes retreated to study. On the oneiric plane, however, I was not a studious patron of the library but one of the librarians—the only one, it seemed, keeping vigil in that desolate institution. I was just sitting there, complacently surveying the shelves of books and laboring under the illusion that in my idleness I was performing some routine but very important function. This did not continue very long—nothing does in dreams—though the situation was one that already seemed interminable.

What shattered the status quo, initiating a new phase to the dream, was my discovery that a note scrawled upon a slip of paper had been left on the well-ordered surface of my desk. It was a request for a book and had been submitted by a library patron whose identity I puzzled over, for I had not seen anyone put it there. I fretted about this scrap of paper for many dream-moments: had it been there even before I sat down at the desk and had I simply overlooked it? I suffered a disproportionate anxiety over this possible dereliction. The imagined threat of a reprimand of some strange nature terrorized me. Without delay I phoned the back room to have the person on duty there bring forth the book. But I was truly alone in that dream library and no one answered what was to my mind now an emergency appeal. Feeling a sense of urgency in the face of some imaginary deadline, and filled with a kind of exalted terror, I snatched up the request slip and set out to retrieve the book myself.

In the stacks I saw that the telephone line was dead, for it had been ripped from the wall and lay upon the floor like the frayed end of a disciplinary whip. Trembling, I consulted the piece of paper I carried with me for the title of the book and call-number. No longer can I remember that title, but it definitely had something to do with the name of the city, suburb of a sort, where Quinn's and my apartment was located. I proceeded to walk down a seemingly endless aisle flanked by innumerable smaller aisles between the lofty bookshelves. Indeed, they were so lofty that when I finally reached my destination I had to climb a high ladder to reach the spot where I could secure the desired book. Mounting the ladder until my shaking hands gripped the highest rung, I was at eye level with the exact call-number I was seeking, or some forgotten dream-glyphs which I took to be these letters and digits. And like these symbols, the book I found is now hopelessly unmemorable, its shape, color, and dimensions having perished on the journey back from the dream. I may have even dropped it, but that was not important.

What was important, however, was the dark little slot created when I withdrew the volume from its rank on the shelf. I peered in, somehow knowing I was supposed to do this as part of the book-retrieving ritual. I gazed deeper . . . and the next phase of the dream began.

The slot was a window, perhaps more of a crack in some dream-wall or a slit in the billowing membrane that protects one world against the intrusion of another. Beyond was something of a landscape—for lack of a more suitable term—which I viewed through a narrow rectangular frame. But this landscape had no earth and sky that hinged together in a neat line at the horizon, no floating or shining objects above to echo and balance their earthbound counter shapes below. This landscape was an infinite expanse of depth and distance, a never-ending morass deprived of all coherence, a state of strange existence rather than a chartable locus, having no more geographical extension than a mirage or a rainbow. There was definitely something in my sight, elements that could be distinguished from one another but impossible to fix in any kind of relationship. I experienced a prolonged gaze at what is usually just a delirious glimpse, the way one might suddenly perceive some sidelong illusion which disappears at the turn of the head, leaving no memory of what the mind had deceptively seen.

The only way I can describe the visions I witnessed with even faint approximation is in terms of other scenes which might arouse similar impressions of tortuous chaos: perhaps a festival of colors twisting in blackness, a tentacled abyss that alternately seems to glisten moistly as with some horrendous dew, then suddenly dulls into an arid glow, like bone-colored stars shining over an extraterrestrial desert. The vista of eerie disorder that I observed was further abetted in its strangeness by my own feelings about it. They were magnified dream-feelings, those encyclopedic emotions which involve complexities of intuition, sensation, and knowledge impossible to express. My dream-emotion was indeed a monstrous encyclopedia, one that described a universe kept under infinite wraps of deception, a dimension of disguise.

It was only at the end of the dream that I saw the colors or colored shapes, molten and moving shapes. I cannot remember if I felt them to be anything specific or just abstract entities. They seemed to be the only things active within the moody immensity I stared out upon. Their motion somehow was not pleasant to watch—a bestial lurching of each color-mass, a legless pacing in a cage from which they might escape at any moment. These phantasms introduced a degree of panic into the dream sufficient to wake me.

Oddly enough, though the dream had nothing to do with my roommate, I woke up calling his name repeatedly in my dream-distorted voice. But he did not answer the call, for he was not home at the time.

I have reconstructed my nightmare at this point for two reasons. First, to show the character of my inner life during this time; second, to provide a context in which I could appreciate what I found the next day in Quinn's room.

When I returned from classes that afternoon, Quinn was nowhere to be seen, and I took this opportunity to research the nightmares that had been visiting our apartment in Nortown. Actually I did not have to pry very deeply into the near-fossilized clutter of Quinn's room. Almost immediately I spied on his desk something that made my investigation easier, this something being a spiral notebook with a cover of mock marble. Switching on the desk lamp in that darkly curtained room, I looked through the first few pages of the notebook. It seemed to be concerned with the sect Quinn had become associated with some weeks before, serving as a kind of spiritual diary. The entries were Quinn's meditations upon his inward evolution and employed an esoteric terminology which must remain largely undocumented, since the notebook is no longer in existence. Its pages, as I recall them, outlined Quinn's progress along a path of offbeat enlightenment, a tentative peering into what might have been merely symbolic realms.

Quinn seemed to have become one of a jaded philosophical society, a group of arcane deviates. Their *raison d'être* was a kind of mystical masochism, forcing initiates toward feats of occult daredevilry—"glimpsing the inferno with eyes of ice," to take from the notebook a phrase that was repeated often and seemed a sort of chant of power. As I suspected, hallucinogenic drugs were used by the sect, and there was no doubt that they believed themselves communing with strange metaphysical venues. Their chief aim, in true mystical fashion, was to transcend common reality in the search for higher states of being, but their stratagem was highly unorthodox, a strange detour along the usual path toward positive illumination. Instead, they maintained a kind of blasphemous fatalism, a doomed determinism which brought them face to face with realms of obscure horror. Perhaps it was this very obscurity that allowed them the excitement of their central purpose, which seemed to be a precarious flirting with personal apocalypse, the striving for horrific dominion over horror itself.

Such was the subject matter of Quinn's notebook, all of it quite interesting. But the most intriguing entry was the last, which was brief and which I can recreate nearly in full. In this entry, like most of the others, Quinn addressed himself in the second person with various snatches of advice and admonishment. Much of it was unintelligible, for it seemed to be obsessed almost entirely with regions alien to the conscious mind. However, Quinn's words did have a certain curious meaning when I first read them, and more so later on. The following, then, exemplifies the manner of his notes to himself:

So far your progress has been faulty but inexorable. Last night you saw the zone and now know what it is like—wobbling glitter, a field of venomous colors, the glistening inner skin of deadliest nightshade. Now that you are actually nearing the plane of the zone, awake! Forget your dainty fantasies and learn to move like the eyeless beast you must become. Listen, feel, *smell* for the zone. Dream your way through its marvelous perils. You know what the things from there may do to you with *their* dreaming. Be aware. Do not stay in one place for very long these next few nights. This will be the strongest time. Get out (perhaps into the great night-light of Nortown)—wander, tramp, tread, somnambulate if you must. Stop and watch but not for very long. Be mindlessly cautious. Catch the entrancing fragrance of fear—and prevail.

I read this brief passage over and over, and each time its substance seemed to become less the fantasies of an overly imaginative sectarian and more a strange reflection on matters by now familiar to me. Thus, I seemed to be serving my purpose, for the sensitivity of my psyche had allowed a subtle link to Quinn's spiritual pursuits, even in their nuances of mood. And judging from the last entry in Quinn's notebook, the upcoming days were crucial in some way, the exact significance of which may have been entirely psychological. Nevertheless, other possibilities and hopes had crossed my mind. As it happened, the question was settled the following night over the

course of only a few hours. This post-meridian adventure—
somehow inevitably—took place amid the dreamy and debased
nightlife of Nortown.

2.

Technically a suburb, at least by any civic definition, Nortown
was not located outside the periphery of that larger city where
Quinn and I attended the university, but entirely within its
boundaries. For the near-indigent student, the sole attraction
of this area is the inexpensive housing it offers in a variety of
forms, even if the accommodations are not always the most
appealing. However, in the case of Quinn and myself, the
motives may have differed, for both of us were quite capable of
appreciating the hidden properties and possibilities of the little
city. Because of Nortown's peculiar proximity to the down-
town area of a large urban center it absorbed much of the big
city's lurid glamour, only on a smaller scale and in a concentrated way. Of course, there were a multitude of restaurants
with bogusly exotic cuisines as well as a variety of nightspots
of bizarre reputation and numerous establishments that existed
in a twilight realm with regard to their legality.

But in addition to these second-rate epicurean attractions,
Nortown also offered less earthly interests, however ludicrous
the form they happened to take. The area seemed a kind of
spawning ground for marginal people and movements. (I
believe that Quinn's fellow sectarians—whoever they may
have been—were either residents or habitués of the suburb.)
Along Nortown's seven blocks or so of bustling commerce,
one may see storefront invitations to personalized readings of
the future or private lectures on the spiritual foci of the body.
And if one looks up while walking down certain streets, there
is a chance of spying second-floor windows with odd symbols
pasted upon them, cryptic badges whose significance is known
only to the initiated. In a way difficult to analyze, the mood of
these streets was reminiscent of that remarkable dream I have
previously described—the sense of dim and disordered land-

scapes evoked by every sordid streetcorner of that city within a city.

Not the least of Nortown's inviting qualities is the simple fact that many of its businesses are active every hour of the day and night, which was probably one reason why Quinn's activities gravitated to this place. And now I knew of at least a few particular nights that he planned to spend treading Nortown's mottled sidewalks.

Quinn left the apartment just before dark. Through the window I watched him walk around to the front of the building and then proceed up the street toward Nortown's business district. I followed when he seemed a safe distance ahead of me. I supposed that if my plan to chart Quinn's movements for the evening was going to fail, it would do so in the next few minutes. Of course, it was reasonable to credit Quinn with an extra sense or two which would alert him to my scheme. All the same, I was not wrong to believe I was merely conforming to Quinn's unspoken wish for a spectator to his doom, a chronicler of his demonic quest. And everything proceeded smoothly as we arrived in the more heavily trafficked area of Nortown approaching Carton, the suburb's main street.

Up ahead, the high buildings of the surrounding metropolis towered around and above Nortown's lower structures. In the distance a pale sun had almost set, highlighting the peaks of the larger city's skyline. The valleyed enclave of Nortown now lay in this skyline's shadows, a dwarfish replica of the enveloping city. And this particular dwarf was of the colorfully clothed type suitable for entertaining jaded royalty. The main street flashed comic colors from an electric spectrum, dizzily hopping foot to foot in its attempt to conquer the nameless boredom of the crowds along the sidewalks. The milling throng—unusual for a chilly autumn evening—made it easier for me to remain inconspicuous.

I almost lost him for a moment when he left the ranks of some sluggish pedestrians and disappeared into a little drugstore on the north side of Carton. I stopped farther down the block and window-shopped for second-hand clothes until he came out onto the street again, which he did a few minutes later, holding a newspaper in one hand and stuffing a flat package of cigars inside his overcoat with the other. I saw him do this in the light flooding out of the drugstore windows, for by now it was nightfall.

Quinn walked a few more steps and then crossed at mid-street. I saw that his destination was only a restaurant with a semicircle of letters from the Greek alphabet painted on the front windows. Through the window I could see him take a seat at the counter inside and spread out his newspaper, ordering something from the waitress who stood with pad in hand. For at least a little while he would be easy to keep track of. Not that I simply wanted to observe Quinn go in and out of restaurants and drugstores the rest of the night. I had hoped that his movements would eventually become more revealing. But for the moment I was gaining practice at being his shadow.

I watched Quinn at his dinner from inside a Middle-Eastern import store located across the street from the restaurant. I could observe him easily through the store's front display window. Unfortunately I was the only patron of this musty place, and three times a bony, aged woman asked if she could help me. "Just looking," I said, taking my eyes from the window momentarily and glancing around at a collection of assorted trinkets and ersatz Arabiana. The woman eventually went and stood behind a merchandise counter, where she kept her right hand tenaciously out of view. For possibly no reason at all I was becoming very nervous among the engraved brass and ruggy smells of that store. I decided to return to the street, mingling along the crowded but strangely quiet sidewalks.

After about a half-hour, at approximately quarter to eight, Quinn came out of the restaurant. From down the street and on the opposite side I watched him fold up the newspaper he was carrying and neatly dispose of it in a nearby mailbox. Then, a recently lit cigar alternating between hand and mouth, he started north again. I let him walk half a block or so before I crossed the street and began tailing him once more. Although nothing manifestly unusual had yet occurred, there now seemed to be a certain promise of unknown happenings in the air of that autumn night.

Quinn continued on his way through the dingy neon of Nortown's streets. But he now seemed to have no specific destination. His stride was less purposeful than it had been, and he no longer looked expectantly before him but gawked aimlessly about the scene, as if these surroundings were unfamiliar or had altered in some way from the condition of previous visits. The overcoated and wild-haired figure of my roommate gave me the impression he was overwhelmed by something around him. He looked up toward the roof-ledges of buildings as though the full weight of the black autumn sky were about to descend. Absent-mindedly he nudged into a few people and at some point lost hold of his cigar, scattering sparks across the sidewalk.

Quinn turned at the next corner, where Carton intersected with a minor sidestreet. There were only a few places alive with activity in this area, which led into the darker residential regions of Nortown. One of these places was a building with a stairway leading below the street level. From a safe position of surveillance I saw Quinn go down this stairway into what I assumed was a bar or coffeehouse of some sort. Innocent as it may have been, my imagination impulsively populated that cellar with patrons of fascinating diversity and strangeness. Suppressing my fantasies, I confronted the practical decision of whether or not to follow Quinn inside and risk shattering his illusion of a lonely mystic odyssey. I also speculated that perhaps he was meeting others in this place, and possibly I would end up following multiple cultists, penetrating their esoteric activities, such as they may have been. But after I had cautiously descended the stairway and peered through the smeary panes of the window there, I saw Quinn sitting in a distant corner . . . and he was alone.

"Like peeping in windows?" asked a voice behind me. "Windows are the eyes of the soulless," said another. This twosome looked very much like professors from the university, though not those familiar to me from the anthropology department. I followed these distinguished academics into the bar, thereby making a less obvious entrance than if I had gone in alone.

The place was dark and crowded and much larger than it

looked from outside. I sat at a table by the door and at a strategic remove from Quinn, who was seated behind a half-wall some distance away. The décor around me looked like that of an unfinished basement or a storage room. There were a great number of flea-market antiquities hanging from the walls, and dangling from the ceiling were long objects that resembled razor strops. After a few moments a rather vacant-looking girl walked over and stood silently near my table. I did not immediately notice that she was just a waitress, so unconvivial was her general appearance and manner.

At some point during the hour or so that I was allowed to sit there nursing my drink, I discovered that if I leaned forward as far as possible in my chair, I could catch a glimpse of Quinn on the other side of the half-wall. This tactic now revealed to me a Quinn in an even greater state of agitated wariness than before. I thought he would have settled down to a languid series of drinks, but he did not. In fact, there was a cup of coffee, not a glass of spirits, sitting at his elbow. Quinn seemed to be scrutinizing every inch of the room for something. His nervous glances once nearly focused on my own face, and from then on I became more discreet.

A little later on, not long before Quinn's and my exit, a girl with a guitar wandered up onto a platform against one wall of the room. As she made herself comfortable in a chair on the platform and tuned her instrument, someone switched on a single spotlight on the floor. I noticed that attached to the front of the spotlight was a movable disc divided into four sections: red, blue, green, and transparent. It was now adjusted to shine only through the transparent section.

The entertainer gave herself no introduction and started singing a song after lethargically strumming her guitar for a moment or so. I did not recognize the piece, but I think any song would have sounded unfamiliar as rendered by this performer, whose voice compared in my imagination to that of a feeble-minded siren locked away somewhere and wailing pitifully to be set free. That the song was intended as mournful I could not doubt. It was, however, a very foreign and disorienting kind of mournfulness, as if the singer had eavesdropped on some exotic and grotesque rituals for her inspiration.

She finished the song. After receiving applause from only a single person somewhere in the room, she started into another number which sounded no different from the first. Then, about a minute or so into the weird progress of this second song, something happened—a moment of confusion—and seconds later I found myself back on the streets.

What happened was actually no more than some petty mischief. While the singer was calling feline-voiced to the lost love of the song's verses, someone sneaked up near the platform, grabbed the disc attached to the front of the spotlight, and gave it a spin. A wild kaleidoscope ensued. The swarming colors attacked the singer and those patrons at nearby tables. The singing continued, its languishing tempo off-sync with the speedy reds, blues, and greens. There was something menacing about the visual disorder of those colors gleefully swimming around. And then, for a brief moment, the colorful chaos was eclipsed when a silhouette hurriedly stumbled past, moving between my table and the singer on the platform. I almost missed seeing who it was, for my eyes were averted from the general scene. I let him make it out the door, which he seemed to have some trouble opening, before dashing from the place myself.

When I emerged from the stairway onto the sidewalk, I saw Quinn standing at the corner on Carton. As he paused to light a cigar, I kept my place in the shadows until he proceeded up the street.

We walked a few blocks that were profusely decorated with neon signs streaming across the night. I was diverted by the sequentially lit letters spelling out E-S-S-E-N-C-E LOUNGE, LOUNGE, LOUNGE; and I wondered what secrets were revealed to those anointed by the priestesses of MEDEA'S MASSAGE.

Our next stop was a short one, though it also threatened the psychic rapport Quinn and I had been so long in establishing. Quinn entered a bar where a sign outside advertised for persons who desired work as professional dancers. I let a few moments pass before following Quinn into the place. But just as I stepped within the temporarily blinding darkness of the bar, someone shouldered me to one side in his haste to leave. Fortunately I was standing in a crowd of men waiting for seats inside, and Quinn did not seem to take note of me. In addition, his right hand—with cigar—was visoring his eyes or perhaps giving his brow a quick massage. In any case, he did not stop but charged past me and out the door. As I turned to follow him in his brusque exit, I noticed the scene within the bar, particularly focusing on a stage where a single figure gyred about— clothed in flashing colors. And gazing briefly on this chaotic image, I recalled that other flurrying chaos at the underground club, wondering if Quinn had been disturbed by this second confrontation with a many-hued phantasmagoria, this flickering and disorderly rainbow of dreams. Certainly he seemed to have been repulsed in some way, causing his furious exit. I exited more calmly and resumed my chartings of Quinn's nocturnal voyage.

He next visited a number of places into which, for one reason or another, I was wary to follow. Included among these stops was a bookstore (not an occult one), a record shop with an outdoor speaker that blared madness into the street, and a lively amusement arcade, where Quinn remained for only the briefest moment. Between each of these diversions Quinn appeared to be getting progressively more, I cannot say *frantic*, but surely . . . watchful. His once steady stride was now interrupted by half-halts to glance into store windows, frequent hesitations that betrayed a multitude of indecisive thoughts and impulses, and a faltering uncertainty in general. His whole manner of movement had changed, its aspects of rhythm, pace, and gesture adding up to a character-image radically altered from his former self. At times I could even have doubted that this was Jack Quinn if it had not been for his unmistakable appearance.

Perhaps, I thought, he had become subliminally aware of someone being always at his back, and that, at this point in his plummet to an isolated hell, he no longer required a companion or could not tolerate a voyeur of his destiny. But ultimately I had to conclude that the cause of Quinn's disquiet was something other than a pair of footsteps trailing behind him. There was something else that he seemed to be seeking, searching out clues in the brick and neon landscape, possibly in some signal condition or circumstance from which he could derive guidance for his movements that frigid and fragrant October night. But I do not think he found, or could properly read, whatever sign it was he sought. Otherwise the consequences might have been different.

The reason for Quinn's lack of alertness had much to do with his penultimate stop that evening. The time was close to midnight. We had worked our way down Carton to the last block of Nortown's commercial area. Here, also, were the northern limits of the suburb, beyond which lay a stretch of condemned buildings belonging to the surrounding city. This part of the suburb was similarly blighted in ways both physical and atmospheric. On either side of the street stood a row of attached buildings whose height sometimes varied dramatically. Many of the businesses on this block were not equipped with outside lights or failed to employ the ones they had. But the lack of outward illumination seldom signified that these places were not open for business, at least judging by the comings and goings on the sidewalks outside the darkened shops, bars, small theaters, and other establishments. Casual pedestrian traffic at this end of the suburb had seemingly diminished to certain determined individuals of specific taste and destination. Street traffic too was reduced, and there was something about those few cars left parked at the curbs that gave them a look of abandonment, if not complete immobility.

Of course, I am sure those cars, or most of them, were capable of motion, and it was only the most pathetic of fallacies that caused one to view them as sentient things somehow debilitated by their broken-down surroundings. But I think I may have been dreaming on my feet for a few seconds: sounds and images seemed to come to me from places outside the immediate environment. I stared at an old building across the street—a bar, perhaps, or a nameless club of some exclusive membership—and for a moment I received the impression that it was sending out strange noises, not from within its walls but from a far more distant source, as if it were transmitting from remote dimensions. And these noises had a visible aspect too, a kind of vibration in the night air, like static that one could see sparkling in the darkness. But all the while there was just an old building and nothing more than that. I stared a little longer and the noises faded into confused echoes, the sparkling became dull and disappeared, the connection lost, and the place fully resumed its decrepit reality.

The building looked much too intimate in size to afford concealment, and I perceived a certain privacy in its appearance that made me feel a newcomer would have been awkwardly noticeable. Quinn, however, had unhesitantly gone inside. I suppose it would have been helpful to observe him in there, to see what sort of familiarity he had with this establishment and its patrons. But all I know is that he loitered in that place for over an hour. During part of that time I waited at a counter stool in a diner down the street.

When Quinn finally came out he was observably drunk. This surprised me, because I had assumed that he intended to maintain the utmost control of his faculties that evening. The coffee I saw him drinking at that underground club seemed to support this assumption. But somehow Quinn's intentions to hold on to his sobriety, if he had such intentions to begin with, had been revised or forgotten.

I had positioned myself farther down the street by the time he reappeared, but there was much less need for caution now. It was ridiculously easy to remain unnoticed behind someone who could barely see the pavement he walked upon. A police car with flashing lights passed us on Carton, and Quinn exhibited no awareness of it. He halted on the sidewalk, but only to light another cigar. And he seemed to have a difficult time performing this task in a wind that turned his unbuttoned overcoat into a wild-winged cape flapping behind him. Perhaps it was this wind, serving as a kind of guiding force, that led the way to our final stop where a few lights relieved the darkness on the very edge of Nortown.

The lights were those of a theater marquee. And it was also here that we caught up with the revolving beacons of the patrol car. Behind it was another vehicle, a large luxury affair that had a deep gash in its shiny side. Not far away along the curb was a No Parking sign that was creased into an L shape. A tall policeman was inspecting the damaged city property, while the owner of the car that had apparently done the deed was standing by. Quinn gave only a passing glance at this tableau as he proceeded into the theater. A few moments later I followed him, but not before hearing the owner of that disfigured car tell the patrolman that something brightly colored had suddenly appeared in his headlights, causing him to swerve. And whatever it was had subsequently vanished.

Stepping into the lobby of the theater, I noted that it must have been a place of baroque elegance in former days, though now the outlines of the scrolled molding above were blurred by grayish sediment and the enormous chandelier was missing some of its parts and all of its glitter. The glass counter on my right, which no doubt was once filled with boxes of candy and such, had been converted, probably long ago, into a merchandise stand displaying pornographic magazines.

I walked through one of a long line of doors and stood around for a while in the hallway behind the auditorium. Here a group of men were talking and smoking, dropping their cigarettes onto the floor and stepping them out. Their voices almost drowned out the soundtrack of the film that was being shown, the sound emanating from the aisle entrances and humming unintelligibly in the back walls. I looked into the film-lit auditorium and saw only a few moviegoers scattered here and there in the worn seats of the theater, mostly sitting by themselves. By the light of the film I located Quinn within the sparse audience. He was sitting very close to the screen in a front-row seat next to some curtains and an exit sign.

He seemed to be dozing rather than watching the film, and I found it a simple matter to position myself a few rows behind him. By that time Quinn appeared to have lost what was left of his earlier resolve and intensity, and the momentum of that night had all but run out. In the darkness of the theater I began to nod and then fell asleep, much as it seemed Quinn had already done.

I did not sleep for long, though—no more than a few minutes. But during that time I dreamed. However, there was no nightmarish scenery in this dream, no threatening scenarios. Only darkness . . . darkness and a voice. The voice was that of Quinn. He was calling out to me from a great distance, a distance that did not seem a matter of physical space but one of immeasurable and alien dimensions. His words were distorted, as if passing through some medium that was misshaping them, turning human sounds into a beastlike rasping—the half-choking and half-shrieking voice of something in the process of being slowly and methodically wounded. First he called my name several times in the wild modulations of a coarse scream. Then he said, as well as I can remember: "Stopped watching for them . . . fell into their zone . . . where are you . . . help us . . . they're dreaming, too . . . they're dreaming . . . and shaping things with their dreams."

I awoke and the first thing I saw was what seemed a great shapeless mass of colors, which was only the giant images of the film. My eyes focused, and I looked down the rows toward Quinn. He seemed to be slumped over, hunching down, the top of his head much too near his shoulders. A mound of movement struggled on the other side of his seat, emerging sideways into the aisle. It was Quinn, but he was now faintly luminous and diminished in size. The bottom of his overcoat dragged along the floor, its sleeves hanging loose and handless, its collar caving in. The thing fought to take each awkward step, as if it did not have full control of its motion, like a marionette jerking this way and that way as it labored forth. Its glow seemed to be gaining in radiance now, a pulsing opalescent aura that crawled or flowed all around the lumbering dwarf.

I might still be in a dream, I reminded myself. Or this might be a distorted after-vision, a delirious blend of images derived from nightmare, imagination, and that enormous stain of colors at the front of the dark auditorium in which I had just awakened. I tried to collect myself, to focus on the thing that was disappearing behind the thick curtain beneath the lighted exit sign.

I followed, passing through the opening in the frayed, velvety curtain. Beyond it was a cement stairway leading up to a
metal door that was now swinging closed. Halfway up the
stairs I saw a familiar shoe which must have been lost in
Quinn's frantic yet retarded haste. Where was he running and
from what? These were my only thoughts now, without consideration of the pure strangeness of the situation. I had abandoned all connections to any guiding set of norms by which to
judge reality or unreality. However, all that was needed to
shatter this acceptance waited outside—something of total
unacceptability atop a rickety scaffold of estrangement. After
I stepped out the door at the top of the stairs, I discovered that
the previous events of that night had only served as a spring-
board into other realms, a point of departure from a world
now diminishing with a furious velocity behind me.

The area outside the theater was unlit but nonetheless was
not dark. Something was shining in a long narrow passageway
between the theater and an adjacent building. This was where
Quinn had gone. Illumination was there, and sounds.

From around the corner's edge a grotesque light was trickling out, the first intimations of an ominous sunrise over a
dark horizon. I dimly recognized this wavering light, though
not from my waking memory. It grew more intense, now pour-
ing out in weird streams from beyond the solid margin of the
building. And the more intense it grew, the more clearly I
could hear the screaming voice that had called out to me in a
dream. I shouted his name, but the swelling, chromatic brilliance was a field of fear which kept me from making any
move in its direction. What repelled me appeared as a rainbow
in which all natural color had been mutated into a painfully
lush iridescence by some prism fantastically corrupted in its
form. It was an aurora painting the darkness with a shimmering blaze that did not belong to this world. And, in actuality, it
was nothing like these figurative effusions, which are merely a
feeble means of partially fixing a reality incommunicable to
those not initiated to it, a necessary resorting to the makeshift
gibberish of the mystic isolated by his experience and left without a language to describe it.

The entire episode was temporally rather brief, though its phantasmagoric quality made it seem of indefinite duration—the blink of an eye or an eon. Suddenly the brightness ceased flowing out toward me, as if some strange spigot had been abruptly turned off somewhere. The screaming had also stopped. With all caution, I stepped into the passageway I had seen Quinn enter. But nothing was there—nothing to relieve my sense of confusion as to what exactly had happened. (Though not a dilettante of the unreal, I have had my moments of dazed astonishment.) But perhaps there was one thing. On the ground was a burnt-out patch of earth, a shapeless and bare spot that was deprived of the weeds and litter that covered the surrounding area. Possibly it was only a place from which some object had recently been removed, spirited off, leaving the earth beneath it vacant and dead. For a moment, when I first looked at the spot, it seemed to twinkle with a faint luminosity. Possibly I only imagined its outline as being that of a human silhouette, though one contorted in such a way that it might also have been mistaken for other things, other shapes. In any case, whatever had been there was now gone.

And around this barren little swatch of ground was only trash: newspapers mutilated by time and the elements; brown bags reduced by decay to their primal pulp; thousands of cigarette butts; and one item of debris that was almost new and had yet to have any transformations worked upon it. It was a thin book-like box. I picked it up. There were still two fresh cigars in it.

3.

Quinn never returned to the apartment we shared. After a few days I reported him as missing to the Nortown police. Before doing this I destroyed the notebook in his room, for in a fit of paranoia I thought the authorities would find it in the course of their investigations and then ask some rather uncomfortable questions. I did not want to explain to them things that they simply would not believe, especially activities indulged in that final night. This would only have erroneously cast suspicion upon me. Fortunately, those charged with law enforcement in Nortown happened to be quite lax.

After Quinn's disappearance I immediately began looking for another place to live. Although my erstwhile roommate seemed permanently removed from my life, we continued to familiarize in nightmares that were robbing me of sleep. I considered these to be leftover visions of Quinn still haunting the apartment.

While the figure in my dreams bore no resemblance to the missing person named Jack Quinn, or to any person at all, I knew it was him. His shape kept changing, or rather was being changed by those kaleidoscopic beasts. Playing out a scene from some Boschian hell, the tormenting demons encircled their victim and were *dreaming* him. They carried him through a hideous series of transfigurations, maliciously altering the screaming mass of a damned soul. They were dreaming things out of him and dreaming things into him. Finally, the purpose of their transformations became apparent. They were torturing their victim through a number of stages which would ultimately result in his becoming one of them, fulfilling his most fearful and obsessive vision. At some point, I did cease to discern the entity I had known as Quinn and noticed only that there was now one more glittering beast that took its place with the others and frolicked among them.

Such was the end of the dreams I had before leaving the apartment. There have been no others since, at least none that have troubled my own sleep. I cannot say the same for that of my new roommate, who rages in his slumber night after night in the shabby, and quite reasonably priced, little place where we reside. Once or twice he has attempted to communicate to me his strange visions and the company into which they have led him. But I affect only the slightest interest in his adventures. For as a student of anthropology, one of the few of my kind, I must keep a certain distance from my subjects. They are of a rare type, and outright intimacy tends to impact their behavior in ways that could spoil my study of them. In any case, companionship is not what these adventurers in an alternative existence seek. What they desire, like Jack Quinn, are witnesses to their downfall as they plummet into an abyss of nightmares. What they want are chroniclers of their explorations in a hell of their own choosing. And in these roles I am more than willing to accommodate them, for their desires and mine are complementary. Nevertheless, I sometimes feel a tinge of guilt on my side. In truth, I am a parasite who lives off a malady that afflicts them while I remain immune. And the part I play is that of a voyeur. For it is within my power to save them. If only I were moved to do so, I could hold out my hand to them as they hover over the pit. I can only wonder, then, what is the sickness from which I suffer that, like some depraved deity, I elect to let them fall.

THE MYSTICS OF
MUELENBURG

If things are not what they seem—and we are forever reminded that this is the case—then it must also be observed that enough of us ignore this truth to keep the world from collapsing. Though never exact, always shifting somewhat, the *proportion* is crucial. For a certain number of minds are fated to depart for realms of delusion, as if in accordance with some hideous timetable, and many will never be returning to us. Even among those who remain, how difficult it can be to hold the focus sharp, to keep the picture of the world from fading, from blurring in selected zones and, on occasion, from sustaining epic deformations over the entire visible scene.

I once knew a man who claimed that, overnight, all the solid shapes of existence had been replaced by cheap substitutes: trees made of poster board, houses built of colored foam, whole landscapes composed of hair-clippings. His own flesh, he said, was now just so much putty. Needless to add, this acquaintance had deserted the cause of appearances and could no longer be depended on to stick to the common story. Alone he had wandered into a tale of another sort altogether; for him, all things now participated in this nightmare of nonsense. But although his revelations conflicted with the lesser forms of truth, nonetheless he did live in the light of a greater truth: that all is unreal. Within him this knowledge was vividly present down to his very bones, which had been newly simulated by a compound of mud and dust and ashes.

In my own case, I must confess that the myth of a natural

universe—that is, one that adheres to certain continuities whether we wish them or not—was losing its grip on me and gradually being supplanted by a hallucinatory view of creation. Forms, having nothing to offer except a mere suggestion of firmness, declined in importance; fantasy, that misty domain of pure meaning, gained in power and influence. This was in the days when esoteric wisdom seemed to count for something in my mind, and I would willingly have sacrificed a great deal in its pursuit. Hence, my interest in the man who called himself Klaus Klingman; hence, too, that brief yet profitable association between us, which came about through channels too twisted to recall.

Without a doubt, Klingman was one of the illuminati and proved this many times over in various psychic experiments, particularly those of the seance type. In this regard, I need only mention the man who was severally known as Nemo the Necromancer, Marlowe the Magus, and Master Marinetti, each of whom was none other than Klaus Klingman himself. But Klingman's highest achievement was not a matter of public spectacle and consisted entirely in attaining an unwavering acceptance of the spectral nature of things, which to him were neither what they seemed to be nor were they quite anything at all.

Klingman lived in the enormous upper story of a warehouse that had been part of his family's legacy to him, and there I often found him wandering amidst a few pieces of furniture and the cavernous wasteland of dim and empty storage space. Collapsing into an ancient armchair, reposing far beneath crumbling rafters, he would gaze beyond the physical body of his visitor, his eyes surveying remote worlds and his facial expression badly disorganized by dreams and large quantities of alcohol. "Fluidity, always fluidity," he shouted out, his voice carrying through the expansive haze around us, which muted daylight into dusk. The embodiment of his mystic precepts, he appeared at any given moment to be on the verge of an amazing disintegration, his particular complex of atoms ready to go shooting off into the great void like a burst of fireworks.

We discussed the dangers—for me and for the world—of adopting a visionary program of existence. "The chemistry of things is so delicate," he warned. "And this word *chemistry*. What does it mean but a mingling, a mixing, a gushing together? These are things that people fear."

Indeed, I had already suspected the hazards of Klingman's company, and, as the sun was setting over the city beyond the great windows of the warehouse, I became afraid. With an uncanny perception of my feelings, Klingman pointed at me and bellowed: "The worst fear of the race—yes, the world suddenly transformed into a senseless nightmare, horrible dissolution of things. Nothing compares, even oblivion is a sweet dream. You understand why, of course. Why this peculiar threat. These brooding psyches, all the busy minds everywhere. I hear them buzzing like flies in the blackness. I see them as glow worms flitting in the blinding sun. They are struggling, straining every second to keep the sky above them, to keep the sun in the sky, to keep the dead in the earth—to keep all things, so to speak, *where they belong*. What an undertaking! What a crushing task! Is it any wonder that they are all tempted by a universal vice, that in some dark street of the mind a soft voice whispers to one and all: 'Lay down your burden.' Then thoughts begin to drift, a mystical magnetism pulls them this way and that, faces start to change, shadows speak. And sooner or later the sky comes down, melting like wax. But as you know, everything has not yet been lost: absolute terror has proved its security against this fate. Is it any wonder that these beings carry on the struggle at whatever cost?"

"And you?" I asked.

"I?"

"Yes, don't you shoulder the universe in your own way?"

"Not at all," he replied, smiling and sitting up in his chair as on a throne. "I am a lucky one, parasite of chaos, maggot of vice. Where I live all is nightmare, thus a certain nonchalance. I am accustomed to drifting in the delirium of history. And by *history* I include events, and even whole eras, that have never gone on record. Speaking with the dead can be so instructive. They remember what the living have forgotten, or would not know if they could. The true frailty of things. What happened in the old town of Muelenburg, for example. Now *there* was an opportunity, a moment of distraction in which so much was nearly lost forever, so many lost in that medieval gloom, catastrophe of dreams. How their minds wandered in the shadows even as their bodies were seemingly bound to narrow rutted streets and apparently safeguarded by the spired cathedral which was erected between 1365 and 1399. A rare and fortuitous juncture when the burden of the heavens was heaviest— so much to keep in its place—and the psyche so ill-developed, so easily taxed and tempted away from its labors. But they knew nothing about that, and never could. They only knew the prospect of absolute terror."

Klingman smiled, then began giggling, his mind obviously turning inward to converse with itself. Hoping to draw his conversation outward, I said. "Mr. Klingman, you were speaking about Muelenburg. You said something about the cathedral."

"I *see* the cathedral, the colossal vault above, the central aisle stretching out before us. The woodcarvings leer down from dark corners, animals and freaks, men in the mouths of demons. Are you taking notes again? Fine, then take notes. Who knows what you will remember of all this? Or if memory will help you at all? In any case we are already there, sitting among the smothered sounds of the cathedral. Beyond the jeweled windows is the town in twilight."

Twilight, as Klingman explained, had come upon Muelenburg somewhat prematurely on a certain day deep into the autumn season. Early that afternoon, clouds had spread themselves evenly above the region surrounding the town, withholding heaven's light and giving a dull appearance to the landscape of forests, thatched farmhouses, and windmills standing still against the horizon. Within the high stone walls of Muelenburg itself, no one seemed particularly troubled that the narrow streets—normally so cluttered with the pointed shadows of peaked roofs and jutting gables at this time of day—were still immersed in a lukewarm dimness which turned merchants' brightly colored signs into faded artifacts of a dead town and which made faces look as if they were fashioned of pale clay. And in the central square—where the shadow from

the clock-tower of the town hall at times overlapped those cast
by the twin spires of the cathedral on the one hand, or the
ones from high castle turrets looming at the border of the
town on the other—there was only grayness undisturbed.

Where were the minds of the townspeople? How had they
ceased paying homage to the ancient order of things? And
when had the severing taken place that set their world adrift
on strange waters?

For some time they remained innocent of the disaster, going
about their ways as the ashen twilight lingered far too long, as
it encroached upon the hours that belonged to evening and
suspended the town between day and night. Everywhere windows began to glow with the yellow light of lamps, creating
the illusion that darkness was imminent. Any moment, it
seemed, the natural cycle would relieve the town of the prolonged dusk it had suffered that autumn day. How well-
received the blackness would have been by those who waited
silently in sumptuous chambers or humble rooms, for no one
could bear the sight of Muelenburg's twisting streets in that
eerie, overstaying twilight. Even the night watchman shirked
his nocturnal routine. And when the bells of the abbey sounded
for the monks' midnight prayers, each toll spread like an alarm
throughout the town still held in the strange luminousness of
the gloaming.

Exhausted by fear, many shuttered their windows, extinguished lamps, and retired to their beds, hoping that all would
be made right in the interval. Others sat up with a candle,
enjoying the lost luxury of shadows. A few, being itinerants
who were not fixed to the life of the town, broke through the
unwatched gate and took to the roads, all the while gazing at
the pale sky and wondering where they would go.

Whether they kept the hours in their dreams or in sleepless
vigils, all of Muelenburg's citizens were disturbed by something
in the spaces around them, as if some strangeness had seeped
into the atmosphere of their town, their homes, and perhaps
their souls. The air seemed heavier somehow, resisting them
slightly, and also seemed to be flowing with things that could not
be perceived except as swift, shadowlike movement escaping all

sensible recognition, transparent flight which barely caressed one's vision.

When the clock high in the tower of the town hall proved that a nightful of hours had passed, some opened their shutters, even ventured into the streets. But the sky still hovered over them like an infinite vault of glowing dust. Here and there throughout the town the people began to gather in whispering groups. Appeals were soon made at the castle and the cathedral, and speculations were offered to calm the crowd. There was a struggle in heaven, some had reasoned, which had influenced the gross reality of the visible world. Others proposed a deception by demons or an ingenious punishment from on high. Certain persons met secretly in well-hidden chambers and spoke in stricken voices about old deities formerly driven from the earth who were now monstrously groping their way back. And all of these explications of the mystery were true in their own way, though none could abate the dread which had settled upon the town of Muelenburg.

Submerged in unvarying grayness, distracted and confused by phantasmal intrusions about them, the people of the town felt their world dissolving. Even the clock in the town hall tower failed to keep their moments from wandering strangely. Within such disorder were bred curious thoughts and actions. Thus, in the garden of the abbey an ancient tree was shunned and rumors spread concerning some change in its twisted silhouette, something flaccid and rope-like about its branches, until finally the monks doused it with oil and set it aflame, their circle of squinting faces bathing in the glare. Likewise, a fountain standing in one of the castle's most secluded courtyards became notorious when its waters appeared to suggest fabulous depths far beyond the natural dimensions of its shell-shaped basin. The cathedral itself had deteriorated into a hollow sanctuary where prayers were mocked by queer movements among the carved figures in cornices and by shadows streaming horribly in the twitching light of a thousand candles.

Throughout the town, all places and things bore evidence to striking revisions in the base realm of matter: precisely sculptured stone began to loosen and lump, an abandoned cart melded with the sucking mud of the street, and objects in desolate rooms lost themselves in the surfaces they pressed upon, making metal tongs mix with brick hearth, prismatic jewels with lavish velvet, a corpse with the wood of its coffin. At last the faces of Muelenburg became subject to changing expressions which at first were quite subtle, though later these divergences were so exaggerated that it was no longer possible to recapture original forms. It followed that the townspeople could no more recognize themselves than they could one another. All were carried off in the great torrent of their dreams, all spinning in that grayish whirlpool of indefinite twilight, all churning and in the end merging into utter blackness.

It was within this blackness that the souls of Muelenburg struggled and labored and ultimately awoke. The stars and high moon now lit up the night, and it seemed that their town had been returned to them. And so terrible had been their recent ordeal that of its beginning, its progress, and its termination, they could remember . . . nothing.

"Nothing?" I echoed.

"Of course," Klingman answered. "All of those terrible memories were left behind in the blackness. How could they bear to bring them back?"

"But your story," I protested. "These notes I've taken tonight."

"What did I tell you? Privileged information, confidences spoken off the historical record. You know that sooner or later each of the souls who occupied Muelenburg recollected the episode in detail. It was all waiting for them in the place where they had left it—the blackness which is the domain of death."

I remembered the necromantic learning that Klingman had professed and to which I gave no small credence. But this was too much. "Then nothing can be verified, nothing you can produce to back up your story. I thought you might at least conjure a spirit or two. You've never disappointed me before."

"Nor will I disappoint you tonight. Remember, I am one with the dead of Muelenburg . . . and with all who have known the great dream in all its true liquescence. They have spoken to me as I am speaking to you. Many reminiscences imparted by those old dreamers, many drunken dialogues I have held with them."

"Like the drunkenness of this dialogue tonight," I said, openly disdaining his narrative.

"Perhaps, only much more vivid, more real. But the yarn which you suppose I have merely spun has served its purpose. To cure you of doubt, you first had to be made a doubter. Until now, pardon my saying so, you have shown no talent in that direction. You believed every wild thing that came along, provided it had the least evidence whatever. Unparalleled credulity. But tonight you have doubted and thus you are ready to be cured of this doubt. And didn't I mention time and again the dangers? Unfortunately, you cannot count yourself among those forgetful souls of Muelenburg. You even have your mnemonic notes, as if anyone will credit them when this night is over. This is my gift to you. This will be your enlightenment. For the time is right again for the return of fluidity, and for the world's grip to go slack. And later so much will have to be washed away, assuming a renascence of things. Fluidity, always fluidity."

When I left his company that night, abandoning the dead and shapeless hours I had spent in that warehouse, Klingman was laughing like a madman. I remember him slouched in that threadbare throne, his face flushed and twisted, his mouth wailing at some hilarious arcana known only to himself. To all appearances, some ultimate phase of dissipation had seized his soul.

Nevertheless, that I had underrated or misunderstood the power of Klaus Klingman was soon demonstrated to me, though I wish it had not been. But no one else remembers that time when the night would not leave and no dawn appeared to be forthcoming. During the early part of the crisis there were sensible, rather than apocalyptic, explanations proffered everywhere: blackout, bizarre meteorological phenomena, an eclipse of sorts. Later, these myths became useless and ultimately unnecessary. As we had done before, we once again returned to this flimsy world—this world I must now view as a mere vapor of spectral manifestations, appearances cast out of emptiness, an ornamented void. As Klingman had promised, my enlighten-ment would be a lonely one.

For no one else recalls the hysteria that prevailed when the stars and the moon dimmed into blackness. Nor can they sum-mon the least memory of when the artificial illumination of this earth turned weak and lurid, and all the shapes we once knew contorted into nightmares and nonsense. And finally how the blackness grew viscous, enveloping what light remained and drawing us into itself. How many such horrors await in that blackness to be restored to the legions of the dead. For no one else living remembers when everything began to change, no one else with the exception of Klaus Klingman and myself.

In the red dawn following that gruesomely protracted night, I went to the warehouse. Unfortunately the place was unten-anted, save by its spare furnishings and a few empty bottles. Klingman had disappeared, perhaps into that same blackness for which he seemed to have an incredible nostalgia. I, of course, make no appeals for belief. There can be no belief where there is no doubt. This is far from secret knowledge, as if such knowledge could change anything. This is only how it seems, and seeming is everything.

IN THE SHADOW OF
ANOTHER WORLD

Many times in my life, and in many different places, I have found myself walking at twilight down streets lined with gently stirring trees and old silent houses. On such lulling occasions things seem firmly anchored, quietly settled and exceedingly present to the natural eye: over distant rooftops the sun abandons the scene and casts its last light upon windows, watered lawns, the edges of leaves. In this drowsy setting both great things and small achieve an intricate union, apparently leaving not the least space for anything else to intrude upon their visible domain. But other realms are always capable of making their presence felt, hovering unseen like strange cities disguised as clouds or hidden like a world of pale specters within a fog. One is besieged by orders of entity that refuse to articulate their exact nature or proper milieu. And soon those well-aligned streets reveal that they are, in fact, situated among bizarre landscapes where simple trees and houses are marvelously obscured, where everything is settled within the depths of a vast, echoing abyss. Even the infinite sky itself, across which the sun spreads its expansive light, is merely a blurry little window with a crack in it—a jagged fracture beyond which one may see, at twilight, what pervades a vacant street lined with gently stirring trees and old silent houses.

On one particular occasion I followed a tree-lined street past all the houses and continued until it brought me to a single house a short distance from town. As the road before me narrowed into a bristling path, and the path ascended in a swerving course up the side of a hump in the otherwise even landscape, I stood before my day's destination.

Like other houses of its kind (I have seen so many of them outlined against a pale sky at dusk), this one possessed the aspect of a mirage, a chimerical quality that led one to doubt its existence. Despite its dark and angular mass, its peaks and porches and worn wooden steps, there was something improperly tenuous about its substance, as if it had been constructed of illicit materials— dreams and vapor posing as solid matter. And this was not the full extent of its resemblance to a true chimera, for somehow the house projected itself as having acquired its present form through a fabulous overlap of properties. There seemed to be the appearance of petrified flesh in its rough outer surfaces, and it was very simple to imagine an inner framework not of beams and boards, but rather of gigantic bones from great beasts of old. The chimneys and shingles, windows and doorways were thus the embellishments of a later age which had misunderstood the real essence of this ancient monstrosity, transforming it into a motley and ludicrous thing. Little wonder, then, that in shame it would attempt to reject its reality and pass itself off as only a shadow on the horizon, a thing of nightmarish beauty that aroused impossible hopes.

As in the past, I looked to the unseen interior of such a house to be the focus of unknown . . . celebrations. It was my conviction that the inner world of these dwellings participated, after their own style, in a kind of ceremonious desolation—that translucent festivals might be glimpsed in the corners of certain rooms and that the faraway sounds of mad carnivals filled certain hallways at all hours of the day and night. I am afraid, however, that a peculiar feature of the house in question prevented full indulgence in my usual anticipations. My reference here is to a turret built into one side of the house and rising to an unusual height beyond its roof, so that it looked out upon the world as a lighthouse, diminishing the aspect of introspection that is vital to such structures. And near the cone-roofed peak of this turret, a row of large windows appeared to have been placed, as a quite recent modification, around its entire circumference. But if the house was truly employing its windows to gaze outward more than within, what it saw was nothing.

For all the windows of the three ample stories of the house, as well as those of the turret and that small octagonal aperture in the attic, were shuttered closed.

This was, in fact, the state in which I anticipated finding the house, since I had already exchanged numerous letters with Raymond Spare, the present owner.

"I thought you would arrive much sooner," Spare said on opening the door. "It's almost nightfall and I was sure you understood that only at certain times . . ."

"My apologies, but I'm here now. Shall I come in?"

Spare stepped aside and gestured theatrically toward the interior of the house, as if he were presenting one of those dubious spectacles that had earned him a substantial livelihood. It was out of an instinct for mystification that he had adopted the surname of the famed visionary and artist, even claiming some blood or spiritual kinship with this great eccentric. But tonight I was playing the skeptic, as I had in my correspondence with Spare, so that I might force him to earn my credence. There would have been no other way to gain his invitation to witness the phenomena that, as I understood from sources other than the illusionistic Spare, were well worth my attention. Unexpectedly, my host was mundane in appearance, which made it difficult to keep in mind his reputation for showmanship, his gift for trumped-up histrionics.

"You have left everything as he had it before you?" I asked, referring to the deceased former owner whose name Spare never disclosed to me, though I knew it all the same. But that was of no importance.

"Yes, very much as it was. Excellent housekeeper, all things considered."

Spare's observation was regrettably true: the interior of the house was immaculate to the point of being suspect. The great parlor in which we now sat, as well as those other rooms and hallways that receded into the house, exuded the atmosphere of a plush and well-tended mausoleum where the dead are truly at rest. The furnishings were dense and archaic, yet they betrayed no oppressive awareness of other times, no secret conspiracies

with departed spirits, regardless of the unnatural mood of twilight created by fastidiously clamped shutters which admitted
none of nature's true twilight from the outside world. The clock
that I heard resonantly ticking in a nearby room caused no sinister echoes to sound between dark, polished floors and lofty, un-
cobwebbed ceilings. Absent was all fear or hope of encountering
a malign presence in the cellar or an insane shadow in the attic.
Despite a certain odd effect created by thaumaturgic curios
appearing on a shelf, as well as a hermetic chart of the heavens
nicely framed and hanging upon a wall, no hint of hauntedness
was evoked by either the surfaces or obscurities of this house.

"Quite an innocent ambiance," said Spare, who displayed
no special prowess in voicing this thought of mine.

"Astonishingly so. Was that part of his intention?"

Spare laughed. "The truth is that this was his original intention, the genesis of what later occupied his genius. In the
beginning . . ."

"A spiritual wasteland?"

"Exactly," Spare confirmed.

"Sterile but . . . safe."

"You understand, then. His reputation was for risk not retreat.
But the notebooks are very clear on the suffering caused by his
fantastic gifts, his incredible sensitivity. He required spiritually
antiseptic surroundings, yet was hopelessly tempted by the
visionary. Again and again in his notebooks he describes himself
as 'overwhelmed' to the point of madness. You can appreciate
the irony."

"I can certainly appreciate the horror," I replied.

"Of course, well . . . tonight we will have the advantage of
his unfortunate experience. Before the evening advances much
further I want to show you where he worked."

"And the shuttered windows?" I asked.

"They are very much to the point," he answered.

The workshop of which Spare had spoken was located, as
one might have surmised, in the uppermost story of the turret
in the westernmost part of the house. This circular room could
only be reached by climbing a twisting and tenuous stairway

into the attic, where a second set of stairs led up into the turret. Spare fumbled with the key to the low wooden door, and soon we had gained entrance.

The room was definitely what Spare had implied: a workshop, or at least the remains of one. "It seems that toward the end he had begun to destroy his apparatus, as well as some of his work," Spare explained as I stepped into the room and saw the debris everywhere. Much of the mess consisted of shattered panes of glass that had been colored and distorted in strange ways. A number of them still existed intact, leaning against the curving wall or lying upon a long work table. A few were set up on wooden easels like paintings in progress, the bizarre transformations of their surfaces left unfinished. These panes of corrupted glass had been cut into a variety of shapes, and each had affixed to it—upon a little card—a scribbled character resembling an oriental ideograph. Similar symbols, although much larger, had been inscribed into the wood of the shutters that covered the windows all around the room.

"A symbology that I cannot pretend to understand," Spare admitted, "except in its function. Here, see what happens when I remove these labels with the little figures squiggled on them."

I watched as Spare went about the room stripping the misshapen glyphs from those chromatically deformed panels of glass. And it was not long before I noticed a change in the general character of the room, a shift in atmospherics as when a clear day is suddenly complicated by the shadowy nuances of clouds. Previously the circular chamber had been bathed in a twisted kaleidoscope of colors as the simple lights around the room diffused through the strangely tinted windowpanes. But the effect had been purely decorative, an experience restricted to the realm of aesthetics, with no implications of the spectral. Now, however, a new element permeated the room, partially and briefly exposing qualities of quite a different order in which the visible gave way to the transcendental. What formerly had appeared as an artist's studio, however eccentric, was gradually inheriting the aura of a stained-glass cathedral, albeit one that had suffered some obscure desecration. In certain places upon the floor, the ceiling, and the circular wall with the shuttered windows, I perceived through those prismatic lenses vague forms which seemed to be struggling toward visibility, freakish outlines laboring to gain full embodiment. Whether their nature was that of the dead or the demonic—or possibly some peculiar progeny generated by their union—I could not tell. But whatever class of creation they seemed to occupy at the time, it was certain that they were gaining not only in clarity and substance, but also in size, swelling and surging and expanding their universe toward an eclipse of this world's vision.

"Is it possible," I said, turning to Spare, "that this effect of magnification is solely a property of the medium through which . . ."

But before I could complete my speculation, Spare was rushing about the room, frantically replacing the symbols on each sheet of glass, dissolving the images into a quivering translucence and then obliterating or masking them altogether. The room lapsed once again into its former state of iridescent sterility. Then Spare hastily ushered me back to the ground floor, the door to the turret room standing locked behind us.

Afterward he served as my guide through the other, less crucial rooms of the house, each of which was sealed by dark shutters and all of which shared in the same barren atmosphere—the aftermath of a strange exorcism, a purging of the grounds which left them neither hallowed nor unholy, but had simply turned them into a pristine laboratory where a fearful genius had practiced his science of nightmares.

We passed several hours in the small, lamplit library. The sole window of that room was curtained, and I imagined that I saw the night's darkness behind the pattern. But when I put my hand upon that symmetrical and velvety design, I felt only solidity on the other side, as if I had touched a coffin beneath its pall. It was this barrier that made the world outside seem twice darkened, although I knew that when the shutters were opened I would be faced with one of the clearest nights ever seen.

For some time Spare read to me passages from the notebooks whose cryptography he had broken. I sat and listened to a voice that was accustomed to speaking of miracles, a well-practiced tout of mystical freakshows. Yet I also detected a grave sincerity in his words, which is to say that his usual unruffled patter contained dissonant overtones of fear.

"We sleep," he read, "among the shadows of another world. These are the unshapely substance inflicted upon us and the prime material to which we give the shapes of our understanding. And though we create what is seen, yet we are not the creators of its essence. Thus nightmares are born from the impress of ourselves on the life of things unknown. How terrible these forms of specter and demon when the eyes of the flesh cast light and mold the shadows which are forever around us. How much more terrible to witness their true forms roaming free upon the land, or in the most homely rooms of our houses, or frolicking through that luminous hell which in pursuit of psychic survival we have named the heavens. Then we truly waken from our sleep, but only to sleep once more and shun the nightmares which must ever return to that part of us which is hopelessly dreaming."

After witnessing some of the phenomena which had inspired this hypothesis, I could not escape becoming somewhat entranced with its elegance, if not with its originality. Nightmares both within and around us had been integrated into a system that seemed to warrant admiration. However, the scheme was ultimately no more than terror recollected in tranquility, a formula reflecting little of the mazy trauma that had initiated these speculations. Should it be called revelation or delirium when the mind interposes itself between the sensations of the soul and a monstrous mystery? Truth was not an issue in this matter, nor were the mechanics of the experiment (which, even if faulty, yielded worthy results), and in my mind it was faithfulness to the mystery and its terror that was paramount, even sacred. In this the theoretician of nightmares had failed, fallen on the lucid blade of theories that, in the end, could not save him. On the other hand, those wonderful symbols that Spare was at a loss to illuminate, those crude and cryptic designs, represented a genuine power against the mystery's madness, yet could not be explained by the most esoteric analysis. As the erstwhile owner of the house knew, we truly live in the shadow of another world, one which he designed his residence either to shut out or reveal as he chose, but which in the end overtook him before he had a chance to shutter for good those windows that disclosed the deranged and terrible quiddity of existence.

"I have a question," I said to Spare when he had closed the volume he held on his lap. "The shutters elsewhere in the house are not painted with the signs that are on those in the turret. Can you enlighten me?"

Spare led me to the window and drew back the curtains. Very cautiously he pulled out one of the shutters just far enough to expose its edge, which revealed that something of a contrasting color and texture composed a layer between the two sides of the dark wood.

"Engraved upon a panel of glass placed inside each shutter," he explained.

"And the ones in the turret?" I asked.

"The same. Whether the extra set of symbols there are precautionary or merely redundant . . ."

His voice had faded and then stopped, though the pause did not seem to imply any thoughtfulness on Spare's part.

"Yes," I prompted, "precautionary or redundant."

For a moment he revived. "That is, whether the symbols were an added measure against . . ."

It was at this point that Spare mentally abandoned the scene, following within his own mind some controversy or suspicion, a witness to a dramatic conflict being enacted upon a remote and shadowy stage.

"Spare," I said in a somewhat normal voice.

"Spare," he repeated, but in a voice that was not his own, a voice that sounded more like the echo of a voice than natural speech. And for a moment I asserted my pose of skepticism, placing none of my confidence in Spare or in the things he had thus far shown me, for I knew that he was an adept of pasteboard visions, a medium whose hauntings were of mucilage and gauze. But how much more subtle and skillful were the present effects, as though he were manipulating the very atmosphere around us, pulling the strings of light and shadow.

"The clearest light is now shining," he said in that hollow, tremulous voice. "Now light is flowing in the glass," he spoke, placing his hand upon the shutter before him. "Shadows gathering against . . . against . . ."

And it seemed that Spare was not so much pulling the shutter away from the window as trying to push the shutter closed while it slowly opened further and further, allowing a strange radiance to leak gradually into the house. It also appeared that he finally gave up the struggle and let another force guide his actions. "Flowing together in me," he repeated several times as he went from window to window, methodically opening the shutters like a sleepwalker performing some obscure ritual.

Ransoming all judgment to fascination, I watched him pass through each room on the main floor of the house, executing his duties like an old servant. Then he ascended a long staircase, and I heard his footsteps traversing the floor above, evenly pacing from one side of the house to the other. He was now a night watchman making his rounds in accordance with a strange design. The sound of his movements grew fainter as he progressed to the next floor and continued to perform the services required of him. I listened very closely as he proceeded on his somnambulistic course into the attic. And when I heard the echoes of a distant door as it slammed shut, I knew he had gone into that room in the turret.

Engrossed in the lesser phenomenon of Spare's suddenly altered behavior, I had momentarily overlooked the greater one of the windows. But now I could no longer ignore those phosphorescent panes which focused or reflected the incredible brilliance of the sky that night. As I followed Spare's circuit about the main floor, I saw that each room was glowing with the superlunary light that was outlined by each window frame. In the library I paused and approached one of the windows, reaching out to touch its wrinkled surface. And I felt a lively rippling in the glass, as if there actually were some force flowing within it, an uncanny sensation that my tingling fingertips will never be able to forget. But it was the scene beyond the glass that finally possessed my attention.

For a few moments I looked out only upon the level landscape that surrounded the house, its open expanse lying desolate and pale beneath the resplendent heavens. Then, almost inconspicuously, different scenes or fragments of scenes began to intrude upon the outside vicinity, as if other geographies of the earth were being superimposed upon the local one, composing a patchwork of images that might seem to have been the hallucinated tableaux of some cosmic tapestry.

The windows—which, for lack of a more accurate term, I must call *enchanted*—had done their work. For the visions they offered were indeed those of a haunted world, a multi-faceted mural portraying the marriage of insanity and metaphysics. As the images clarified, I witnessed all the intersections which commonly remain unseen to earthly sight, the conjoining of planes of entity which should exclude each other and should no more be mingled than is flesh with the inanimate objects that surround it. But this is precisely what took place in the scenes before me, and it appeared that there existed no place on earth that was not the home of a spectral ontogeny. In brief, the whole of the world was a pageant of nightmares.

Sunlit bazaars in exotic cities thronged with faces that were transparent masks for insectoid countenances; moonlit streets in antique towns harbored a strange-eyed slithering within their very stones; dim galleries of empty museums sprouted a ghostly mold that mirrored the sullen hues of old paintings; the land at the edge of oceans gave birth to a new evolution transcending biology and remote islands offered themselves as a haven for forms having no analogy outside of dreams; jungles teemed with beast-like shapes that moved beside the sticky luxuriance as well as through the depths of its pulpy warmth; deserts were alive with an uncanny flux of sounds which might enter and animate the world of substance; and subterranean landscapes heaved with cadaverous generations that had sunken and merged into sculptures of human coral, bodies heaped and unwhole, limbs projecting without order, eyes scattered and searching the darkness.

My own eyes suddenly closed, shutting out the visions for a moment. And during that moment I once again became aware of the sterile quality of the house, of its "innocent ambiance." It was then that I realized that this house was possibly the only place on earth, perhaps in the entire universe, that had been cured of the plague of phantoms that raged everywhere. This achievement, however futile or perverse, now elicited from me tremendous admiration as a monument to Terror and the stricken ingenuity it may inspire.

And my admiration intensified as I pursued the way that Spare had laid out for me and ascended a back staircase to the second floor. For on this level, where room followed upon room through a maze of interconnecting doors which Spare had left open, there seemed to be an escalation in the optical power of the windows, thus heightening the threat to the house and its inhabitants. What had appeared, through the windows of the floor below, as scenes in which spectral monstrosities had merely intruded upon orthodox reality, were now magnified to the point where that reality underwent a further eclipse: the other realm became dominant and pushed through the cover of masks, the conceal-ment of stones, spread its moldy growths at will, generating apparitions of the most feverish properties and intentions, erect-ing formations that enshadowed all familiar order.

By the time I reached the third floor, I was somewhat pre-pared for what I might find, granted the elevating intensity of the visions to which the windows were giving increasingly greater force and focus. Each window was now a framed phan-tasmagoria of churning and forever changing shapes and colors, fabulous depths and distances opening to the fascinated eye, grotesque transfigurations that suggested a purely supernatural order, a systemless cosmogony reeling with all the caprice of the immaterial. And as I wandered through those empty and weirdly lucent rooms at the top of house, it seemed that the house itself had been transported to another universe.

I have no idea how long I had been enthralled by the chaotic fantasies imposing themselves upon the unprotected rooms of my mind. But this trance was eventually interrupted by a com-motion emanating from an even higher room—the very crown of the turret and, as it were, the cranial chamber of that many-eyed beast of a house. Making my way up the narrow, spiraling stairs to the attic, I found that there, too, Spare had unsealed the octagonal window, which now seemed the gazing eye of some god as it cast forth a pyrotechnic craze of colors and gave a frenzied life to shadows. Through this maze of illusions I followed the voice which was merely a vibrating echo of vocal utterance, the counterpart in sound to the swirling sights around me. I climbed the last stairway to the door leading into the turret, listening to the reverberant words that sounded from the other side.

"Now the shadows are moving in the stars as they are moving within me, within all things. And their brilliance must reach throughout all things, all the places which are created according to the essence of these shadows and of ourselves . . . *This house is an abomination, a vacuum and a void. Nothing must stand against . . . against . . .*"

And with each repetition of this last word it seemed that a struggle was taking place and that the echoing alien voice was fading as the tone of Spare's natural voice was gaining dominance. Finally, Spare appeared to have resumed full possession of himself. Then there was a pause, a brief interim during which I considered a number of doubtful strategies, anxious not to misuse this moment of unknown and extravagant possibilities. Was it merely the end of life that faced one who remained in that room? Could the experience that had preceded the disappearance of that other visionary, under identical circumstances, perhaps be worth the strange price one would be asked to pay? No occult theories, no arcane analyses, could be of any use in making my decision, nor justly serve the sensations of those few seconds, when I stood gripping the handle of that door, waiting for the impulse or accident that would decide everything. All that existed for the moment was the irreducible certainty of nightmare.

From the other side of the door there now came a low, echoing laughter, a sound which became louder as the laughing one approached. But I was not moved by this sound and did nothing except grip the door handle more tightly, dreaming of the great shadows in the stars, of the strange visions beyond the windows, and of an infinite catastrophe. Then I heard a soft scraping noise at my feet; looking down, I saw several small rectangles projecting from under the door, fanned out like a hand of cards. My only action was to stoop and retrieve one of them, to stare in mindless wonderment at the mysterious symbol which decorated its face. I counted the others, realizing that none had been left attached to the windows within the room in the turret.

It was the thought of what effect these windows might have, now that they had been stripped of their protective signs and stood in the full glare of starlight, that made me call out to Spare, even though I could not be sure that he still existed as his former self. But by then the hollow laughter had stopped, and I am sure that the last voice I heard was that of Raymond Spare. And when the voice began screaming—*the windows,* it said, *pulling me into the stars and shadows*—I could not help trying to enter the room. But now that the impetus for this action had arrived, it proved to be useless for both Spare and myself. For the door was securely locked, and Spare's voice was fading into nothingness.

I can only imagine what those last few moments were like among all the windows of that turret room and among orders of existence beyond all definition. That night, it was to Spare alone that such secrets were confided; he was the one to whom it fell—by some disaster or design—to be among the elect. Such privileged arcana, on this occasion at least, were not to be mine. Nevertheless, it seemed at the time that some fragment of this experience might be salvaged. And to do this, I believed, was a simple matter of abandoning the house.

My intuition was correct. For as soon as I had gone out into the night and turned back to face the house, I could see that its rooms were no longer empty, no longer the pristine apartments I had lamented earlier that evening. As I had thought, these windows were for looking *in* as well as out. And from where I stood, the sights were now all inside the house, which had become an edifice possessed by the festivities of another world. I remained there until morning, when a cold sunlight settled the motley phantasms of the night before.

Years later I had the opportunity to revisit the house. In conformity with my intuition, I found the place bare and abandoned: every one of its window frames was empty and there was not a sign of glass anywhere. In the nearby town I discovered that the house had also acquired a bad reputation. For years no one had gone near it. Wisely avoiding the enchantments of hell, the citizens of the town have kept to their own little streets of gently stirring trees and old silent houses. And what more can they do in the way of caution? How can they know what it is their houses are truly nestled among? They cannot see, nor even wish to see, that world of shadows with which they consort every moment of their brief and innocent lives. But often, perhaps during the visionary time of twilight, I am sure they have sensed it.

THE COCOONS

Early one morning, hours before sunrise, I was awakened by Dr. Dublanc. He was standing at the foot of my bed, lightly tugging on its layered covers. In my quasi-somnolent state, I was convinced for a moment that a small animal was prancing about on my bedclothes, its movements signifying some nocturnal ritual unknown to higher forms of life. Then I saw a gloved hand twitching in the glow of the streetlight outside my window. Finally, I identified the silhouette, shaped by a hat and overcoat, of Dr. Dublanc.

I switched on the nightstand lamp and sat up to face the well-known intruder. "What's wrong?" I asked as if in protest.

"My apologies," he said in a rather unapologetic tone. "There is someone I want you to meet. I think it might be beneficial for you."

"If that's what you say. But can't it wait? I haven't been sleeping well as it is. Better than anyone you should know that."

"Of course I know. I also know other things," he asserted, betraying his annoyance. "The gentleman I want to introduce to you will be leaving the country very soon, so there is a question of timing."

"All the same . . ."

"Yes, I know—your nervous condition. Here, take these."

Dr. Dublanc placed two egg-shaped pills in the palm of my hand. I put them to my lips and then swallowed a half-glass of water that was on the nightstand. I set down the empty glass next to my alarm clock, which emitted a soft grinding noise due to some unknown mutations of its internal mechanism. My eyes became fixed by the slow, even movement of the second hand, but Dr. Dublanc, in a quietly urgent voice, brought me out of my trance.

"We should really be going. I have a taxi waiting outside."

So I hurried, thinking that I would end up being charged for this excursion, cab fare and all.

Dr. Dublanc had left the taxi standing in the alley behind my apartment building. Its headlights beamed rather weakly in the blackness, scarcely guiding us as we approached the vehicle. Side by side, the doctor and I proceeded over the uneven pavement and through blotched vapors emerging from the fumaroles of several sewer covers. I could see the moon shining between the close rooftops, and I thought that it subtly shifted phases before my eyes, bloating a bit into fullness. The doctor caught me staring.

"It's not going haywire up there, if that's what is bothering you."

"But it seemed to be changing."

With a growl of exasperation, the doctor pulled me after him into the cab.

The driver appeared to have been stilled into a state of dormancy. Yet Dr. Dublanc was able to evoke a response when he called out an address to the hack, who turned his thin rodent face toward the back seat and glared briefly. For a time we sat in silence as the taxi coasted through a series of unpeopled avenues. At that hour the world on the other side of my window seemed to be no more than a mass of shadows wavering at a great distance. The doctor touched my arm and said, "Don't worry if the pills I gave you seem to have no immediate effect."

"I trust your judgment," I said, only to receive a doubtful glance from the doctor. "Well, it would help if you told me why we're sitting in the back of a taxi at this hour. Just who are we going to see that's so important? What's the mystery?"

"No mystery," the doctor replied. "We're going to see a former patient of mine. Not to say that some unfortunate aspects do not still exist in his case. For certain reasons I will be introducing him to you as 'Mr. Catch,' though he's also a doctor of sorts—a brilliant scientist, in fact. Primarily I would like you to view a document relating to his work. A film, to be precise.

It's something quite remarkable. And possibly beneficial—to you, I mean. That's all I can say at the moment."

I nodded as if this disclosure had satisfied me. Then I noticed how far we had gone, almost to the opposite end of the city, if that was possible in what seemed a relatively short period of time. (I had forgotten to wear my watch, and this negligence somewhat aggravated my lack of orientation.) The district in which we were now traveling was of the lowest order, a landscape without pattern or substance, especially as I viewed it by moonlight.

There might be an open field heaped with debris, a devastated plain where bits of glass and scraps of metal glittered. Occasionally a solitary building of some indiscernible nature stood out in this wasteland, a skeletal structure with all markings of identity scraped off its bones. And then, turning a corner, one left behind this lunar spaciousness and entered a densely tangled nest of houses, the dwarfish and the great all tightly nestled together and all eaten away, disfigured. Even as I watched them through the taxi's windows they appeared to be carrying on their corruption, mutating in the dull light of the moon. Roofs and chimneys elongated toward the stars, dark bricks multiplied and bulged like tumors upon the façades of houses, entire streets twisted themselves along some unearthly design. Although a few windows were filled with light, however sickly, the only human being I saw was a derelict crumpled at the base of a traffic sign.

"Sorry, doctor, but this may be too much."

"Just hold on to yourself," he said, "we're almost there. Driver, pull into that alley behind those houses."

The taxi joggled as we made our way through the narrow passage. On either side of us were high wooden fences beyond which rose so many houses of such impressive height and bulk, though of course they were still monuments to decay. The cab's headlights were barely up to the task of illuminating the cramped little alley, which seemed to become ever narrower the further we proceeded. Suddenly the driver jerked us to a stop to avoid running over an old man slouched against the fence, an empty bottle lying at his side.

"This is where we get out," said Dr. Dublanc. "Wait here for us, driver."

As we emerged from the taxi I pulled at the doctor's sleeve, whispering about the expense of the fare. He replied in a loud voice, "You should worry more about getting a taxi to take us back home. They keep their distance from this neighborhood and rarely answer the calls they receive to come in here. Isn't that true, driver?" But the man had returned to that dormant state in which I first saw him. "Come on," said the doctor. "He'll wait for us. This way."

Dr. Dublanc pushed back a section of the fence that formed a kind of loosely hinged gate, closing it carefully behind us after we passed through the opening. On the other side was a small backyard, actually a miniature dumping ground where shadows bulged with refuse. And before us, I assumed, stood the house of Mr. Catch. It seemed very large, with an incredible number of bony peaks and dormers outlined against the sky, and even a weathervane in some vague animal-shape that stood atop a ruined turret grazed by moonlight. But although the moon was as bright as before, it now appeared to be considerably thinner, as if it had been worn down just like everything else in that neighborhood.

"It hasn't altered in the least," the doctor assured me. He was holding open the back door of the house and gesturing for me to approach.

"Perhaps no one's home," I suggested.

"The door's unlocked. You see how he's expecting us?"

"There don't appear to be any lights in use."

"Mr. Catch likes to conserve on certain expenses. A minor mania of his. But in other ways he's quite extravagant. And by no means is he a poor man. Watch yourself on the porch—some of these boards are not what they once were."

As soon as I was standing by the doctor's side he removed a flashlight from the pocket of his overcoat, shining a path into the dark interior of the house. Once inside, that yellowish swatch of illumination began flitting around in the blackness. It settled briefly in a cobwebbed corner of the ceiling, then ran down a blank battered wall and jittered along warped floor moldings. For a moment it revealed two suitcases, quite well used, at the bottom of a stairway. It slid smoothly up the stairway banister and flew straight to the floors above, where we heard some scraping sounds, as if an animal with long-nailed paws was moving about.

"Does Mr. Catch keep a pet?" I asked in a low voice.

"Why shouldn't he? But I don't think we'll find him up there."

We went deeper into the house, passing through many rooms which fortunately were unobstructed by furniture. Sometimes we crushed bits of broken glass underfoot; once I inadvertently kicked an empty bottle and sent it clanging across a bare floor. Reaching the far side of the house, we entered a long hallway flanked by several doors. All of them were closed and behind some of them we heard sounds similar to those being made on the second floor. We also heard footsteps slowly ascending a stairway. Then the last door at the end of the hallway opened, and a watery light pushed back some of the shadows ahead of us. A round-bodied little man was standing in the light, lazily beckoning to us.

"You're late. You're very late," he chided while leading us down into the cellar. His voice was high-pitched yet also quite raspy. "I was just about to leave."

"My apologies," said Dr. Dublanc, who sounded entirely sincere on this occasion. "Mr. Catch, allow me to introduce—"

"Never mind that 'Mr. Catch' nonsense. You know well enough what things are like for me, don't you, doctor? So let's get started, I'm on a schedule now."

In the cellar we paused amid the quivering light of candles, dozens of them positioned high and low, melting upon a shelf or an old crate or right on the filth-covered floor. Among the surrounding objects, I could see that an old-fashioned film projector had been set up on a table toward the center of the room, and a portable movie screen stood by the opposite wall. The projector was plugged into what appeared to be a small electrical generator humming on the floor.

"I think there are some chairs about that you can sit on," said Mr. Catch as he threaded the film around the spools of the projector. Then for the first time he spoke to me directly. "I'm not sure how much the doctor has explained about what I'm going to show you. Probably very little."

"Yes, and deliberately so," interrupted Dr. Dublanc. "If you just roll the film I think my purpose will be served, with or without explanations. What harm can it do?"

Mr. Catch made no reply. After blowing out some of the candles to darken the room sufficiently, he switched on the projector, which was a rather noisy mechanism. I worried that whatever dialogue or narration the film might contain would be drowned out between the whirring of the projector and the humming of the generator. But I soon realized that this was a silent film, a cinematic document that in every aspect of its production was thoroughly primitive, from its harsh light and coarse photographic texture to its nearly unintelligible scenario.

It seemed to serve as a visual record of a scientific experiment, a laboratory demonstration in fact. The setting, nevertheless, was anything but clinical—a bare wall in a cellar which in some ways resembled, yet was not identical to, the one where I was viewing this film. And the subject was human: a shabby, unshaven, and unconscious derelict who had been propped up against a crude grayish wall. Not too many moments passed before the man began to stir, perhaps awakening from a deep stupor. However, the movements he made did not appear to be his own. More specifically, they seemed to be the spasmodic twitchings of some energy that *inhabited* the old tramp. One of his legs wiggled for a second. Then his chest heaved and collapsed. Soon his head began to wobble, and it kept on wobbling, as if something was making its way through the derelict's scalp, rustling among long greasy locks. Part of it finally poked upwards—a thin sticklike thing. More of them emerged, dark wiry appendages that were bristling and bending and reaching for the outer world. At the end of each was a pair of slender snapping pincers. What ultimately broke through that shattered skull, pulling itself out with a wriggling motion of its many new-born arms, was approximately the size and proportions of a spider monkey. It had tiny translucent wings which fluttered a few times, glistening but useless, and seemed to be in an emaciated condition. When it twisted its head toward the camera, it stared into the lens with malicious eyes and seemed to be chattering with its beaked mouth.

I whispered to Dr. Dublanc: "Please, I'm afraid that—"

"Exactly," he hissed back at me. "But you need to face certain realities so that you may free yourself from your fear of them."

Now it was my turn to give the doctor a dubious look. I was not blind to the fact that he was practicing a highly unconventional form of therapeutics, to say the least. And our presence in that cellar—that cold swamp of shadows in which candles flickered like fire-flies—seemed to be as much for Dr. Dublanc's benefit as it was for mine, if "benefit" is the proper word in this case.

"You might indulge me on occasion," I said.

"Shhh. Watch the film."

It was almost finished. After the creature had hatched from its strange egg, it proceeded very rapidly to consume the grubby derelict, leaving only a collection of bones attired in cast-off clothes. Picked perfectly clean, the skull leaned wearily to one side. And the creature, which earlier had been so emaciated, had grown rather plump with its feast, becoming bloated and meaty like an overfed dog. In the final sequence, a net was tossed into the scene, capturing the gigantic vermin and dragging it off camera. Then whiteness filled the screen and the film was flapping on its reel.

"So what did you think?" said the doctor. No doubt noticing that I was still under the spell of what I had just seen, he snapped his fingers in front of my face. I blinked and then looked at him in dazed silence. Taking advantage of the moment, he tried to lend a certain focus or coloration to the events of the film. "You must understand," he explained, "that the integrity of material forms is only a prejudice. This is not to mention the substance of those forms, which is an even more dubious state of affairs. That a monstrous insect could burst forth from the anatomy of a human being should be no cause for consternation. Your prejudices about a clockwork world of sunrise schedules and lunar routines have been a real obstacle in the therapy I've been practicing with you. You've put me in the position of having to cater to your anxiety that the world is not *ruled by regularity*. But it's time you realized that nothing is bolted down, so to speak. And no more is that thing which we call the mind, with its craving for evermore novel sensations and perceptions. You could learn a great deal from Mr. Catch. I know that I have. Of course, I still recognize that there remain some unfortunate aspects to his case—there was only so much I could do for him—but nonetheless I think that he has gained rare and invaluable knowledge, the consequences notwithstanding.

"His research had taken him into areas where, how should I say, where the shapes and levels of phenomena, the multiple planes of natural existence, revealed their ability to establish new relationships with one another . . . to become interconnected, as it were, in ways that we never thought possible. At some point everything became a blur for him, a sort of pandemonium of forces, a phantasmagoria of possibilities which he eagerly engaged. We can have no idea of the tastes and temptations that may emerge or develop in the course of such work . . . a curious hedonism that could not be controlled. Oh, the vagaries of omnipotence, breeder of indulgence. Well, Mr. Catch retreated in panic from his own powers, yet he could not put the pieces back as they had been: unheard of habits and responses had already ingrained themselves into his system. The worst sort of slavery, but how persuasively he spoke of the euphoria he had known, the infinitely diverse sensations beyond all common understanding. It was just this understanding that I required in order to free him of a life that, in its own fashion, had become as abysmal and problematic as your own—except that his pathology existed at the opposite pole. Some middle ground must be established, some balance. How well I understand that now! This is why I have brought you two together. This is the only reason, however it may seem to you."

"It seems to me," I replied, "that Mr. Catch has snuck out on us. Personally, I hope we've seen the last of him."

Dr. Dublanc emitted the shadow of a laugh. "Oh, he's still in the house. You can be sure of that. Let's take a look upstairs."

He was, in fact, not far at all. Stepping into that hallway of closed doors at the top of the cellar stairs, we saw that one of those doors was now partially open and the room beyond it was faintly aglow. Without announcing us, Dr. Dublanc slowly pushed back the door until we could both see what had happened inside.

It was a small unfurnished room with a bare wooden floor upon which a candle had been fixed with its own drippings. The candlelight shone dimly on the full face of Mr. Catch, who seemed to have collapsed in a back corner of the room, lying somewhat askew. He was sweating, though it was cold in the room, and his eyes were half-closed in a kind of languorous exhaustion. But something was wrong with his mouth: it seemed to be muddied and enlarged, sloppily painted into a clown's oversized grin. On the floor beside him were, to all appearances, the freshly ravaged remains of one of those creatures in the film.

"You made me wait too long!" he suddenly shouted, opening his eyes fully and straightening himself up for a moment before his posture crumbled once again. He then repeated this outburst: "You couldn't help me and now you make me wait too long."

"It was in order to help you that I came here," the doctor said to him, yet all the time fixing his eyes on the mutilated carcass on the floor. When he saw that I had observed his greedy stare he regained himself. "I'm trying to help both of you the only way you can be helped. Tell him, Mr. Catch. Tell him how you breed those amazing individuals and enable them to induce the most rapturous exaltation, bliss on the brink of apotheosis."

Mr. Catch groped in his pants pocket, pulled out a large handkerchief, and wiped off his mouth. He was smiling idiotically, quite obviously intoxicated by his recent feast, and with difficulty worked himself to a standing position. His body now seemed even more swollen and bulbous than before, really not quite human in its proportions. After replacing his handkerchief in one pocket, he reached down into the other, digging around inside it. "It's really too much to go into detail," he explained in a voice that had become placid. "What should I say? Much of it is a psychic matter. Hence, my appeal to the doctor. The rest involves some chemical formulations to instigate what is essentially a universal process of transfiguration, the so-called miracle of creation in all its forms. A catalyzing agent is introduced into the subject by insemination or ingestion." With a kind of giddy pride, he held out his open hand. In the thick pad of his palm I could see two tiny objects that were shaped like eggs. "The larvae of the gods," he said with a hint of awe in his voice.

I turned abruptly to the doctor. "The pills you gave me."

"It was the only thing that could be done for you. I've tried so hard to help you both."

"I had suspected something was up," said Mr. Catch, now reviving himself from his stupefaction. "I should never have brought you into this. Don't you realize that it's difficult enough without involving your own patients. The derelicts are one thing, but this is quite another. I'm sorry I ever involved you in my predicament. Well, my suitcases are packed. It's your operation now, doctor. Let me by, time to go."

Mr. Catch maneuvered himself from the room, and a few moments later the sound of a door being slammed echoed throughout the house. The doctor kept close watch on me, waiting for some reaction, I suppose. Yet he was also listening very intently to certain sounds emanating from the rooms around us. The noise of restless skittering was everywhere.

"You understand, don't you?" asked the doctor. "Mr. Catch isn't the only one who has waited too long . . . far too long. I thought by now the pills would have had their effect."

I went into my pocket and removed the two little eggs which I had failed to swallow earlier. "I can't claim that I had much faith in your methods," I said. Then I tossed the pills at Dr. Dublanc who, speechless, caught them. "You won't mind if I return home by myself."

Indeed, he was probably relieved to see me go. In the course of treating Mr. Catch, the doctor had apparently also become a hideous degenerate, a wholly unbalanced specimen in need of the most radical therapy himself. As I traced my way back through the house I heard him running about opening door after door, finally crying out with a pitiful delight, "There you are, you beauties. There you are."

Although the doctor himself now seemed hopeless, I think that his therapeutic strategy may have been somewhat beneficial in my case, or at least given me a glimpse of how I could meet the demoniac undercurrents of existence halfway. For during those first few moments on that hazy morning, when the taxi edged out of the alley and passed through that neighborhood of deteriorating houses, I felt myself attain the middle ground Dr. Dublanc spoke of—the balancing point between an anxious flight from the abyss and the temptation to plunge into it. There was a great sense of escape, as if I could exist serenely outside the grotesque ultimatums of creation, an entranced spectator casting a clinical gaze at the chaotic tumult both around and within himself.

But the feeling soon evaporated. A genuine cure for the quandaries of an inconstant existence is exceedingly rare. "Could you go a little faster?" I said to the driver, for it seemed to me that we were making no progress in our leave from that district in which all order had dissipated. Things again appeared to be changing, ready to burst forth from their sagging cocoons and take on uncertain forms. Even the pale morning sun seemed to be wavering from its proper proportions.

At the end of the ride, I was content to pay the extraordinary fare and return to my bed. The following day I started looking for a new doctor.

THE VOICE OF THE DREAMER

THE NIGHT SCHOOL

Instructor Carniero was holding class once again.

I discovered this fact on my return from a movie theater. It was late and I thought, "Why not take a short cut across the grounds of the school?" This thought led to a whole train of thoughts that I often pondered, especially when I was out walking at night. Mainly these thoughts were about my desire to know something that I was sure was real about my existence, something that could help me in my existence before it was my time to die and be put into the earth to rot, or perhaps have my cremated remains drift out of a chimney stack and sully the sky. Of course, this desire was by no means unique to me. Nonetheless, I had spent quite a few years, my whole life it seemed, seeking to satisfy it in various ways. Most recently, I had sought some kind of satisfaction by attending the classes of Instructor Carniero. Though I had not attended his classes for very long, he seemed to be someone who could reveal what was at the bottom of things. Lost in my thoughts, then, I left the street I was walking along and proceeded across the grounds of the school, which were vast and dark. It was quite cold that night, and when I looked down the front of my overcoat I saw that the single remaining button holding it together had become loose and possibly would not last much longer. So a short cut on my return from that movie theater appeared to be the wise move.

I entered the school grounds as if they were only a great park located in the midst of surrounding streets. The trees were set close and from the perimeter of that parcel of land I could not see the school hidden within them. *Look up here*, I thought I heard someone say to me. When I did look up, I saw that the branches overhead were without leaves, and through their intertwining mesh the sky was fully visible. How bright and dark it was at the same time. *Bright* with a high, full moon shining among the spreading clouds, and *dark* with the shadows mingling within those clouds—a slowly flowing mass of mottled shapes, a kind of unclean outpouring from the black sewers of space.

I noticed that in one place these clouds were leaking down into the trees, trickling in a narrow rivulet across the wall of the night. But it was really smoke, dense and dirty, rising up to the sky. A short distance ahead, and well into the thickly wooded grounds of the school, I saw the spastic flames of a small fire among the trees. By the smell, I guessed that someone was burning refuse. Then I could see the misshapen metal drum spewing smoke, and the figures standing behind the firelight became visible to me, as I was to them.

"Class has resumed," one of them called out. "He's come back after all."

I knew these were others from the school, but their faces would not hold steady in the flickering light of the fire that warmed them. They seemed to be smudged by the smoke, greased by the odorous garbage burning in that dark metal drum, its outer surface almost glowing from the heat and flaking off in places.

"Look there," said another member of the group, pointing deeper into the school grounds. The massive outline of a building occupied the distance, a few of its windows sending a dim light through the trees. From the roof of the building a number of smokestacks stood out against the pale sky.

A wind rose up. It droned noisily around us and breathed a crackling life into the fire in the decayed metal drum. I tried to shout above the confusion of sounds. "Was there an assignment?" I cried out. But they appeared not to hear me, or perhaps were ignoring my words. When I repeated the question they briefly glanced my way, as if I had said something improper. I left them hunched around the fire, assuming they would be along. The wind died, and I could hear someone say the word "maniac," which was not spoken, I realized, either to me or about me.

Instructor Carniero, in his person, was rather vague to my mind. I had not been in his class very long before some disease— a terribly serious affliction, one of my fellow students hinted— had caused his absence. So what remained, for me, was no more than the image of a slender gentleman in a dark suit, a gentleman with a darkish complexion and a voice thick with a foreign accent. "He's a Portuguese," someone told me. "But he's lived almost everywhere." And I recalled a particular phrase of reproof he used to single out those of us who had not been attending to the diagrams he was incessantly creating on the blackboard. "Look up here," he would say. "If you do not look, you will learn nothing—you will be nothing." A few members of the class never needed to be called to attention in this manner, a certain small group who had been longtime students of the instructor and without distraction scrutinized the unceasing series of diagrams he would design upon the blackboard and then erase, only to construct again, with slight variation, a moment later.

Although I cannot claim that these often complex diagrams were not directly related to our studies, there were always extraneous elements within them which I never bothered to transcribe into my own notes for the class. They were a strange array of abstract symbols, frequently geometric figures altered in some way: various polygons with asymmetrical sides, trapezoids whose sides did not meet, semicircles with double or triple slashes across them, and many other examples of a deformed or corrupted scientific notation. These signs appeared to be primitive in essence, more relevant to magic than mathematics. The instructor marked them in an extremely rapid hand upon the blackboard, as if they were the words of his natural language. In most cases they formed a border around a familiar diagram allied to chemistry or physics, enclosing it and sometimes, it seemed, transforming its sense. Once a student questioned him regarding what seemed his apparently superfluous embellishment of these diagrams. Why did Instructor

Carniero subject us to these bewildering symbols? "Because," he answered, "a true instructor must share everything, no matter how terrible or lurid it might be."

As I proceeded across the grounds of the school, I noticed certain changes in my surroundings. The trees nearer to the school looked different from those in the encompassing area. These were so much thinner, emaciated and twisted like broken bones that had never healed properly. And their bark seemed to be peeling away in soft layers, because it was not only fallen leaves I trudged through on my way to the school building, but also something like dark rags, strips of decomposed material. Even the clouds upon which the moon cast its glow were thin or rotted, unraveled by some process of degeneration in the highest atmosphere of the school grounds. There was also a scent of corruption, an enchanting fragrance really— like the mulchy rot of autumn or early spring—that I thought was emerging from the earth as I disturbed the strange litter strewn over it. This odor became more pungent as I approached the yellowish light of the school, and strongest as I finally reached the old building itself.

It was a four-story structure of dark scabby bricks that had been patched together in another era, a time so different that it might be imagined as belonging to an entirely alien history, one composed solely of nights well advanced, an after-hours history. How difficult it was to think of this place as if it had been constructed in the usual manner. Far easier to credit some fantastic legend that it had been erected by a consort of demons during the perpetual night of its past, and that its materials were pilfered from other architectures, all of them defunct: ruined factories, ravaged mausoleums, abandoned orphanages, penitentiaries long out of use. The school was indeed a kind of freakish growth in a dumping ground, a blossom of the cemetery or the cesspool. Here it was that Instructor Carniero, who had been everywhere, held his class.

On the lower floors of the building a number of lights were in use, weak as guttering candles. The highest story was blacked out, and many of the windows were broken. Nevertheless, there was sufficient light to guide me into the school, even if the main hallway could hardly be seen to its end. And its walls appeared to be tarred over with something which exuded the same smell that filled the night outside the school. Without touching these walls, I used them to navigate my way into the school, following several of the greater and lesser hallways that burrowed throughout the building. Room after room passed on either side of me, their doorways filled with darkness or sealed by wide wooden doors whose coarse surfaces were pocked and peeling. Eventually I found a classroom where a light was on, though it was no brighter than the swarthy illumination of the hallway.

When I entered the room I saw that only some of the lamps were functioning, leaving certain areas in darkness while others were smeared with the kind of greasy glow peculiar to old paintings in oil. A few students were seated at desks here and there, isolated from one another and silent. By no means was there a full class, and no instructor stood at the lectern. The blackboard displayed no new diagrams but only the blurred remnants of past lessons. I took a desk near the door, looking at none of the others as they did not look at me. In one of the pockets of my overcoat I turned up a little stub of a pencil but could find nothing on which to take notes. Without any dramatic gestures, I scanned the room for some kind of paper. The visible areas of the room featured various items of debris without offering anything that would allow me to transcribe the complex instructions and diagrams demanded by the class. I was reluctant to make a physical search of the shelves set into the wall beside me because they were very deep and from them drifted that heady fragrance of decay.

Two rows to my left sat a man with several thick notebooks stacked on his desk. His hands were resting lightly on these notebooks, and his spectacled eyes were fixed on the empty lectern, or perhaps on the blackboard beyond. The space between the rows of desks was very narrow, so I was able to lean across the unoccupied desk that separated us and speak to this man who seemed to have a surplus of paper on which one could take notes, transcribe diagrams, and, in short, do whatever scribbling was demanded by the instructor of the class.

"Pardon me," I whispered to the staring figure. In a single, sudden movement, his head turned to face me. I remembered his pitted complexion, which had obviously grown worse since our class last met, and the eyes that squinted behind heavy lenses. "Do you have any paper you could share with me?" I asked, and was somehow surprised when he shifted his head toward his notebooks and began leafing through the pages of the topmost one. As he performed this action, I explained that I was unprepared for the class, that only a short time before did I learn it had resumed. This happened entirely by chance, I said. I was coming home from a movie theater and decided to take a short cut across the school grounds.

By the time I was finished illuminating my situation, the other student was searching through his last notebook, the pages of which were as solidly covered with jottings and diagrams as the previous ones. I observed that his notes were different from those I had been taking for Instructor Carniero's course. They were far more detailed and scrupulous in their transcriptions of those strange geometric figures which I considered only as decorative intrusions in the instructor's diagrams. Some of the other students' notebook pages were wholly given over to rendering these figures and symbols to the exclusion of the diagrams themselves.

"I'm sorry," he said. "I don't seem to have any paper I could share with you."

"Well, could you tell me if there was an assignment?"

"That's very possible. You can never tell with this instructor. He's a Portuguese, you know. But he's been all over and knows everything. I think he's out of his mind. The kind of thing he's been teaching should have gotten him into trouble somewhere, and probably did. Not that he ever cared what happened to him, or to anyone else. That is, those that he could influence, and some more than others. The things he said to *us*. The lessons in measurement of cloacal forces. Time as a flow of sewage. The excrement of space, scatology of creation. The voiding of the self. The whole filthy integration of things and the *nocturnal product,* as he called it, drowning in the pools of night."

"I'm afraid I don't recall those concepts," I confessed.

"You're new to the class. To tell the truth, you don't seem to understand what the instructor is teaching. But soon enough he will get through to you, if he hasn't already. You can never know. He's very captivating, the instructor. And always ready for anything."

"I was told that he recovered from the sickness that caused his absence, and that he was back teaching."

"Oh, he's back. He was always ready. Did you know that the class is now being held in another part of the school? I couldn't tell you where, since even I haven't been with Instructor Carniero as long as some of the others. To tell the truth, I don't care where it's being held. Isn't it enough that we're here, in this room?"

I had little idea how to answer this question and understood almost nothing of what the man had been trying to explain to me. It did seem clear, or at least very possible, that the class had moved to a different part of the school. But I had no reason to think that the other students seated elsewhere in the room would be any more helpful on this point than the one who had now turned his spectacled face away from me. Wherever the class was being held, I was still in need of paper on which to take notes, transcribe diagrams, and so forth. This could not be accomplished by staying in that room where everyone and everything was degenerating into the surrounding darkness.

For a time I wandered about the hallways on the main floor of the school, keeping clear of the walls which certainly were thickening with a dark substance, an odorous sap with the intoxicating potency of a thousand molting autumns or the melting soil of spring. The stuff was running from top to bottom down the walls, leaking from above and dulling the already dim light in the hallways.

I began to hear echoing voices coming from a distant part of the school I had never visited before. No words were decipherable, but it sounded as if the same ones were being repeated in a more or less constant succession of cries that rang hollow in the halls. I followed them and along the way met up with someone walking slowly from the opposite direction. He was dressed in dirty work clothes and almost blended in with the

shadows which were so abundant in the school that night. I
stopped him as he was about to shuffle straight past me. Turning an indifferent gaze in my direction was a pair of yellowish
eyes set in a thin face with a coarse, patchy complexion. The
man scratched at the left side of his forehead and some dry
flakes of skin fell away. I asked him:

"Could you tell me where Instructor Carniero is holding
class tonight?"

He looked at me for some moments, and then pointed a finger at the ceiling. "Up there," he said. "Look up there."

"On which floor?"

"The top one," he answered, as if a little amazed at my
ignorance.

"There are a lot of rooms on that floor," I said.

"And every one of them is his. Nothing to be done about
that. But I have to keep the rest of this place in some kind of
condition. I don't see how I can do that with him up there."
The man glanced around at the stained walls and let out a single, wheezing laugh. "It only gets worse. Starts to get to you if
you go up any further. Listen. Hear the rest of them?" Then he
groaned with disgust and went on his way.

But by that point I felt that any knowledge I had amassed—
whether or not it concerned Instructor Carniero and his night
classes—was being taken away from me piece by piece. The
man in dirty work clothes had directed me to the top floor of
the school. Yet I remembered seeing no light on that floor
when I first approached the building. The only thing that
seemed to occupy that floor was an undiluted darkness, a
darkness far greater than the night itself, a consolidated darkness, something clotted with its own density. "The *nocturnal
product*," I could hear the spectacled student reminding me in
a hollow voice. "Drowning in the pools of night."

What could I know about the ways of the school? I had not
been in attendance very long, not nearly long enough, it seemed.
I felt myself a stranger to my fellow students, especially since
they revealed themselves to be divided in their ranks, as though
among the degrees of a secret society. I did not know the
coursework in the way some of the others seemed to know it

and in the spirit that the instructor intended it to be known. My turn had not yet come to be commanded by Instructor Carniero to look up at the hieroglyphs on the blackboard and comprehend them fully. So I did not understand the doctrines of a truly septic curriculum, the science of a spectral pathology, philosophy of absolute disease, the metaphysics of things sinking into a common disintegration or rising together, flowing together, in their dark rottenness. Above all, I did not know the instructor himself: the places he had been . . . the things he had seen and done . . . the experiences he had embraced . . . the laws he had ignored . . . the troubles he had caused . . . the fate that he had incurred, gladly, upon himself and others.

I was now close to a shaft of stairways leading to the upper floors of the school. The voices became louder, though not more distinct, as I approached the stairwell. The first flight of stairs seemed very long and steep, not to mention badly defined in the dim light of the hallway. The landing at the top of the stairs was barely visible for the poor light and unreflecting effluvia that here moved even more thickly down the walls. But it did not appear to possess any real substance, no sticky surface or viscous texture as one might have supposed, only a kind of density like heavy smoke, filthy smoke from some smoldering source of expansive corruption. And it carried the scent of corruption as well as the sight, only now it was more potent with the nostalgic perfume of autumn decay or the feculent muskiness of a spring thaw.

I climbed another flight of stairs, which ascended in the opposite direction from the first, and reached the second floor. Each of the four stories of the school had two flights of stairs going in opposite directions between them, with a narrow landing that intervened before one could complete the ascent to a new floor. The second floor was not as well-lighted as the one below, and the walls there were even worse: their surface had been wholly obscured by that smoky blackness which seeped down from above, the blackness so richly odorous with the offal of worlds in decline or perhaps with the dark compost of those about to be born, the primeval impurity in which all things are founded, the native putridity.

On the stairs that led up to the third floor I saw the first of them—a young man who was seated on the lower steps of this flight and who had been one of the instructor's most assiduous students. He was absorbed in his own thoughts and did not acknowledge me until I spoke to him.

"The *class?*" I said, stressing the words into a question.

He gazed at me calmly. "The instructor suffered a terrible disease, a monumental disease." This was all he said. Then he returned within himself and would not respond.

There were others similarly positioned higher on the stairs or squatting on the landing. The voices were still echoing in the stairwell, chanting a blurred phrase in unison. But the voices did not belong to any of these students, who sat silent and entranced amid the scattered pages torn from their voluminous notebooks. Pieces of paper with strange symbols on them lay scattered everywhere like fallen leaves. They rustled as I walked through them toward the stairs leading to the highest story of the school.

The walls in the stairwell were now swollen with a blackness that was the very face of a plague—pustulant, scabbed, and stinking terribly. It was reaching to the edges of the floor, where it drifted and churned like a black fog. Only in the moonlight that shone through a hallway window could I see anything of the third floor. I stopped there, for the stairs to the fourth were deep in blackness. Only a few faces rose above it and were visible in the moonlight. One of them was staring at me, and, without prompting, spoke.

"The instructor is holding class again despite his terrible disease. Can you imagine? He is able to suffer anything and has been everywhere. Now he is in a new place, somewhere he has not been." The voice paused and the interval was filled by the many voices calling and crying from the total blackness that prevailed over the heights of the stairwell and buried everything beneath it like tightly packed earth in a grave. Then the single voice said: "The instructor died in the night. You see? He is with the night. You hear the voices? They are with him. And he is with the night. The night has spread itself within him. He who has been everywhere may go anywhere with the disease of the night. Listen. The Portuguese is calling to us."

I listened and finally the voices became clear. *Look up here,* they said. *Look up here.*

The fog of blackness had now unfurled down to me and lay about my feet, gathering there and rising. For a time I could not move or speak or form any thoughts. Inside me everything was becoming black. The blackness was quivering in my bones, eating away at them, making everything black within my body. It was holding me, and the voices were saying, "Look up here, look up here." And I began to look. But I aborted my gesture before it was completed. I was already too close to something I could not endure, that I was not prepared to endure. Even the blackness quivering inside me could not go on to its end. I could not remain where I was nor look up to the place where the voices called out to me.

Then the blackness seemed to exude from my being, washing itself out of me, and I was no longer inside the school but outside it, almost as if I had suddenly awakened there. Without looking back, I retraced my steps across the grounds of the school, forgetting about the short cut I had meant to take that night. I passed those students who were still standing around the fire burning in an old metal drum. They were feeding the bright flames with pages from their notebooks, pages scribbled to blackness with all those diagrams and freakish signs. Some of those among the group called out to me. "Did you see the Portuguese?" one of them shouted above the noise of the fire and the wind. "Did you hear anything about an assignment?" another voice cried out. And then I heard them all laughing among themselves as I made my way back to the streets I had left before entering the school grounds. I moved with such haste that the loose button on my overcoat finally came off by the time I reached the street outside the grounds of the school.

As I walked beneath the streetlights, I held the front of my overcoat together and tried to keep my eyes on the sidewalk before me. But I might have heard a voice bid me, "Look up here," because I did look, if only for a moment. Then I saw the sky was clear of all clouds, and the full moon was shining in the black spaces above. It was shining bright and blurry, as if coated with a luminous mold, floating like a lamp in the great sewers of the night. The *nocturnal product*, I thought, drowning in the pools of night. But these were only words I repeated without understanding. My desire to know something that I was sure was real about my existence, something that could help me in my existence before it was my time to die and be put into the earth to rot, or perhaps have my cremated remains drift out of a chimney stack and sully the sky—that would never be fulfilled. I had learned nothing, and I was nothing. Yet instead of disappointment at my failure to fulfill my most intense desire, I felt a tremendous relief. The urge to know the fundament of things was now emptied from me, and I was more than content to be rid of it. The following night I went to the movie theater again. But I did not take a short cut home.

THE GLAMOUR

It had long been my practice to wander late at night and often to attend movie theaters at this time. But something else was involved on the night I went to that theater in a part of town I had never visited before. A new tendency, a mood or penchant formerly unknown to me, seemed to lead the way. How difficult to say anything precise about this mood that overcame me, because it seemed to belong to my surroundings as much as to myself. As I advanced farther into that part of town I had never visited before, my attention was drawn to a certain aspect of things—a fine aura of fantasy radiating from the most common sights, places and objects that were both blurred and brightened in my gaze.

Despite the lateness of the hour, there was an active glow cast through many of the shop windows I passed. Along one particular avenue, the starless evening was glazed by these lights, these diamonds of plate glass set within old buildings of dark brick. I paused before the display window of a toy store and was entranced by a chaotic tableau of preposterous excitation. My eyes followed several things at once: the fated antics of mechanized monkeys that clapped tiny cymbals or somersaulted uncontrollably; the destined pirouettes of a music-box ballerina; the grotesque wobbling of a newly sprung jack-in-the-box. The inside of the store was a Christmas-tree clutter of merchandise receding into a background that looked shadowed and empty. An old man with a smooth pate and angular eyebrows stepped forward to the front window and began rewinding some of the toys to keep them in ceaseless gyration.

While performing this task he suddenly looked up at me, his face expressionless.

I moved down the street, where other windows framed little worlds so strangely picturesque and so dreamily illuminated in the shabby darkness of that part of town. One of them was a bakery whose window display was a gallery of sculptured frosting, a winter landscape of swirling, drifting whiteness, of snowy rosettes and layers of icy glitter. At the center of the glacial kingdom was a pair of miniature people frozen atop a many-tiered wedding cake. But beyond the brilliant arctic scene I saw only the deep blackness of an establishment that was closed for the night. Standing outside another window nearby, I was uncertain if the place was open for business or not. In the background, a few figures were positioned here and there within faded lighting reminiscent of an old photograph, though it seemed they were beings of the same kind as the window dummies of this store, which apparently trafficked in dated styles of clothing. Even the faces of the manikins, as a glossy light fell upon them, wore the placidly enigmatic expressions of a different time.

I saw no one enter or exit the many doors along the sidewalks where I strolled that night. A canvas awning that some proprietor had neglected to roll up for the night was flapping in the wind. Nevertheless, as I have described, there reigned a vitality of enterprise everywhere I looked, and I felt the kind of acute anticipation that a child might experience at a carnival, where each lurid attraction incites fantastic speculations, while unexpected desires arise for something which has no specific qualities in the imagination yet seems to be only a few steps away. Thus my mood had not abandoned me but only grew stronger, a possessing impulse without object.

Then I saw the marquee for a movie theater, though not one I intended to patronize. For the letters spelling out the name of the theater were broken and unreadable, while the title on the marquee was similarly damaged, as if stones had been thrown at it, a series of attempts made to efface the words that I finally deciphered. The feature being advertised was called *The Glamour*.

When I reached the front of the theater I found that the row of doors forming the entrance had been barricaded by cross-wise planks with notices posted upon them warning that the building had been condemned. This action was apparently taken some time ago, judging by the weathered condition of the boards that blocked my way and the dated appearance of the notices stuck upon them. As I was about to proceed on my way, however, I saw that the marquee was illuminated, wretchedly aglow with a light that I previously thought was a reflection from a nearby streetlamp. It was beneath this same streetlamp that I now noticed a double-faced sign propped up on the side-walk, an inconspicuous little board that read: ENTRANCE TO THE THEATER. Beneath these words was an arrow pointing into an alleyway which separated the theater from the remaining buildings on the block. Peeking into this dark open-ing, this aperture in the otherwise solid façade of that particu-lar street, I saw only a long, narrow corridor with a single light set far into its depths. The light shone with a strange shade of purple, like that of a freshly exposed heart, and appeared to be positioned over a doorway leading into the theater. It had long been my practice to attend late performances at movie theaters—this is what I reminded myself. But whatever reservations I felt at the time were easily overcome by a new surge of the mood I was experiencing that night in a part of town I had never vis-ited before.

The purple lamp did indeed mark a way into the theater, casting its arterial light upon a door that reiterated the word "ENTRANCE." Stepping inside, I entered a tight hallway where the walls glowed a deep pink, very similar in tint to that little beacon in the alley but more reminiscent of a richly blooded brain than a beating heart. At the end of the hallway I could see my reflection in a ticket window, and approaching it I noticed that those walls so close to me were veiled from floor to ceiling with what appeared to be cobwebs. This gos-samer material was also strewn upon the carpet leading to the ticket window, wispy shrouds that did not scatter when I walked over them, as if they had securely bound themselves to the carpet's worn and shallow fiber, or were tightly combed into it, sparse hairs sticking to the scalp of an old corpse.

There was no one behind the ticket window, no one I could
see in that small space of darkness beyond the blur of purple-
tinted glass in which my reflection was held. Nevertheless, a
ticket was protruding from a slot beneath the semi-circular
cutaway at the bottom of the window, sticking out like a paper
tongue. A few hairs lay beside it.

"Admission is free," said a man who was now standing in
the doorway beside the ticket booth. His suit was well-fitted
and neat, but his face appeared somehow a mess, bristling
over all its contours. His tone was polite, even passive, when
he said, "The theater is under new ownership."

"Are you the manager?" I asked.

"I was just on my way to the rest room."

Without further comment he drifted off into the darkness of
the theater. For a moment something floated in the empty
space he left in the doorway—a swarm of filaments like dust
that scattered or settled before I stepped through. And in those
first few seconds inside, all I could see were the words "rest
room" glowing above a door as it slowly closed.

I maneuvered with caution until my sight became sufficient
to the dark and allowed me to find a door leading to the auditorium of the movie theater. But once inside, as I stood at the
summit of a sloping aisle, all previous orientation to my surroundings underwent a setback. The room was illuminated by
an elaborate chandelier centered high above the floor, as well
as a series of light fixtures along either of the side walls. I was
not surprised by the dimness of the lighting nor by its hue,
which made shadows appear faintly bloodshot—a sickly, liver-
ish shade that might be witnessed in an operating room where
a torso lies open on the table, its entrails a palette of pinks and
reds and purples . . . diseased viscera imitating all the shades
of sunset.

However, my perception of the theater auditorium remained
problematic not because of any oddities of illumination but for
another reason. While I experienced no difficulty in mentally
registering the elements around me—the separate aisles and
rows of seats, the curtain-flanked movie screen, the well-noted
chandelier and wall lights—it seemed impossible to gain a sense

of these features in simple accord with their appearances. I saw nothing that I have not described, yet the round-backed seats were at the same time rows of headstones in a graveyard; the aisles were endless filthy alleys, long desolate corridors in an old asylum, or the dripping passages of a sewer narrowing into the distance; the pale movie screen was a dust-blinded window in a dark unvisited cellar, a mirror gone rheumy with age in an abandoned house; the chandelier and smaller fixtures were the facets of murky crystals embedded in the clammy walls of an unknown cavern. In other words, this movie theater was merely a virtual image, a veil upon a complex collage of other places, all of which shared certain qualities that were projected into my vision, as though the things I saw were possessed by something I could not see.

But as I lingered in the theater auditorium, settling in a seat toward the back wall, I realized that even on the level of plain appearances there was a peculiar phenomenon I had not formerly observed, or at least had yet to perceive to its fullest extent. I am speaking of the cobwebs.

When I first entered the theater I saw them clinging to the walls and carpeting. Now I saw how much they were a part of the theater and how I had mistaken the nature of these long pale threads. Even in the hazy purple light, I could discern that they had penetrated into the fabric of the seats in the theater, altering the weave in its depths and giving it a slight quality of movement, the slow curling of thin smoke. It seemed the same with the movie screen, which might have been a great rectangular web, densely woven and faintly in motion, vibrating at the touch of some unseen force. I thought: "Perhaps this subtle and pervasive *wriggling* within the theater may clarify the tendency of its elements to suggest other things and other places thoroughly unlike a simple auditorium, a process parallel to the ever-mutating images of clouds." All textures in the theater appeared similarly affected, without control over their own nature, but I could not clearly see as high as the chandelier. Even some of the others in the audience, which was small and widely scattered, were practically invisible to my eyes.

Furthermore, there may have been something in my mood

that night, given my sojourn in a part of town I had never visited before, that influenced what I was able to see. And this mood had become steadily enhanced since I first stepped into the theater, and indeed from the moment I looked upon the marquee advertising a feature entitled *The Glamour*. Having taken my place among the quietly expectant audience of the theater, I began to suffer an exacerbation of this mood. Specifically, I sensed a greater proximity to the point of focus for my mood that night, a tingling closeness to something quite literally *behind the scene*. Increasingly I became unconcerned with anything except the consummation or terminus of this abject and enchanting adventure. Consequences were evermore difficult to regard from my tainted perspective.

Therefore I was not hesitant when this focal point for my mood suddenly felt so near at hand, as close as the seat directly behind my own. I was quite sure this seat had been empty when I selected mine, that all the seats for several rows around me were unoccupied. And I would have been aware if someone had arrived to fill this seat directly behind me. Nevertheless, like a sudden chill announcing bad weather, there was now a definite presence I could feel at my back, a force that pressed itself upon me and inspired a surge of dark elation. But when I looked around, not quickly yet fully determined, I saw no occupant in the seat behind me, or in any seat between me and the back wall of the theater. I continued to stare at the empty seat because my sensation of a vibrant presence there was unrelieved. And in my staring I perceived that the fabric of the seat, the inner webbing of swirling fibers, had composed a pattern in the image of a face—an old woman's face with an expression of avid malignance—floating amidst wild shocks of twisting hair. The face itself was a portrait of atrocity, a grinning image of lust for sites and ceremonies of mayhem. And it was formed of those hairs stitching themselves together.

All the stringy, writhing cobwebs of that theater, as I now discovered, were the reaching tendrils of a vast netting of hairs. And in this discovery my mood of the evening, which had delivered me to a part of town I had never visited before and to that very theater, only became more expansive and defined, taking in scenes of graveyards and alleyways, reeking sewers and musty corridors of insanity as well as the immediate vision of an old theater that now, as I had been told, was under new ownership. But my mood abruptly faded, along with the face in the fabric of the theater seat, when a voice spoke to me. It said:

"You must have seen her, by the looks of you."

A man sat down one seat away from mine. It was not the same person I had met earlier; this one's face was nearly normal, although his suit was littered with hair that was not his own.

"So did you see her?" he asked.

"I'm not sure what I saw," I replied.

He seemed almost to burst out giggling, his voice trembling on the edge of a joyous hysteria. "You would be sure enough if there had been a private encounter, I can tell you."

"Something was happening, then you sat down."

"Sorry," he said. "Did you know that the theater has just come under new ownership?"

"I didn't notice what the show times are."

"Show times?"

"For the feature."

"Oh, there isn't any feature. Not as such."

"But there must be . . . something," I insisted.

"Yes, there's something," he replied excitedly, his fingers stroking his cheek.

"What, exactly? And these cobwebs . . ."

But the lights were going down into darkness. "Quiet now," he whispered. "It's about to begin."

Soon the screen before us glowed a pale purple in the blackness and vague images unaccompanied by sound began to take form upon it, as if a lens were being focused on a microscopic world. To be sure, the movie screen might have been a great glass slide upon which were projected to gigantic proportions a landscape of organisms normally hidden from our sight. But as these visions coalesced and clarified, I recognized them as something I had already seen, more accurately *sensed*, in that theater. The images were appearing on the screen as if a pair of disembodied eyes was moving within venues of profound morbidity and degeneration. Here was the purest essence of those places I had felt were superimposing themselves on the genuinely tangible aspects of the theater—those graveyards, alleys, grimy corridors, and subterranean passages whose spirit had intruded on another locale and altered it. Yet the places now revealed on the movie screen were without an identity I could name: they were the fundament of the sinister and seamy regions which cast their spectral ambiance on the reality of the theater but which were themselves merely the shadows, the superficial counterparts, of a deeper, more obscure realm. Farther and farther into it we were being taken.

The all-pervasive purple coloration could now be seen as emanating from the labyrinth of a living anatomy: a compound of the reddish, bluish, palest pink structures, all of them morbidly inflamed and lesioned to release a purple light. We were being guided through a catacomb of putrid chambers and cloisters, the most secreted ways and waysides of an infernal land. Whatever these spaces may once have been, they were now habitations for ceremonies of a private sabbat. The hollows in their fleshy, gelatinous integuments streamed with something like moss, a fungus in flimsy strands that were threading themselves into translucent tissue and quivering beneath it like veins. It was indeed the sabbat ground, secret and unconsecrated, but it was also the theater of a mad surgery. The hair-thin sutures stitched among the yielding entrails, unseen hands designing unnatural shapes and systems, weaving a nest in which the possession would take place, a web wherein the bits and pieces of the anatomy could be consumed at leisure. There seemed to be no one in sight, yet everything was scrutinized from an intimate perspective, the viewpoint of that invisible surgeon, the weaver and web-maker, the old puppet-master who was setting a helpless creature with new strings and placing him under the control of a new owner. And through eyes unknown we witnessed the work being done.

Then those eyes began to withdraw, and the purple world of the organism receded into purple shadows. When the eyes finally emerged from where they had been, the movie screen was filled with the face and naked chest of a man. His posture was rigid, betraying a state of paralysis, and his gaze was fixed, yet strikingly alive. "She's showing us," whispered the man who was sitting nearby me. "That horrible witch has taken him. He cannot feel who he is any longer, only her presence within him."

This statement, at first sight of the possessed, seemed to be the case. Certainly such a view of the situation provided a terrific stimulus to my own mood of the evening, urging it toward culmination in a type of degraded rapture, a seizure of debauched panic. Nonetheless, as I stared at the face of the man on the screen, he became known to me as the one I encountered in the vestibule of the theater. The recognition was difficult, however, because his flesh was now even more obscured by the webs of hair woven through it, thick as a full beard in spots. His eyes were also quite changed and glared out at the audience with a ferocity that suggested he indeed served as the host of great evil. But all the same, there was something in those eyes that belied the fact of a complete transformation—an awareness of the bewitchment and an appeal for deliverance. Within the next few moments, this observation assumed a degree of substance.

For the man on the movie screen regained himself, although briefly and in limited measure. His effort of will was evident in the subtle contortions of his face, and his ultimate accomplishment was modest enough: he managed to open his mouth in order to scream. Of course no sound was projected from the movie screen, which only played a music of images for eyes that would see what should not be seen. Thus, a disorienting effect was created, a sensory dissonance which resulted in my being roused from the mood of the evening, its spell over me echoing to nothingness. Because the scream that resonated in the auditorium had originated in another part of the theater, a place beyond the auditorium's towering back wall.

Consulting the man who was sitting near me, I found him oblivious to my comments about the scream within the theater. He seemed neither to hear nor see what was happening around him and what was happening to him. Long wiry hairs were sprouting from the fabric of the seats, snaking low along their arms and along every other part of them. The hairs had also penetrated into the cloth of the man's suit, but I could not make him aware of what was happening. Finally I rose to leave, because I could feel the hairs tugging to keep me in position. As I stood up they ripped away from me like stray threads pulled from a sleeve or pocket.

No one else in the auditorium turned away from the man on the movie screen, who had lost the ability to cry out and relapsed into a paralytic silence. Proceeding up the aisle I glanced above at a rectangular opening high in the back wall of the theater, the window-like slot from which images of a movie are projected. Framed within this aperture was the silhouette of what looked like an old woman with long and wildly tangled hair. I could see her eyes gazing fierce and malignant at the purple glow of the movie screen. And from these eyes were sent forth two shafts of the purest purple light that shot through the darkness of the auditorium.

Exiting the theater the way I had come in, it was not possible to ignore the words "rest room," so brightly were they now shining. But the lamp over the side door in the alley was dead; the sign reading ENTRANCE TO THE THEATER was gone. Even the letters spelling out the name of the feature that evening had been taken down. So this had been the last performance. Henceforth the theater would be closed to the public; somehow I knew this to be true.

Also closed, if only for the night, were all the other businesses along that particular street in a part of town I had never visited before. Despite the fact that they had been lit up before, even the ones that had shut their doors at that late hour, the shop windows were now dark. And how sure I was that behind each one of those dark windows I passed was the even darker silhouette of an old woman with glowing eyes and a great head of monstrous hair.

THE VOICE
OF THE CHILD

THE LIBRARY
OF BYZANTIUM

FATHER SEVICH'S VISIT

In whatever corner of our old house I happened to find myself, I could always sense the arrival of a priest. Even in the most distant rooms of the upper floors, those rooms which had been closed up and which were forbidden to me, I would suddenly experience a very certain feeling. The climate of my surroundings then became inexplicably altered in a manner at first vaguely troublesome and afterward rather attractive. It was as if a new presence had invaded the very echoes of the air and entered into the mellow afternoon sunlight casting its glow upon dark wooden floors and the pale contortions of ancient wallpaper. All around me invisible games had begun. My earliest philosophy regarding the great priestly tribe was therefore not a simple one by any means; rather, it comprised a thick maze of propositions, a labyrinthine layering of systems in which abstract dread and a bizarre sort of indebtedness were forever confronting each other. In retrospect, then, the prelude to Father Sevich's visit seems to me as crucial, and as introductory to later events, as the visit itself. So I have no qualms about lingering upon these lonely moments.

For much of that day I had been secluded in my room, intently pursuing a typical activity of my early life and in the process badly ravaging what previously had been a well-made bed. Having sharpened my pencil innumerable times, and having worn down a thick gray eraser into a stub, I was ready to give myself up as a relentless failure. The paper itself seemed to defy me, laying snares within its coarse texture to thwart my every aim. Yet this rebellious mood was a quite recent manifestation: I had been allowed to fill in nearly the entire scene before this breakdown in relations between myself and my materials.

The completed portion of my drawing was an intense impression of a monastic fantasy, evoking the cloistral tunnels and the vaulted penetralia without attempting a guide-book representation of them. Nevertheless, the absolute precision of two specific elements in the picture was very much on my mind. The first of these was a single row of columns receding in sharp perspective, a diminishing file of rigid sentinels starkly etched into the surrounding gloom. The second element was a figure who had hidden himself behind one of these columns and was peering out of the shadows at something frightful beyond the immediate scene. Only the figure's face and a single column-clutching hand were to be rendered. The hand I executed well enough, but when it came to the necessary features of fear which needed to be implanted on that countenance—there was simply no way to capture the desired effect. My wish was to have every detail of the unseen horror clearly readable in the physiognomy of the seer himself, a maddening task and, at the time, a futile one. Every manipulation of my soft-pointed pencil betrayed me, masking my victim with a series of completely irrelevant expressions. First it was misty-eyed wonder, and then a kind of cretinous bafflement. At one point the gentleman appeared to be smiling in an almost amiable way at his imminent doom.

Thus, one may comprehend how easily I succumbed to the distraction of Father Sevich's visit. My pencil stopped dead on the paper, my eyes began to wander about, checking the curtains, the corners, and the open closet for something that had come to play hide-and-seek with me. I heard footsteps methodically treading down the long hallway and stopping at my bedroom door. My father's voice, muffled by solid wood, instructed me to make an appearance downstairs. There was a visitor.

My frustrations of that afternoon must have disadvantaged me somewhat, because I completely fell into the trap of expectation: that is, I believed our caller was only Father Orne, who often dropped by and who served as a kind of ecclesiastical familiar of our family. But when I descended the stairs and saw that strange black cloak drooping down from the many-pegged rack beside the front door, and when I saw the wide-brimmed hat of the same color hanging beside it like an age-old companion, I realized my error.

From the parlor came the sound of soft conversation, the softest part of which was supplied by Father Sevich himself, whose speaking voice was no more than a sleepy whisper. He was seated, quite fairly, in one of our most expansive arm-chairs, toward which destination my mother maneuvered me as soon as I entered the room. During the presentation I was silent, and for a few suspenseful moments afterward continued to remain so. Father Sevich thought that I was fascinated into muteness by his fancy walking stick, and he said as much. At that moment the priest's voice was infiltrated, to my amazement, by a foreign accent I had not previously noticed. He handed his cane over to me for examination, and I hefted the formidable length of wood a few times. However, the real source of my fascination lay not in his personal accessories, but in the priest's own person, specifically in the chalky-looking texture of his round face.

Invited to join the afternoon gathering, I was seated in a chair identical to the one supporting Father Sevich's bulk, and angled slightly toward it. But my alliance to this group was in body only: I contributed not a word to the ensuing conversation, nor did I understand those words that now filled the parlor with their drowsy music. My concentration on the priest's face had wholly exiled me from the world of good manners and polite talk. It was not just the pale and powdery cast of his complexion, but also a certain emptiness, a look of incompleteness that made me think of some unfinished effigy in a toymaker's work-shop. The priest smiled and squinted and performed several other common manipulations, none of which resulted in a true facial expression. Something vital to expression was missing, some essential spirit in which all expressions are born and evolve toward their unique destiny. And, to put it graphically, his flesh simply did not have the appearance of flesh.

At some point my mother and father found an excuse to leave me alone with Father Sevich, presumably to allow his influence to have a free rein over me, so that his sacerdotal presence might not be adulterated by the secularity of theirs. This development was in no way surprising, since it was my parents' secret hope that someday my life would take me at least as far as the seminary, if not beyond that into the purple-robed mysteries of priesthood.

In the first few seconds after my parents had abandoned the scene, Father Sevich and I looked each other over, almost as if our previous introduction had counted for naught. And soon a very interesting thing happened: Father Sevich's face under-went a change, one in favor of the soul which had formerly been interred within his most obscure depths. Now, from out of that chalky tomb emerged a face of true expression, a mas-terly composition of animated eyes, living mouth, and newly flushed cheeks. This transformation, however, must have been achieved at a certain cost; for what his face gained in vitality, the priest's voice lost in volume. His words now sounded like those of a hopeless invalid, withered things reeking of medi-cines and prayers. What their exact topic of discourse was I'm not completely sure, but I do recall that my drawings were touched upon. Father Orne, of course, was already familiar with these fledgling works, though I do not recall that he ever expressed admiration for them. Nonetheless, it seemed that something in their pictorial nature had caused him to mention them to his colleague who was visiting us from the old coun-try. Something had caused Father Orne to single my pictures out, as it were, among the sights of his parish.

Father Sevich spoke of those scribblings of mine in a highly cir-cuitous and rarefied fashion, as if they were a painfully delicate subject which threatened a breach in our acquaintanceship. I did not grasp what constituted his tortuous and subtle interest in my pictures, but this issue was partially clarified when he showed me something: a little book he was carrying within the intricate folds of his clerical frock.

The covering of the book had the appearance of varnished wood, all darkish and embellished with undulating grains. At first I thought that this object would feel every bit as brittle as it looked, until Father Sevich actually placed it in my hands and allowed me to discover that its deceptive binding was in fact extremely supple, even slippery. There were no words on the front of the book, only two thin black lines which intersected to create a cross. On closer examination, I observed that the horizontal beam of the cross had, on either end, squiggly little extensions resembling tiny hands. And the vertical beam appeared to widen at its vertex into something like a little bulb, so that the black decoration formed a sort of stick man.

At Father Sevich's instruction, I randomly opened the book and thumbed over several of its incredibly thin pages, which were more like layers of living tissue than dead pulp. There seemed to be an infinite number of them, with no possibility of ever reaching the beginning or the end of the volume merely by turning over the pages one by one. The priest warned me to be careful and not to harm any of these delicate leaves, for the book was very old, very fragile, and unusually precious.

The language in which the book was written resisted all but imaginary identifications by one who was as limited in years and learning as I was then. Even now, memory will not permit me to improve upon my initial speculation that the book was composed in some exotic tongue of antiquity. But its profusion of pictures alleviated many frustrations and illuminated the darkness of the book's secret symbols. In these examples of the art of the woodcut, I could almost read the texts composing the book, every one of which seemed devoted to wearing away at a single theme: *salvation through suffering*.

It was this chamber of sacred horrors that Father Sevich believed would catch my eye and my interest. How few of us, he explained, really understood the holy purpose of such images of torment, the divine destiny toward which the paths of anguish have always led. The production, and even the mere contemplation, of these volumes of blessed agony was one of the great lost arts, he openly lamented. Then he began to speak about a certain library in the old country. But his words were now lost on me. My attention was already wandering along its own paths, and my eye was inextricably caught by the dense landscape of these old woodcuts. One scene in particular appeared exemplary of the book's soul.

The central figure in this illustration was bearded and emaciated, with his head bowed, hands folded, and knees bent. Contracted in an attitude of prayerful pleading, he seemed to be suspended in mid-air. All around this bony ascetic were torturing demons, surprisingly effective owing to, or perhaps despite, the artist's brutal technique and the sparseness of precise detail. An exception to this general rule of style was a single squatting devil whose single eye had clusters of perfect little eyes growing out of it; and each of the smaller eyes had its own bristling lashes that sprouted like weeds, an explosion of minute grotesquerie. The ascetic's own eyes were the focus of his particular form: stark white openings in an otherwise dark face, with two tiny pupils rolling deliriously heavenward. But what was it about the transports written on this face which inspired in me the sense of things other than fear or pain, or even piety? In any event, I did find inspiration in this terrible scene, and tried to make an imprint of it upon the photographic plates of my memory.

With a tight grip of my index finger and thumb, I was holding the page on which this woodcut was reproduced when Father Sevich unexpectedly snatched the book out of my hands. I looked up, not at the priest but at my mother and father now returning to the parlor after their brief and calculated absence. Father Sevich was gazing in the same direction, while blindly stashing the little book back in its place. So he must not have noticed the thin leaf which was loosely draped over my fingers and which I immediately concealed between my legs. At any rate, he said nothing about the mishap. And at the time I could not imagine that any power on earth could perceive the loss of a single page from the impossibly dense and prodigious layers of that book. Certainly I was safe from the eyes of Father Sevich, which had once again become as dull and expressionless as the plaster complexion of his face.

Shortly thereafter the priest had to be on his way. With fascination I watched as he assembled himself in our foyer, donning his cloak, adjusting his huge hat, and propping up his large body with his walking stick. Before leaving, he invited us all to visit him in the old country, and we promised to do so should our travels ever take us to that part of the world. While my mother held me close to her side, my father opened the door for the priest. And the sunny afternoon, now grown windy and overcast, received him.

FATHER SEVICH'S RETURN

The stolen woodcut from the priest's prayer book, as I came to think of it, was not the solution I thought it would be. Although I suspected that it possessed certain inspirational powers, a modest fund of moral energy, I soon found that the macabre icon withheld its blessings from outsiders. I had not then considered that a sacred image of this kind would have such a secretive nature, for I was more infatuated with the profane lessons I believed it could teach—above all, how I might provide my faceless man in the monastery with a countenance of true terror. However, I learned no such lessons and was forced to leave my figure in an unfinished state, a ridiculously empty slate which I remained unable to embellish with the absolute horror of an offstage atrocity. But the picture, I mean the one in the prayer book, did have another and unsuspected value for me.

Since I had already established a spiritual rapport with Father Sevich, I could not obstruct a certain awareness of his own mysteries. He soon became connected in my mind with unarticulated narratives of a certain kind, stories in the rough, and ones potentially epic, even cosmic, in scope. Without a doubt there was an aura of legend about him, a cycle of mute, incredible lore; and I resolved that his future movements merited my closest possible attention. Such a difficult undertaking was made infinitely easier due to my possession of that single, flimsy page torn from his prayer book.

I kept it with me at all times, protectively enclosed in some wrapping tissue I borrowed from my mother. The initial results were soon in coming, but at the same time they were not entirely successful, considering the expense of this rather prodigal burst of psychic effort. Hence, the early scenes were highly imperfect, visions easily dispersed, fragmentary, some quite near to nonsense. Among them was a visit Father Sevich paid another family, a morose vignette in which the anemic priest seemed to have grown pale to the point of translucency.

And the others involved were even worse: some of them had barely materialized or were visible only as a sort of anthropomorphic mist. There was considerable improvement when Father Sevich was alone or in the presence of only one other person. A lengthy conversation with Father Orne, for example, was projected in its totality; but, as in an improperly lighted photographic scene, the substance of every shape had been watered down into an eerie lividity. Also, given the nature of these visionary endeavors, the entire meeting transpired in dead silence, as if the two clergymen were merely pantomiming their parts.

And in all phases of activity, Father Sevich remained the model visitor from a foreign diocese, laying no new ground for scandal since his brief, though infinitely promising, visit with my parents and me. Perhaps the only occasions on which he threatened to live up to this promise, this pledge to incarnate some of those abstract myths that his character suggested to my imagination, took place during his intervals of absolute privacy. In the most unconscious hours of darkness, when the rest of the rectory's population was in slumber, Father Sevich would leave the austere comforts of his bed and, seating himself at a window-facing desk, would pore over the contents of a certain book, turning page after page and stopping every so often to mouth some of the strange words inscribed upon them. Somehow these were the sentences of his own mysterious biography, a chronicle of truly unspeakable things. In the formation of the priest's lips as he mimed the incantations of a dead language, in the darting movements of his tongue between rows of immaculate teeth, one could almost chart the convoluted chronology of this foreign man.

How alien is the deepest life of another: the unbelievable beginnings; the unimaginably elaborate developments; and the incalculable eons which prepare, which foretell, the multiform phenomena of an uncertain number of years! Much of what Father Sevich had endured in his allotted span could already be read on his face. But something still remained to be revealed in his features, something which the glowing lamp resting upon the desk, joined by the light of every constellation in the visible universe, was struggling to illuminate.

When Father Sevich returned to his homeland, I lost all touch with his life's whereabouts, and soon my own life collapsed back into its established routine. After that weary and fruitless summer had passed, it was time for me to begin another year of school, to encounter once again the oppressive mysteries of the autumn season. But I had not entirely forgotten my adventure with Father Sevich. At the height of the fall semester we began to draw pumpkins with thick orange crayons whose points were awkwardly blunt, and with dull scissors we shaped black cats from the formless depths of black paper. Succumbing to a hopeless urge for innovation, I created a man-shaped silhouette with my paper and scissors. The just proportions of my handiwork even received compliments from the nun who served as our art instructor. But when I trimmed the figure with a tiny white collar and gave it a crudely screaming mouth—there was outrage and there was punishment. Without arguing a happy sequence of cause and effect between this incident and what followed, it was not long afterward that the school season, for me, became eventful with illness. And it was during this time of shattered routine, as I lay three days and nights dripping with fever, that I regained my hold, with a visionary grasp that reached across the ocean between us, on the curious itinerary of Father Sevich.

With hat and cloak and walking stick, the old priest was hobbling along rather briskly, and alone, down the narrow, nocturnal streets of some very old town in the old country. It was a fairy-tale vision to which not even the most loving illustrator of medieval legends could do justice. Fortunately, the town itself—the serpentine lanes, the distorted glow of streetlamps, the superimposed confusion of pointed roofs, the thinnest blade of moon which seemed to belong to this town as it belonged to no other place on earth—does not require any protracted emphasis in this memoir. Although it did not give away its identity, either in name or location, the town still demanded a designation of some kind, some official title, however much in error it might be. And of all the names that had ever been attached to places of this world, the only one which seemed proper, in its delirious way, was an ancient name which, after all these years, seems no less fitting and no less ludicrous now than it did then. Unmentionably ludicrous, so I will not mention it.

Now Father Sevich was disappearing into a narrow niche between two dark houses, which led him to an unpaved lane bordered by low walls, along which he traveled in almost total blackness until the pathway opened into a small courtyard surrounded by high walls and lit by a single dull lamp at its center. He paused a moment to catch his breath, and when he gazed up at the night, as if to reconcile his course with the stars above, one could see his face sweating and shining in the jaundiced lamplight. Somewhere in the shadows that were draped and fluttering upon those high walls was an opening. Passing through this doubtful gate, the old priest continued his incredible rambling about the darkest and most remote quarters of the old town.

Now he was descending a stairway of cut stone which led below the level of the town's streets; then a brief tunnel brought him to another stairway which burrowed in a spiral down into the earth and absolute blackness. Knowing his way, the priest ultimately emerged from this nowhere of blackness when he suddenly entered a vast circular chamber. The place appeared to be a tower sunken beneath the town and soaring to a great and paradoxical height. In the upper reaches of the tower, tiny lights glimmered like stars and threw down their illumination in a patternless weave of crisscrossing strands.

The subterranean structure, at whose center Father Sevich now stood, ascended in a series of terraces, each bordered by a shining balustrade made of some golden metal and each circling the perimeter of the inner chamber. These terraces multiplied into the upward distance, contracting in perspective into smaller and thinner circles, blurring together at some point and becoming lost in clouds of shadows that hovered far above. Each level was furthermore provided with numerous and regularly spaced portals, all of them dark, hinting at nothing of what lay beyond their unguarded thresholds. But one might surmise that if this was the library of which the priest spoke, if this was a true repository of such books as the one he had just removed from under his cloak, then those slender openings must have led to the archives of this prodigious athenaeum, suggesting nothing less than a bibliographic honeycomb of unknown expanse and complexity. Scanning the shadows about him, the priest seemed to be anticipating the appearance of someone in charge, someone entrusted with the care of this institution. Then one of the shadows, one of the most sizeable shadows and the one closest to the priest, turned around . . . and three such caretakers now stood before him.

This triumvirate of figures seemed to share the same face, which was almost a caricature of serenity. They were attired very much like the priest himself, and their eyes were large and calm. When the priest held out the book to the one in the middle, a hand moved forward to take it, a hand as white as the whitest glove. The central figure then rested its other hand flat upon the front of the book, and then the figure to the left extended a hand which laid itself upon the first; then a third hand, belonging to the third figure, covered them both with its soft white palm and long fingers, uniting the three. The hands remained thus placed for some time, as if an invisible transference of fabulously subtle powers was occurring, something being given or received. The heads of the three figures slowly turned toward one another, and simultaneously there was a change in the atmosphere of the chamber streaked with the chaotic rays of underworld starlight. And if forced to name this new quality and point to its outward sign, one might draw attention to a certain look in the large eyes of the three care-takers, a certain expression of rarefied scorn or disgust.

They removed their hands from the book and placed them once again out of view. Then the caretakers turned their eyes upon the priest, who had already moved a few steps away from these indignant shadows. But as the priest began to turn his back on them, almost precisely at the mid-point of his pivot, he seemed to freeze abruptly in position, like someone who has just heard his name called out to him in some strange place far from home. However, he did not remain thus transfixed for very long, this statue poised to take a step which is forbidden to it, with its face as rigid and pale as a monument's stone. Soon his black, ankle-high shoes began to kick about as they left the solid ground. And when the priest had risen a little higher, well into the absolute insecurity of empty air, he lost hold of his walking stick; and it fell to the great empty expanse of the tower's floor, where it looked as small as a twig or a pencil. His wide-brimmed hat soon followed, settling crown-up beside the cane, as the priest began tossing and turning in the air like a restless sleeper, wrapping himself up in the dark cocoon of his cloak. Then the cloak was torn away, but not by the thrashing priest. Something else was up there with him, ascending the uncountable tiers of the tower, or perhaps many unseen things which ripped at his clothes, at the sparse locks of his hair, at the interlocking fingers of his hands which were now folded and pressed to his forehead, as though in desperate prayer. And finally at his face.

Now the priest was no more than a dark speck agitating in the greater heights of the dark tower. Soon he was nothing at all. Below, the three figures had absconded to their refuge of shadows, and the vast chamber appeared empty once more. Then everything went black.

My fever grew worse over the course of several more days, and then late one night it suddenly, quite unexpectedly, broke. Exhausted by the ordeals of my delirium, I lay buried in my bed beneath heavy blankets, whose usually numerous layers had been supplemented according to the ministrations of my mother. Just a few moments before, or a few millennia, she had gone out of my room, believing that I was at last asleep. But I had not even come near to sleeping, no more than I approached a normal state of wakefulness. The only illumination in my room was the natural nightlight of the moon shining through the windows. Through half-closed eyes I focused on this light, suspecting strange things about it, until I finally noticed that all the curtains in my room had been tightly drawn, that the pale glow at the foot of my bed was an unnatural phosphorescence, an infernal aura or angelic halo beaming about the form of Father Sevich himself.

In my confusion I greeted him, trying to lift my head from its pillow but falling back in weakness. He showed no awareness of my presence, and for a second I thought—in the hellish wanderings of my fever—that *I* was the revenant, not he. Attempting to take a clearer account of things, I forced open my leaden eyelids with all the strength I could muster. As a reward for this effort, I witnessed with all possible acuity of my inward and outward vision the incorporeal grandeur of the specter's face. And in a moment immeasurable by earthly increments of time, I grasped every detail, every datum and nuance of this visitor's life-history, the fantastic destiny which had culminated in the creation of this infinitely gruesome visage, one whose expression had grown rigid at the sight of unimaginable horrors and petrified into spectral stone. And in that same moment, I felt that I, too, could see what this lost soul had seen.

Now, with all the force of a planet revolving its unspeakable tonnage in the blackness of space, the face turned on its terrible axis and, while it still appeared to have no apprehension of my existence, it spoke, as if to itself alone and to its solitary doom:

Not given back as it had been given, the law of the book is broken. The law . . . of the book . . . is broken.

The specter had barely spoken the last resounding syllables of its strange pronouncement when it underwent a change. Before my eyes it began to shrivel like something thrown into a fire, and without the least indication of anguish it crinkled into nothing, as if some invisible power had suddenly decided to dispose of its work, to crumple up an aborted exercise and toss it into oblivion. And it was then that I felt my own purposes at an intersection, a fortuitous crossroads, with that savage and unseen hand. But *I* would not scorn what I had seen. My health miraculously restored, I gathered together my drawing materials and stayed up the rest of that night recording the vision. At last I had the face I was seeking.

POSTSCRIPTUM

Not long after that night, I paid a visit to our parish church. As this gesture was entirely self-initiated, my parents were free to interpret it as a sign of things to come, and no doubt they did so. The purpose of this act, however, was merely to collect a small bottle of holy water from the handsome metal cistern which dispensed this liquid to the public and which stood in the vestibule of the church. With apologies to my mother and father, I did not on this occasion actually enter the church itself. Gaining the priest-blessed solution, I hurried home, where I immediately unearthed—from the bottom of my dresser drawer—the page torn from Father Sevich's book. Both items, prayer book page and bottle of holy water, I took into the upstairs bathroom. I locked the door and placed the delicate little leaf in the bathroom sink, staring for a few moments at that wonderful woodcut. I wondered if one day I might make amends for my act of vandalism, perhaps by offering something of my own to a certain repository for such treasures in the old country. But then I recalled the fate of Father Sevich, which helped to chase the whole matter from my mind. From the uncorked bottle, I sprinkled the holy water over the precious page spread out at the bottom of the sink. For a few moments it sizzled, exactly as if I had poured a powerful acid on it, and gave off a not unpleasant vapor, an incense reeking of secret denial and privilege. Finally, it dissolved altogether. Then I knew that the game was over, the dream at an end. In the mirror above the sink I saw my own face smiling a smile of deep contentment.

MISS PLARR

It was spring, though still quite early in the season, when a young woman came to live with us. Her purpose was to manage the affairs of the household while my mother was suffering some vague ailment, lingering but not serious, and my father was away on business. She arrived on one of those misty, drizzling days which often prevailed during the young months of that particular year and which remain in my memory as the signature of this remarkable time. Since my mother was self-confined to her bed and my father absent, it was left for me to answer those sharp, urgent rappings at the front door. How they echoed throughout the many rooms of the house, reverberating in the farthest corners of the upper floors.

Pulling on the curved metal door handle, so huge in my child's hand, I found her standing with her back to me and staring deep into a world of darkening mist. Her black hair glistened in the light from the vestibule. As she turned slowly around, my eyes were fixed upon that great ebony turban of hair, folded so elaborately into itself again and again yet in some way rebelling against this discipline, with many shiny strands escaping their bonds and bursting out wildly. Indeed, it was through a straggle of mist-covered locks that she first glared down at me, saying: "My name is . . ."

"I know," I said.

But at that moment it was not so much her name that I knew, despite my father's diligent recitations of it to me, as all the unexpected correspondences I sensed in her physical presence. For even after she stepped into the house, she kept her head slightly turned and glanced over her shoulder through the open door, watching the elements outside and listening with intense expectancy. By then this stranger had already gained a precise orientation amid the world's chaos of faces and other phenomena. Quite literally her place was an obscure one, lying somewhere deep within the peculiar mood of that spring afternoon when the natural gestures of the season had been apparently distanced and suppressed by an otherworldly desolation—a seething luxuriance hidden behind dark battlements of clouds looming above a bare, practically hibernal landscape. And the sounds for which she listened also seemed remote and stifled, shut out by a mute and sullen twilight, smothered in that tower of stone-gray sky.

However, while Miss Plarr appeared to reflect with exactitude all the signs and mannerisms of those days all shackled in gloom, her place in our household was still an uncertainty.

During the early part of her stay with us, Miss Plarr was more often heard than seen. Her duties, whether by instruction or her own interpretation, had soon engaged her in a routine of wandering throughout the echoing rooms and hallways of the house. Rarely was there an interruption in those footsteps as they sounded upon aged floorboards; day and night this gentle crepitating signaled the whereabouts of our vigilant housekeeper. In the morning I awoke to the movements of Miss Plarr on the floors above or below my bedroom, while late in the afternoon, when I often spent time in the library upon my return from school, I could hear the clip-clopping of her heels on the parquet in the adjacent room. Even late at night, when the structure of the house expressed itself with a fugue of noises, Miss Plarr augmented this decrepit music with her own slow pacing upon the stairs or outside my door.

One time I felt myself awakened in the middle of the night, though it was not any disturbing sounds that had broken my sleep. And I was unsure exactly what made it impossible for me to close my eyes again. Finally, I slid out of bed, quietly opened the door of my room a few inches, and peeped down the darkened hallway. At the end of that long passage was a window filled with the livid radiance of moonlight, and within the frame of that window was Miss Plarr, her entire form shaded into a silhouette as black as the blackness of her hair, which was all piled up into the wild shape of some night-blossom. So intently was she staring out the window that she did not seem to detect my observance of her. I, on the other hand, could no longer ignore the force of her presence.

The following day I began a series of sketches. These works first took form as doodles in the margins of my school books, but swiftly evolved into projects of greater size and ambition. Given the enigmas of any variety of creation, I was not entirely surprised that the images I had elaborated did not include the overt portrayal of Miss Plarr herself, nor of other persons who might serve by way of symbolism or association. Instead, my drawings appeared to illustrate scenes from a tale of some strange and cruel kingdom. Possessed by curious moods and visions, I depicted a bleak domain that was obscured by a kind of fog or cloud whose depths brought forth a plethora of incredible structures, all of them somehow twisted into aspects of bizarre savagery. From the matrix of this fertile haze was born a litter of towering edifices that combined the traits of castle and crypt, many-peaked palace and multi-chambered mausoleum. But there were also clusters of smaller buildings, warped offshoots of the greater ones, housing perhaps no more than a single room, an apartment of ominously skewed design, an intimate dungeon cell reserved for the most exclusive captivity. Of course, I betrayed no special genius in my execution of these phantasmal venues: my technique was as barbarous as my subject. And certainly I was unable to introduce into the menacing images any suggestion of certain sounds that seemed integral to their proper representation, a kind of aural accompaniment to these operatic stage sets. In fact, I was not able even to imagine these sounds with any degree of clarity. Yet I knew that they belonged in the pictures, and that, like the purely visible dimension of these works, their source could be found in the person of Miss Plarr.

Although I had not intended to show her the sketches, there was evidence that she had indulged in private viewings of them. They lay more or less in the open on the desk in my bedroom; I made no effort to conceal my work. And I began to suspect that their order was being disturbed in my absence, to sense a subtle disarrangement that was vaguely telling but not conclusive. Finally, upon returning from school one gray afternoon, I discovered a sure sign of Miss Plarr's investigations. For lying between two of my drawings, pressed like a memento in an old scrapbook, was a long, black strand of hair.

I wanted to confront Miss Plarr immediately regarding her intrusion, not because I resented it in any way but solely to seize the occasion to approach this devious eccentric and perhaps draw closer to the strange sights and sounds she had brought into our household. However, at that stage of her term of employment she was no longer so easily located, having ceased her constant, noisy marauding and begun practicing more sedentary or stealthy rituals.

Since there was no sign of her elsewhere in the house, I went directly to the room which had been set aside for her, and which I had previously respected as her sanctum. But as I slowly stepped up to the open doorway I saw that she was not there. After entering the room and rummaging about, I realized that she was not using it at all and perhaps had never settled in. I turned around to continue my search for Miss Plarr when I found her standing silently in the doorway and gazing into the room without fixing her eyes on anything, or anyone, within it. I nevertheless appeared to be in a position of chastisement, losing all the advantage I earlier possessed over this invader of *my* sanctum. Yet there was no mention of either of these transgressions, despite what seemed our mutual understanding of them. We were helplessly drifting into an abyss of unspoken reproaches and suspicions. Finally, Miss Plarr rescued us both by making an announcement she had obviously been saving for the right moment.

"I have spoken with your mother," she declared in a strong voice, "and we have concluded that I should begin tutoring you in some of your weaker school subjects."

I believe that I must have nodded, or offered some other gesture of assent. "Good," she said. "We will start tomorrow."

Then, rather quietly, she walked away, leaving her words to resound in the cavity of that unoccupied room—unoccupied, I may claim, since my own presence now seemed to have been eclipsed by the swelling shadow of Miss Plarr. Nonetheless, this extra-scholastic instruction did prove of immense value in illuminating what, at the time, was my weakest subject: Miss Plarr in general, with special attention to where she had made accommodations for herself in our household.

My tutelage was conducted in a room that Miss Plarr felt was especially suited to the purpose, though her reasoning may not have been readily apparent. For the place she had selected to impart her lessons to me was a small attic located beneath a roof toward the back of the house. The slanted ceiling of that room exposed to us its rotting beams like the ribbing of some ancient seagoing vessel that might carry us to unknown destinations. And there were cold drafts that eddied around us, opposing currents emanating from the warped frame in which a many-paned window softly rattled now and then. The light by which I was schooled was provided by overcast afternoons fading in that window, assisted by an old oil lamp which Miss Plarr had hung upon a nail in one of the attic rafters. (I still wonder where she unearthed that antique.) It was this greasy lamplight that enabled me to glimpse a heap of old rags which had been piled in a corner to form a kind of crude bedding. Nearby stood the suitcase Miss Plarr had arrived with.

The only furniture in this room was a low table, which served as my desk, and a small frail chair, both articles being relics of my early childhood and no doubt rediscovered in the course of my teacher's many expeditions throughout the house. Seated at the center of the room, I submitted to the musty pathos of my surroundings. "In a room such as this," Miss Plarr asserted, "one may learn certain things of the greatest importance." So I listened while Miss Plarr clomped noisily about, wielding a long wooden pointer which had no blackboard to point to. All considered, however, she did deliver a series of quite fascinating lectures.

Without attempting to render the exact rhetoric of her discourse, I remember that Miss Plarr was especially concerned with my development in subjects that often touched upon history or geography, occasionally broaching realms of philosophy and science. She lectured from memory, never once hesitating in her delivery of countless facts that had not reached me by way of the conventional avenues of my education. Yet these talks were nonetheless as meandering as her footsteps upon the cold floor of that attic room, and at first I was breathless trying to follow her from one point to the next. Eventually, though, I began to extract certain themes from her chaotic syllabus. For instance, she returned time and again to the earliest twitchings of human life, portraying a world of only the most rudimentary law but one intriguingly advanced in what she called "visceral practices." She allowed that much of what she said in this way was speculative. In her discussions of later periods, she deferred to the restrictions, while also enjoying the explicitness, of accepted records. Hence, I was made intimate with those ancient atrocities which gained renown for a Persian monarch, with a century-old massacre in the Brazilian backlands, and with the specific methods of punishment employed by various societies often relegated to the margins of history. And in other flights of instruction, during which Miss Plarr might flourish her pointer in the air like an artist's paintbrush, I was introduced to lands whose chief feature was a kind of brutality and an air of exile— coarse and tortuous terrains, deliriums of earth and sky. These included desolate, fog-bound islands in polar seas, countries of barren peaks lacerated by unceasing winds, wastelands that consumed all sense of reality in their vast spaces, shadowed realms littered with dead cities, and sweltering hells of jungle where light itself is tinged with a bluish slime.

At some point, however, Miss Plarr's specialized curriculum, once so novel and engrossing, dulled with repetition. I started to fidget in my miniature seat; my head slumped over my miniature desk. Then her words suddenly stopped, and she drew close to me, laying her rubber-tipped pointer across my shoulder. When I looked up I saw only those eyes glaring down at me, and that black bundle of hair outlined in the dismal light drifting through the attic like a glowing vapor.

"In a room such as this," she whispered, "one may also learn the *proper* way to behave."

The pointer was then pulled away, grazing my neck, and Miss

Plarr walked over to the window. Outside, one of the great mists of that spring obscured the landscape. As if seen through murky sheets of ice, everything appeared remote and hallucinatory. An indeterminate figure herself, Miss Plarr gazed out at a world of shadows bound in place. She also seemed to be listening to it.

"Do you know the sound of something that stings the air?" she asked, swinging her pointer lightly against herself.

I understood her meaning and nodded my compliance. But at the same time I imagined more than a teacher's switch as it came down upon a pupil's body. Sounds more serious and more strange intruded upon the hush of the classroom. They were faraway sounds lost in the hissing of rainy afternoons: immense blades sweeping over vast spaces; expansive wings cutting through cold winds; long whips lashing in darkness. I also heard the sound of things that were "stinging the air" in places beyond all comprehension. These sounds grew increasingly louder. Finally, Miss Plarr dropped her pointer and put her hands over her ears.

"That will be all for today," she shouted.

And neither did she hold class on the following day, nor ever again resume my tutelage.

It seemed, however, that my lessons with Miss Plarr had continued in a different form. Those afternoons in that attic must have exhausted something within me, and for a brief time I was unable to leave my bed. During this period I noticed that Miss Plarr was suffering a decline of her own, allowing the intangible sympathies which had already existed between us to become so much deeper and more entangled. To some extent it might be said that my own process of degeneration was following hers, much as my faculty of hearing, sensitized by illness, followed her echoing footsteps as they moved about the house. For Miss Plarr had reverted to her restless wandering, somehow having failed to settle herself into any kind of repose.

On her visits to my room, which had become frequent and were always unexpected, I could observe the phases of her dissolution on both a material and a psychic level. Her hair now hung loose about her shoulders, twisting itself in the most hideous ways like a dark mesh of nightmares, a foul nest in which her own suspicions were swarming. Moreover, her links to a strictly mundane order had become shockingly decayed, and my relationship with her was conducted at the risk of intimacy with spheres of a highly questionable nature.

One afternoon I awoke from a nap to discover that all the drawings she had inspired me to produce had been torn to pieces and lay scattered about my room. But this primitive attempt at exorcism proved to have no effect, for in the late hours of that same night I found her sitting on my bed and leaning close to me, her hair brushing against my face. "Tell me about those sounds," she demanded. "You've been doing this to frighten me, haven't you?" For a while I felt she had slipped away altogether, severing our extraordinary bond and allowing my health to improve. But just as I seemed to be approaching a full recovery, Miss Plarr returned.

"I think that you're much better now," she said as she entered my room with a briskness that seemed to be an effort. "You can get dressed today. I have to do some shopping, and I want you to come along and assist me."

I might have protested that to go out on such a day would cause me to relapse, for outside waited a heavy spring dampness and so much fog that I could see nothing beyond my bedroom window. But Miss Plarr was already lost to the world of wholesome practicalities, while her manner betrayed a hypnotic and fateful determination that I could not have resisted.

"As for this fog," she said, even though I had not mentioned it, "I think we shall be able to find our way."

Having a child's weakness for prospects of misadventure, I followed Miss Plarr into that fog-smothered landscape. After walking only a few steps we lost sight of the house, and even the ground beneath our feet was submerged under layers of a pale, floating web. But she took my hand and marched on as if guided by some peculiar vision.

And it was by her grasp that this vision was conducted into me, setting both of us upon a strange path. Yet as we progressed, I began to recognize certain shapes gradually emerging around us—that brood of dark forms which pushed through the fog, as if their growth could no longer be contained by it. When I tightened my grip on Miss Plarr's hand—which seemed to be losing its strength, fading in its substance—the vision surged toward clarity. With the aspect of some leviathan rising into view from the abyss, a monstrous world defined itself before our eyes, forcing its way through the surface of the fog, which now trailed in wisps about the structures of an immense and awful kingdom.

More expansive and intricate than my earlier, purely artistic imaginings, these structures sprung forth like a patternless conglomerate of crystals, angular and many-faceted monuments clustering in a misty graveyard. It was a dead city indeed, and all residents were entombed within its walls—or they were nowhere. There were streets of a sort which cut through this chaos of architecture, winding among the lopsided buildings, and yet it all retained an interlocking unity, much like a mountain range of wildly carved peaks and chasms and very much like the mountainous and murky thunderheads of a rainy season. Surely the very essence of a storm inhered in the jagged dynamism of these structures, a pyrotechnics that remained suspended or hidden, its violence a matter of suspicion and conjecture, suggesting a realm of atrocious potential—that infinite country which hovers beyond fogs and mists and gray heaping skies.

But even here something remained obscure, a sense provoked of rites or observances being enacted in concealment. And this peculiar sense was aroused by certain sounds, as of smothered cacophonous echoes lashing out in black cells and scourging the lengths of blind passages. Through the silence of the fog they gradually disseminated.

"Do you hear them?" asked Miss Plarr, though by then they had already risen to a conspicuous stridency. "There are rooms we cannot see where those sounds are being made. Sounds of something that stings the air."

Her eyes seemed to be possessed by the sight of these rooms she spoke of; her hair was mingling with the mist around us. Finally, she released her hold on my hand and drifted onward.

There was no struggle: she had known for some time what loomed in the background of her wandering and what waited her approach. Perhaps she thought this was something she could pass on to others, or in which she might gain their company. But her company, her *proper* company, had all the time been preparing for her arrival elsewhere. Nevertheless, she had honored me as the heir of her visions.

The fog swept around her and thickened once again until there was nothing else that could be seen. After a few moments I managed to gain my geographical bearings, finding myself in the middle of the street only a few blocks from home.

Soon after the disappearance of Miss Plarr, our household was again established in its routine: my mother made a strong recovery from her pseudo-illness and my father returned from his business excursion. The hired girl, it seemed, had vacated the house without giving notice, a turn of events that caused little surprise in my mother. "Such a flighty creature," she said about our former housekeeper.

I supported this characterization of Miss Plarr, but offered nothing that might suggest the nature of her flight. In truth, no word of mine could possibly have brought the least clarity to the situation. Nor did I wish to deepen the mysteries of this episode by revealing what Miss Plarr had left behind in that attic room. For me this chamber was now invested with a dour mystique, and I revisited its drafty spaces on several occasions over the years. Especially on afternoons in early spring when I could not close my ears to certain sounds that reached me from beyond a gray mist or from skies of hissing rain, as if somewhere the tenuous forms of spirits were thrashing in a dark and forsaken world.

THE VOICE OF
OUR NAME

THE SHADOW AT THE
BOTTOM OF THE WORLD

Before there occurred anything of a truly prodigious nature, the season had manifestly erupted with some feverish intent. This, at least, was how it appeared to us, whether we happened to live in town or somewhere outside its limits. (And traveling between town and countryside was Mr. Marble, who had been studying the seasonal signs far longer and in greater depth than we, disclosing prophecies that no one would credit at the time.) On the calendars which hung in so many of our homes, the monthly photograph illustrated the spirit of the numbered days below it: sheaves of cornstalks standing brownish and brittle in a newly harvested field, a narrow house and wide barn in the background, a sky of empty light above, and fiery leafage frolicking about the edges of the scene. But something dark, something abysmal always finds its way into the bland beauty of such pictures, something that usually holds itself in abeyance, some entwining presence that we always know is there. And it was exactly this presence that had gone into crisis, or perhaps had been secretly invoked by small shadowy voices calling out in the midst of our dreams. There came a bitter scent into the air, as of sweet wine turning to vinegar, and there was a hysteric brilliance flourished by the trees in town as well as those in the woods beyond, while along the roads between were the intemperate displays of thorn apple, sumac, and towering sunflowers that nodded behind crooked roadside fences. Even the stars of chill nights seemed to grow delirious and take on the tints of an earthly inflammation. Finally, there was a moonlit field where a scarecrow had been left to watch over ground that had long been cleared yet would not turn cold.

Adjacent to the edge of town, the field allowed full view of itself from so many of our windows. It lay spacious beyond tilting fence-posts and under a bright round moon, uncluttered save for the peaked silhouettes of corn shocks and a manlike shape that stood fixed in the nocturnal solitude. The head of the figure was slumped forward, as if a grotesque slumber had overtaken its straw-stuffed body, and the arms were slackly extended in a way that suggested some incredible gesture toward flight. For a moment it seemed to be an insistent wind which was flapping those patched-up overalls and fluttering the worn flannel of those shirt sleeves. And it would seem a forceful wind indeed which caused that stitched-up head to nod in its dreams. But nothing else joined in such movements: the withered leaves of the cornstalks were stiff and unstirring, the trees of the distant woods were in a lull against the clear night. Only one thing appeared to be living where the moonlight spread across that dead field. And there were some who claimed that the scarecrow actually raised its arms and its empty face to the sky, as though declaring itself to the heavens, while others thought that its legs kicked wildly, like those of a man who is hanged, and that they kept on kicking for the longest time before the thing collapsed and lay quiet. Many of us, we discovered, had been nudged from our beds that night, called as witnesses to this obscure spectacle. Afterward, the sight we had seen, whatever we believed its reason, would not rest within us but snatched at the edges of our sleep until morning.

And during the overcast hours of the following day we could not keep ourselves from visiting the place around which various rumors had hastily arisen. As pilgrims we wandered into that field, scrutinizing the debris of its harvest for augural signs, circling that scarecrow as if it were a great idol in shabby disguise, a sacred avatar out of season. But everything upon that land seemed unwilling to support our hunger for revelation, and our congregation was lost in fidgeting bemusement. (With the exception, of course, of Mr. Marble, whose eyes, we recall, were gleaming with perceptions he could not offer us in any words we would understand.) The sky had hidden itself behind a leaden vault of clouds, depriving us of the crucial element of pure sunlight which we needed to fully burn off the misty dreams of the past night. A vine-twisted stone wall along the property line of the farm was the same shade as the sky, while the dormant vines themselves were as colorless as the stone they enmeshed like a strange network of dead veins. But this calculated grayness was merely an aspect of the scene, for the colors of the abundant woods along the margins of the landscape were undulled, as if those radiant leaves possessed some inner source of illumination or stood in contrast to some deeper shadow which they served to mask.

Such conditions no doubt impeded our efforts to come to terms with our fears about that particular field. Above all these manifestations, however, was the fact that the earth of those harvested acres, especially in the area surrounding the scarecrow, was unnaturally warm for the season. It seemed, in fact, that a late harvest was due. And some insisted that the odd droning noises that filled the air could not be blamed on the legions of local cicadas but indeed rose up from under the ground.

By the time of twilight, only a few stragglers remained in the field, among them the old farmer who owned this suddenly notorious acreage. We knew that he shared the same impulse as the rest of us when he stepped up to his scarecrow and began to tear the impostor to pieces. Others joined in the vandalism, pulling out handfuls of straw and stripping away the clothes until they had exposed what lay beneath them—the strange and unexpected sight.

For the skeleton of the thing should have been merely two crosswise planks. We verified this common fact with its maker, and he swore that no other materials had been used. Yet the shape that stood before us was of a wholly different nature. It was something black and twisted into the form of a man, something that seemed to have come up from the earth and grown over the wooden planks like a dark fungus, consuming the structure. There were now black legs that hung as if charred and withered; there was a head that sagged like a sack of ashes upon a meager body of blackness; and there were thin arms stretched like knobby branches from a lightning-scorched tree. All of this was supported by a thick, dark stalk which rose from the earth and reached into the effigy like a hand into a puppet.

And as that sunless day began to dim, our vision was still held by that thing which dangled ominously in the dusk. Its composition appeared to be of the blackest earth, of earth that had gone stagnant somewhere in its depths, where a rich loam had festered into a bog of shadows. Soon we realized that each of us had fallen silent, entranced by a deep blackness which seemed to absorb our sight but which exposed nothing to scrutiny except an abyss in the outline of a man. Even when we ventured to lay our hands on that mass of darkness, we found only greater mysteries. For there was almost no tangible aspect to it, merely a hint of material sensation, barely the feel of wind or water. It seemed to possess no more substance than a few shifting flames, but flames of only the slightest warmth, black flames that have curled together to take on the molten texture of spoiled fruit. And there was a vague sense of circulation, as though a kind of serpentine life swirled gently within. But no one could stand to keep his hold upon it for long before stepping away.

"Damn the thing, it's not going to be rooted to my land," said the old farmer. Then he walked off toward the barn. And like the rest of us he was trying to rub something from the hand that had touched the shriveled scarecrow, something that could not be seen.

He returned to us with an armory of axes, shovels, and other implements for uprooting what had grown upon his land, this eccentricity of the harvest. It would seem to have been a simple task: the ground was curiously soft all around the base of that black growth and its tenuous substance could hardly resist the wide blade of the farmer's axe. But when the old man swung and tried to split the thing like a piece of firewood, the blade would not cleave. The axe entered and was closed upon, as if sunk within a viscous mire. The farmer pulled at the handle and managed to dislodge the axe, but he immediately let it fall from his hands. "It was pulling back on me," he said in a low voice. "And you heard that sound." Indeed, the sound which had haunted the area all that day—like innumerable insects laughing—did seem to rise in pitch and intensity when the thing was struck.

Without a word, we began digging up the earth where that thick black stalk was buried. We dug fairly deep before the approaching night forced us to abandon our efforts. Yet no matter how far down we burrowed, it was not far enough to reach the bottom of that sprouting blackness. Furthermore, our attempts became hindered by a perverse reluctance, as in the instance of someone who is hesitant to have a diseased part of his own body cut away in order to keep the disease from spreading.

The clouds of that day had lingered to hide the moon, and in the darkness our voices whispered various strategies, so that we might yet accomplish what we had thereto failed in doing. Nor did any of our words now rise above a whisper, although none of us would have said why this was so.

The great shadow of a moonless night encompassed the landscape, preserving us from seeing the old farmer's field and what was tenanted there. And yet so many of the houses in town were in vigil throughout those dark hours. Soft lights shone through curtained windows along the length of each street, where our trim wooden homes seemed as small as dollhouses beneath the dark rustling depths of the season. Above the gathered roofs hovered the glass globes of streetlamps, like little moons set inside the dense leaves of elms and oaks and maples. Even in the night, the light shining through those leaves betrayed the festival of colors seething within them, blazing auras which had not faded with the passing days, a plague of colors that had already begun to infect our dreams. This prodigy had by then become connected in our minds with that field just outside of town and the strange growth which there had taken root.

Thus, a sense of urgency led us back to that place, where we found the old farmer waiting for us as the frigid aurora of dawn appeared above the distant woods. Our eyes scanned the frost-powdered earth and studied every space among shadows and corn shocks spread out over the land, searching for what was no longer present in the scene. "It's gone back," the farmer revealed to us. "Gone into the earth like something hiding in its shell. Don't walk there," he warned, pointing to the mouth of a wide pit.

We gathered about the edge of this opening in the ground, gazing into its depths. Even full daybreak did not show us the bottom of that dark well. Our speculations were brief and futile. Some of us picked up the shovels lying nearby, as if to begin the long duty of filling in the great aperture. "No use in that," said the farmer. He then found a large stone and dropped it straight down the shaft. We waited and waited; we put our heads close to the hole and listened. But all we seemed to hear were remote, humming echoes, as of countless voices of insects chattering unseen. Finally, we covered the hazardous pit with some boards and buried the makeshift enclosure under a mound of soft dirt. "Maybe there'll be some change in the spring," someone said. But the old farmer only chuckled. "You mean when the ground warms up? Why do you think those leaves aren't falling the way they should?"

It was not long after this troubling episode that our dreams, which formerly had been the merest shadows and glimpses, swelled into full phase. Yet they must not have been dreams entirely, but also excavations into the season which had inspired them. In sleep we were consumed by the feverish life of the earth, cast among a ripe, fairly rotting world of strange growth and transformation. We took a place within a darkly flourishing landscape where even the air was ripened into ruddy hues and everything wore the wrinkled grimace of decay, the mottled complexion of old flesh. The face of the land itself was knotted with so many other faces, ones that were corrupted by vile impulses. Grotesque expressions were molding themselves into the darkish grooves of ancient bark and the whorls of withered leaf; pulpy, misshapen features peered out of damp furrows; and the crisp skin of stalks and dead seeds split into a multitude of crooked smiles. All was a freakish mask painted with russet, rashy colors—colors that bled with a virulent intensity, so rich and vibrant that things trembled with their own ripeness.

But despite their gross palpability, there remained something spectral at the heart of our new dreams. It moved in shadow, a presence that was *in* the world of solid forms but not *of* it. Nor did it belong to any other world that could be named, unless it was to that realm which is suggested to us by an autumn night when fields lay ragged in moonlight and some wild spirit has entered into things, a great aberration sprouting forth from a chasm of moist and fertile shadows, a hollow-eyed howling malignity rising to present itself to the cold emptiness of space and the pale gaze of the moon.

And it was to that moon we were forced to look for comfort when we awoke trembling in the night, overcome by the sense that another life was taking root within us, seeking its ultimate incarnation in the bodies we always dreamed were our own and inviting us into the depths of an extraordinary harvest.

Certainly there was some relief when we began to discover, after many insecure hints and delvings, that the dreams were not a sickness restricted to solitary individuals or families but in fact were epidemic throughout the community. No longer were we required to disguise our uneasiness as we met on the streets under the luxuriant shadows of trees that would not cast off their gaudy foliage, the mocking plumage of a strange season. We had become a race of eccentrics and openly declared an array of singular whims and suspicions, at least while daylight allowed this audacity.

Honored among us was that one old fellow, well known for his oddities, who had anticipated our troubles weeks beforehand. As he wandered about town, wheeling the blade-sharpening grindstone by which he earned his living, Mr. Marble had spoken of what he could "read in the leaves," as if those fluttering scraps of lush color were the pages of a secret book in which he perused gold and crimson hieroglyphs. "Just look at them," he urged passersby, "bleeding their colors like that. They should be bled dry, but now they're making pictures. Something inside trying to show itself. They're as dead as rags now, all limp and flapping. But something's still in there. Those pictures, do you see them?"

Yes, we saw them, though somewhat belatedly. And they were not seen only in the chromatic designs of those deathless leaves. They could show themselves anywhere, if always briefly. Upon a cellar wall there might appear an ill-formed visage among the damp and fractured stones, a hideous impersonation of a face infiltrating the dark corners of our homes. Other faces, leprous masks, would arise within the grain of paneled walls or wooden floors, spying for a moment before sinking back into the knotty shadows, withdrawing below the surface. And there were so many nameless patterns that might spread themselves across the boards of an old fence or the side of a shed, engravings all tangled and wizened like a subterranean craze of roots and tendrils, an underworld riot of branching convolutions, gnarled ornamentations. Yet these designs were not unfamiliar to us . . . for in them we recognized the same outlines of autumnal decay we saw our dreams.

Like the old visionary who sharpened knives and axes and curving scythes, we too could now read the great book of countless colored leaves. But still he remained far in advance of what was happening deep within us all. For it was he who manifested certain idiosyncrasies of manner that would later appear in so many others, whether they lived in town or somewhere outside its limits. Of course, he had always set himself apart from us by his waywardness of speech, his willingness to utter pronouncements of dire or delightful curiosity. To a child he might say: "The sight of the night can fly like a kite," while someone older would be told: "Doesn't have arms, but it knows how to use them. Doesn't have a face, but it knows where to find one."

Nevertheless, he plied his trade with every efficiency, pedaling the mechanism that turned the grindstone, expertly honing each blade and taking his pay like any man of business. Then, we noticed, he seemed to become distracted in his work. In a dull trance he touched metal implements to his spinning wheel of stone, careless of the sparks that flew into his face. Yet there was also a wild luminousness in his eyes, as of a diamond-bright fever burning within him. Eventually we found ourselves unable to abide his company, though we now attributed this merely to some upsurge in his perennial strangeness rather than to a wholly unprecedented change in his behavior. It was not until he no longer appeared on the streets of town, or anywhere else, that we admitted our fears about him.

And these fears necessarily became linked to the other disruptions of that season, those extravagant omens which were gaining force all around us. The disappearance of Mr. Marble coincided with a new phenomenon, one that finally became apparent in the twilight of a certain day when all of the clustering and tenacious foliage seemed to exude a vague phosphorescence. By nightfall this prodigy was beyond skepticism. The multicolored leaves were softly glowing against the black sky, creating an untimely nocturnal rainbow which scattered its spectral tints everywhere and dyed the night with a harvest of hues: peach gold and pumpkin orange, honey yellow and winy amber, apple red and plum violet. Lustrous within their leafy shapes, the colors cast themselves across the darkness and were splattered upon our streets and our fields and our faces. Everything was resplendent with the pyrotechnics of a new autumn.

That night we kept to our houses and watched at our windows. It was no marvel, then, that so many of us saw the one who wandered about the town on that iridescent eve, and who joined in its outbursts and celebrations. Possessed by the ecstasies of a dark festival, he moved in a trance, bearing in his hand that great ceremonial knife whose keen edge flashed a thousand glittering dreams. He was seen standing alone beneath trees whose colors shined upon him, staining his face and his tattered clothes. He was seen standing alone in the yards of our houses, a rigid scarecrow concocted from a patchwork of shadows. He was seen stalking beside high wooden fences that were now painted with a quivering glow. Finally, he was seen at a certain intersection of streets at the center of town.

By then, we knew what needed to happen. The slaughtering beast had come for its own. A season was upon us out of all seasons, and an aberration had risen that did not belong to the course of life we had always known. It grew out of the earth in a farmer's field, and beneath it was a bottomless hole that we covered with a mound of dirt, thereby denying a hungering presence what it asked of us. Unsated, it would now take what it desired. As frightened as we were, we also felt resentment and outrage. From the beginning, there was an exchange to which we had resigned ourselves: that which is given must one day be given back. In time the eternal darkness would arrive, as each of our lives was reclaimed at its end and went back to the earth that had borne our bodies and sustained them with its plenty. But the phenomenon we confronted seemed nothing less than a premature craving, a greed surpassing our covenant with earth's estate. What we were forced to stipulate, then, was another, perhaps more fundamental, order of being than our species had suspected, even a betrayal or deception on the part of creation itself. All that was left to us was to wonder: who knows all that is innate to this world, or to any other? Why should there not be something buried deep within appearances, something that wears a mask to hide itself behind the visibility of nature?

But whatever it was that secreted itself in outward shapes mattered less to us that night than the plan it had conceived for an expertly whetted blade and the possessed hand that held it. We had no illusions that our fate could be evaded or opposed. For if the power or entity that had seized our land could exercise its will as we had seen, what was there that it could not do? And now it was rousing itself to a furor. More than ever, the trees burned with an eerie incandescence, and the chittering noises that commanded the sultry air began rising to a pitch of vicious laughter. As Mr. Marble stood in the center of town, he eyed our houses in turn, the matter of his mind seemingly focused on where the blood would begin and how voracious would be the ravening demanded by whatever mystery empowered him as its brutal servant.

Like any group of persons who feel a sure sense of imminent mayhem, each of us hoped that it might pass us by and the worst would be visited on others. Cowards all, we prayed to be overlooked in the coming massacre. But our shame was not long-lived. Voices began to call from the street to those of us who were still in hiding. "He's gone," someone said. "We saw him go off into the woods." He had raised his knife, it was reported, but his hand trembled, as if he was fighting against it. Then he walked off past the town limits. "More like staggered," said a woman who was holding a spatula like a weapon. "You'd think he was walking in a windstorm that way he leaned forward, pushing and pushing. I was afraid that he'd tumble back into Main Street." A man who came late to the scene avowed to all of us that if Mr. Marble had stayed any longer, he was going to approach him and say, "Take me and spare the others. Blood is blood." It was not difficult to see through his fabrication.

For some hours, we huddled in the center of town, waiting to see if Mr. Marble would return. The trees around us seemed to be fading in their radiance, and the night was quiet, the din of shrill vibrations in the air having abated entirely. A few at a time, we turned back to our houses, which had now lost their reek of moldering shadows, and gradually the town succumbed to a dreamless sleep. Somehow we all felt assured that what we feared would happen that night would not come to pass.

Yet at daybreak it became evident that something had indeed happened during the night. Everywhere the earth had at last turned cold. And the trees now stood bare of leaves, all of which lay dark and withered upon the ground, as if their strangely deferred dying had finally overtaken them in a sudden rage of mortification. We searched both the town and countryside for any remaining sign of the appalling season we had endured. And it was not long before Mr. Marble was discovered.

The corpse reposed in a field, stretched face-down across a mound of dirt and alongside the remains of a dismantled scarecrow. When we turned over the body we looked upon open eyes as colorless as that ashen autumn morning. Then we marked that the figure's left arm had been slashed to the bone by the knife still gripped in its right hand.

Blood had flowed over the earth and blackened the flesh of the self-murdered man. But those of us who handled that limp, nearly weightless body, dipping our fingers into the dark wound, found nothing at all that had the feeling of blood. We knew very well, of course, what that shadowy blackness did feel like. We knew what had found its way into the man before us and dragged him into its savage world. His affinity with the immanent schemes of existence had always been much deeper than ours. So we buried him deep in a bottomless grave.